The ACCUSED

CRAIG PARSHALL

HARVEST HOUSE™ PUBLISHERS

EUGENE, OREGON

Cover by Left Coast Design, Portland, Oregon

This novel is a work of fiction. Names, characters, places, and incidents are either the product of the author's imagination or are used fictitiously. It is the intent of the author and publisher that all events, locales, organizations, and persons portrayed herein be viewed as fictitious.

THE ACCUSED
Copyright © 2003 by Craig L. Parshall
Published by Harvest House Publishers
Eugene, Oregon 97402
www.harvesthousepublishers.com

Library of Congress Cataloging-in-Publication Data
Parshall, Craig, 1950–
    The accused / Craig Parshall.
        p. cm. — (Chambers of justice ; bk. 3)
    ISBN 0-7369-1173-1 (pbk.)
    1. Chambers, Will (Fictitious character)—Fiction. I. Title.
PS3616.A77A64 2003
    813'.54—dc21
                                                                    2003004365

Printed in the United States of America

05 06 07 08 09 10 11 / BC-KB / 10 9 8 7 6 5 4

To the memory of my father, Richard Palmer Parshall,
who served as a catapult officer in the United States Navy in World War II
on the USS Makin Island, *a Casablanca Class escort aircraft carrier,*
during the fierce battles in the Pacific theater.

And to my father-in-law, Vince DiFrancesca,
who ably served as a PFC in the United States Army Air Force
in the same war, on the Marianas and other Pacific islands.

And finally, to my brother, Richard Parshall,
who served in Vietnam as a first lieutenant in the United States Army,
and whose return—as was regrettably true of too many of
our brave soldiers in that conflict—was greeted
with far less honor than his dedicated service deserved.

Acknowledgments

Much like the first two novels in this series, this one is a legal thriller and a love story of sorts—as well as a spiritual odyssey. But unlike the others, it is a tale of war. It describes the journey of a military hero faced with enduring the personal, as well as the geopolitical, crucible that results from a tragic exercise of judgment during our War on Terrorism. As a result, I relied heavily on the expertise of men who have served our nation in the armed forces, and whose keen insights, I hope, have kept this tale within the bounds of realism. I am profoundly in their debt.

David Tanks, a 25-year military veteran and an expert in matters of missile and satellite defense, as well as national security, gave me superb pointers on overall military logistics—as well as some great technology information. Thomas Rumping, a retired Marine Corps intel officer, combat pilot, and counterterrorism expert, and now a defense and security consultant (and an aspiring author in his own right), was incredibly helpful—especially in the operational aspects of the military assault that leads to the criminal case at the center of this story. And I also owe much thanks to Lt. Col. M.J.K. Maher, U.S.M.C., Judge Advocate—Marine Corps HQ. My experience in criminal defense of U.S. Marines at Quantico has been, admittedly, very limited—and Lt. Col. Maher filled in the numerous lapses when it came to the Article 32 proceeding. I have tremendous admiration for the U.S. Marine Corps, the other branches of service, and our intelligence agencies. I hope this story confirms that admiration. If there are any failures in military accuracy, they are solely mine—and are not the responsibility of these men who shared with me their time, expertise, and the fruits of their brave service to our nation.

Marilyn Clifton, as always, brought her Marine Corps experience—and her paralegal acumen—to bear on this project, more, perhaps, than any other to date. I am in debt to her and to Sharon Donehey, who slaved on this manuscript under crippling deadlines. Lastly, thanks to Janet, my wife, for lovingly putting up with the life of a lawyer/writer. Our life together continues to inspire the most important things that are written here.

1

INSIDE THE BLACK HOOD that was tied over his head, Frederick Kilmer, United States Secretary of Commerce, was sucking in the stale air. His face was dripping with sweat in the moist heat of the Mexican jungle. He was tied up in the back of a vehicle—that much he knew. And it was moving fast over potholes and ditches, jarring his teeth together with each bump. Wherever it was, this road was not paved.

He also knew that two of his captors were with him as well. He could hear the two Middle Eastern men banging their automatic weapons on the metal surface he was sitting on and talking excitedly together.

In his dark, confused world, Kilmer was clinging to the image of his wife with her gentle smile, who was still back in their condo in Bethesda, Maryland. And the image of his two lovely daughters, who were attending college—sitting in the quiet safety of a classroom somewhere, listening to a lecture on Restoration literature or perhaps on the current theories of political science. The idea of never seeing his family again was almost too overpowering to comprehend.

But he was smart—and he knew the score. And he knew these terrorists had gotten this far—and they were not afraid to go further. To find some forsaken part of the Yucatán jungle—haul him out—and then slowly torture him while one of them grinned behind the eyepiece of a video camera, capturing his gruesome death for all the world to witness. That was the worst part—the thought that his wife and daughters might see that.

Kilmer did not know that the driver of the old, rusty pickup truck they were in and the man on the front seat next to him—separated from the camper shell on the back by a window—were both heavily armed Colombians. Unlike the others, they were in it strictly for the money. Speeding in front of the truck driven by the Colombians was a late-model Mercedes with four other Middle Eastern men.

In just a mile or so both vehicles would arrive at an even narrower dirt road that would lead them to a path through the nearly impenetrable Yucatán interior, within a canopy of jungle so dense that helicopters could not find them.

But before that, the Mercedes began slowing down unexpectedly. Up ahead, at the side of the road, there was a crumbling, deserted café with empty windows, sagging walls, and a faded sign that read "¡Mucho Gusto!" Beside the café there was something in the road. The pickup truck slowed too.

Then the drivers saw it. A taxicab with its hood open—and jumper cables leading from its engine to under the open hood of an old bus. The bus and the cab were blocking the entire width of the road—so close to the thick, vine-covered trees on both sides that no car could pass.

A Mexican man of medium height was standing in front of the taxi. A taller man, with his back to the approaching vehicles, was bending over the engine of the bus. He was wearing a straw hat and a multicolored poncho.

The leader, in the Mercedes, stuck his head out and motioned frantically back toward the Colombians as the vehicles stopped about fifty feet from the taxi and the bus.

The Colombian driver jumped out with his weapon in this hand, yelling and cursing. "Move it now or you die!" he screamed. Soon the other man dashed out of the truck, joining in the yelling.

The man in front of the taxi nodded solemnly, looked at his companion, and raised his hands slowly over his head—moving around to the other side of the car.

But the bigger man did not move—his back was still to the Colombians.

The Colombian driver fired a round—sending two bullets through the multicolored cape and missing the man's torso by inches.

But the man in the hat and the cape did not move, except to turn slightly to view the bullet holes in the fabric—much like a bull would glance at a fly on his flank.

Neither the Colombians nor the terrorists in the Mercedes were looking toward the rear—where an American special operations agent in black assault coveralls had scurried out of the abandoned café, straight to the back of the truck. The windows of the camper shell were covered with dirty curtains, so he reached his position without detection.

He took a metal canister filled with pressurized, reconstituted halothane gas and clamped its rubber feet to the truck's gate, holding it in place.

Then he fed a rubber hose into an opening at the corner of the rear window where it met the gate and turned the control knob on. The odorless, tasteless gas poured into the compartment that housed Secretary Kilmer and his two captors.

But up at the front—by the bus—the four men in the Mercedes were getting nervous. Then the driver of that car slammed it into gear and, throwing dirt and stones, spun it in a half circle and sped off in the opposite direction. The American special ops agent scuttled underneath the truck as the car flew past.

The two Colombians were still staring at the man in the hat and cape, who was not moving. They began laughing and taunting him as they walked closer—"Loco, loco!"

Then he stood up straight. And turned around fully and faced them.

That was when the Colombians stopped laughing. The man in the hat had an iron-hard expression on his face. And he was not a Mexican—he looked like an American.

Caleb Marlowe, Colonel, United States Marine Corps, pulled his Beretta pistol from under his cape and sent two deadly rounds into the chest of one of the Colombians, then turned the fury of his weapon on the other terrorist. The injured man managed to get off one shot after he was wounded by Marlowe, but was finished off as he tried to escape by the gunfire from two more members of the unit, who were shooting from their hidden positions in the café.

The gas in the back of the truck had partially overcome the two men guarding Kilmer—but they still managed to swing open the gate, though dazed and drugged, and started shooting randomly.

A third special ops sniper put both of them down with one bullet apiece.

The operative at the rear of the truck pulled Frederick Kilmer out. He yanked off the black hood and allowed him to breathe in fresh air for a few minutes. Then his rescuer started talking.

"Secretary Kilmer," the man said slowly and calmly, "I am Master Sergeant Mike Rockwell—with a special unit from the United States. Can you understand me?"

Kilmer nodded.

"Sir," the sergeant said, "you are safe now."

In a few hours the secretary would be talking to his wife on the telephone while she sobbed in utter relief. His daughters—still at college—would learn later of his kidnapping and successful rescue.

Colonel Caleb Marlowe shucked off his hat and poncho and shouted to his special operations unit—who were all assembling around the pickup truck and surveying the dead terrorists.

"Okay, you bunch of heroes—game's not over yet. We've got to get those last four bad guys who just got away."

Marlowe thought he knew the risks of that second phase of the operation. Their mission was to locate and kill four terrorists somewhere in the jungles of southern Mexico. It would not be easy. And it was guaranteed to be dangerous. For Marlowe and his unit, that much just came with the territory.

But there was also something, even for Marlowe, that was yet unknown: evil in its brutal design—and waiting.

What he did not know and could not have anticipated was the unexpected toll that was about to be exacted—as during some horrible, blood-cult ceremony before a stone god.

In the sweltering green overgrowth of the Yucatán jungle, Caleb Marlowe, brave American warrior, was about to face the darkest sacrifice of all.

2

ON THE SEVENTH FLOOR OF THE LUXURY HOTEL, Fiona stood before the sliding glass door in her bathing suit, combing out her wet tangle of dark hair. She padded barefoot over to the door, slid it open, and stepped out onto the balcony. As she did, her senses were greeted by the roaring crash of the ocean surf far below.

The trim, thirty-six-year-old woman leaned against the railing, and inhaled the mixed scent of sea air and the grilled shrimp that were being prepared somewhere down at the poolside café. The sun was hot, and the clear sky faded into the edges of an ocean brilliant with different blues—light crystal blue by the white beaches and stretching to the sandbar fifty yards out—then intensifying into aquamarine, and finally, from that point all the way out to the horizon, a glistening dark blue, like the surface of sparkling sapphire.

She glanced down at the gold band that adorned her left hand and the diamond that accompanied it. She had been on her honeymoon for only ten days. But so much had changed. So many lessons learned, in such a short time—heart knowledge in the ways of friendship, passion, intimacy, and love. As she felt the ocean breeze and contemplated the paradox of having fallen in love with the man she had, she found herself laughing out loud.

A mariachi band began playing below. She gazed out at the ocean again, catching a glimpse of a red, yellow, and blue sail gliding over the ocean.

She walked back in and picked up her watch from the desk. Her husband, Will Chambers, had been gone only forty minutes now.

She smiled at that and at how she was already longing for his presence. How could she have ever doubted that the two of them should be married and spend the rest of their lives together?

Of course there had been the usual communication problems…and the near impossibility of scheduling time together. The latter was particularly challenging, given the fact that Fiona already had an established music career as a gospel singer and recording artist, and that Will was a forty-three-year-old globe-trotting trial lawyer. But her greatest fear had always been the unseen, usually unmentioned, but ever-present ghost of Will's first wife, Audra.

Fiona didn't know whether it was Will's love for Audra or her tragic murder that had made his forgetting and moving beyond her death so difficult.

But in those last ten days all doubts had vanished. Fiona was convinced her relationship with Will was no product of coincidence. It was the result of divine matchmaking.

She had waited thirty-six years for the right man. She had had to be certain. But now she was. Not just because Will had come full circle—from an agnostic, former ACLU lawyer to a Bible-toting Christian. Beyond even that. God's hand in their first meeting and in their courtship had been so clearly evident.

She glanced over at the television, which had been left on with the volume turned down.

Only one cloud darkened the incandescence of their honeymoon. The violence and chaos of the outside world had still managed to invade their lives.

Fiona studied the INN news report and the ticker tape of information passing across the bottom of the screen. She was searching, now, for some recent news about the kidnapping of Secretary of Commerce Kilmer. She reached down and turned the volume up. But there was nothing new. It was the same news that had been flooding the television for the last twelve hours—that the Secretary of Commerce had been captured by a cell group of terrorists who were using Mexico as their base. They had spirited him out of a hotel in Cancún, Mexico, during an economic conference. Two Secret Service agents had been killed, and one injured.

At the hotel where Will and Fiona were staying in Cozumel, an island only some forty miles from Cancún, the kidnapping had resulted in a security alert. All of the guests had been ordered to stay on the grounds.

It was no inconvenience to Fiona and Will because this was the last forty-eight hours of their honeymoon. Besides that, Fiona felt secure. Looking back on her husband's extraordinary brushes with terrorism and violence in the past, she felt safe with him.

Then a news reporter, live from Cancún, appeared on the screen. She shared the breaking news:

> Just minutes ago it was announced there has been a break in the hostage crisis here in Cancún, Mexico. Secretary of Commerce Frederick Kilmer, who was kidnapped by a terrorist cell group operating in Mexico, has now been released, and he is safely in the custody of U.S. officials. We are now being told that his release was secured yesterday by an American military strike force that attacked the kidnappers as they were heading through the Yucatán jungles around dawn. Several of the terrorists were killed, but four escaped.
>
> There is no information yet about the identity of the terrorist group. However, unconfirmed sources tell us that it may have ties to the al-Aqsa Jihad—the terrorist organization linked with the late Abdul el Alibahd. Government sources withheld information about the rescue for nearly twelve hours because American special operation forces were still pursuing the remaining terrorists.

Fiona heard the door unlocking, and it swung open. Will was standing in the doorway with his island shirt unbuttoned in the front, wearing a pair of shorts and sandals. On his face was a broad smile.

"Great news," he said. "The guy at the desk says the security hold is lifted. Apparently Kilmer has been released. The American military came in and got it done."

Fiona explained she had just heard the same news on the television.

"We can now make outgoing phone calls," Will said. "I thought I would call my office and let them know we're okay. Then maybe you can call your dad and tell him the same thing."

He was going to grab the phone, but he noticed the smile on Fiona's face and the look in her eye. He strode over to her, gathered her up in his arms, and gave her a long kiss. Their bodies melded together.

"Isn't married life great?" Will asked with a smile.

"I was just thinking the same thing—out there on the balcony—looking at the ocean and thinking how wonderful it was that the Lord brought us together," Fiona responded.

And then she added, "But I was just wondering something…"

"What?"

"Well—I was just wondering, during these first few days of our marriage—whether there is anything about me that has surprised you."

"Yeah," Will said, laughing. "You don't like seafood. Now I think that is probably going to be the *only* thing the two of us will ever seriously disagree on!"

Then he turned quiet. "So—what did you find about me that surprised you?"

Fiona thought for a moment. "That you were on the boxing team in college. That surprised me."

"Why?"

"Oh—just the picture of you as a campus liberal. Pacifist. Antiwar. The whole picture doesn't match with the fellow who gets into a sport so he can break somebody else's nose!"

"Well, I didn't really tell you the whole story. My dad was a welterweight boxing champ in college. And he was the world's biggest political liberal. So—like father, like son."

"You know, something else struck me while I was waiting for you."

"Like what?"

"How are the two of us going to work out our impossible schedules so we can live happily ever after?"

Her husband smiled.

"I know we can do that—we are going to *have* to do that."

"And I know we will. Actually, I was just thinking that the forty minutes you were downstairs just now was the longest we had been separated in the last ten days. And it was killing me!"

Will laughed and looked into her eyes and at her dimpled cheeks. He pulled her to himself again and gave her another long, lingering kiss.

"Go ahead—make your phone call to your office," Fiona said, "and I will call Da after you're through."

She walked over to her suitcase, which was already open on the bed, and started throwing some clothes into it.

Will dialed his office and got Hilda, his secretary. She and everyone in the office had been tremendously worried, she explained, since Cozumel was close to the terrorist activity at Cancún.

Will assured her they were fine.

"Any urgent messages for me?"

There was an awkward pause at the other end, and then Hilda responded, "Well…nothing that can't wait until you get back."

"I know that tone of voice. Give me the bad news—what do I need to know?"

"Truly," she said, trying to smooth things over, "it can wait, Will. Really, I think you ought to wait on this."

"Come on, Hilda. I'm a big boy. If there is something, let me know right now."

Will's tone and his conversation had caught Fiona's attention. She had stopped packing her suitcase and was staring intently at him.

"Look, Will, you are there on your honeymoon. For heaven's sake, take advantage of your time with your dear wife. Fiona deserves it. You certainly deserve it. That detective can talk to you when you get back."

"Detective? What are you talking about?"

"See," Hilda said with resignation. "You always get me going, and then I say something I shouldn't."

"Out with it," Will said. "Come on, what is it?"

After another slight pause, his secretary sighed and then began to explain.

"A detective from the DC police department called. It is about Audra. Said he's got some information on the guy who killed her. It doesn't change a thing. I don't even know why he called now. But he wanted you to know. Apparently, the person who did it was in prison and confessed to his cellmate. But now the guy is dead. And that is the end of the story. I wish I didn't have to tell you. And I'm sorry you asked me."

Will sat down in a chair next to the telephone and ran his hand through his hair.

"Did they tell you anything else?"

"No. That was it. He wants you to call him when you get back to town, and he will fill you in on, I suppose, some more details."

And then Hilda added a few words of advice.

"Will, you've got a beautiful, precious wife. Fiona loves you like crazy. All that with Audra is past. Let the dead bury their dead. I'm not saying this right, but I think you know what I mean."

"Thanks," he responded, but his voice was breaking a bit and was barely audible.

He hung the phone up and stared out into space blankly.

Fiona came over and sat down on the carpet in front of him, her hands on his knees.

"Tell me, darling, what is it?"

"Audra. A detective in DC called to say they found out who did it. The guy was in prison—for something else, I guess—he was killed. But before that, he admitted to his cellmate that he'd murdered Audra."

Fiona looked into her husband's face, which was flinty and unmoved by emotion now. There was a hardness to his expression she had not seen before.

"I am sorry," she said. "I know how hard it is every time you have to relive that."

Will thought a minute and struggled for some diplomatic way to say what he needed to say. But euphemisms were not going to help.

"Look," he started out. "When Audra died I went through the whole gamut. Shock. Soul-scorching grief. Emptiness. Anger. Resignation. Bitterness. Everything. But then something really surprised me. What was left after all of that."

"Left?" Fiona asked. "What do you mean?"

"I mean…that I had nothing but willful rage. Strange, isn't it? But I can't stand the idea that the animal who killed her is now dead. Because I had this lingering desire. This nasty, unforgiving prayer that someday I would meet the guy. And then I could take out my own revenge."

He glanced at his wife with a tired, distant look. "That sounds pretty twisted, doesn't it?"

Fiona rose to her feet, and as she did, she bent forward and kissed her husband on the forehead. She had nothing to say. What she wanted to say—but didn't—was that, for a fleeting instant, Will had looked like someone else. Like a man who was still stuck in limbo between the past and the future—and who could not fully commit to the present…or to her.

Fiona turned and walked to the suitcase, her back to Will. She did it partly because she was stunned by her husband's words about revenge and rage. But mostly she did it so she could hide the tears that were now filling her eyes.

3

ON ISLA HOLBOX, A TINY ISLAND a few miles offshore from the Yucatán Peninsula of Mexico, Colonel Caleb Marlowe, commanding officer of BATCOM, was looking through the window of the Mexican federal police building. His face was as unmoving as granite. His eyes were searching the police grounds for the approaching military police detail.

Marlowe was forty-three, but beneath his camouflage utilities, he had the hardened body of a twenty-five-year-old athlete. Something in his eyes and the lines in his face, however, revealed the aging process that comes with command decisions over life, death, survival, and destruction. Now he was trying to figure out how to survive the tragic consequences of his command decision of the day before.

At the other end of the room, Master Sergeant Mike Rockwell and Staff Sergeant Billy Baker, both under Marlowe's command in the recent assault on the fleeing terrorists, were trying to remain at ease on a cheap plastic couch.

Baker leaned over and tried to ask Rockwell a question in a hushed voice. But his companion motioned for him to be silent, and then stood to his feet.

"Sir, permission to take a smoke break?" he asked, brandishing a cigar and a lighter.

Marlowe turned only slightly from his watch at the window, smiled, and nodded. The two men put on their covers, stepped outside, and closed the door behind them. There were a few members of the Mexican police lounging outside the barracks, leaning on their rifles.

Rockwell fingered his cigar and then slipped it back into his pocket. "I don't want you talking in front of the colonel."

"All right, so tell me now. What's coming down? I have a right to know. I am a member of this unit," Baker insisted.

"In a couple of minutes you are about to see the most decorated Marine I know—and probably the best warrior, pound for pound, in the American military—apprehended by a chaser detail. Some colonel from the Office of the Staff Judge Advocate is coming down here to put him into custody and take him back to Quantico."

"What happened back at Chacmool last night—that was not his fault," Baker protested.

"Colonel Marlowe was the ground force commander in that mission. When you are in charge, everything is your fault," Rockwell countered, with no emotion.

"You're saying the colonel blew it?"

The master sergeant turned his head quickly and gave Baker a withering glare.

"After all you've been through, all your training, you still don't get it? Every one of us knew the risks. I've never seen anything go quite so bad, so quick, as it did back there in Chacmool. We were being played like a fiddle. But that doesn't change the fact that it looks like they're picking the colonel to pay the fiddler."

"And you're sure about the identity of the people who took the fire inside that house?"

"The colonel went in himself—you saw that—and he made the ID and the body count. When I learned who we had hit in there, I just about puked."

Baker just shook his head. Then he spoke up again.

"How long have you been with the colonel?"

"From the beginning," Rockwell replied. "Back when they used to call him Colonel God and Guts."

"Good description."

"Well, you know what he's like. He's a fierce believer in the chain of command—the Commandant of the Marine Corps, the Secretary of the Navy, the Secretary of Defense, the President. The only difference is, his chain goes way up—all the way up to God Almighty. That is sort of where the buck starts and stops for him."

Then Rockwell glimpsed the MP detail approaching the barracks. The two men hustled to the door and bolted inside, quickly taking positions behind Colonel Marlowe and standing at attention. Marlowe straightened his utilities. The door swung open.

To their surprise, the detail was being lead by Lieutenant General Cal Tucker from the Pentagon. Behind Tucker was Colonel Ronald Stickton, followed by two chasers—members of the military police. The two chasers saluted Marlowe.

The colonel and his two unit sergeants snapped to attention.

"At ease, gentlemen," General Tucker said. "Colonel Marlowe, step aside with me for a moment, please."

Tucker stepped to the other side of the room with Marlowe. Before speaking, he pursed his lips slightly and clenched his jaw.

"Caleb," he began, "this is not the kind of ending I wanted for all of this. I read the debriefing your men gave about the incident in Chacmool. It raises a whole lot of questions and doesn't give a lot of answers. From this point on, I have to be careful about what you and I discuss. You knew you were on your own when you accepted the second phase of that mission."

Marlowe nodded silently.

"And in this mess you've got very little backup. I will do what I can, but that may not be very much. There are some issues here that are beyond my authority. They are detailing defense counsel back at Quantico for you. I think it is going to be Major Douglas Hanover—good man, good military lawyer. But if you take my advice, I think you also ought to retain your own civilian legal counsel."

"Why is that, sir?"

"Just my recommendation," Tucker replied.

Then he reached his big hand out and gave Caleb Marlowe a firm handshake.

"Good luck, son."

The general wheeled around and exited the barracks quickly.

Colonel Ronald Stickton stepped quickly over to Marlowe's position and stood in front of him.

"Colonel Caleb Marlowe," Stickton began in a loud and official tone, "you are hereby apprehended as authorized under the rules for courts-martial. After being taken into custody, you will be transported to the Marine Corps Base, Quantico, where you will be subject to a formal investigation under charges and specifications that I am now delivering to you."

With that, Stickton removed the paperwork from his clipboard and handed it stiffly to Colonel Marlowe.

"These are the charges and specifications preferred against you. Two Charges, with four specifications under each Charge. The first Charge is Article 118, murder, with one specification for each victim. The second Charge is Article 119, manslaughter, specifications same."

As Sergeant Baker heard the charges and specifications, he gave Sergeant Rockwell a slight side-glance. But the other man's gaze remained straight ahead and unbroken.

As Stickton recited Colonel Marlowe's procedural rights, General Tucker was halfway to the waiting helicopter at the small landing strip on the federal police grounds. His aide-de-camp stepped up and followed him.

"Jimmy," Tucker said back to his aide, "get me the CG over at Marine Corps Base, Quantico, Brigadier General Landon."

The aide nodded and followed the general to the helicopter. There he paused at the cockpit and yelled something to the crew chief.

As the helicopter departed, it drew the gaze of a small crowd of Mexican police. Some of them were chuckling and pointing as it rose up and finally disappeared out of sight.

4

WILL CHAMBERS WAS WAITING IN THE LOBBY of the District of Columbia police department, just outside the office of Captain Jenkins. He could have talked to him on the phone about the matter of Audra's murder. But Will chose to come in person, thinking perhaps it would give closure. But now he was doubting that. Instead, he admitted to himself, his decision to meet directly with the police captain had more to do with his instincts as a trial lawyer. He wanted to eyeball the man—take in his demeanor, his gestures, his facial expression.

And in a face-to-face meeting, Will would be able to probe deeper. To find out what was not being discussed. To read between the lines.

Jenkins strode into the lobby. He was wearing a smartly starched white shirt. His badge was polished, and his pants were neatly pressed. He had the no-nonsense look of business about him—all police procedure.

He reached out his hand to Will.

"Mr. Chambers, I don't know if you remember me," he began. "I think we spoke on the phone a few times during the initial investigation into your wife's death. I am sorry we have to meet again in such unfortunate circumstances. Won't you come in?"

Will nodded, shook his hand and followed him into his office.

The captain flipped open the file on his desk, leaned back slightly in his chair, and then folded his hands in his lap and began talking.

"How long had you and your former wife been separated at the time of her murder?"

"Less than a year."

"She left you?"

"Yes," Will responded, puzzled at the approach the other man was using—particularly if the purpose of their conversation was to close the file on Audra's death.

"Mr. Chambers, before I share with you the information that has just come to light about her assailant, I just wanted to know, whether in the years since our investigation—have you, yourself, come across any additional information about your wife? Anything that might shed light on the circumstances of her murder? People, or organizations, that she had contact with shortly before her death?"

Will studied the man carefully. It seemed clear he did not consider this a closed file. As a matter of fact, his questions gave Will the impression this was a case that—for some reason—was being actively investigated.

"I don't have any more information," the lawyer said. "I don't have anything to add to what I told investigating officers at the time. Now, why don't you share with me the details of what you told my secretary? Who is this guy who murdered Audra?"

"The guy's name was Horace Dudlow. His alias was Buddy. He was doing time for armed robbery in the state penitentiary in Nebraska. He had a substantial rap sheet. Shortly before his death in prison he told his cellmate about a murder he had committed. He said he had killed an attractive blond woman in an apartment in Georgetown. His details of the murder—how he killed your wife—matched the information we had. So we took a closer look at this guy. He had been in the Washington, DC, area at the time of the murder. His details about the crime fit all the physical evidence we had. And most importantly, he had a motive that also matched the crime."

"Motive?" Will asked, his body tensed and leaning forward in the chair toward the captain. "What do you mean by that?"

"Dudlow was a member of a neo-Nazi group up in Brooklyn. It was the same group that you had basically bankrupted through a civil suit you had brought against them on behalf of a Jewish family they had terrorized. The leader of the group was the owner of a trucking company. As I understand it, after you bankrupted the group and the company, their leader was later convicted criminally, and the trucking line was taken over by the Jewish family and operated thereafter by them—right?"

The lawyer nodded—in a stunned daze.

"We don't know anything more that ties the murder back to the neo-Nazi group. But we are checking into that. Dudlow didn't tell his cellmate anything about the involvement of the group. He just shared the details of the murder. But we suspect that the motive was probably retaliation."

Will was still reeling, trying to make sense of the shocking news he had just heard. "Retaliation for what?" he asked.

"Against you," Jenkins said plainly. "For ruining their organization financially and helping to lead to the criminal conviction of their leader, who, as you know, is still serving a lengthy prison term."

Will was staring ahead. His lips parted slightly—but no words came out.

"I am sorry this news has hit you just off the heels of your honeymoon. I was very happy, of course, to find out that you had remarried. It's too bad all of this had to come back up when it did."

The lawyer raised his eyes, struggling to study the captain's face. The other man was glancing down at the file that lay on his desk.

After a few moments of awkward silence Will spoke up. "Your investigation is not closed on Audra's murder, is it?"

"I am afraid not."

"Captain, there is something you know that I don't know. What information haven't you told me?"

"Mr. Chambers…Dudlow did say one more thing to his cellmate."

"And what was that?" Will asked, his face now hard, his eyes locked on the police captain.

"Dudlow said there was another man with him in the apartment at the time of the murder. Somebody who was with him. We don't have a name…no ID. We don't have any idea who it was. But we are certainly going to try to find out. We are checking every lead we've got back to the white supremacy group. Friends, and criminal associates Dudlow came in contact with. I guarantee you, Mr. Chambers, we will leave no stone unturned."

But that was no consolation to Will. As he shook hands with the captain and walked out of the office, he felt as if he had taken a hit with a baseball bat to his solar plexus. All the life in his body seemed to have been drained out.

It was clearly no accident that Dudlow, the man responsible for Audra's vicious murder, had had links to the same neo-Nazi group Will had vanquished in his civil suit years before.

And the implications of that were something Will was not prepared to handle. As he made his way down to the parking structure to his '57 Corvette convertible, he felt as if he were walking through a bad dream. The slow, topsy-turvy disassembling of his life in the weeks and months following Audra's death…the near-collapse of his professional and personal life in the years after that…he had finally believed it was all behind him after his spiritual conversion—and then when he had met Fiona and they had fallen in love.

But now it was all rushing back at him. The demons…the ghosts that had haunted him…the victories he thought he had won over alcohol, over despair, over his bitterness against the world at large and his petty opponents in his former law firm, who had ended up ousting him and forcing him out on his own—all that was now spreading its shadow like some long, nightmarish solar eclipse, where there was no guarantee the sun would shine again or the night would end.

As he numbly guided his car onto the interstate, the awful realization was beginning to settle in.

It was not just Audra's death.

The reality now breaking in on Will was starkly simple in its horrible implication. His obsessive pursuit of justice—his legal triumph over the white supremacist haters—had been the cause of Audra's torture and death. That had been the price tag.

It was a cruel joke. He had negotiated a deadly quid pro quo—a lawsuit victory in exchange for Audra's life—and he hadn't even known it.

How could he survive with the knowledge of that grotesque barter? How could he live with himself?

As he inched his Corvette into the gridlocked traffic exiting the Beltway, Will stared at his cell phone, which was lying on the passenger seat.

He couldn't call Fiona. He wanted to…but he couldn't. He felt as if he were drowning. But to call Fiona—to reach out frantically for her—that would mean pulling her down into the vortex…like a swimmer pulling his rescuer down into the cold, icy deep.

He wanted to pray, but that too seemed a metaphysical impossibility. His mind would not work. His lips would not open. It was if the laws of nature had conspired against his ability to think, or speak, or even cry out to God.

The Lord of all time and space—the divine Father who had reached down, plucked him out of the abyss and saved his soul so concretely and certainly—now, was he powerless to rescue Will out of the one place that so horrified him?

5

IT WAS FIVE O'CLOCK IN THE AFTERNOON. But as usual, many of the staffers within the cavernous Dirksen Senate Office Building were still busy at work. The worker bees in the congressional offices—young, bright, and energetic—had learned to absorb the endless hours. When budget battles flared or special legislation of overriding national importance arose—or just before recess when a myriad of business was being done before members of Congress would fly back to their constituencies in their home districts—that was when the pace could be brutal.

But the staff of Senator Jason Bell Purdy didn't mind the long hours. What they did find irritating was their new boss's habit of disregarding deadlines, appointments, or schedules for the sake of his own personal comfort or individual interests.

The chief of staff, the legislative assistant, and the press secretary had been waiting since three-thirty. They knew the senator was not on the floor voting. In fact, he was out taking another long lunch. The staff meeting, which Purdy himself had set for that time, was now on hold while the staff awaited the arrival of the newest member of the United States Senate.

For Jason Bell Purdy, schedules were something to be kept or broken depending on whim and personal desire. Such were the consequences of his upbringing as the grandson of a former Georgia governor and heir to the vast Purdy fortune, which controlled a healthy chunk of Georgia politics.

Purdy's chief claim to fame was his co-ownership of a professional baseball franchise, coupled with his ranking as richest man in the state.

As the senator meandered down the halls of the Dirksen Building he tugged slightly at his starched white collar and tightly knotted red-white-and-blue tie. The formal trappings of the Senate were something he was having to get used to. If it were up to him, he would stroll into his office every day wearing a golf shirt, khakis, and canvas boating shoes.

As he glided into his office, his staff quickly grabbed notepads, clipboards, and briefing books, and scurried in. The three staffers sat in the brown leather chairs in a semicircle around the ornate mahogany desk. Purdy slipped off his blue silk suit coat, hung it up on the brass coat rack, and then plopped into his overstuffed leather executive chair and swung both feet up on the desk.

"Hey, Myron," he called glibly. "Give me the box score here."

The chief of staff flipped through his legal pad and began a rapid-fire recitation of the status of his Senate office.

Purdy had upcoming meetings with several contingencies of constituents, a half dozen different lobbyists, followed by a briefing by his legislative assistant on several items of pending legislation. But he had failed to return a phone call from the chief of staff of Senator Wayne O'Brien, Chairman of the Senate Armed Services Committee and chair of the Subcommittee on Counterterrorism.

"Would you like me to get Senator O'Brien's office on the line right now?" Myron asked.

"Hey, let's not rush the gun on this thing," Purdy replied. "I have a feeling O'Brien just wants me to do some Chinese laundry for him. He's tossing me nuts for the squirrels. I've been waiting for a decent leadership assignment on the Counterterrorism Subcommittee since I got here."

"Senator," the legislative assistant said diplomatically, "your selection, as a freshman senator, to the Subcommittee on Counterterrorism is a real coup. From what I know, it certainly takes time to build ethos with the other senators. I'm sure in a short period of time that Senator O'Brien and his colleagues on our side of the aisle are going to recognize your value."

"Jimmy—with all due respect—don't patronize me, now. I'm telling the three of you that we gotta get some distinguishing assignments— we need some blue-ribbon issues to sink our teeth into. Otherwise, you boys and girls are going to end up with the shortest congressional careers of any staffers in the Beltway—when election time comes up and I get a whopping because we haven't done anything significant during what's left of my appointment term."

Linda, his press secretary, smiled and then volunteered her thoughts.

"Senator, how about that Mexico incident?"

"That's what I'm talking about!" Purdy said, pulling his feet off the desk and slapping the top of the desk with his hand. "That Mexico deal is *exactly* what I'm talking about. We got some kind of massacre that's going on down there. The Pentagon's not telling us. Everybody's scratching their heads over that. I can smell a feeding frenzy on this deal. We got that group of marines—what do you call that, a...you know, a small group..."

"A squad?" Myron asked with a wry smile.

"That's exactly right," Purdy continued. "This squad of marines goes down there and shoots up a bunch of innocent people. Now I know we've gotta tip our hats to them for the rescue of our Secretary of Commerce. And I do tip my hat—I thank God for his safe rescue. But this colonel—what's his name?"

"Marlowe. Colonel Caleb Marlowe," Linda, the press secretary, said.

"Right. Colonel Caleb Marlowe. He needs to be investigated. I think there is some slime on the bottom of this pond. I think the Pentagon is trying to make some kind of covert move—or maybe even the White House—I've just got that sense. They're not telling us the full story."

"With all due respect," Jimmy, the LA said, "Chairman O'Brien has got that as his number-one agenda item—"

"I don't want to hear what Chairman O'Brien has on his little shopping list," Purdy snapped back. "I'm here to tell you what's on the top of my list. And this is what I want for Christmas, little boys and girls, so listen up—I want a Senate subcommittee hearing—I want to chair it, and I want to look into this Mexico massacre and this whole Marine Corps incident. And I want that to happen."

The senator dismissed his chief of staff and legislative assistant but asked his press secretary to stay.

After the two male staff members left, Jason Bell Purdy grabbed the crystal golf ball off of the brass golf-ball holder on his desk and poised it between his index finger and thumb.

"Linda—you have any plans tonight? I was hoping we could order in some Chinese food—go over some of these press releases that need to go out tomorrow."

"Sure," the young press secretary said, with a tinge of hesitation in her voice.

"Why don't you go order the food—I've got a call I need to make."

She stood up dutifully and left his office, closing the door behind her.

Then Purdy grabbed his cell phone and punched the number for Howard John "Howley" Jubb.

Jubb picked up the cell phone in his black Hummer as he was nearing downtown Atlanta.

"Hey," Purdy said. "Jason calling. I want you to be by your landline at ten o'clock tonight. I've got to talk to you about something."

"Are you sure?" Jubb asked. "I was heading into the city to have some fun tonight."

"Change of plans. Be by your landline. I need you to start thinking about contacts we might have down in Mexico. I've gotta have you do an investigation for me. I need some inside stuff on that Mexican shoot-up down there in the Yucatán involving the marines. Think about some of the banditos down there who are willing to give us some information."

"Sure—I'll be by the phone. We'll work it out then. Say," Jubb added, "are you all settled in in your new house up there in Chevy Chase?"

"Yeah—I sure am. I'll have you over some time. We'll bring you out here to DC."

"Sure," Jubb replied, sounding as if he didn't believe it. "I thought when you went east, I was going east with you."

"We'll talk about it. See ya."

Linda knocked on the door, and Purdy told her to open it.

She poked her head in and asked, "What kind of Chinese do you want?"

The senator smiled and leaned back in his chair. "Sweet and sour," he said. "Just like me."

6

WILL CHAMBERS SLOWLY WHEELED OFF the country road and onto the long, winding driveway that led to his home. His house was perched atop a rise in the Virginia countryside that had, since the Civil War, been called Generals' Hill. The newly built structure was a huge, split-log house looking over to the Blue Ridge Mountains. Will had it built after his pre–Civil War mansion had burned to the ground a year-and-a-half after Audra's death.

As he slowly motored up the driveway, his tires crunching in the gravel, Will glanced up toward the front of the porch that wrapped around the house. He noticed Fiona's Saab convertible parked there.

Fiona's meeting with her business manager and agent must have ended earlier than they thought, Will mused. In anticipation of her meeting running late, he had picked up some deli sandwiches and soup for a late-night dinner. But he wasn't hungry now. And he wasn't even sure what he was going to tell his wife about his meeting with the DC police department. Communication was key to their relationship…he knew that. At the same time, what he had to share seemed destined only to cast gloom and chaos into the middle of their marriage.

For a few moments Will sat in his car with the engine running, staring at the front door of the log house. Then something at the door caught his eye.

Fiona swung the front door open and stepped out onto the porch. She was still wearing a baseball cap with her hair tucked under it. She must have just arrived.

She waved with one hand, hesitantly, and then peered toward Will. Then she broke into a broad smile. Sweeping the baseball cap up off her head, she let her dark hair cascade down and motioned for her husband to come in.

Will grabbed the grocery bag of food and trudged up the varnished wood steps that led to the porch. Fiona was in the doorway and didn't wait for him to enter. She surrounded him with her arms and gave him a big, long kiss. Then she led him into the large open kitchen and sat him down, and then sat down across from him at the large oak table. The last light of day was now streaming through the skylights and, off in the distance, the sun was setting with a brilliant outpouring of red and pink.

Fiona urged her husband to tell her everything about his meeting with the police.

Will went through it all in cold, factual detail. The death of the inmate...his confession as one of the assailants involved in Audra's murder...the certainty of his involvement...and the existence of another perpetrator who, as of yet, had not been located. And, with crushing finality, he described the likely motivation for the murder—his successful lawsuit against the neo-Nazi organization in New York.

As he talked, Fiona held her peace. But he knew she wanted to speak—to respond to what he was telling her. He had learned to detect the signs—she would purse her lips together slightly and her eyes would begin dancing.

After he had finished he held his hands open but said nothing, as if to indicate he had said his piece—and there was nothing more to say.

"And?" Fiona said, her voice rising slightly in a question.

"And..." he answered, "that's it. That's all I know. That's all they told me."

Another few seconds of silence went by, and then she spoke again.

"And?" she added, this time more emphatically.

"And what?" Will said, staring at the kitchen table.

"*And*—what is going on inside you as you're dealing with all of this?" she asked with a slight edge of irritation in her voice.

"I don't know," he responded vaguely. "I have absolutely no idea how I'm feeling right now."

A few seconds of silence went by, and then Fiona continued.

"I'm not your dentist—and I'm not going to pull teeth. You're my husband, I'm your wife. You need to open up and tell me what's really on your heart."

"And how would I do that?" he said curtly. "Okay, here goes—I feel like somebody has just kicked me in the gut. I feel like somebody has taken a butcher knife and stuck it into my heart. That's how I feel. That's where I'm at. So—what good is it going to do to lay all that out in front of you? Let's just leave it alone."

"It's called marriage," she said with passion and a little catch in her voice. "I'm just...stupefied."

"About what?"

"That you—an attorney whose profession requires him to argue the fine points of the law, a lawyer who has vindicated the down-trodden and has righted the injustices in cases around the nation, a man who has escaped death several times, a man who is apparently fearless about everything—has neither the desire, nor the courage, to look his wife in the face and tell her the truth about how he is really feeling about this news from the police."

Will pushed himself back from the table with a wry chuckle.

"You know, we've got this mixed up...you're the one who ought to be the trial lawyer."

"Please don't patronize me." Fiona continued to probe. "I want to really hear what's going on in your heart."

"You sure about that?" he asked with some hesitation.

"I'm absolutely sure, darling." She laid her hand on his.

"Okay—how about this? I feel like I'm living in two dimensions. A parallel universe. I'm here in this house with you. I love you madly. But it was here, on top of this very hill, in that one-hundred-and-fifty-year-old mansion Audra and I were fixing up, where we were loving and trying to make a life for ourselves. Yes, she did leave me. But I was convinced—maybe I'm still convinced—that if the murder wouldn't have happened, she would have come back and we would have patched things up and stayed together. So I guess what I'm saying is...if it makes any sense...I feel like I'm living out multiple personalities—like I'm walking through a house of mirrors in some twisted carnival."

His wife was silent and cocked her head. And then she spoke.

"Will...I love you. But you need to listen to me on this. No matter how large this big log house is, it's not big enough for the three of us. Audra doesn't fit in this house—or our lives. You're married to *me*. Whatever you need to do to come to grips with that...you're going to have to do it. I will not share my house, or my marriage, or my bed with some phantom."

Fiona stood up and turned to walk away, but then she looked back.

"Just let me know when you choose *our life together* as the life you want to live."

7

COLONEL CALEB MARLOWE'S VOICE at the other end of the telephone was direct and unemotional.

"Mr. Chambers, where do we stand—about your representing me?"

"Well, Colonel Marlowe, I may need time to think about it. I'm not really clear on why you called me. These are military charges, under the court-martial jurisdiction of the military."

"Yes, that's correct. Mr. Chambers, how many military cases have you handled before?"

"Well, Colonel, just one," Will replied.

"And what was that case about?"

"It was a long time ago. I represented a naval officer in San Diego. I think the charges were 'conduct injurious to the good order of the military'—something like that."

"Why was he charged?"

"Because he had made some statements critical of the military."

"How did the case end up?"

"Well, we won. Beginner's luck, I guess."

"How did you get the case?"

"That was back when I worked with the ACLU. Back when I was young and foolish."

The other man didn't see the humor in that.

"But since then," Will added, "I've experienced a major shift in my worldview—a spiritual realignment, you might say."

Marlowe kept pressing. "I would like you to represent me as civilian counsel in these charges. All I need to do is meet you in person and size you up, eyeball-to-eyeball."

"Like I said," the lawyer replied, "I may need some time to think about this. These are serious charges. How many charges of murder, did you say?"

"Two charges—four specifications on each charge. Each specification represents one of the four victims."

"Colonel, to put it to you straight—there are a number of lawyers inside the Beltway that do a lot more military criminal defense than I do. With charges as serious as these, you may want to consider that."

"To repeat myself, Mr. Chambers, I want you to represent me as civilian counsel. I have military counsel already detailed to my defense. The two of you would work together. All I need to do is meet with you in person."

"So you're asking for a snap decision from me?"

"With all due respect," Marlowe replied, "in the marines we have a rule—it's called the seventy-percent rule. Have you ever heard of it?"

"Can't say I have."

"Well, it goes something like this: If you have to make a critical decision, better to be seventy-percent correct at the right time than to be one-hundred-percent correct when it's too late."

"Then let me ask you a question," Will responded.

"Take a shot."

"Why are you so insistent on retaining me as your legal counsel?"

"A couple of reasons. One in particular. But I'd rather discuss that with you in person."

The lawyer paused. He flipped open his calendar and glanced at the next two months. His schedule was only moderately filled—he had tried to leave it as light as possible following his return from his honeymoon. The most time-consuming matter was the lawsuit against General Kurtzu Nuban, the despot and ruler of Sudan. Nuban had been responsible for the torture and death of several American missionaries, and Will was representing their families. He and the government of Sudan had hired two large Washington, DC, law firms to defend him. For the last year those two firms had been trying to bury Will in an avalanche of paperwork, technical objections, and jurisdictional arguments. He would have to gear up for a major hearing on the jurisdictional issue in a few weeks. But other than that, his calendar was relatively clear. He was convinced he could fit in Colonel Marlowe's case.

"All right—I'll tentatively agree to represent you. But when we meet in person and I get the facts of your case, if for any reason I do not feel comfortable taking on this matter, I reserve the right to bail out immediately."

"That's affirmative," Marlowe said. "They've got me in custody—confined to the grounds here at Quantico. You'll have to come up here. I'll arrange for a conference room and have military defense counsel at that meeting. I'll call you tomorrow to let you know which building we'll be meeting at."

"I'll wait for your call."

"One other thing," the colonel added.

"What is it?"

"As far as my case…where it goes from here…and the possibility of plea-bargaining—I just want to let you know what my position is. Up front."

"What?"

"As we go into this, I've determined a level of acceptable losses."

"And—what level of loss are you willing to accept in your case?"

Colonel Marlowe did not hesitate.

"None, counselor. None."

8

In The Hague, Netherlands, Francine Les Forges, prosecutor of the United Nations International Criminal Court, was meeting with her deputy prosecutor, Atavar Strinsky. The prosecutor had her back turned and was speaking on the phone at her large, gleaming, stainless-steel desk. She smoothed her black hair with one hand.

Atavar was a young, pale-faced international law prosecutor in his second year at the ICC. While he waited for his boss to finish her telephone conversation, he glanced around her room. He had seen the pictures and plaques many times before. The framed photograph of her before the French Supreme Court of Appeals. Several framed newspaper clippings from the *London Times* and *Le Monde,* as well as articles from the *New York Times* and the *International Herald.* They all described the war crimes trial of Slobodan Milosevic, where she had been the youngest deputy assistant prosecutor on the case. On the other wall there was a large framed calligraphy in multiple colors saying the same thing in ten different tongues:

THERE WILL BE NO GLOBAL PEACE
WITHOUT GLOBAL JUSTICE

A few minutes later, Les Forges hung up and swung around in her large executive chair, facing Atavar.

"So," she began, "you said you have a referral for me."

"This is the matter," he began, "that I told you about. From Mexico. The incident down in the Yucatán. I sent you over the e-file on this."

"Yes, I took a look at that. I think this is premature. But I have to tell you I am very intrigued. Quite interested. This could be a superb case for the ICC. Don't you see? This was an unparalleled act of aggression by a small combat force of American marines—I believe they were marines. I'm not sure. Do you know whether they were?"

Atavar shook his head. "Ms. Les Forges, we are not entirely certain about that. We believe that the commanding officer is an officer with the U.S. Marines. But as to whether or not this was a unit of the marines…for some reason the information isn't very clear on that."

"Well, never mind—that is not important. The United States decided to penetrate the borders of the sovereign State of Mexico in pursuit of what it has described as a cell of terrorists. But *without* permission—before committing an assault on a civilian house. The result?"

Atavar started to rustle through the papers on his lap, mistaking the prosecutor's rhetorical statement for a question.

"The result?" she continued, her hands waving in the air as if she were conducting a small orchestra. "Four Mexican nationals killed in an attack that certainly appears barbaric."

"There is something you should know," her deputy spoke up.

"What?" the prosecutor snapped.

"This really isn't a formal referral. It's more like an inquiry."

"Please explain that to me. What are you saying?" she demanded.

"The state party—here, Mexico—has not formally referred this matter to our office for possible prosecution. The Deputy Minister of the Interior called and merely wanted to find out whether we would be willing to look into this if it *were* formally referred."

Les Forges' face grew animated. She snatched a cigarette out of her desk and lit it with a silver lighter, ignoring the no-smoking regulation in the ICC building.

"You see?" she began, standing up and straightening her suit brusquely. And then she started walking around the room as she talked. "The state party bureaucrats, they are cowards. They don't want to commit to making a formal referral. So they call us—you see how they call us this way? Prying. Insinuating. Implying. Asking us whether we would do *this*, if they refer *that*. Would we prosecute this case if they refer the following facts to us? And I ask them to verify with a formal referral. And they turn me down because they lack the political courage to send these formal charges to the ICC. They're afraid that the ICC may just begin doing its job to police the world—and begin punishing the atrocities of bully nations."

Les Forges was off on her favorite diatribe—impugning "bully nations" and seeking to expand the power of the ICC to prosecute war crimes. Strinsky had heard it all before. He wouldn't mind it if he thought—deep down—that the prosecutor really believed what she said. But he didn't think that. She would chain-smoke her French cigarettes, strutting and lecturing her staff—without moral conviction. It all seemed a little like a schoolgirl who recited her Latin lessons from Virgil's *Aeneid* with gusto…but failed to understand, or even care, what she was reciting.

Atavar was suddenly aware that the prosecutor was standing and staring at him, one arm across her chest and the other straight up in the air, her fingers wriggling the cigarette nervously.

"I told him that I would talk to you," he said, breaking the uncomfortable pause. "And that's what I have done. I told him we likely could not do anything without a formal referral with the formal backing of the president of Mexico. And of course, there's that situation of instability in the Mexican presidency—"

"Of course. Exactly. That is exactly what I am talking about!" Les Forges broke out again, flicking her ashes on the carpet. "Like so many other countries, there is a fractured political base in Mexico. President Alienda is hanging on by his fingertips. The insurgent party is clamoring for him to get tough. For him to tell the United States that Mexico is no longer its poor little pack donkey south of the border. It is a full-fledged member of the international community."

"What do you want me to tell him?"

"Tell him…" she began, pausing to pick a piece of tobacco off her tongue and flick it with her painted nails, "tell him that we need a formal referral from the office of the president of Mexico. Tell him that. Until then—we do not give impromptu opinions about what we might do if a hypothetical set of facts is referred to us. I want a formal referral. And then we will act."

"Well," Atavar added, "we would also need the jurisdictional prerequisite before we could act anyway."

"Of course. Certainly. That goes without saying," Les Forges replied curtly. "And as for that—we will simply wait and watch."

As she strolled to the large glass window overlooking the plaza below, she took a long drag of her cigarette and then exhaled slowly before she spoke again.

"Before too long, we will see, I trust, the true face of American arrogance."

9

WILL WAS MOTORING DOWN THE LONG avenue that was flanked by thick woods. After a secluded stretch of roadway he approached the guard shack bordering the Marine Corps base at Quantico. He pulled up and produced his identification.

"I'm on my way to the Legal Defense office," the lawyer explained.

The armed sentry glanced at his clipboard. "Who are you here to see, sir?"

"Major Douglas Hanover."

The sentry nodded and waved him on.

After more woods, Will drove slowly uphill through the maze of barracks, administrative buildings, and winding streets that compose the self-enclosed military compound. After making his way up the hill to the vicinity of the parade deck, he parked in front of the building that housed the Judge Advocate's office.

Snatching his briefcase he trotted into the single-story building. As he entered the lobby he noticed a glum-looking marine seated on one of the plastic lobby chairs with his hands folded in front of him. He reported to the information desk.

"Sir, Major Hanover will be with you shortly," the marine at the desk said.

Will glanced around the lobby and saw the large sign over the entrance:

WHEN JUSTICE IS DONE
THE GOVERNMENT ALWAYS WINS

The lawyer waited ten minutes, and then a marine officer in a crisp tan-and-green uniform strode over and shook his hand firmly.

41

"I'm Major Doug Hanover. I'm detailed defense counsel for Colonel Marlowe."

Hanover appeared to be in his mid-thirties. He had a marine "high and tight" haircut and wore glasses.

"If you'll follow me," he went on, "Colonel Marlowe is waiting in my office."

Will followed the major down a short hallway, and the two of them ducked into a small, cramped office with stacked boxes of files, a small bookcase with a handful of books and manuals, and one small window that overlooked a physical-training field.

Seated in a chair in front of the desk was the colonel. He stood to his feet immediately and gave the lawyer a bone-crushing handshake.

Will studied Marlowe's square, rugged face. He had dark circles under his eyes, but gave him a slight smile.

As the colonel released his vise grip, Will sat down next to him in front of Hanover's desk. Marlowe was the first to speak.

"Mr. Chambers, you and I have something in common."

"Oh?"

"That snake Abdul el Alibahd."

Major Hanover had a quizzical look on his face.

"Mr. Chambers here has earned my respect as a civilian combatant," Marlowe explained to Hanover. "About two years ago he was captured by Abdul el Alibahd. Held hostage in connection with some case he was handling. Mr. Chambers escaped to tell the tale."

"I hate to interrupt a highly decorated marine, particularly when he's in the process of pinning medals on me," Will said, smiling. "But the truth is—I didn't really escape from el Alibahd. He released me. It was all part of this bizarre situation—he wanted me to deliver a message for him. Because I held some value, he released me to be a messenger boy. That's basically it."

"You're being modest, Mr. Chambers," Marlowe countered. "I have some inside information about this character."

"Oh?" Will said. "What information?"

The colonel leaned toward Will and gave him a slow, enigmatic smile. "I was on the mission, along with some Delta Force boys and another specialized unit, when we apprehended el Alibahd and carried him off on a stretcher. He was dying of cancer at the time we captured him. He died shortly after that. We killed his bodyguards during the capture. I was later debriefed by the FBI. Your name came up because they were following up on your story about being released by el Alibahd. Apparently you told them that he had wanted you to deliver some *jihad* message to billionaire Warren Mullburn."

"Yeah, that's right," Will said. "And I did. And as between el Alibahd and Mullburn...I don't know who was scarier."

Major Hanover redirected the conversation.

"Mr. Chambers, do you do a lot of military defense?"

"Hardly any," Will admitted without hesitation. "And that's why I was reluctant to get involved in this case. These are horrendous charges."

Then the lawyer looked Marlowe in the eye.

"Colonel, this is a potential capital case. If you're convicted of premeditated murder you could be facing the death penalty."

The colonel straightened up quickly.

"I know you told me you hadn't handled many military cases. That's not the first consideration. It was more important to me what kind of man you were."

Then he reached into his pocket, pulled out a crumpled magazine article, and started reading. "This is an article published last year in the *Trial Court Digest*—about a case you handled down in Delphi County, Georgia, last year:

> Virginia lawyer Will Chambers has established an impressive record of winning difficult civil liberties cases against imposing odds. But recently, he has also added a new qualification to his list of credentials—survivor of bizarre episodes of incarceration and kidnapping.

> While representing a mother wrongfully charged with child abuse, Chambers was jailed for contempt of court by a local circuit judge. The Georgia Supreme Court wasted no time reversing the contempt order and ordering Chambers' immediate release, but not before he had been inexplicably transferred to an auxiliary jail facility that resembled something out of Cold War Russia. While there, Chambers was subjected to electric shock by a sadistic guard, as well as a severe beating at the hands of an inmate.

Fortunately, he escaped without permanent injury and went on to win an acquittal for his client.

Prior to that, while representing Angus MacCameron, a fundamentalist preacher, in a defamation case brought by the late, renowned Harvard scholar, Dr. Albert Reichstad, Chambers was tracked down and captured by henchmen of the Middle Eastern terrorist mastermind Abdul el Alibahd. Chambers managed to survive that brush with death also."

Hanover's eyes had widened, but he said nothing.

"So you see," Marlowe continued, "that's the kind of guy I want representing me in a trial for my life—somebody who has successfully survived extreme, high-risk situations."

"And Major Hanover could certainly help bring you up to speed with the Rules for Courts-Martial in the Uniform Code of Military Justice," the colonel added.

After a moment's pause Major Hanover threw in a comment. "And for what it's worth, I'd appreciate the opportunity to work with you jointly on this defense."

Marlowe was studying Will keenly, waiting for his response.

"All right," the attorney said slowly. "Then I think we've got a team. Major Hanover, I'm going to rely on you for the procedural points. When can I get a complete copy of the discovery that prosecution trial counsel has in hand?"

"I've already got our office burning copies. There's a huge volume of paperwork here that I will get to you in the next day or so. Copies of all their evidence and investigations. Copies of investigation reports from the Naval Criminal Investigation Service, which was assigned to make the immediate military investigation before the charges and specifications were preferred. Also some DOD stuff. But there is a problem."

"What kind of problem?" Will asked.

"This kind of problem," Colonel Marlowe responded, passing a Department of Defense message to the attorney. "The communications center just delivered it to me today."

Will studied the message, glancing at the top. It was from the Deputy Secretary of Defense, and was also copied to the General Counsel of the Department of Defense and to the Commandant, U.S.

Marine Corps. Will also noted that it was likewise copied to the Commander, U.S. Special Operations Command.

The correspondence ordered Colonel Marlowe *not* to discuss any element of the hostage rescue of the Secretary of Commerce with any person, including both civilian legal counsel and detailed military counsel. Marlowe was further instructed in the letter not to divulge any details or factual information on the nature of his unit—or any information related to the military configuration, composition, or "ultimate" mission of the unit to which he had been assigned at the time of the hostage rescue and subsequent counterterrorist operation.

After Will had studied the message he glanced over at his new client, who returned his gaze—expressionless except for one slightly raised eyebrow.

"So they're playing the national-security card on us," Marlowe said.

"Where does that leave us?" the attorney asked. "How much information can we get now? I see us obtaining very little about the underlying facts. They've blindfolded us, and now they're walking us down a dark alley."

"Here's the way I see this. Until we get some further direction on this, there's not much I can tell you about what went on down there in Mexico. These are my orders. And I'm obeying them."

Will tapped his index finger on the letter. "I think we've got to get a clarification of the terms and conditions of this gag order." Then he scanned down the message again to the last paragraph, which read,

> You are to consider this a direct order from the Secretary of Defense. The restrictions placed on you under the terms of this letter are based upon matters of the highest national security.

After Will thought for another moment he continued. "I see the order in this message prohibiting you, Colonel Marlowe, from discussing anything with your defense counsel about the actual hostage rescue of the Secretary of Commerce. I'm presuming that would include things like logistics, the informants you used, and the actual mission itself. But, what happened in the Yucatán *after* the rescue—that's what you're charged with. While you were pursuing the terrorists."

Then he turned back to Major Hanover. "Major, why don't you contact OSD and talk to someone in the general counsel's office? See if you can get a clarification, in writing, that would permit us to go into the details of the terrorist pursuit that *followed* the hostage rescue."

"Yes, sir, I agree," Hanover replied. "I'll send a message this afternoon."

The major rose to his feet, apologizing and indicating that he had to get to a hearing in five minutes.

Will and Hanover shook hands quickly as he grabbed his file and asked Marlowe for permission to leave.

Will still had the message from the Secretary of Defense in his hand. He lifted it up to Colonel Marlowe. "This national-security directive is going to make it awfully difficult for me to represent you."

"Did you ever serve in the military?" Marlowe asked.

Will shook his head.

"But you do understand chain of command?"

The attorney nodded.

"Civilians are always criticizing the military because we're supposedly one-track-minded—always focused on following orders. But the thing about warfare is, it's total chaos. The only source of order in that chaos comes from the orders that are given…and the orders that are followed."

Then the colonel's face took on a stern, thoughtful expression. "One of the other reasons I hired you, Mr. Chambers, is because I found out you were a man who walks with the Lord."

Will reached into his brown leather briefcase and pulled out a pocket Bible. He lifted it up in his hand so that Marlowe could see it. "These are my marching orders," he said with a smile. "And I do understand chain of command."

"That's good," the other man responded. And then his eyes took on more intensity as he spoke. "Joshua. Chapter one, verse eighteen— 'Anyone who rebels against your command and does not obey your words in all that you command him, shall be put to death.' That was God's battle plan for Joshua as he led the army into Canaan."

The colonel rose to his feet. "Mr. Chambers, I had lawful orders from the President of the United States, through the Department of Defense, through the chain of command, to execute that mission in Mexico. That's exactly what I did. I consider that a command from God because God made me a marine—in *this country*, subject to the lawful authority of this government under a system instituted by God. I followed those orders. And as a result…well…things went real bad."

Marlowe grimaced, and grew quiet.

"Bad," Will noted. "Meaning four people dead. Civilians. Nonterrorists."

"Much worse," his client said quietly. "The four dead were people I knew. Carlos Fuego, a friend of mine for many years, and his beautiful wife, and his two little children were shot to death—blown apart—as a result of my order to my unit."

The attorney was unsure how to respond to that. For a moment, what Marlowe had just said—his brutally clear assessment that his orders had caused the death of an entire innocent family—struck home. Will didn't understand, at that early stage of the case, why things had gone so catastrophically wrong when Marlowe's special operations unit had attacked a small house in the Yucatán jungle. But something was very clear to him.

His client—for good or bad—was facing the fact that his actions had had fatal results. Why was Will unwilling—or unable—to do the same thing regarding Audra? Why couldn't he start dealing with his responsibility for her death—rather than trying to cram it into the farthest corner of his mind?

While the lawyer was still deep in thought, the colonel broke the silence.

"I'm not a murderer," he said. "What happened in our attack…that was unintended…I had no idea Carlos and his family would get hit in there. But…" Marlowe rubbed the back of his neck and considered what he was going to say next. He walked over to the window and stared out.

"But I have to figure out how I live with that…" And then his voice trailed off as he added, "…and how I am going to finish my mission."

Will rose to his feet. Marlowe turned, and the two looked at each other—eye-to-eye.

"And what mission would that be?"

"I can't divulge that," the colonel replied.

He then shook hands firmly with Will, took the message back, put it back in its folder, and turned to leave.

"Colonel," Will said as his client was preparing to depart.

Marlowe turned.

"In that same chapter, God also commanded something else. Joshua and his soldiers were commanded to also obey the entire law of Moses. Including the command not to commit murder."

"Point taken," the colonel said, and he then squared his shoulders and left the room.

Will grabbed his briefcase. As he was leaving the building he wondered who the real opponent in this case would be. The U.S. government bringing the charges? A zealous trial counsel prosecuting the case for the military? Or perhaps even the White House? As he crossed the road overlooking the Quantico compound, heading to his car, he wondered if there was yet another possibility. His most difficult opposition might not come from any of those sources.

Will was beginning to think that the ultimate battle might be with his own client.

10

WILL HAD GONE TO HIS OFFICE in Monroeville, Virginia, early that morning.

However, he was having a hard time focusing as he sat at the desk. He stared at the papers in front of him. But he was thinking of something else.

He was still dealing with the aftermath of a dream he had had the night before. It had been about Audra.

The two of them had been together in a crowded room. Perhaps it had been a party of some kind. But he had been unable to hear what she was saying. Then a policeman had entered the room, smiling. Suddenly he had been aware that a gun was being pointed directly at his wife. He had tried to reach it, but his arms had felt as though they had been tied to his sides. His feet had been immovable, as if paralyzed. The police officer had been staring straight ahead—oblivious to the threat. The gun had fired—Audra had fallen back slowly, almost gracefully, with her arms outstretched—reaching out for something—or someone. Will had tried to scream, but no words had come out.

When he had awakened, he had been cloaked with a suffocating feeling of dread. At breakfast Fiona had said she had known he was dealing with something, but Will had shrugged it off. He'd decided not to tell Fiona about his dream. But she'd been able to see that it was gnawing at him, from the inside out.

Will looked again at the twelve-inch stack of documents on his desk that had been delivered from his military co-counsel at Quantico. It was time to get to work—regardless of how he felt.

His first task was to plow through the discovery production—the declassified documents that the government was willing to release. FBI agents and representatives of the Defense Intelligence Agency (DIA) had spent a day with him at his office, questioning him and gathering background information. In order for him to get access to the full scope of documents in Marlowe's case, he had to receive a top-secret security clearance.

Yet he knew that, even with such a clearance, he might still be barred from reviewing key documents in light of the gag order that the Defense Department had placed on his client.

As he paged through the documents, Will collected them into three categories.

The first group seemed innocuous. These were the records contained in Marlowe's officer qualification record regarding his educational and military background, his adjustments in pay scale, and his promotions. There were hundreds of entries relating to his assignments to various bases in the early part of his career. He also noticed that the colonel had been married. There were papers verifying a divorce action filed by his wife, Kathy, some ten years before. He saw no evidence that his client had remarried.

In the second group of documents Will caught a glimpse of the bone-crushing, nerve-shattering training regimen Marlowe had undergone in his metamorphosis from a skilled marine into one of the world's most deadly special operations commandos.

To Will, a typical civilian, the training experience defied description. The whole thing looked like one long bizarre ritual of pain.

Marlowe had trained with First Special Forces Operational Detachment—Delta Force—in the rugged terrain of Camp Dawson, West Virginia.

The colonel also voluntarily submitted himself to the unimaginable rigors of the Navy Seals' BUD/S qualifying program—including its "drown-proofing" exercise (being thrown into an extra-deep pool with his hands tied behind his back) and "hell week"—marching, running, and dodging hazards for days on end, without sleep and while shivering in water-drenched utilities.

With the Army Rangers, he had crawled for weeks through the swamps of Georgia, pulling leeches off of his body, avoiding alligators, and sharing fetid black-water pools with snakes.

Marlowe had become an expert in every weapon produced by the American military, in many produced by the Russians, the Brits, the Europeans, and in a host of those peddled by underground arms dealers.

He had been schooled in several language groups, submitted himself as a "victim" to authentic prison-camp torture exercises, and experienced the bad end of advanced psychological warfare.

Such was the information that the attorney was permitted to read. The details of many of the other training programs had been deleted or crossed out with black marker. He could only imagine the harrowing survival experiences that lay within the classified—and unrevealed—records.

The last group of documents was the only one that had direct relevance to the current charges. But Will shook his head in disbelief as he leafed through page after page of blank documents, with all but a few sentences here and there on each page concealed as "classified."

Most of the records were from the Naval Criminal Investigative Service, which had done a preliminary investigation into the Mexico incident. There was a shorter report from the DIA. The only portion of that report not excised was a brief geographical description of the area where the attack had taken place. The house that had been the site of the military operation was located near a small village called Chacmool, less than five miles away from the ancient Mayan ruins at Chichén Itzá. The house itself was isolated within a section of the dense Yucatán jungle.

There was also a CIA report. However, every word within the body of the report had been redacted.

After reviewing everything Will was able to piece together only a few basic details of the incident at Chacmool.

Marlowe had been leading a small unit of commandos who were in pursuit of a group designated only as AAJ. However, the events leading up to the nighttime attack—and indeed, information about the strike on the house itself—had been deleted from the documents produced to the defense.

Will turned to the autopsy protocol. Four bodies had been recovered from the site. One male adult, one female adult, and two children, ages ten and seven.

There was a knock at the door of his office.

Jacki Johnson, the senior legal associate in Will's office, stepped in with a smile. An attractive black woman, she had long been a part of Will's legal career—including a few ups and numerous downs. Her husband, Howard, taught history at Capitol College just north of Washington, DC.

"I just wanted to make sure you saw my memo on the Sudan case—the one about the defector from General Nuban's regime."

"You mean the PhD?" Will asked.

Jacki nodded and began to explain. "His name is Dr. Ibrahim Agabba. He was part of the administration before Nuban's military coup. They kept him on for some reason. But Agabba must have stuck out like a sore thumb—he actually had a seminormal human rights record. He finally escaped from Sudan and relocated down in North Carolina. He just got appointed to a teaching post at Duke University in Durham. I think he might be a valuable source of information in the lawsuit. Oh, and I will be taking two weeks off with my hubby starting next week."

"Why don't you do some of the groundwork in setting up a deposition of Dr. Agabba?" Will said. "Give him a call down there at Duke. Start furrowing the ground. When you get some more information about his current situation, let me know. And then we can schedule this deposition down there."

Then Will paused.

"What was that last thing you mentioned?"

"It's called a *vacation*. It's also called a *marriage*. These two things do go together. You ought to try it some time!"

Jacki smiled and then closed the door behind her. Will wanted to find some humor in that, but couldn't—so he turned back to the stack of files from Quantico. He stared for a minute at the pages of documents consisting mostly of blank spaces where information, details, and facts had once been located—but which had now been removed beyond his reach.

Will felt as if he were wandering in a jungle with no sense of direction. In order to effectively defend Colonel Marlowe there was something he needed. He had to get his hands on some kind of legal compass so he could figure out where it was he was wandering, and what minefields might lie ahead.

11

SENATOR WAYNE O'BRIEN, a wide and tall man with a full mane of gray-and-white hair, was seated on the couch of his spacious Senate office. He smiled broadly as his secretary poured coffee for him and for Jason Bell Purdy, who was seated in the chair across from him.

After the secretary left, O'Brien took a sip of his coffee, put the cup down on the china saucer, and leaned back on the couch and looked at Purdy. O'Brien was a ruddy-faced man with an easy manner with people. But during his long career representing the state of Georgia, he had also acquired the fine art of knowing when and where to address an issue with the force of a blunt axe.

"Jason, I appreciate you coming over here to talk this through. I did get your e-mail. And I got the follow-up phone call from your staffer. The fact is, though, I have no intention of giving you a chairmanship over any of our subcommittees. I've made up my mind, and there's very little use discussing it."

Purdy's foot bobbed nervously as he pursed his lips and squinted slightly at the older man.

"I'm very sorry to hear that. But I do not intend to let it rest there. I was led to believe, when I was appointed to fill out the term in this seat, that I would get at least one committee position of distinction. I've been waiting. And I'm still waiting."

"Well, perhaps I need to remind you," O'Brien intoned in his deep Georgia drawl, "that I did not favor you as the appointment to fill the term of Senator Hartley. That decision was made against my recommendation. Nevertheless, you and I are United States senators, representing the same state. As such, I want a good working relationship. In addition, we're supposed to be part of the same political party. That also ought to bring us together and give us some common ground. There's a lot you can learn. Just be patient. Expend your energies being a good senator. A good *freshman* senator. Do a lot of watching and listening. Represent your constituents. And the rest will take care of itself."

"With all due respect," the younger man said with clear agitation in his voice, "that is not the way things happen in politics. Not in the statehouse in Georgia. Not inside the Beltway in Washington, DC. And I'm sure you're smart enough and experienced enough to know that. So—let me just say this—I do plan on pushing this. And pushing it hard."

"Look, Jason," O'Brien said, trying to reason with him, "you bring no military or intelligence experience to the Senate. There is no good reason under the sun why I ought to appoint you as chair of that committee. Besides, that incident down in Chacmool is far too sensitive for a freshman senator to investigate. When you've been around the block a few times, you'll get the chairmanship of *some* committee, I can promise you that. As it is, I told you that I will make you a *member* of the Subcommittee on Counterterrorism. That in itself is a real honor for a freshman senator like you."

"I am not going to let this rest. I am going to challenge you on this," Purdy countered with his jaw slightly cocked.

O'Brien was now seething.

"Well now, Jason, why don't you go ahead and challenge me? Why don't you go to the party leadership? I'm sure they're gonna put a lot of stock in the whims and fancies of a freshman senator. Or better yet— why don't you air your grievance at the next party caucus? I'm sure they're going to want to hear what you have to say."

Now Purdy's face was flushed. The older man had just touched on a sore nerve. Jason Bell Purdy had been chastised soundly at the last caucus for arriving ten minutes late.

"You and I do come from the same state," Purdy replied with icy deliberation. "That means you need voters and you need money. And I have a lot of control—a lot of power in our state—and you know it."

"Don't threaten me, Jason." O'Brien chuckled. "I know the way your family used money. I know the favors you've done folks—and the favors you expect to collect. I don't like the way you play the game. I surely don't. But I really don't think you want to cross me, Jason. If this becomes a political blood feud I can guarantee you I will pin you to the mat in less than five seconds. Jason, you're a lightweight."

Purdy had heard enough. He rose quickly, not extending his hand to the older man.

"I am sorry for the direction this is heading," he snarled as he headed for the door.

O'Brien rose slowly and watched Purdy's back as he exited. In the corridors of the diplomatic and courtly Senate, Purdy's threatening conduct would normally be considered the unforgivable sin. On the other hand, the older senator knew that, like any other rogue bull, his younger colleague could do some damage.

O'Brien's goal now was simple—to use his cunning to lead the bull out to pasture without getting gored.

12

IN THE PROSECUTION SECTION OF THE OFFICE of the Staff Judge Advocate at the Quantico marine base, Colonel Ronald Stickton was conducting a strategy session with his chief investigator. The subject was the Chacmool deaths. Stickton was the assigned trial counsel, who would prosecute. The case promised to be one of the more closely watched court-martial proceedings in Marine Corps history. Stickton flipped through his massive file with the confidence of a man who had a good grasp of the obvious—that this one case could make his military career.

Special Agent Fred Brooks of the Naval Criminal Investigative Service, a middle-aged civilian in a suit and tie, had a cup of coffee in his hand, and he was aimlessly searching the drawers and cabinets of the conference room for some sugar.

"Fred, did you get a chance to get an update from the federal police down in Mexico?" Stickton asked.

Brooks discovered a lone packet of Sweet 'n' Low. He tore it open, dumped it into his cup, and turned to the other man.

"They told me they were shipping off the bullet fragments so we could do our ballistics. Not exactly critical, considering the other evidence we've got."

"True," the colonel answered, "but it's important to tie that up. Even though we've got overwhelming proof that Marlowe and his unit were in place, shooting tne victims to the point of death. We've recovered at least—what is it?—one of the weapons used by the AAJ?"

"Actually two. We've got the Uzi—that's ironic, isn't it? Arab terrorists from al-Aqsa Jihad using an Israeli-made automatic weapon? So we've got that, and we also found the semi-automatic pistol the bad guys left behind. When I was down there, it didn't look likely that any of the wounds to the four victims were tied to those weapons."

"All the same, we need to finish the ballistics matchup of the bullet fragments in the bodies with the weapons fired by Marlowe and his unit." Stickton tapped his pen on the table, then added, "You know my mama—when she cooks the Thanksgiving turkey, after she stuffs it, the last thing she does is sew it up. This ballistics will be the last sew-up we need to do on this turkey."

"Who are you calling a turkey? Colonel Marlowe? Or this assignment?" Brooks asked, stirring his coffee slowly.

"You didn't hear me call anybody a turkey," Stickton snapped back.

"Colonel, I thought you marines always stuck together—even when you're prosecuting each other in a general court-martial."

"I'm trial counsel—not defense counsel. My job is to do my duty for the corps and for my country. The way I see it," the colonel continued, "this is going to be a wake-up call to DOD about these Rambo groups."

"Speaking of that," Brooks responded, "when are we getting some identifying information on who Colonel Marlowe's guys were actually taking orders from? When can we stop calling it 'the unit' and find out the actual military designation and configuration of that group?"

"DOD has a gag order on defense counsel and trial counsel as well. Theirs is more severe than ours. The only limit on us involves evidence relating to the background and military identity of the special forces unit. The only other requirement is that we send the DOD legal liaison a preview of all the evidence we're intending to introduce at the Article 32 hearing. We have to tag everything we suspect may be sensitive. Then they screen the summary themselves and make their own independent determination on any evidence too sensitive to present."

"Well," Brooks said, glancing at his watch, "we need to get cracking on this. I've got an investigation off base at eleven hundred."

Stickton turned back to his discovery file. He glanced at the paper on top. "Okay. Here's the checklist," he said, running down the memo. "Number one. We've got the statements from the four other members of the unit. Colonel Marlowe refused to give a statement. Did you get anything from him down in Mexico besides the perennial name, rank, and serial number?"

"Actually," Brooks noted, "I didn't do the interrogations in Mexico. Remember? I finally got a crack at them on the USS *Nathan Hale*. It was being used as the command post for the operation."

"Yes, that's right," the colonel said. "They flew Marlowe and two of his men back to Isla Holbox so the Mexicans could see me serving the charges and apprehending him—I suppose that was to calm the international tensions. Then they dispatched the other two—Rockwell and Baker—back to the ship."

Brooks continued. "The ship's captain stonewalled me at first. It took me six hours and a dozen different phone calls from the *Hale* before I was able to interrogate the other four men. As you know, Thompson was seriously injured—he was shot at the scene—and was down in the sick bay. He was doped up, and I decided not to interrogate him until later. The other three wouldn't talk until they got direct orders from Marlowe."

"See—this is the kind of zombie commando stuff I don't like. Those guys were military personnel, presumably under the jurisdiction of the United States Marine Corps. This was a military investigation. They shouldn't be taking their orders from their former commanding officer—an officer who is confined to quarters and who's being investigated for multiple specifications of possible capital murder."

"Well, the point is, Colonel Marlowe did give them the go-ahead to give statements."

"That's correct—but only after demanding that any charge be placed on him—and that no charges were to be preferred against the members of his unit. That's arrogance."

"Some folks might call it leadership," Brooks countered, smiling.

"And what would you know about leadership over at NCIS?" The colonel gave a sardonic chuckle.

The special agent smiled again, opened his file, and pulled out his investigative report. As he scanned it he summarized his findings out loud.

"So, the hit list starts with the statements from three of the team members. All three confirmed they were positioned outside the house under Colonel Marlowe's command that night. They all confirmed that Marlowe gave the order. They all indicated he was in charge of making a decision based on the recon reports he had. They said he knew the rules of engagement because he had explained it to each of them—and those rules clearly indicated, on this assignment, that the 'locate and destroy' mission against the AAJ was secondary to the avoidance of civilian casualties. That the house was clearly a civilian home on the edge of the jungle—according to the members of his team, the colonel stated that his main source was the CIA operative who he ended up gunning down inside the house. All three confirmed there were shots fired by one of the terrorists who had exited the house.

"And that's when Marlowe gave the order to open fire. They also confirmed that Marlowe had thermal imaging, but no one knows what he saw. Which raises the question, why he didn't see that some of the bodies were different shapes—that there were two children in there? And finally, the colonel was the first one, and the *only* one, who actually entered the building."

"That's crucial," Stickton commented. "At least two of his team members confirmed—I think it's in one of the statements that you took—that Marlowe ducked in the house quickly, and ten seconds later he was out of there ordering the rest of his team *not to enter* the home or inspect the casualties. But of course, there is also the hugely important factor regarding what Marlowe did immediately after he exited the house."

"One thing that puzzled me," Brooks broke in. "How did the federal police arrive on the scene so soon? It was my conclusion they were on the scene within five minutes of the shooting. I thought the Mexican police were left out of the loop on this thing. They got there even before the helos showed up."

"Don't know," the trial counsel said. "As I looked over the reports from the federal police—that's number two on my memo here—I didn't come up with a straight answer. But you know the way the Mexican police operate. There's so much inside stuff—so much partnership with the criminal elements…deals cut with the local drug gangs…they probably knew about the operation going down even though the U.S. government didn't tell them."

"That's another thing," Brooks noted. "I had a question about the diagrams of the scene and the location of the bodies as indicated in the federal police reports. "

With that he pulled out the diagram of the room drawn by the Mexican police. Five stick bodies—four civilians and one terrorist—were noted in various positions. A photograph was also attached.

"The diagram—even the photograph—shows the bodies arrayed around a kitchen table in the middle of the room," Brooks continued. "It just seemed to me that—taking the trajectory of the bullets as they were coming from two directions—this kind of a configuration would be a rather strange way for the bodies to drop."

"Which means what?"

"I'm not sure," Brooks replied. "Just an observation."

"Well—from what I can see—each of those bodies took multiple hits. Twenty, thirty shots or other fragments into each body. So," Stickton continued, "because we know that the bullets in the bodies belong to the weapons fired by Marlowe's men—and because he gave a reckless order—I'm not sure how critical it really is, what the position of the civilians inside the house was at the moment of firing. Plus, that only plays to our advantage anyway. The more obvious their position was to Marlowe, the more culpable he is. But even if their position was hidden from his view, we know that he had a reasonable belief that there might be civilians in the house."

"You're talking about the tape?"

"Exactly. I've listened to it myself several times. It is clear and unambiguous. One of his men—I think it may have been Master Sergeant Rockwell—suggests some closer recon before they start a full-scale assault. Anyway, Marlowe says no, gives the order—and it's clear on the tape: 'I'm assuming the risk of collateral damage here—fire!'"

Special Agent Brooks glanced down at his notes. Then he looked out the window of the barracks building. Glancing back at Stickton, he spoke. "I just feel like there's something we need to know about what was going on inside that little shack ten seconds before the firing began."

"Disagree—my focus is somewhere else."

"Oh?"

"My focus is on Colonel Marlowe's knowledge when he gave the order to rain down death on Carlos Fuego, and on Carlos's wife and two little children."

Brooks looked at the photograph taken by the Mexican police and shook his head with a grimace.

"Something else that doesn't add up—Fuego had been a close friend of Marlowe's for more than ten years. Marlowe was the best man at his wedding."

"Carlos Fuego was also a CIA operative within Mexico," Stickton rapped out. "Let's not forget that little detail."

Brooks hadn't forgotten that fact. But in the big picture, it really didn't matter to him. Certainly, after he had investigated Caleb Marlowe's background...his decorated service...his character...he didn't believe that this marine would coldly execute his best friend along with his family just because they were in the way of his counterterrorism mission.

Yet two things seemed undeniable and painfully clear. First, that Marlowe had given the crucial order. And second, that four innocent people who had no business being there, had been directly in the line of fire.

For Brooks, this was reason enough for charges to be initially preferred. And for Colonel Stickton, it was enough to seek referral to a general court-martial...and then await the boost to his career that he felt would most certainly result.

13

THE SKY WAS BLUE, AND THERE WAS A CRISP FEEL to the morning air as Will wandered out onto the front porch. He looked out to the Blue Ridge Mountains that softly bordered the horizon. The cloud bank that had covered the foothills and the valleys at first light was beginning to dissipate.

He sipped from his steaming mug of coffee. Then he descended the stairs and walked around to the backyard.

There, Fiona was crouched down in the flower garden that wound along the back of the house and up to the path that led to the woods and fields beyond. She was wearing a sun hat and one of Will's work shirts with the shirttails hanging out, reaching down to mid-thigh.

She had been digging furiously with a hand trowel but stopped when Will approached.

"Hey, mister." She glanced at the large mug in Will's hand. "Okay—be honest—am I making decent coffee yet?"

"Honey," he said, assuming his television commercial voice, "have you switched brands? This is one great cup of coffee!"

"Oh, come on," Fiona said playfully, "tell me the truth. The first time I made coffee for you, you said it was far too weak. I have to keep reminding myself you prefer it like battery acid."

"All right," he replied with a smile. "Here's the straight scoop—you really do make a great cup of coffee. I have no complaints in that department. Now that I think about it, I have no complaints about my life with you at all."

He bent down and kissed his wife slowly, full on the mouth, and then moved his face back, still keeping it close to hers.

"Life with you is great. I'm really glad we've got a quiet weekend together. Aren't you?"

Fiona nodded and smiled broadly.

"So what are you thinking as you're digging out here in your garden?" he asked.

"You know, it's funny the things that go through your mind when you're working outside. I love working with my flowers. Digging in the moist ground. The smell of the earth. You know what keeps going through my mind?"

Will shook his head.

"I keep thinking of Pearl S. Buck—*The Good Earth*."

Then she cocked her head slightly and looked deep into Will's eyes. "So, my darling, what's on your mind this morning?" She suspected there was some silent interior struggle—but he wasn't letting on to it.

"Until I am at least halfway into my first cup of coffee," he replied, "I doubt if you'd find a single brainwave on an EEG."

His wife smiled back at him with a look of complacent disbelief. He felt a twinge of guilt. He was not being honest with her—not really. And he knew she was perceptive enough to detect it.

He had awakened that morning, as he had several previous mornings, overwhelmed with thoughts about Audra's murder—and the fact that an accomplice was still on the loose. He had tried to push those thoughts out of his mind. He worried that this had become an obsession—a psychological quicksand from which he found himself unable to escape. He had prayed to God for a mind that would be purified of the rage and the crushing guilt that seemed to overwhelm him.

He stood up slowly.

"I think I'm going to grab my chainsaw and cut up some of those hardwoods that have fallen. They'll make good firewood."

Fiona nodded and went back to her digging, thinking that perhaps hauling around tree limbs and cutting through logs would be a good emotional relief for her husband, if nothing else.

Will picked up the chainsaw in the garage. He put on his leather work gloves and, laying the chainsaw in the wheelbarrow, made his way up the path, stopping when he reached the middle of the woods that rose gently up from the back of the house.

He started trimming the small branches off a felled tree and then laid it on a stump and started cutting the trunk into segments, the wood fragments spitting out from the whining blade.

Will loved the smell of freshly cut wood.

After he had cut up the entire tree he clicked off his chainsaw and took a moment to glance down at Fiona, who was still digging busily in the ground. He glanced off into the distance where the sun was illuminating the soft mountaintops in a variety of velvet green colors.

But then, out of nowhere, a thought intruded. He had tried to contact Captain Jenkins at the DC police department during the week and had been told he would be back on duty that Saturday. Will had wanted to get an update on the investigation.

Why don't you give it a rest? he thought to himself.

He grabbed his axe and began quartering the freshly cut logs. As he brought the blade down onto the round end of each log, cracking it in two, his mind kept gnawing on the same thought.

Finally he tossed the axe down, stripped off his gloves, and tossed them into the wheelbarrow. He walked down the woods past Fiona and into the back door of the house.

Picking up the phone, he dialed the DC police department. A dispatcher answered. She indicated that Captain Jenkins was in and asked Will to hold. After a few seconds the captain answered.

"Counselor, what can I do for you?"

"Just wondering whether there's anything new on the investigation. I'd really like to know what you folks are doing about getting an ID on that second man."

"Like I said before," Jenkins said, with a bit of fatigue in his answer, "we will let you know when there are any new developments. We're going through all the standard stuff. We're doing due diligence—going back over the original file on this case. Reviewing everything. We've got a couple leads. Nothing significant. But if anything pops, I promise we will give you a call immediately. Now until then, why don't you go on with your life? Enjoy your marriage to your beautiful wife. Keep up with things in your law practice.

"You know, this could be a very long and tedious process before we're ever able to get a positive ID. What we are really doing here is reopening a cold case file. Rest assured—we are tracking down every lead. Now, let us do the worrying. I will let you know the minute we get any further information."

As the conversation ended and Will put the phone down, he turned and saw Fiona staring at him from across the kitchen.

She pulled her sunbonnet off. There was a funny look on her face.

"Who are you calling?" she asked gently.

"DC police. Just trying to keep tabs on their investigation."

Fiona pursed her lips together, but said nothing.

"Okay—say it," Will said.

"You know," she began, "we were outside and you kissed me. And you said how glad you were we had this weekend together. Just the two of us. With the difficulties in our schedules and in our lives, having this kind of time is precious. But we really aren't having this weekend together, are we? It's not just the two of us, is it?"

She tossed her gloves and sunbonnet on the chair and walked over to the stove.

"How about I make us a big brunch—I'm starving." She did not turn around.

"How about if I help you?" Will said, stepping over toward her.

She wheeled around quickly.

"Don't bother. I'm glad to do it. Why don't you go back and finish splitting the logs?"

He could see the look in her eyes. Although they'd only been married a short time, he knew that look. She was trying to be patient—to be the dutiful wife—but she was stretched to the breaking point.

Walking over, Will put his hands on her shoulders and kissed her on the cheek.

"I do love you, Fiona. I love you more than life itself."

She partially turned toward him and, with a glance to the side, smiled a half-smile.

"And I love you," she said with no expression in her voice.

Will turned, left the kitchen, and began walking up the hill to the woods.

It all seemed so awkward, the see-saw cycles of their relationship. Married, he was now wandering in the wilderness of intense human interaction, a place where there were no clean fact patterns, no precisely worded black-letter rules—no detailed, codified regulations. Those things belonged to the abstractions of law—not the realities of love. He thought back to the first time his father had taken him out, as a young boy, to learn how to hit a golf ball. The ball had seemed so ridiculously small, and the golf swing his father was trying to teach him had seemed so laughably unnatural.

I guess I just need to keep my focus—and keep swinging, he thought to himself.

14

"So—YOU HAVE TO REMEMBER THAT an Article 32 hearing is not a general court-martial. It is simply an investigation conducted by an investigating officer—an IO—who investigates the charges to determine if they are in proper form, if there is sufficient evidence to support them, if there are additional potential charges—and finally, he makes a recommendation as to disposition. Those findings and recommendations are then forwarded to the convening authority—in this case, the base commanding general—who then makes the decision on whether or not to make a referral to a general court-martial."

Will Chambers nodded to Major Hanover, who, with Caleb Marlowe beside him, continued laying out the legal geography.

"And because this is only a preliminary investigation to determine whether the matter should be referred to the general for a general court-martial, we have to face the question of whether or not Colonel Marlowe should testify in his own behalf. He cannot be compelled to do so. That's a decision we have to make."

Will nodded again and then chimed in, addressing Marlowe.

"Colonel, Major Hanover and I have discussed this. We both feel, at least at this point, that you have nothing to gain—and everything to lose—by testifying at the Article 32 hearing. If this goes to a court-martial, you could present your defense through your own testimony at that time. We're hoping we can get these charges dropped before then."

"One thing bothers me with your recommendation," Marlowe responded, "about my not testifying at the Article 32."

"What's that?" Will asked.

"I'm the only person on this planet…the only one that went into that house and saw Carlos, and his wife, Linda, and his two little children.

I'm also the only one who talked to Carlos the day before the assault, when he told me that safe house was where the AAJ would be hiding. That makes my testimony absolutely critical. And if that's the case, then maybe I should testify."

Hanover and Will both shook their heads simultaneously.

"Colonel, I don't think so," Will said. "Although we're trying to get dismissal of these charges, we also want to get discovery of the trial counsel's case. Beyond that, we don't want to tip our hand before the court-martial case about the theory of our defense."

"Well, if we don't get my side of the story through my testimony at the Article 32," Marlowe said, "then how is the general going to rule in our favor and keep this case from being referred to a court-martial?"

"Sir, what the Colonel has to understand," Hanover explained, "is that the general has a little discretion in deciding whether or not this matter should be referred. He looks at the evidence, he looks at the extenuating circumstances, he looks at the appropriateness of the charges—the whole context—in making that determination. Mr. Chambers here and I both believe we can do a fairly good job of presenting your defense without locking you in by testifying."

Marlowe nodded. But he had a look on his face that indicated that he was deferring—reluctantly—to the advice of his two legal counsel.

Will leaned forward and picked up on something that the colonel had said.

"But your comments do raise a question. And that is, what you really did see that night."

The lawyer turned to Major Hanover.

"What is the status on that gag order based on national security? Has DOD waived its prior restriction on us discussing all of those matters with Colonel Marlowe?"

"Not entirely," Hanover answered. "I received a message today from DOD indicating we are free to discuss the occurrence at Chacmool, but nothing that preceded it—and absolutely nothing about the military designation of Colonel Marlowe's team—or the chain of command that led, ultimately, to the colonel's order to open fire on the house."

After only a moment of reflection, it became very clear to Will what the parameters were regarding his ability to get information from his client. And it was equally obvious where he needed to start first.

"All right, Colonel—this is it," Will began. "Start from the point where you and your team were getting into position at Chacmool. Start there."

There were a pitcher of water and a few cups on the table in the defense conference room. Marlowe took the pitcher and filled one of the styrofoam cups halfway.

He said nothing, but took a few gulps from the cup and then set it down. After looking into Will's face he turned and studied Major Hanover, but still said nothing.

Then he turned to look at Will again. But now the marine tilted his head just slightly as he did. As if he were a time traveler who was about to explain some ancient and horrible event, one that his attorneys would never fully grasp. Colonel Marlowe was about to unveil a bloody enigma of sacrifice and death.

15

Mᴀʀʟᴏᴡᴇ ʙᴇɢᴀɴ ʀᴇᴄᴏᴜɴᴛɪɴɢ the incident that had occurred deep in the Yucatán jungle of Mexico. His hands were quiet in his lap and he stared straight ahead. He spoke precisely, calmly—but his voice was monotone.

He and his team had been given the mission of tracking down and killing the surviving members of the group of terrorists who had kidnapped Secretary of Commerce Kilmer. From what they could tell, there were four remaining members of AAJ—al-Aqsa Jihad. The fleeing men had been traced to an area near the ancient Mayan ruins of Chichén Itzá. According to information made available to Marlowe, a few miles northwest of Chichén Itzá, just outside a small village called Chacmool, there was a probable safe house that the AAJ cell group was using.

The colonel had been in contact with Special Forces Command in Tampa, Florida, and with a navy vessel off the Yucatán Peninsula, to coordinate incoming intelligence leading up to the attack...

As he and his squad were being airlifted across the shadowy canopy of the Yucatán jungle, Marlowe studied the faces of the men. Master Sergeant Mike Rockwell had already served on several missions with him—Afghanistan and Operation Allied Forge in Kosovo, as well as Operation Desert Thunder in Saudi Arabia and Kuwait, and more recently in classified operations in Iraq and North Korea. Rockwell, as usual, was expressionless, but he nodded ever so slightly toward the colonel when their eyes met.

Next to him was Staff Sergeant Billy Baker, a much younger but lean and tough warrior. Next to Marlowe on the helicopter bench was Corporal Hank Thompson, the least experienced but the best marksman among the five of them…and an expert in explosives. At the end of the bench was navy Chief Petty Officer Mark Dorfman. The colonel had handpicked them from the ranks of the Navy Seals, Delta Force, Army Rangers, and Marine Expeditionary Units. As the helicopter skimmed over the top of the trees, the crew chief gave the five-minute sign.

Marlowe gave the five-minutes-out signal to the team and motioned for them to check their equipment.

The members of his team adjusted their slim-line headsets, and the colonel gave a test to all four. All gave affirmative signs that their headgear was hot and communications were open.

The leader then snapped open his laptop computer, punched in the key code, and waited. After only a few seconds, the screen suddenly gave him the message he was waiting for.

INTEL OP CF CONFIRMS SAFE HOUSE JUST NORTHWEST OF CHICHÉN ITZÁ, ON THE EDGE OF CHACMOOL VILLAGE. COORDINATES FOLLOW. STILL WORKING ON SECOND CONFIRMATION VIA SIGINT.

The colonel knew who the "intel op cf" was. This was CIA agent Carlos Fuego, a longtime friend. In fact, Marlowe had been the best man at Carlos's wedding to his beautiful bride, Linda. The agent was a Mexican national with a long record of faithful service to the CIA, primarily within Mexico. Fuego and Marlowe had first met during the Persian Gulf War when the agent had been temporarily assigned to assist special operations forces. He would trust his life to him—and he knew his information was absolutely credible.

He had known only, with few details, that the agent had had the safe house under surveillance for some time. Fuego had also managed to penetrate deep within an AAJ–Mexico connection that had developed. And, unlike many CIA operatives, Fuego had actually been encouraged to proceed with his marriage plans and raise a family so he would blend more easily into the Mexican culture.

The second confirmation of the location of the safe house had not yet arrived. The NSA—National Security Agency—had its ECHELON system programmed to identify and immediately alert its operators to any cell-phone transmission intercepts from the group's leader,

Abu Adis—the successor of Abdul el Alibahd—because Carlos Fuego had managed to obtain Adis's cell-phone number. Any attempt by the terrorists to use that cell phone would be detected by one of NSA's SIGINT satellites. For this operation, the Advanced Orion satellite positioned high above Latin America was expected to make the intercept.

The helicopter was nearing the drop zone: the courtyard of the Mayan ruins of Chichén Itzá, which lay between the main plaza, the ancient ball court, and the sacred well—*cenote sagrado*—which was approximately two hundred yards to the north.

Then suddenly the computer screen flashed a message.

CELL-PHONE CONFIRMATION NUMBER ORIGINATING FROM SAFE HOUSE—LOCATION CONFIRMED—COORDINATES MATCH.

That was it. Adis had made a call from his cell phone from within the safe house, and it had been instantly picked up and located from above the Earth. Now, with two confirmations, one from Carlos and the other from satellite hardware, the team was ready to strike.

Marlowe gave the signal for the team to prepare to fast-rope from fifty feet up when the helicopter reached the drop position. The team rappelled down with lightning speed. Behind them, in the pale moonlight, stood the huge pyramid with its steps leading up to the area where, fifteen hundred years before, the Mayans had sliced out the hearts of their victims and presented them, still drenched in blood, to the stone statue of the god Chacmool.

The warriors moved swiftly and inconspicuously through the jungle and within thirty minutes they were nearing the small house occupied by the terrorists.

On command from Marlowe, the other four took their positions.

Dorfman, armed with an M240G machine gun, began to work his way around the left side of the house, while Thompson, armed with an M16 rifle/M203 grenade-launcher combination, crawled toward the right and occupied a concealed firing position under some bushes. Both Dorfman's and Thompson's task was to prevent any terrorist from escaping. The other three comprised the assault team. Rockwell was armed with a 12-gauge Mossberg. He would blow the door open with the shotgun. Baker would then toss in a single concussion grenade and those two—joined by Marlowe in the lead—would make entrance.

That plan, though, like any other plan, was based on uncertain assumptions. The logistics presumed there were no guards and they would meet no initial resistance.

But when the assault team members had taken up their positions about five meters apart—behind some cover approximately thirty meters in front of the house, the door suddenly swung open.

A man stepped out quickly with what appeared to be an automatic weapon. He glanced around and then turned as if he were going to walk back inside. But he suddenly whirled and fired a short burst in the direction of Thompson, who was prone on the ground. Over his headset, Marlowe heard him give a guttural groan. He had been hit.

The colonel clicked on his thermal-imaging scope and directed it at the house. He saw several blurred human images running within the building. As he finished adjusting the scope he could distinguish four stationary figures in seated positions.

Rockwell whispered frantically, "Colonel, have Thompson take him out with one shot and then let's do a close-up recon of the house."

"Negative," Marlowe replied. "Open fire! Take this guy down and put everything you have into that house—I'm assuming the risk of collateral damage here—fire!"

The guard was still standing with his gun pointed toward Thompson when a blast of buckshot ripped into him. Weapons fire began to rake through the masonry walls, the front door, and the closed window shutters from different angles so as to cross the pattern being stitched by the machine gun. Thompson managed to fire a grenade through a ragged opening in a front shutter, and the house trembled with the explosion. Meanwhile, Rockwell opened up an M72 LAW and fired a rocket at the lower-right front wall of the house, opening another hole with its shaped charge but also releasing a lethal spray of masonry fragments in the interior. Thompson managed to empty his M16 through the new opening, his angle of fire sweeping through any remaining dead spaces.

After a couple of minutes of intense fire, Marlowe determined that nothing could possibly still be alive inside and ordered, "Cease fire!

"Mike one, Mike two—go!" he commanded as he jumped to his feet and ran toward the corner of the house. Rockwell and Baker were close behind him. Charging through the door opening, the colonel jumped over the body of the dead man, a beam of light from his weapon illuminating the gloom within.

But then his brain went numb. His body, though, through years of training, did all the right things—he checked immediately to his left and right to make sure the room was secure. He could hear the other two men approaching from behind.

In a flash his eyes had fixed on the four bodies on the ground. They had been tied to chairs, which had toppled away from the table as their occupants had been hit by the terrible rain of bullets, grenade fragments, and masonry chips. But these were not enemy combatants lying on the ground, their bodies ripped and shredded by flying metal. Marlowe was sickened. A child...two children. There was blood on the floor, blood spattered on the walls. And a woman...a beautiful young woman...it was Linda, Carlos's wife. As her body lay on the floor in its chair, little recognizable was left of her torso or below...though, dreadfully, her face was perfectly intact. Little was left of Carlos's face. His bound body had been ripped apart. Conspicuously tied around his neck was his CIA identification tag.

Marlowe whirled as Rockwell entered the doorway and put his hand in front of the other man's face.

"Out! Out now! This has gone down bad!" As he shoved Rockwell and Baker out, they could hear sirens coming—several of them—and could glimpse perhaps five or six flashing lights in the darkness. The Mexican police—they were racing down the dirt road toward the house. How had they found out? Who had tipped them off?

Marlowe barked commands to head for the assembly area at Chichén Itzá, where they were to be picked up.

Rockwell—the biggest and strongest of the group—had Thompson in a fireman's carry as they double-timed through the thick tangle of Yucatán jungle. No one spoke. But Marlowe could hear the huffing and puffing of each of the men through his headset. He switched the channel and gave a command for the navy helicopter to meet them in five minutes.

By the time the team had reached the pickup zone, the helicopter was already there, sitting on the grass with its blades whirling. They loaded Thompson in first and the other four men jumped in.

As the helicopter took off, Rockwell leaned forward and peered at his leader. Then, tearing off his Kevlar vest and his headset, he threw them to the deck and then leaned forward again, staring at the colonel, wanting—wishing for an answer on what had happened—why things had gone so bad so quickly.

But Marlowe said nothing. He leaned his head back against the metal skin of the helicopter and looked down through the open door—down onto the towering stairs, illuminated by moonlight, that led to the pyramid erected to the bloodthirsty gods of the Mayans. The multistaired stone structure was getting smaller...until it started to disappear into the dark expanse of the jungle as they sped away.

Off in the distance, north of Chichén Itzá, the colonel could see flashing lights penetrating the night. The squad cars had ringed the small house. And the federal police were now entering...beholding the massacre.

He was already thinking ahead. About what this would mean for his men—and for the United States government. He was already thinking about how he, and he alone, would insist on shouldering responsibility for this special operations catastrophe...

And that was it. As Marlowe finished his narrative, Major Hanover and Will Chambers were eyeing him without speaking.

Will broke the silence.

"You say they were all tied to chairs. If the police report—"

"Sir, the federal police diagram of the scene—" Hanover interjected, "it didn't show that."

"In fact," Will added, "it shows the outlines of the bodies on the floor in positions that are inconsistent with being tied to a chair. Further, the chairs don't appear in the photographs, nor do they appear in the diagram."

The colonel cocked his head again and looked at Will—as if he was losing patience with the lawyer's inability to understand the deeper secrets of this dark tragedy.

"Of course the police report didn't show that," he said. "And did you look at the autopsy report?"

Will nodded. "Yes—and there was no mention of any abrasions or cuts to the wrists of any of the victims that would be consistent with being tied with rope."

"Of course," Marlowe repeated. "The autopsy report was done by a local doctor under the jurisdiction of the federal police."

"What happened to the rest of the terrorists?" Will asked.

The colonel's face tightened as he answered.

"There was a door."

"A door, sir?" Hanover asked.

"A trapdoor in the floor," Marlowe continued. But now he was clearly troubled as he went forward with his description.

"A small, square trapdoor in the floor, about two yards from where the bodies lay. It was pretty clear the terrorists must have exited down it—I'm sure it led some distance away from the house. By the time I noticed it, though, we could hear the sirens and the federal police were approaching."

Will leaned forward. "So, you made a deliberate choice to avoid the federal police?"

Marlowe nodded.

Hanover picked up the thread. "Sir, was that a critical part of your mission—to avoid contact with the Mexican government or Mexican nationals?"

"Exactly. Don't ask me who gave me my orders—you know I can't answer that."

Will was beginning to size up his client's defense—and the prospects were disheartening. His story about the four civilian victims being tied to chairs—like ducks in a shooting gallery—was contradicted by the report, the diagram, and the photographs of the Mexican police, who had arrived at the scene only moments after the team had abandoned the site.

Beyond that, the colonel had rejected Sergeant Rockwell's suggestion to kill the lookout at the front door quietly and then do a close-up reconnaissance before attacking. And then there was the matter of Marlowe ordering his unit to flee from the approaching Mexican police.

But there was something else. Something that troubled Will down to the pit of his stomach.

"Colonel, there's something else I need to ask you. Just moments before the attack you said that you would assume the responsibility for 'collateral damage.' What did you mean by that?"

Marlowe took a few long seconds before he answered. And when he did, he was fingering the styrofoam cup on the conference table in front of him.

"I meant that if there was collateral damage to other persons, it was my call."

"Sir, what other persons?" Hanover broke in, his voice tight.

"In the event there was a civilian noncombatant in the house."

"You knew there might be a civilian noncombatant in the house when you ordered your unit to fire upon it?" Will asked. His body was tensing, and he was leaning forward on the table.

"I knew there might be at least one person inside…one civilian not formally associated with the cell group. I was aware of that."

"Who?" Will and Hanover asked almost simultaneously.

But the colonel shook his head. "I cannot answer that."

"Why not?" Will asked protestingly.

"It has nothing to do with the DOD directive," his client barked.

"You've got to give that information to us. It's critical, " Will shot back.

"Mr. Chambers," Marlowe bulleted out, "I don't have to tell you anything. Now, this interview is over." As his client stood to leave, as if on cue, Major Hanover jumped to attention, followed by Will, who stood there not knowing quite why he also had sprung up. The colonel gave a nod to them and quickly exited the room.

The two lawyers looked at each other with the same idea. Just when they thought they had been getting to the core of the case, they had discovered something very different…that they had been unwrapping a mystery, only to find another riddle.

16

JASON BELL PURDY CLOSED THE sliding French doors to the library of his Chevy Chase brownstone.

"Jason, I appreciate you inviting me out to Maryland." Howley Jubb was at the bar pouring himself a drink.

"Hey," Purdy responded, "like I said—I've been meaning to bring you out here for a long time. Things just got crazy. Real busy. Is your hotel room okay?"

"Yeah, nice suite. I appreciate it."

Purdy plopped down on the couch, kicked off his shoes, and stretched out his legs.

"So, what do you have for me? What did you dig up south of the border?"

"I think I've got the whole package almost wrapped up for you."

The seated man's eyes brightened, and he gave out a whoop.

"Hey—great work, Howley! Give me the details."

"Well, first I was going to have Susie back at the office type up a report for you. But her kid got sick. So I didn't get a chance to have her do it before I flew out of Atlanta."

Purdy's expression changed to a scowl and he straightened up on the couch.

"Hey—hey. Nothing in writing. *Nothing*. What's wrong with you, Howley? You're going to have some secretary type this stuff up? All this is *verbal only*."

"Fine, fine. No problem," Jubb said, sipping from his glass. "How dumb do you think I am? All the really sensitive stuff I was going to put in code."

"Hey—forget the code stuff. I'm in Washington, DC. We've got guys walking around with badges who break codes all the time. We've

78

got people looking for paper on each other constantly. You get the point?"

"Sure," Jubb said with a half smile, as he sat down in a chair opposite the couch. "So, like I was saying, things are looking very good. My contacts down there tell me that this group—al-Aqsa Jihad, the AAJ—has been operating in Mexico. Some of the folks in the Mexican government even know about it. They tell me there's been a change of attitude about the U.S. from bad to worse. There's a group down there called the Independent Revolutionary Party—the IRP—it's really building a lot of support. And of course the federal police and some of the judges and government folks in Mexico City have been playing ball with drug dealers for a long period of time."

"Why would somebody in the government let the AAJ operate in the country?" Purdy asked.

"Can't figure that out yet. But it's apparently a fact."

"So how about this massacre deal down at Chacmool?"

"Okay, you've got to go back to the kidnapping down at Cancún first. The way the Mexicans look at it, the American military and some sort of mysterious special ops group were already on their way down there—maybe even within the borders—when the kidnapping happened. Anyway, the commando unit was already close by.

"So they're moving into position when the White House calls Mexico City and says we're going in—we're saving the Secretary of Commerce with or without your permission. But we would like your permission—so how about it? So the Mexicans figure, hey, this is a cabinet-level kidnapping—we can't fool around with this. So they give a kind of halfhearted approval for the military operation to be run by the Americans. The Mexicans are only there to provide background information, as requested. But basically, it's—you Mexicans get out of the way—the Americans are coming and we're going to take care of this."

"Alright, all that's fine," Purdy said. "Secretary Kilmer is rescued. But what happens next? What did Mexico have to say about the Americans tracking down these AAJ people and trying to kill them?"

"That's where it gets really good. The Mexicans never gave the American military—or the White House for that matter—permission to hunt these guys down. They consider that the prerogative of Mexico. Some of the government officials really got ticked off at the way this came down. They're talking about their country being treated like the new Afghanistan where America just walks all over it, calls the shots, shoots the guns, and directs the campaign. Like I said, you got to remember that Mexico feels like—for whatever reason—it's got the ability to start showing off its chest hairs. But that's not the best."

"Oh?"

"There's this thing called a status of forces agreement. In the past, there was this working relationship between Mexico and the United States in terms of us being able to send our troops down there as long as we sort of checked in routinely with the government when we crossed the border. Well, apparently—and I don't know the details— but it looks like no formal agreement was ever reached, or it didn't get signed. Or they were still negotiating when this thing came down.

"The Mexicans feel they really have a chokehold on the White House on this deal. My guess is, they're going to try to crank up the heat on this—you know, get some big economic boost out of the fact they could embarrass the White House over the incident because they never gave permission for American commandos to track down and try to kill this cell group on Mexican soil."

"What do we know about this American commando unit?"

"Don't know that," Jubb responded. "You told me you got all the stuff on the court-martial that's pending against this Caleb Marlowe— you've got all that stuff."

"Yeah, right," Purdy said. "I've got that. But I want something more. Tell me something about this AAJ activity down in Mexico. Are they working with anybody?"

"Well, they are. There's been some contact and some trading back and forth between the AAJ and some drug group. Remember a number of years ago there was a drug business—they were really doing well—it was Hezbollah buying pseudoephedrine and then selling it to fund its activities. They were doing business down in Mexico. But the DEA busted them while they were doing this crackdown—excuse the expression…"

Purdy laughed loudly.

"Yeah, I remember. We talked about that."

"Right. Well, the DEA cracked down on Hezbollah and some of these guys who were selling pseudoephedrine, which is used in crystal meth. So apparently, after these guys from Hezbollah and the drug dealers got busted, AAJ moves in and picks up where they left off."

"What about the proof that the Mexican government has about the massacre?"

"The Mexicans feel like they have a great case. Everything they've got says that Marlowe told his guys to shoot at everything moving in the house, including the civilians who ended up getting killed. You know, like a scene out of *The Wild Bunch*. All their federal police reports and investigations show that."

"Alright—now to the big question—our friend Senator O'Brien. What's the deal on that?"

"Well, I checked every source that I could get my hands on. I even had a tail put on him for a long time. But I couldn't find anything dirty on this guy. He's clean. He's one of these upright guys."

"So—is that the end of the story?"

Howley Jubb smiled and shook his head.

"No—not by a long shot. This is where it really gets good. I put the word out everywhere I could that we were looking for trash on O'Brien. I didn't get anything like that. But then I made some calls. I got connected to some pretty unpleasant Russian dudes. They work in some very nasty Internet stuff."

"So?" Purdy asked with an air of irritated boredom.

"So they can put some of that nasty—and I might add, illegal— stuff into O'Brien's computer. I'm talking remote intrusion—"

"Hey, hey," Purdy called out, "whoa. I don't want details. Zero information. Got it? Just make the guy embarrassed enough to deal with me—okay? And no rough stuff."

"Sure, Jason. I read you."

Purdy jumped off the couch and stretched. He took the glass out of Jubb's hand and walked it over to the minibar, where he poured out the remaining contents into the sink.

"Okay, Howley—here's the way it lies. You get to work on this. You find a place to rent for a couple weeks here in the DC area. But I don't want you anywhere near me in Chevy Chase, you understand?"

Jubb stood up and nodded.

"You keep me informed—verbally and in person, on a regular basis, on just one thing—how soon this is going down. But if at any time I start feeling uncomfortable about this, I want you to pull the plug…with no jeopardy. Got it?"

"Sure, I've got it all," Jubb said, cocking an eyebrow. "And look—if this thing goes down well, then you and I can talk about bumping me up a bit. And I don't just mean money. I mean giving me a place on the East Coast. A place with you out here, close to where the action is."

"Sure," the other man said with a grin. "But let's not get ahead of ourselves. You're just teeing up. Let's see if you hit onto the fairway or into the rough."

As Jubb headed for the front door Purdy corrected him.

"No, not through the front. I want you out the back door."

Howley Jubb shrugged and shook his head sardonically. This was classic Jason Bell Purdy, and he knew it.

As the door closed behind Jubb, Purdy was feeling the rush. He was a little anxious because he didn't know whether to trust Jubb's Russian contacts—and the shadowy strike against Senator O'Brien, over which he had little control. On the other hand, he liked the anonymity. He liked the ability to give a plausible denial if the trail ended up getting too close to him.

And even more important, he loved the knowledge that, so soon after arriving in Washington, DC, he was becoming a deal maker…and a king breaker.

He poured himself a drink, but as he did so, he heard a noise in the doorway leading to the study.

Linda, his press secretary, was in the doorway, wearing one of his bathrobes.

"Jason—are you done with your phone call yet?"

"Sure, honey. Listen, time for you to go. I need some sleep tonight. And you need to bunk somewhere else."

Her eyes narrowed, and she turned and walked away quickly. But not before slamming the glass door so hard that Purdy thought it might shatter.

"Women," he muttered to himself as he took a big gulp from his glass.

17

THE AQUA-BLUE HELICOPTER WITH the Global Petroleum logo on the side was setting itself down gently on the helipad of the oil platform. Thirty miles off the coast of Mexico, the weather was clear and the ocean was calm.

The door opened and a man in a dark suit with an open collar and a briefcase stepped out. Then came Warren Mullburn, billionaire and engineering genius, man of letters and cultural guru. Though he was medium in height, his muscular build gave him an energetic presence, and his balding head lent him an intellectual air. A radiant smile lit up his tanned, youthful features as he stepped out and surveyed the platform. Then he thrust his hand into that of the Mexican official who was awaiting him.

Following Mullburn, one of his assistants scurried out followed by two bodyguards, and they all took their positions next to him.

"Señor Mullburn, it is so very good to see you and to welcome you to our joint venture. Won't you follow me to the elevator? I will take us down to the meeting room." The official and all the just-arrived party crammed inside the freight elevator, which slowly took them down to the first level.

"I was not sure whether we would have the privilege of your personal attendance at this meeting. I know how very important your time is—and how busy you are around the world," the Mexican said.

Mullburn smiled. "You will find that I have a very hands-on management style," he quipped, "particularly when it comes to oil exploration."

"Well, I'm very pleased—no—actually, I'm ecstatic that the geophysical crude locator system has been such a remarkable success. This deposit is beyond enormous. That system worked a hundred times better than traditional oil exploration techniques. It succeeded beyond our wildest dreams," the official said.

"It ought to," Mullburn said, smiling again. "I designed it."

All of the occupants of the elevator responded with hearty laughter.

As they stepped out, the official stopped on the metal-caged catwalk and turned to his guest.

"But I do have one question for you, Señor Mullburn."

"And what is that?"

"Regarding the news I am hearing about possible criminal prosecution…that you may be extradited back to the United States on serious charges. This is very troubling to us, of course. We simply look to you for assurance that this matter will not affect our working relationship."

Mullburn beamed confidently and placed his hand on the other man's shoulder.

"You are Mexico's greatest geological expert in regard to oil, are you not?"

The official nodded politely.

"Then I will give you a parable—and you answer me. What are the forces that produce the petroleum you and I seek so vigorously?"

"Well, intense pressure deep within the earth over substantial periods of time."

"Precisely." Mullburn's tone was full of self-satisfaction. "The philosopher Hegel pointed out the same thing, but in more abstract terms. He told us that when two great, opposing forces meet in politics, civilization, or ideas, the result is not destruction. Rather, it is transformation. When great ideologies conflict, they create a new synthesis—a new idea. When pressures meet equal and opposite pressures, the result is a synthesis that creates energy."

The Mexican official was still waiting for the punchline. Mullburn sighed when he realized that his impromptu disciple was not catching the drift.

"Don't you see?" Mullburn said with a tinge of exasperation. "This threat of criminal prosecution against me—the scandalous lies about me—this is simply a useful coefficient of political pressure, even though it is being applied by those who desire my destruction. But rather than my destruction, a new energy—a new geopolitical power—is about to be created. And you and I, Señor, will be there at its birth."

After a struggle to express some enthusiasm over these cryptic ruminations, the official opened the door to the control center of the oil platform and gestured for Mullburn and his entourage to enter.

The billionaire entered first. After him came one of his assistants, who then unzipped a pocket in his briefcase and retrieved a calculator. With it he would estimate how many millions of barrels of petroleum this site would soon start to yield.

And at the same time, he would be calculating just how quickly Warren Mullburn was about to become the richest man in the world.

18

Back at his office, Will finally received the return call from his private investigator, Tiny Heftland. The attorney had left a message on Tiny's office voice mail, asking him for assistance in the case, and had sent pertinent documents from the file. Having used Tiny often in past cases, Will had just presumed that he would be able to retain him on this case as well. But after several days of silence, Will had begun to get worried.

And then the call came in.

"Man, I really feel lousy leaving you on the hook. I mean, I've been planning to get back with you after you sent me that stuff on the military case—but I have been hopping faster than a three-legged dog lately—work has really kept me busy," Heftland said at the other end of the line.

"Don't worry about it," Will replied. "But I do need you and me to get up to speed really quickly on this case against Marlowe."

"Matter of fact, I've read through everything you sent me. Not pretty. Sounds like something wicked went down there in old Mexico."

"So...how's your Spanish?"

"Yeah, I did get your message about flying down there. My schedule's open. Are you still holding the ticket for tomorrow?"

"Yes. Major Hanover got permission from the Mexican police for us to visit the scene of the shootout. They weren't real excited about it, but Major Hanover got some pressure applied through the American embassy and the State Department."

"Speaking of the Mexicans, I used to have a contact—not in the Yucatán per se—but in Mexico City. I used him a couple of years ago on a case where I was tailing a husband who was cheating on his wife.

He'd married her in Las Vegas and then turned around and married somebody else shortly after that down in Mexico. Nice guy, huh?"

"Have you touched base with your contact about this case?" Will asked.

"We've been exchanging messages. I'm supposed to speak to him today. I've got your memo with the points you wanted to check out with the Mexican authorities—you know, very quietly—about a trap being set for the U.S. commandos, not only by the AAJ, but with the assistance of the Mexicans. I'm going to start checking that out with my guy down there. He's traveling down to Cancún to meet us when we arrive."

As he hung up, Will was pleased that the trip with Tiny was a go. He wasn't sure what he would find—or even what to expect—when they surveyed the scene. But he did have an overwhelming sense of certainty that he needed to be there—in person—and walk the actual route that Marlowe and his men had taken, from the drop-off point near the Mayan ruins to the scene of the incident and back.

The attorney leaned back in his black leather chair and gazed out his office window at the church steeple across the street and the red brick buildings that surrounded it. The summer tourist season in Monroeville was over, and the streets were quiet now. This was the time when he enjoyed the historical charm of the city the most.

He got up and walked over to the window, leaning his arms on the sill, and gazing out at the eighteenth-century, cream-painted church spire.

For a moment he reflected back on the dramatic shift that his life had taken—from being a skeptical, cynical lawyer, a man whose life was quickly disintegrating into alcoholism and despair, to his present state as the husband of a beautiful gospel singer, whose faith and generosity of heart had inspired him to be a better man.

Just a few years ago he had sat on the carpet, right there in front of his desk—broken, amazed, yet certain that he must acknowledge and accept the reality of God—and the convincing proof and immutable truth that Jesus was both Lord and Savior.

In the time that had passed since that cataclysmic event—after that first awkward, groping prayer—Will had become keenly aware of the inward transformation.

He had been able to order his life from the inside out—from the core of spiritual peace he had been granted, out into his law practice, his friendships, and the externals of daily living.

Yet there were still challenges. One of them was to be the kind of man he felt Fiona deserved. Lately he had felt himself letting go of the past—not entirely—but slowly and progressively.

Over the last few days he had started to direct his mind away from the investigation into Audra's death. The last time he had really dug his fingers into that issue was when he had called Captain Jenkins, that Saturday at home with Fiona.

Will's reverie was interrupted when he recalled that he should check with Fiona on his trip to Mexico. Right now would be the time—she was at home handling a series of conference calls with her manager and some promoters, working on a schedule for her next concert tour.

The phone rang only twice.

"Hey, lover," Will said brightly when Fiona picked up. "How are your conferences going?"

"You called me at a perfect time. I've got a couple minutes before my next call comes in."

"Say—you remember I said I might have to travel down to Mexico this week, depending on whether I could hook up with Tiny?"

"Sure, I remember," she said quietly.

"Well, I got ahold of him and we have tickets booked for tomorrow. I'm going to confirm with my travel agent that everything's a go."

"I can't say I'm excited about being separated. But I know you've got to do what you've got to do in this case. You said you were going to be gone only a couple of days?"

"Yeah, we're coming back in four days. Two days of travel, and two days down there at the site."

Just then they heard a click on the line.

"I'm sure that's the next conference call coming in," Fiona said.

"Listen, there's something else I want to suggest. Keep me in the loop on this next concert tour. I'd like to travel with you for at least part of it."

"Oh, wow!" she said, overjoyed. "I would absolutely love that. Thank you, darling. We're going to have so much fun!"

Will told her how much he loved her, and he hung up.

There was only one major challenge that Will had to overcome before the two of them could do some traveling together on the concert tour.

All he had to do, first, was exonerate a highly decorated marine colonel in a quadruple murder case whose secrets were—thus far—wrapped and hidden from view like a corpse in a shroud.

19

Will and Tiny flew together from Reagan National Airport in Washington to Mexico. They landed at the Aeropuerto Internacional de Cancún. Will couldn't help but think of his honeymoon with Fiona at Isla Cozumel, just south of Cancún.

On the flight, the two men had strategized on their approach to the quick, two-day investigation. Tiny was going to rent a car and drive the short distance inland to San Rafael. There he was going to meet with his Mexican contact, who was to come down from Mexico City, and try to glean as much information as he could on the inside Mexican view of the shoot-out at Chacmool.

Tiny's contact, a shadowy character who went only by the name of Hermán, was engaged in an import–export business. Tiny knew he had regular contact with some of the drug gangs and Yucatán jungle bandits. He also had a good working relationship with the Mayan population—the dominant demographic group in the area—as well as with some high-ranking officials.

Will would take a taxi down Federal Highway 180 into the jungles of the Yucatán, where he would first stop off at Chichén Itzá and the spot where Marlowe and his commandos had been dropped off and had made their way through the jungle to the house on the outskirts of Chacmool.

Hermán had arranged for the taxicab driver to act as a guide for Will—and had assured Tiny he was reliable and knowledgeable. He did add, however, that Will should bring a pocketful of American dollars—not pesos, as that denomination was ever plummeting because of the unstable Mexican economy.

The driver, a middle-aged Mexican with missing teeth and a broad smile, went only by the name Pancho. He greeted Will at the airport with a smile and a two-handed handshake, quickly grabbing his bags and tossing them into his taxi.

The cab itself was a vintage Cadillac convertible of uncertain color—ranging somewhere between silver-gray, black, and purple, with an attempted repaint job that appeared not to have taken. The vehicle had no doors, which, Pancho assured Will, aided in good ventilation.

As the attorney started out on the several-hour trip, his guide offered to sell him a bottle of Coke, which he conveniently kept in a styrofoam cooler in the backseat.

"Five dollar—one bottle—American dollar only," Pancho said with a smile, showing the gap in his teeth.

Settling himself into the front seat next to his driver, Will snorted and shook his head. *Five dollars for a bottle of soda—this guy must think I'm stupid,* he mused to himself.

They quickly left the beautiful beaches and international hotels of the Cancún beach area and entered the jungle.

After less than an hour they were driving on a poorly maintained two-lane road and were surrounded by all-but-impenetrable green forest that rose up in tangled trunks of tan-and-beige jungle trees and undergrowth. As they drove, the jungle seemed to grow closer, encompassing the highway and blocking the fierce sun.

Pancho was chain-smoking, breaking the silence occasionally only to point out a small village here, or perhaps a dilapidated gas station there…one belonging to a friend of a relative of a friend.

It wasn't very long before Will's lightweight Hawaiian shirt was drenched in sweat, his hair damp, and droplets of sweat were falling from his nose and eyebrows. Soon he was reaching into his wallet with disgust and pulling out five-dollar bills, which Pancho stuffed merrily in his top pocket as he invited his passenger to retrieve the bottles of Coke from the cooler himself.

Will figured he should have known that Pancho had a soda racket when he first entered the car and noticed a bottle opener permanently screwed to the dashboard.

"Tell me something, Pancho," he addressed the other man. "Are you Mayan?"

Pancho shook his head.

"No—but I've got a lot of friends who are Mayans. We call them Indians down here."

"We're going to Chichén Itzá first, right?"

The Mexican smiled and nodded. "You're not *turista*, are you?" he asked. "You're a lawyer—down here on a law case, huh?"

"Yes—after that we're going to Chacmool, right?"

Pancho nodded again.

"Now, after Chichén Itzá," Will continued, "we're going to walk through the jungle together. On a path I'm going to show you from some notes I've got. It leads to a house on the outskirts of Chacmool—okay?"

Pancho stopped smiling, and he flipped his cigarette out of the car and gave Will a quizzical look.

"Walk through the jungle? Don't think that's a good idea. We've got the car—we'll drive there."

Will shook his head violently.

"No—you and I have to take a path through the jungle, exactly as I instruct us. You need to go along with me in case there are some Mexican police who ask what we're doing."

"That's going to cost you extra—fifty American dollars."

Apparently, Hermán's advice to Tiny had been no exaggeration. Will was glad he had brought a huge pile of American bills in his pocket.

He tried to glance at his file on the way to the Mayan ruins, but the wind blowing through the side openings where doors used to be threatened to rip the pages from his hands.

When they got to the town of Valladolid, Pancho pulled into a gas station, bragging that Valladolid was one of the biggest cities in the area. But Will found it a sleepy provincial Mexican town. There was a market at its center, and a sixteenth-century—according to his tourist book—Spanish church dominated the central square. Several skinny, brown-skinned boys—Mayans, perhaps—were playing baseball behind the gas station, and a little girl in a dirty dress stared at him as he stepped out of the Cadillac and stretched. He smiled at her, but her wide eyes remained unblinking, and she played with her dress nervously and then ran away.

"There are good hotels—clean rooms, very beautiful—if you want to stay here for the night," Pancho said, climbing back in and starting the car. "Only twenty-five miles or so now. We soon get to the ruins."

"How do the Mayans get along with the Mexicans?" Will asked.

The driver shrugged. After a few moments he answered.

"Still problems—the Indians still have a few uprisings—fights with the police. They don't think the government takes care of them. They think the government..." he thought for a minute for the right word. "...That the government pushes them down—steps on them," he continued.

Slowing down, Pancho pulled off the main highway onto a side road that led toward the ruins. They stopped at a tourist gate with a booth, where a guard let them through.

After they parked the car, Will grabbed the diagram he'd made from his briefcase and asked Pancho to lock the case in the trunk. He stuffed the diagram in his pocket, and they trudged off toward the ruins.

The attorney glanced at his watch. Time was short. But by retracing Marlowe's steps right up to the site of the killing, he hoped to dislodge some hidden piece of evidence—anything.

What he really wanted to do was to climb inside Marlowe's head to learn what he had known that night. Barring that, a walk through the hot Mexican jungle would have to suffice.

20

"THERE'S WHERE I WANT TO START," Will said, pointing to the towering El Castillo, the same Mayan pyramid that Marlowe and his men had approached in their helicopter, and from which the top of the jungle canopy could be viewed. Beyond El Castillo was the clearing where the U.S. team had been dropped, a spot where, at night, there would have been no observers.

"So we're going to walk through the jungle to Chacmool?" Pancho asked with a smile.

Will nodded, and then caught his companion's drift as he beckoned with his right hand and rubbed his thumb and forefinger together. The lawyer handed him a fifty-dollar bill and then tightened the laces of his rubber-soled hiking boots.

Pancho led Will across the grounds. To their left was the mammoth El Castillo, and to their right was the Temple of the Warriors, a large, square, stone structure with carved images and glyphs around its base, shapes that were still mostly recognizable, though rubbed almost smooth by one hundred thousand rains over fifteen hundred years.

"There—there!" his companion shouted, pointing to the top of the temple. He pulled out a small pair of binoculars and handed them to Will.

"Chacmool—the god Chacmool!"

As they walked by, Will looked up at the platform at the top of the temple and saw a stone image—reclining, with its head turned sideways toward the viewer—the god Chacmool, in whose lap was a flat, stone surface.

"Do you see his lap?" Pancho asked.

The lawyer nodded.

"The hearts of victims—human sacrifice—were placed in the lap of Chacmool." Pancho then gave Will a grin that exposed several of his missing teeth.

As they walked between El Castillo and the Temple of the Warriors, Will saw the large open area where the helicopter must have landed. He glanced at the diagram he had drawn after his conference with Colonel Marlowe.

Then he surveyed the area. He concluded that the commandos, after being dropped off from the helicopter, must have run straight ahead to the edge of the jungle, along the left side of a large open area about a hundred yards down from his position.

"What is that?" he asked, pointing ahead to a vast opening in the jungle floor off in the distance.

"*Cenote sagrado*—the sacred well of sacrifice," Pancho said as they walked quickly toward its edge. Then he added, "I give you this tour of the Mayans free of charge!"

They walked over to the edge of the mammoth, gaping chasm. It was ringed with stones, like the teeth of a dark and forbidding mouth—a natural well hundreds of feet across. Will peered down into its dark abyss, a black hole that defied the light.

"Did they use this for sacrifices?" he asked.

"Yes—tie the victims down with weights and throw them in. There is deep water at the bottom. But it is spring-fed from way down in the earth. So they cannot drain it. Many artifacts—many old things brought up. Skulls. Skeletons. The Mayans believed if they threw you in the well and you lived, then you were a god—or maybe a very powerful leader."

"How deep is this?" Will pointed down into the dark, airless depths.

His companion shrugged. "Hard to say. But very deep—very dangerous."

Stepping back from the gaping hole in the earth, Will wondered at a culture that was based on the sacrifice of innocent human life.

As they left the well and headed for the edge of the jungle, Pancho pointed over to a spot beyond the Temple of the Warriors.

"Sometime you should look over there at the ball court. There they played games—very much like jai alai, but a little bit like basketball too—and if you lose the game..." He took his thumb and quickly struck it across his throat from side to side. "They would cut your head off!" he said with a smile.

When they entered the deep undergrowth, heading toward the house that lay on the outskirts of the village of Chacmool, Pancho started using the machete he had brought along. At first he was able to pick a moderately open path through the jungle and only occasionally had to cut through vines.

"It's good that you have boots," he said. "Watch where you step, and don't put your hands on the trees—the snakes like to sleep there."

Occasionally Will glanced at his compass to make sure they were still taking the same direction that Marlowe and his commandos had taken.

The colonel had said that there had been a near full moon that night, but even so, with the thick jungle canopy above, Will wondered how they had been able to navigate so quickly. Marlowe had told him they had small flashlights attached to their headgear. But even so, it must have been rough going by night.

Here and there Will heard the screech of a jungle bird and caught sight of a flamboyantly colored cockatoo on a tree. He was drenched with sweat from the damp heat of the jungle and was taking increasingly large gulps from his water bottle. The foliage was getting thicker and more intense, and the vines were now almost impenetrable. Pancho was working hard, chopping and clearing the vines ahead with the machete. He was panting, and his pace was getting slower.

They felt a suffocating, almost strangling sensation, being surrounded by the hot, damp walls of vegetation.

And then, quite suddenly, they broke through to a dirt road. Will glanced down at his diagram and pointed over to the right. There, about a hundred feet from the edge of the road—which was walled by jungle on each side—was a small structure. He knew this was it. And beyond the little house, approximately two miles further down, was the beginning of the village of Chacmool.

He took out his diagram, which was damp with sweat, and glanced at it to make sure this was the location. The two men walked over to the front of the little yard, which was filled with weeds and scrub brush.

"You stay here," Will said to his guide. There were several sawhorse barricades set up around the perimeter of the house, with a sign in Spanish.

"Hey, Señor," Pancho yelled. "The sign says no trespass—by order of police."

Will nodded but walked ahead toward the front door. As he approached he was able to see the full extent of the destruction that had been rained down on this little house. The windows had all been shot out, and the cement base, wooden walls, and tin roof were perforated and blasted open with an infinite number of bullet holes. Some of the sunlight piercing through the jungle canopy found its way in through a few of the bullet holes and streamed out again in shafts. At the door there was a small concrete slab which was stained with red.

The front door had a padlock on it, so, after putting on his gloves, Will gingerly took a few of the remaining jagged pieces of glass from the window and stepped through the opening. He turned on his flashlight and glanced around the room.

There was a putrid stench, as if he had entered a tomb that had not been opened for centuries. Even with only his flashlight to illuminate the inside, he could tell that the blood everywhere had never been cleaned up. There were several scattered chairs and a cheap wooden table in the center of the room. In the middle of the floor there was a wooden trapdoor, which he lifted. He cast the flashlight beam down a rough-hewn ladder that rested on a dirt floor at the bottom.

He climbed down the ladder until his feet hit the dirt. At first he could see no opening that led from the small space. Then he saw a tunnel, perhaps two-and-a-half feet square, leading away from the ladder. Squatting down and shining his light into it, he saw an occasional piece of wood reinforcement on the inside of a roughly cut earthen passageway. There were vines hanging down here and there from the earthen roof.

Satisfied that he had located the escape route of the al-Aqsa Jihad terrorists, he scampered up the ladder and closed the trapdoor behind him.

Will experienced a vast feeling of relief when he finally climbed out of the window of that sweltering, oppressive place. Pancho was waiting for him, smoking a cigarette.

"We go back on the road this time?"

"Right," Will answered. "We can take the road back."

"The jungle—much thicker—much more work than I thought," his guide said, opening his hand toward Will.

The lawyer dug in his pocket and pulled out a crumpled twenty-dollar bill. He was going to thank Pancho for bringing him, but something stopped him. How could he be thankful for a trip into this jungle nightmare…where the stench of death still hung in the air like a poisonous cloud.

On the way back the two were quiet. Then Will asked his companion a question.

"Have you heard anything about what happened back at that house—the gunfight with the terrorists?"

Pancho shrugged.

"Have you heard any information about the terrorists—the banditos—or about who was killed inside?"

The other man turned toward Will, but he was not smiling.

Thrusting his hand into his pocket, the American pulled out a wad of twenty-dollar bills.

But Pancho shook his head, put both hands up as if to ward something off, and then quickened his pace to go ahead of Will, down the dirt road.

21

ON THE WAY BACK TO THE YUCATÁN COAST, Will had Pancho pull over when they reached the town of Valladolid. He found a phone in a hotel lobby and called Tiny, who was nervously waiting for him in his room at the airport motel.

"Will, buddy, glad you called." The large private investigator was fanning himself with the room-service menu. "Listen," Tiny continued, "I feel like a sitting duck here. After I met with Hermán, I noticed that I was being followed by a couple of creepy-looking guys. I think I need to split the airport area here and head inland until we fly out tomorrow."

Will suggested that Tiny make his way to Valladolid—to the Hacienda Montejo, a hotel a few blocks down from the old San Bernardino Church. He agreed, and said he thought he could give his trailers the slip.

By the time Tiny arrived, the sun was going down and the jungle heat was subsiding. They met in the hotel restaurant, a whitewashed, partly open veranda with shuttered windows that split the last glimmer of sunset into gold and yellow shafts of light as it streamed through the slats.

Outside, the banana trees were swaying in a gentle breeze that had just come up. The big investigator was halfway through his plate of *pollo pibil* when he started reciting the results of the meeting with his contact.

"Okay, first," he said with his mouth half-full, "my guy said that the word was out about the commando strike against the safe house before it ever happened. But he was vague about it—that's all he could say. So it's very possible that your marine guy was being set up."

"What about the federal police—what role did they play in this?"

"Not sure—I mean, kidnapping and drug-running is like a cottage industry down here, and a lot of the Mexican cops are in on it. Hermán acted real jittery about giving me the lowdown on the role of the government in this, except to say that the political buzz down here is maximum stinko when it comes to the U.S.A."

"What do you mean?"

"Well," Tiny said, wiping his mouth with his napkin, "he says all the government bigwigs are talking trash against America. Especially our military. Which—you know—ticked me off, as a proud veteran myself."

"Where's this coming from?"

"A lot of talk about the popular power of the Independent Revolutionary Party down here. Actually, it's building up a lot of steam up in Mexico City and also down in the south, around Chiapas, where the IRP has the backing of a militant radical group called the EZLN—the National Liberation Army. But the IRP isn't exactly the hometown team here in the Yucatán—where they've got all the Mayans. The Mayan Indians have been fighting the Spanish and the Mexicans—for hundreds of years. So they're not buying into any of the pro-Mexican nationalism—regardless of the party."

"So, how does al-Aqsa Jihad fit in?"

"Oh, that," the detective said, leaning back from the table. "Yeah, well, it's like…how can I put it? It's like a heavyweight championship—picture Blackbeard the Pirate meets Saddam Hussein. I mean, who do you root for, you know? The Jihad cell group is down here running drugs to keep their movement in the money and also to get closer to the American borders. At the same time, Mexico has not done much to kick them out. In fact, there's some talk about sympathy for the Jihad—but Hermán didn't give details."

"So the terrorists are dealing drugs?" Will asked.

"Big-time. Hey—just remembered—there's an American drug guy in on this. I wrote his name down."

With that, Tiny pulled a piece of paper from his pocket and handed it to Will.

After glancing at it, the lawyer raised an eyebrow and threw a smirk at the other man.

"'Victor Viper'? That's his name?"

Tiny laughed out loud.

"Yeah. Not likely to be the name that mommy and daddy gave him. Obviously an alias. According to my contact, this guy is not nice. Anyway, he has sort of disappeared from the scene recently. Bottom line, Hermán thinks that the Jihad cell is still operating down here."

Will had been listening carefully, but wasn't sure what he thought of Tiny's information—certainly nothing sounded groundbreaking. "Anything else?" he asked.

"One thing—now take this for what it's worth."

"What?"

"Well," Tiny said, "my guy says there's something big and very bad...that's going to happen."

Will looked at the detective with bewilderment.

"What are you talking about?"

"That's all he could tell me."

"Bad—in what way?"

"Bad, like being dead is bad."

"And who is this bad thing supposedly going to happen to?"

"Don't know. But Hermán was not joking about it."

"How did it come up?"

"When we were talking about the AAJ."

"Do you think he was talking about a target in the U.S.? Americans being hit by terrorists?"

"It did occur to me."

That last bit of intelligence seemed, to Will, to be extraordinarily *un*intelligible. And its relevance, if any, to the defense of Caleb Marlowe was mystifying in the extreme.

Nevertheless, it was a chilling—though obscure—warning. Will felt as if he had just stumbled on an ancient, indecipherable message—a brutal prophecy carved in stone, previously hidden by the overgrowth of the jungle.

22

BACK AT QUANTICO, WILL AND Major Hanover were preparing for the upcoming hearing and conferring with Colonel Marlowe. When Will recounted the information he had received from Tiny Heftland, his client jotted down notes studiously.

Then Will and Hanover turned their attention to the accused marine officer.

"Sir, why didn't you follow Master Sergeant Rockwell's suggestion?" Hanover asked. "Take out the guard, and then one of you approach the house and make a close-up recon?"

"Maybe we could have taken him out when he was on the front porch. But I figured it would be just a matter of seconds before the rest of his group would realize he wouldn't have come back. Not only was I trying to accomplish the mission, I was also trying to avoid any loss to our team."

"And what was the mission?" Will asked.

"Like I said before, to locate and eliminate the cell group we had tracked—the bad guys who had participated in the attempted kidnapping of Secretary Kilmer."

Will followed up. "Was there any thought given to capture? Wouldn't there have been some value in trying to interrogate these guys?"

"Negative. The intel reports we already had indicated that it would be difficult, if not impossible, to take any of them alive. They were known to carry both self-detonated and remotely detonated explosives. The idea was that they would defy capture and blow themselves up—taking us with them. The one guard we took down was strapped with explosives."

Will continued probing. "I'm not sure if you answered Major Hanover's question. Why not have one of your guys get up to that window to see who was inside?"

"In addition to what I've already told you," Marlowe said, "there was another obvious problem with that—it was lights-out inside the house. I had the heat sensor and I could see bodies in there. That's all we could tell."

"But your thermal-imaging screen showed that four of those bodies were stationary, and in sitting positions?"

At first the colonel's face seemed expressionless. Then his eyes twitched slightly and the corners of his mouth tightened ever so slightly. He stared at his hands, which were lying on top of the conference table. When he finally spoke, his voice was constricted, choked with emotion.

"Those four thermal images were Carlos. My good friend Carlos. And his beautiful young wife. And their two young children."

The colonel raised his head and stared Will in the eyes. "And there's something else…" He was having trouble talking.

"Something else," he continued. "For an instant—maybe it was even a fraction of an instant—I noticed that two of the four body images on my scope looked smaller…much smaller…than the other two."

"So you knew there might be children sitting in the middle of the room before you ordered a cross fire of weapons that would tear them apart?" Will asked bluntly.

His client paused. "I…I can't say that was my thought. Things happened very quickly. You have orders…a mission…concern about controlling a very fluid environment. One of the guards had apparently already detected our position and fired at one of our men, hurting him badly. Here we are about to be detected, and the whole mission's going to go bad. I know that we've got a cell group of four people—"

"Exactly," Will said, pushing harder. "One guard outside, and four sitting in the middle of the room. That makes a total of five people. So did you ask yourself—who the fifth person was?"

"Oh, yes—I asked myself that…and that's when I gave the order."

"Who did you think it was? Another terrorist? A civilian? You said earlier that you knew there might be a noncombatant in the group— but you were willing to assume the risk of 'collateral damage,' right?"

"I can't tell you who I thought it was."

"Because of the DOD gag order?"

"Not just that. There are things that you don't know…that you can't know…and I'm still bound by orders that go way beyond this."

Will leaned back in his chair. Marlowe looked tired and burdened.

"Tell me something," the attorney said. "What are the questions you are asking yourself right now?"

The colonel took only a second, perhaps two, before answering.

"Giving orders—making the command decision—that's what I've been trained for and what I'm built for. But you give the orders—and then there's the other part. You have to take responsibility for the orders you give. That doesn't just mean facing a superior officer's questions, a board of inquiry, or even a court-martial. It means living in that decision every minute, every day. It means going to bed every night…seeing the bodies of your best friend and his wife and his two little children chopped up by the assault you ordered. And when you wake up the next morning the ghosts are there. Standing at the edge of your bed in your room. They greet you in the morning and they're with you all day."

Marlowe stopped suddenly, as if he were calculating the degree to which he would make himself vulnerable. After a few seconds he continued.

"From what I know about you, a lawyer who walks with God, you know something about forgiveness. I thought I did. If I made a mistake—if I had a lapse in judgment—or even if it wasn't my fault, still I'm the one responsible for giving the order. Whatever the truth is…I know in my head Jesus hung on the cross to forgive that. I know the Bible tells me all of that was taken care of at the cross. And I've asked for forgiveness for not having seen a way around this…for not having been ahead of the curve to figure out that we might be double-crossed, and that we might have been led into a trap.

"But—you see—the fact is, sometimes now I find it difficult to look in the mirror. There's a person out there with my name, rank, and serial number who looks a lot like me. Well, you see, in a way, I hate that guy—and want him dead. So I'm just like the walking dead. I don't know if you can possibly understand that. But you asked me, so that's my answer."

For some reason, quite unexpectedly, it all rushed back to Will. He had always been good at achieving a level of professional detachment, and cold, objective analysis. Even in his most emotionally charged cases he always kept himself at arm's length because he told himself that, like a surgeon, he could best operate on critical patients if he could keep them from grabbing ahold of his insides.

But now the attorney was feeling something else. This decorated career marine officer had lived a life that couldn't have been further from his own...yet now there was a connection. Something had been touched...deeply disrupted...in Will. He thought he had managed to distance himself from the guilt over Audra's murder. But now he was wondering whether he had just been giving himself a cheap, ready-made solution...through distraction.

Had he missed the signals? In the back of his memory, he knew, there was something more awful than he wanted to recall. Yet it kept clawing its way to the surface...One of the witnesses in the case he had brought against the neo-Nazi group in New York had warned him that this was a group that would always pay back, an eye for an eye—that if Will was successful in breaking these domestic terrorists, he should be prepared for retribution—against him, or his family.

Will had never shared that with Audra. He had considered the warning, but then had rejected it as a kind of urban legend about the group. And there was also something else—his confidence...maybe even arrogance...that if he was on the right side of truth and justice, then he and Audra, and their lives, would be protected.

And when Will recalled his failure to ask Audra to come back after she had moved out...his ignoring that inner voice that kept telling him to patch things up and bring her back...those were the thoughts that gave him a dreadful sense of responsibility for what happened. He knew there was a likelihood that his actions, or his failure to act, had been a factor in the brutal death of the woman he loved. And that is when his cold, computerlike sense of logic would flash the message on the screen of his brain—the message he could not ignore: *You are responsible. You will have to live with this.*

There was something in Will's face, in his eyes, that showed he had fixed on a dark, forbidding place...an abyss where he was struggling with ghosts of his own.

During the preceding silence, Colonel Marlowe had been looking intently at Will. Now he straightened up in his chair and gave his lawyer a smile of recognition.

"On the other hand," the officer said quietly, "maybe you do understand."

23

MAJOR HANOVER WAS ALREADY in the military courtroom at Quantico when Will Chambers arrived. Colonel Marlowe was standing next to the defending officer. Both were dressed in their marine "Charlie" uniforms. Marlowe's chest was covered with a block of ribbons. Though intellectually aware of it because of his work on the case, somehow Will had never fully appreciated the extent of his client's service to his country. As he shook Marlowe's hand, he wanted to say something—a thank-you perhaps—but before he could, the other man greeted him.

"Counselor," he said, shaking his hand firmly, "I'm privileged to have you representing me today—you too, Major Hanover."

"No," Will replied, "the honor is mine, Colonel."

As the two advocates unpacked their briefcases and stacked their notebooks and manuals on the counsel table, Will surveyed the courtroom. It was blandly military. Within a few minutes Colonel Stickton, the government trial counsel, strode in. He shook hands all around. He had the Deputy Director of the Staff Judge Advocate from Headquarters, U.S. Marine Corps with him. They were followed by Special Agent Fred Brooks, the chief NCIS man on the case.

Hanover, Will, and Marlowe huddled together quietly at their counsel table.

"Just remember what we indicated to you about the purpose of this proceeding today—an Article 32 hearing is just a preliminary hearing to determine whether or not there's probable cause for the matter to be referred to a general court-martial," the major explained to Will as Marlowe nodded his head.

"The investigating officer—the IO—who acts like the judge in this proceeding, is going to hear the evidence." Hanover continued directing his comments at Will. "And then the IO will issue a report with his findings and a summary of the proceedings. If he finds probable cause to refer this matter, he has to state the evidence and the reasons that support that. But ultimately, the decision doesn't belong to the IO—it belongs to the convening authority. That's the commanding general here at Marine Corps base—Brigadier General Landon—who will have to sign off on any recommendation for a formal court-martial referral."

"Who is our IO?" Will inquired.

"Lieutenant Colonel Howard Rogers—he's the civil law officer for the Marine Corps here at Quantico—he was detailed to this proceeding," Hanover replied.

A military court reporter scurried in and began setting up. After a few moments of silence, IO Rogers stepped into the courtroom from behind the bench, and the room quickly snapped to attention.

"Be seated. This investigation is convened by the commanding general under Article 32. I am the investigating officer, Lieutenant Colonel Howard Rogers, United States Marine Corps. This matter is referenced Colonel Caleb R. Marlowe, accused. Does the accused acknowledge receipt and advisement of the charges and specifications?"

Major Hanover rose and indicated in the affirmative.

"If the investigating officer please," he continued, "I'd also like to introduce attorney Will Chambers of Virginia, privately retained civilian defense counsel, who will be acting as co-counsel for the accused."

"Welcome to the United States Marine Corps," the lieutenant colonel said.

Both trial counsel and defense counsel reserved opening statements.

The prosecution's first witness was Corporal Hank Thompson. The corporal was still nursing injuries from the mission, and his left arm was in a shoulder restraint.

Initially, Will sized Thompson up as a confident, emotionless witness. But as Colonel Stickton led him through his initial questioning, Will noticed a nervous gesture—the corporal would periodically, though subtly, tuck his chin quickly toward his neck. Thompson gave his rank, serial number, and a brief explanation of his military history. He had been with the Army Rangers when he had been transferred on special duty to the Office of Special Operations to serve under Colonel Marlowe.

"And so you were transferred to the command of Colonel Caleb Marlowe, USMC?"

"That's correct, sir. Assigned to BATCOM, a special covert counter-terrorism unit."

Thompson's overexpansive description sent an electric charge through the courtroom.

Stickton immediately bent down and consulted in a hushed tone with his co-counsel, as Special Agent Brooks stretched over the table so he could listen in on the huddle.

Will quickly turned to Hanover and whispered, "I thought there was a restriction on any testimony relating to the military configuration of Marlowe's unit—or its actual identity. What's this 'BATCOM' thing?"

His partner nodded vigorously and added, "I can't understand this—I can't believe that Colonel Stickton did not brief Thompson on this. I suggest we don't object."

"Considering that we're only at a probable-cause stage here, I recommend that we *do* object," Will countered. "We ought to err on the side of caution in terms of additional evidence coming in. This is a two-edged sword—it could cut both ways."

But Hanover was insistent—no objection. Will complied, and the two attorneys leaned back in their chairs and waited for the trial counsel to continue.

Stickton stood straight up, with his fingertips resting lightly on the top of his table.

"If we may continue," he said. "Let's move on. Corporal Thompson, were you involved in a military mission near the vicinity of a village in southern Mexico, in the Yucatán, known as Chacmool—code name for the mission, 'Snake Hunt'?"

Thompson nodded enthusiastically. "Yes, sir, that's correct."

"Who was your commanding officer?"

"Colonel Marlowe."

"What time did you arrive at your position for the assault?"

"Sir, it was zero three hundred hours."

"And what was the designated target?"

"Sir, our mission was to locate and eliminate four terrorists who were known to have participated in the attempted kidnapping of Secretary of Commerce Kilmer. Our intel had indicated that they had retreated through the jungle to a safe house on the outskirts of the village of Chacmool."

"Would you please describe to this investigation the members of your unit, the weapons with which they were armed, and their positions at the mission site?"

"Well, sir," the corporal began, "I set up in a concealed position under some brush and trees about seventy-five feet from the southeast corner of the house. From this position I could see the front of the house, which faced south, and also place fire along the east side of the house in case anyone tried to escape in that direction. I had standard-issue special-operations gear and was armed with an M203 grenade launcher mounted under an M16 rifle. To my left about ten or fifteen meters, and slightly to the rear of me, was Colonel Marlowe, hidden behind some cover. He and the rest of us were waiting for Chief Petty Officer Dorfman to set up the machine-gun position at the rear of the house before starting operations.

"The colonel was armed with a 9mm H&K MP5 submachine gun with silencer. About four or five meters to his left—directly south of the front door—was Master Sergeant Rockwell. His position also had good cover. He was equipped with a Mossberg 12-gauge shotgun. He was also carrying an M72 LAW—a collapsible light antitank weapon. We carried it along in case we encountered any fortified positions.

"Swinging to the top of Rockwell's left about four or five meters was Staff Sergeant Baker. He was armed with standard-issue special-operations gear and concussion grenades, as well as a 9mm H&K MP5 submachine gun with silencer, the same as Colonel Marlowe. He was also behind cover—about a hundred feet south of the southwest corner of the house.

"Chief Petty Officer Dorfman, who was equipped with an M240G medium machine gun, was in the vicinity of the northwest corner of the house. He was moving to take up a position from which to cover the back—in case anyone tried to escape out the back door. From that position he would also be able to observe and cover the west side of the house while the assault team was inside.

"Sir, I guess I should add that all of the weapons, except the shotgun and the LAW, were equipped with some type of night-vision sighting device."

Strickton moved to the next question. "What was your mission task?"

"Sir, to locate and eliminate the terrorists I just referred to."

"And tell me," the trial counsel asked, fingering a copy of the NCIS report in his left hand as he spoke, "what was the planned mission brief of this attack?"

"Sir, assuming there was no prior alert, no activity on the outside, then Master Sergeant Rockwell was to approach the front door, and if the front door was locked, blow it open. At that point he was to be followed immediately by Staff Sergeant Baker, who was to toss in a concussion grenade—and after the detonation, Colonel Marlowe was to lead Master Sergeant Rockwell and Staff Sergeant Baker into the building. Chief Dorfman and I were to maintain our positions and create covering fire if necessary from the outside—also, if there were any escapees through the rear or side of the house, we were to take them down immediately."

"And was that plan executed?"

"Well, sir," Thompson responded, tucking his chin down slightly, "not exactly."

"And what do you mean by that? What happened, if anything, that prevented that plan from being executed?"

"Sir, we were interrupted by a lookout, who exited the building from the front and stood guard on the front porch."

"And did that lookout fire in the direction of any of the members of your team?"

"Yes, sir, that's exactly what happened," the corporal said, pointing to his bandaged shoulder.

"Question—you were hit by two separate rounds?"

"Yes, sir, but I was still conscious and able to fire."

"Did your commanding officer, Colonel Marlowe, take any action to hit the guard first?"

"No, sir, that was not the order."

"What was the order?"

Thompson shifted a little in his seat, tucked his chin down quickly, and replied, "The order, sir, was for everyone to open fire immediately—

to empty our clips into the lookout and into all aspects of that house. We were to kill everything in sight, sir."

Will glanced at Stickton and knew that the coup de grace was coming. If the colonel was smart, he would put in one last line of questioning. One final dagger into the defense case.

"Tell me, Corporal Thompson," the trial counsel continued. "In the intervening seconds between the time that the lookout fired in your direction and the time that Colonel Marlowe ordered the members of your unit to commence firing, was there any fire coming out of the building toward any of your positions?"

Thompson thought for a second and shook his head.

"No, sir, he fired a short burst. That was it. Then it was quiet."

"And quiet for how long between the time that the lookout fired and the time Colonel Marlowe ordered your unit to hit that house?"

Thompson thought for a moment again.

"A few seconds—I'm not sure how many, sir."

"More than two seconds?"

"Maybe, sir."

"More than five seconds?"

Thompson shifted in the chair and glanced over at Colonel Marlowe.

"The questions are coming from this table, not Colonel Marlowe's table," Stickton barked.

Thompson snapped his attention back to his questioner.

"Possibly more than five, sir, but I doubt it."

"Corporal Thompson, who was the best marksman in your unit?"

"Sir, every member of the team is an expert marksman and sniper-trained. However, the last time we all fired for qualification, I had the best score."

"Then you were the best marksman in your unit, is that correct?"

"I suppose so, sir," Thompson replied reluctantly.

"Based on your past observations of your team's shooting skills, would any of you have much difficulty hitting a target the size of a quarter from one hundred feet out?"

"No, sir—we could actually hit dimes at that close a range."

"But Colonel Marlowe never ordered you to take that lookout down—which would have been an easy task for you, right?"

The corporal's eyes gazed off in the distance for just an instant, but then he looked back at Stickton.

"The fact is, sir," Thompson said, "Colonel Marlowe ordered suppressing fire down on that house, after taking out the lookout—I took that to be an order to kill the lookout first."

"True or false," Stickton demanded, his voice rising and filling the room, "Colonel Marlowe did *not* order any of you to take out that lookout with a single shot?"

"That's correct."

"Had Colonel Marlowe ordered, from one hundred feet away you could have placed one shot in that lookout's head with relative ease under normal conditions—and no one inside that house would have been threatened."

The corporal hesitated. His face tightened, as if he were about to hand a club to a pencil-pushing desk jockey who would use it to bludgeon his mentor and hero.

Finally he spoke up.

"I suppose so, sir…all of that is true, except—"

"Thank you, Corporal Thompson," Stickton snapped. "That's all, Corporal."

24

As WILL STEPPED OVER TO THE podium to cross-examine Corporal Thompson, he knew that his questioning would have to be limited, narrow, and very focused. He would have to show that it would not have been feasible for Thompson, after being hit, to have made an accurate single shot to take down the lookout. Thus, if Marlowe had given a more cautious order, it wouldn't have worked.

Further, the corporal was the youngest among the members of Marlowe's team—and perhaps the most easily led. If Will opened up a troublesome area by asking too-broad questions, the young man might inadvertently say something that would undermine the defense.

"Corporal Thompson, I'd like to direct your attention," the attorney began, "to your testimony of a few minutes ago relating to the weapons being carried by the various team members. You testified that both Colonel Marlowe and Staff Sergeant Baker were carrying MP5 sub-machine guns with silencers. Are you qualified on the MP5 submachine gun?"

"Yes, I am—in fact, I usually carry an MP5 in the field. I was armed with an M16 and an M203 grenade launcher for this operation just in case we ran into an unplanned-for situation, sir."

"So is it safe to say that you are an expert on the MP5?"

"Certainly, sir."

Will got a pensive look on his face. "Corporal Thompson, I am not an expert on weapon systems, but it seems to me that if someone wanted to take out the guard who ended up shooting you, spraying the front of the house with automatic-weapons fire would be sure to alert those inside of your presence—is that so?"

Colonel Stickton was looking at Will with a puzzled expression.

Thompson hesitated. "But...you *wouldn't* be spraying the house with bullets, sir—the MP5 has a selector switch that allows you to fire either single-shot or fully automatic. So either the colonel or Sergeant Baker could have killed that lookout with one shot!"

Stickton was looking down at the counsel table, trying not to gloat. He was wondering why Marlowe had bothered to bring in civilian counsel if he was just going to help prove the prosecution's case.

"Now, back to the weapon you were carrying—if Colonel Marlowe had ordered you to take down that man with a single shot from your M16, you might have had the marksmanship to do that under normal conditions. I noticed that Colonel Stickton asked you about your ability to fire a shot under *normal* conditions, am I correct?"

"Sir, that's how the lawyer there for the prosecution put it—right."

"But under the *actual combat conditions* at the time of the Chacmool incident, you had been hit in the shoulder and were seriously injured, is that correct?"

"Absolutely."

"Considering the injury to your shoulder, would that not have affected your ability to take out the lookout with one shot—to absolutely take him down with a single round?"

"No doubt about it, sir."

Will was gambling that Colonel Stickton would press the point that a left-shoulder injury wouldn't hamper a right-handed marksman. He knew he had set the trap. Now the only question was whether Stickton was going to thrust his hand into it.

It wouldn't take very long for Will to find out.

The trial counsel strode to the podium and spoke quickly and firmly.

"Is it correct that you were shot in your left shoulder?"

"Yes sir, that's right."

"Are you right-handed?"

"Yes, sir, I am right-handed—yes."

"And you shoot—trigger finger and aiming hand—all on the right side?"

"Well...I'm right-handed—and I fire right-handed—yes, sir."

Then the colonel got ready to launch his final volley.

"That bullet in your left shoulder didn't stop you from emptying the entire clip of your M16 into the house after you were shot—is that correct? You were still capable of precision shooting?"

Thompson grimaced a little bit and then answered.

"Yes—I suppose. I did get all my rounds off…that's right, sir."

Stickton stepped down from the podium, seeming satisfied.

But Will bounded back to the podium for re-cross-examination.

"About your firing that M16—" he began, "how were you able to fully expend your ammunition? Did your M16 have a bipod support?"

Thompson smiled at that.

"No, sir, but I was able to use the grenade launcher as a prop and get off a full clip even though I had been shot in the left shoulder. I could get away with using just my right arm because the grenade launcher provided the necessary support."

"But would that system of support have been adequate for more precise shooting—like a single shot to the head of that lookout?"

"No, sir. No marksman would want to use a sloppy kind of prop like that for a sniper shot—especially if he were already injured."

Will had planned to stop there. He felt he had done some moderate damage to the prosecution's proof. But he decided to ask one more question.

"Do you know how that lookout was able to detect your position, considering the fact that you had approached the house with stealth and under cover? Did it appear to you that the lookout was expecting you?"

Thompson leaned forward, seeming ready to answer quickly and eagerly, but he was interrupted by Colonel Stickton, who jumped to his feet.

"Objection—will the investigating officer please note prosecution's objection. Not only is the question improper as to form, but it's also asking this witness to comment on the state of mind of a man who is now dead."

"Noted," Colonel Rogers fired back. Then he turned to Will Chambers.

"Counselor, there was no way, from his position and based on his limited capacity for observation, that the corporal could have reasonably formed an opinion on *why* that lookout fired at his position. Mr. Chambers, you're finished with this witness."

Will managed a smile and a polite nod, and he resumed his seat at counsel table. The IO's rebuke had some bite to it, but like the sting of a wasp, it was not likely to cause any real damage. He still felt confident that he had kicked some of the props out from under the trial counsel's use of Corporal Thompson.

Yet he knew there was still a major problem. The evidence from each succeeding witness would prove to be increasingly more troublesome to his client's defense. Considering the fact that he could not risk calling the colonel to testify at this early stage of the case, aggressive cross-examination of the prosecution's case was his only weapon. But that was not going to be easy—because Marlowe was refusing to disclose everything he knew. It was beginning to look as if Will Chambers would have to perform a marksman's job—while wearing a blindfold.

25

"CHIEF DORFMAN, PRIOR TO Colonel Marlowe's giving you the order to open fire, did you see or hear any weapon fired from the inside of the house out to your position?"

"No, sir—I guess what you're asking is...whether anyone was shooting at me before we started shooting at them. The answer is no. There were no shots fired from the inside of the house—at least nothing I could see toward *my* position—before I commenced firing. I had heard shots coming from the front of the house. That's when Thompson was hit."

"And was there a window near your position—where you were lying due north of the building?"

"Yes, there was a large square window to the right of the back door."

"And when Colonel Marlowe gave you the order to fire, what was your target?"

"I fired through the window, then through the door, and then I sprayed the rest of my round in a horizontal, zigzag line from side to side along the house."

"And the M240G you were carrying is a large-caliber gun?"

"Yes, sir. Large-caliber."

"And that weapon sends a very punishing fire, capable of taking down four or five targets in quick fashion?"

"Sir, if you hit your target with the M240G, it's not going to be standing very long."

"One last question, Chief Dorfman..." the trial counsel said. "If you've got a group of terrorists who are holding civilian hostages in a small room—in the same room as the terrorists themselves—and you're shooting blindly into a window that opens into that room—is the M240G machine gun the best weapon to use?"

Major Hanover rose to his feet and objected on the grounds that Chief Dorfman had not been the commanding officer of the mission—nor had he been qualified as an expert in making command decisions in that kind of a mission.

Colonel Rogers noted the objection but directed that the question be answered.

Dorfman thought for a moment, then cocked his head slightly to the side as he began answering.

"Sir, I suppose…if you've got a small room with hostages and terrorists and they're all together within your target—the M240G doesn't really discriminate. It doesn't have the precision of some of the smaller-caliber automatic weapons. So let me say that we didn't know there were hostages—"

"Nonresponsive. I ask that the investigating officer note the nonresponsive nature of the witness's answer. That is all, Chief Dorfman," Colonel Stickton said as he walked to the prosecution table.

On cross-examination Hanover quickly established that Dorfman had had no idea that there might be civilians in the house. Then Hanover moved to his second line of questioning.

"Was the house darkened?"

"Yes, that is correct, sir. There weren't any lights on that I could see."

"And did it appear that there was a curtain drawn over the window on the north side—the side where you were positioned?"

"Yes, sir—it looked like there was some kind of a drape across the window. I couldn't see through it."

Stickton stepped back to the podium.

"If Colonel Marlowe knew there might be one or more civilians inside that house, prior to his order for your unit to commence firing into it—if that was true, apparently Colonel Marlowe never let you in on that fact, is that correct?"

Dorfman stared down at his hands, which were folded in his lap. After a moment of reflection he answered.

"I suppose that would be right…yes, sir."

26

WHILE PREPARING FOR THE ARTICLE 32 hearing, Will had asked Colonel Marlowe what kind of witness Staff Sergeant Billy Baker would make.

Marlowe chuckled a bit and then described Baker as "Mr. Gung-Ho."

That description was right on target.

As the trial counsel led Baker through his questioning, the witness sat steel-spine rigid in the chair and snapped his answers out with military precision.

Colonel Stickton asked the sergeant to describe the rules of engagement as articulated by Colonel Marlowe immediately before hitting the drop zone that night.

"Sir, the rules of engagement, as explained by our commanding officer, Colonel Marlowe, were threefold."

"Why don't you describe for us what those three rules were?"

"Sir, those three rules of engagement were as follows—first, no shots were to be fired until and unless commanded by Colonel Marlowe. Next, if we met any resistance, and on Colonel Marlowe's command, we were to use absolute and unrestrained deadly force. Third, we were to be on the alert for the presence of hostages or civilian noncombatants. In the event that we had a positive identification of any such hostages or civilian noncombatants, we were to avoid casualties."

"In other words," Stickton asked, "the third rule—to avoid civilian losses—that rule was to trump the other two, is that right?"

"I'm not sure I understand the Colonel's question, sir—perhaps the Colonel could more fully explain it."

"Well, Sergeant Baker, here's my question—if you, or any other member of your team, determined there might be civilians in that house, then you were to refrain from the use of force even if Colonel Marlowe commanded you to use force—is that right?"

"Negative, sir. Colonel Marlowe was in complete command of the mission. He gave the orders—we followed them. We were to fire down on that house only on his command, and when his order came, we had to follow it."

"Well, what if you spotted some civilians there in the house—then what would you do?"

"That decision, sir, was to be made by Colonel Marlowe. We were to report the presence of any civilian noncombatants to him, and then he was to make the command decision."

"And these rules of engagement were clearly described by the colonel to you in your mission briefing prior to your descent into the drop zone, correct?"

"Yes, sir. That's correct. Colonel Marlowe clearly outlined the rules of engagement. He always made his orders crystal clear to all of his team."

"So, according to what Colonel Marlowe told you before you reached the house on the outskirts of Chacmool, he was the one to make the decision about authorizing deadly force if someone raised an issue concerning the presence of civilians at the scene, is that right?"

"Sir, the decision about civilian noncombatants was Colonel Marlowe's decision. He was in command. He made the decision."

"Now, Sergeant Baker, did you see or hear any signs of the presence of civilians in or about that house before Colonel Marlowe gave his command to commence firing?"

"Negative, sir—I saw and heard no signs of civilians."

"But someone else raised the issue of civilians inside the house—is that correct?"

Baker had maintained his rigid posture in the witness stand so far throughout the questioning. But with this last inquiry from Colonel Stickton, the witness's shoulders slumped slightly. His head did a small, momentary bob up and down.

"Would the Colonel repeat the question, sir—I'm not sure what the Colonel is getting at."

"Sergeant Baker, did someone else in your mission mention to Colonel Marlowe that there might be civilians inside that house?"

"Affirmative, sir. Someone did."

"And who was that?"

Will and Major Hanover both jumped to their feet simultaneously. Hanover recited the objection that the question was based on hearsay and asked the investigating officer to note it in the record.

But Colonel Rogers directed that the question be answered.

"I do not recall the question—I need the question repeated, sir."

The trial counsel repeated the question.

"Sir, the fact is," Baker replied, "someone did make a reference to civilians before Colonel Marlowe gave the order to fire."

"And please tell the investigating officer who that person was."

"Sir, the person who made that remark—it happened just before Colonel Marlowe gave the order to open fire. I heard it on my headset. But I also was looking at that person at the time the comment was made because he was on the south side of the house to the right of my position. When I heard the voice, I looked over—and I saw who it was. It was Master Sergeant Rockwell making that comment to the colonel, sir."

"So your testimony at this hearing," Stickton said, jabbing his finger in the air toward Baker, "is that *after* Master Sergeant Rockwell raised the issue of civilians, Colonel Marlowe nevertheless gave the order for all of the members of your team to commence firing—that is, use deadly force—is that what you're saying?"

"Sir, I'm not sure I'd put it that way—"

"Staff Sergeant Baker, yes or no—is that what you're saying—is that what happened?"

Baker straightened up in the stand, glanced over at Colonel Marlowe, then refocused on Colonel Stickton.

"Sir, that is what happened."

Major Hanover's cross-examination was deliberately short and confined.

"You did not see any civilians, is that correct?"

"Yes, sir, that is correct. I saw zero civilians before we opened fire."

"You were standing close to Master Sergeant Rockwell, is that correct?"

"We were only ten or fifteen feet apart."

"And did Master Sergeant Rockwell indicate to you—or to anyone—before he made that comment to Colonel Marlowe—that he saw, or perceived in any way, the presence of civilians at that scene?"

"No, sir, Master Sergeant Rockwell didn't say anything about seeing civilians."

"So would it be accurate to say that you have no idea why he made that comment about civilians?"

"Yes, sir, that's correct."

"Is it correct that the only person your team had encountered at the house up to that point, was the terrorist who had stepped out of the front door and then fired in the direction of Corporal Thompson—is that correct?"

"Yes, sir—that is one-hundred-percent correct."

Hanover rested his cross-examination, but Stickton marched back to the podium.

"Sergeant Baker, were you able to determine whether there were civilians inside that house?"

"Not exactly...not with my own eyes."

"And that is because," Stickton continued, "Colonel Marlowe was the first to enter the building, and he immediately turned to you and Master Sergeant Rockwell and ordered you not to enter the house, is that correct?"

"Sir, he did ask us not to enter and then told us to leave the site."

"In fact, at that time there was the sound of police sirens approaching, and Colonel Marlowe ordered your entire unit to flee the scene and double-time back to the pickup zone—is that correct?"

Baker lowered his head a little as he thought. His eyes then looked out at some unfixed point beyond the courtroom. His face was drawn, and he blinked slowly and then answered.

"Colonel Marlowe ordered us to immediately evacuate the scene and go to the assembly area where we were met by the helo—that's correct, sir."

As Baker descended the witness stand and walked toward Colonel Marlowe, their eyes locked, and a small nod was given from warrior to warrior as the sergeant walked by the defense table and through the courtroom.

27

MASTER SERGEANT ROCKWELL SMILED before he answered the question posed by Colonel Stickton.

"Yes, sir, that's correct—I've had the privilege of serving under Colonel Marlowe's command in a number of missions."

"Would you inform the tribunal of the last four missions?"

"Does the Colonel mean...before Operation Snake Hunt in Mexico?"

Stickton nodded. "Yes," he added, "the four missions that preceded the incident at Chacmool, Mexico."

"Well, sir," Rockwell began in his South Carolina drawl, "it was the Afghan war—Operation Enduring Freedom—then Operation Iraqi Freedom, and then missions within North Korea and Syria later on. The last two missions are classified."

"And prior to the incident in Mexico, on the four missions you described—what was your command structure?"

"Two of the four before Mexico were all part of MEU(SOC)missions—Marine Expeditionary Unit, Special Operations Capable—the tip of the spear, sir. The last two, as I said, are classified."

"And you understood, under the rules of engagement, that your unit was to be on the alert for the possible presence of civilians, is that correct?"

"Yes, sir, in that kind of mission that is always a matter of concern—that's correct."

"Now, let's consider the Chacmool incident. From your position on the side of the target house did you, in fact, have visual contact with any civilians before Colonel Marlowe's order to commence firing?"

"No, sir—no civilians at all. Zero civilians by visual contact."

"Now, Sergeant Rockwell," the trial counsel continued, straightening up behind the podium, "did you have *nonvisual* intelligence that there might be civilians within the main room of that small house?"

"Well, sir, the Colonel is going to have to define *civilians*..."

Stickton bristled, then bulleted his next question.

"By *civilians*, I mean the accepted and customary definition of the word—a definition you ought to be well acquainted with, Sergeant Rockwell. I mean nonuniformed individuals who are not part of an organized military unit, and whose status is as noncombatants in an armed conflict. Did you have any intelligence of any persons meeting that definition present inside that house that night?"

"Sir, I'm not sure how to answer that question—"

Colonel Stickton left the podium, stepped directly in front of Sergeant Rockwell, and did not let him finish his answer.

"If there's any element of my question that you do not understand, Master Sergeant, please indicate *exactly* what you don't understand and I will rephrase it. But if you do understand it, you are to answer this question now—within that building, according to intelligence that you had been provided prior to commencing fire, were there any civilians as I've defined them?"

"Sir, the problem with the question as it is being put to me is the bit about noncombatants. This is a new kind of war. Our enemy is terrorism, which operates through small armies of terrorists whose roles shift between civilian noncombatants, civilian combatants, and members of organized military units."

"Did you have any intelligence that suggested, even indirectly, that persons not officially associated with al-Aqsa Jihad—the terrorists you were pursuing—were present in that house before the shooting began?"

"Sir, not personally, no."

Colonel Stickton paused a minute and considered Rockwell's answer. It was clear to the trial counsel that Rockwell, in his answers, was attempting to flank him.

"Did you have any indication that Colonel Marlowe had intelligence that persons not formally associated with al-Aqsa Jihad—the terrorists you were pursuing—might also be in that house?"

"Sir, Colonel Marlowe never indicated to me that he had confirming information, from any intelligence source, that there might be persons in that house who had no connection with al-Aqsa Jihad."

"But Colonel Marlowe *did* tell you—that one or more Mexican nationals who were unarmed might be present. Is that correct?"

The sergeant raised his eyebrows slightly and leaned toward Stickton.

"Sir, Colonel Marlowe never told me he had such intelligence—if that's what the Colonel is asking, sir…"

"But the fact is, Master Sergeant, that after the lookout fired in the direction of Corporal Thompson, you immediately communicated to Colonel Marlowe on your headset, suggesting that Thompson get a shot off to take the sniper down and then one of you do a close-up recon of the house—is that correct?"

"Sir, I said something close to that—I don't recall the exact words."

"But Colonel Marlowe rejected that, correct?"

"The colonel…had a better appreciation for the situation and ordered us to take out the lookout and lay down suppressing fire on the house." With that, Rockwell gave a half-smile in the direction of Colonel Marlowe.

The trial counsel picked up on this immediately. "Master Sergeant, do you find something amusing about the tragedy at Chacmool—about the four innocent civilians, including a CIA operative, who were killed?"

Sergeant Rockwell turned his gaze slowly back toward Stickton. His gaze penetrated the other man's, and he answered with restrained emotion.

"*Sir*—Carlos Fuego was a very close friend of Colonel Marlowe—as was Carlos's wife, Linda. Colonel Marlowe would not have harmed a hair on either of their heads, let alone their two little children, for anything in this world."

"Is that so? Then why did he tell you that he would accept the 'collateral damage' to civilians in that house when he ordered the four members of your unit to commence firing with deadly force?"

Rockwell had been sitting straight in the witness chair with his hands folded in his lap, but now he leaned toward Stickton and tilted his head slightly forward—as if he were about to dress down a new recruit who had just made a training blunder with a dummy hand grenade.

"The Colonel wondered why I was smiling a minute ago. The fact is, I have spent enough time in combat with Colonel Marlowe to know when this man has information I don't—when he's making command decisions with facts and considerations that my big South Carolina skull does not contain. It is my firm belief—for what it's worth—that Colonel Marlowe had information that there were going to be one or more collaborators with al-Aqsa Jihad inside that house. I can't prove anything—can't tell you why—but I do know that he did not antici-pate...nobody could...that we were about to be led into a trap that night, something you haven't bothered to ask me about—"

"I ask that Master Sergeant Rockwell be admonished," Stickton barked.

Colonel Rogers quickly turned to the sergeant.

"Master Sergeant Rockwell, may I remind you that your attitude and your answers border on insubordination for this hearing and for trial counsel, a senior officer. You will refrain from answering questions that aren't being asked—and you will limit your answers to those ques-tions that are being asked, do you understand me?"

Rockwell nodded, calm again, and quickly added, "Sir—yes, sir."

But Stickton decided not to pursue any further questioning of Rockwell. As it stood—Rockwell's outburst had, in his opinion, served the prosecution well. It showed that the only basis that Colonel Mar-lowe might have had for his command decision to fire on the house was based on pure speculation and guesswork on the sergeant's part.

But as Stickton was halfway back to the prosecution counsel table, he changed his mind and quickly returned to the podium for one last question.

"Just to make sure the record is absolutely clear on this—Colonel Marlowe did tell you that he was willing to assume all 'collateral damage' as a result of his order to commence firing, is that correct?"

"Yes, sir," Sergeant Rockwell answered.

As Stickton stepped back to counsel table, Will rose to his feet. He knew that if he was unable to mitigate these two devastating words—*collateral damage*—his client could be facing the death sentence.

28

As WILL CHAMBERS APPROACHED THE podium, he paused for a full half-minute before starting a terse, focused examination of Master Sergeant Rockwell. He felt as if a border battle had just broken out...and he was but a messenger running along the battle line, avoiding bullets flying from each direction. The point was to get the message delivered without getting caught in the cross fire.

"Sergeant Rockwell," Will began slowly, "your prior tours of duty under Colonel Marlowe's command gave you a reason to trust his judgment, is that correct?"

"Sir, absolutely. I found his military judgment to have always been sound and in the best tradition of the United States Marine Corps."

"Did Colonel Marlowe indicate to you, at any time before reaching the drop zone, that he had received intelligence from Carlos Fuego, in his capacity as a CIA operative, relative to this mission?"

"Yes, sir, he did. In his pre-mission briefing, the colonel told our unit that the primary source of information that had verified the location of the safe house and its connection with the terrorists, was CIA operative Carlos Fuego. Mr. Fuego had been working within Mexico for a substantial period of time, developing contacts and information regarding an ongoing collaboration between Mexican nationals and terrorists of Middle Eastern origin, particularly al-Aqsa Jihad."

"And to your knowledge, was there a second verification that Colonel Marlowe received pin-pointing this particular house just outside of the village of Chacmool, as the haven for al-Aqsa Jihad?"

"Sir, absolutely. Colonel Marlowe received an encrypted message on his laptop that United States spy satellites had verified an outgoing call from the cell phone of the ringleader of al-Aqsa Jihad, and that the call had originated from that same house."

"Now, fast-forwarding to the house—the scene of the shooting—did Colonel Marlowe explain to you what he meant by 'collateral damage'?"

"No, sir."

"But did you have some reason to think that the colonel may have intended that term to represent a unique situation?"

"I…yes, I think that's right, sir," Rockwell responded.

"All right, let's go back to the briefing on the helicopter ride to the drop zone. Did Colonel Marlowe at any time give the impression that he was privy to information that could not be shared with the mission team?"

"Yes, sir. He certainly did."

Stickton's co-counsel was frantically trying to whisper something to him, but the colonel was waving him off, trying to rivet his attention on this new information that was now surfacing—evidence that had not been discovered during the NCIS investigation.

Will knew that he was approaching the precipice, the edge of inestimable depth and danger. He could go very little further, perhaps only a few more inches, in his questioning.

Based on the information that Tiny Heftland had rooted out during their visit to Mexico, and partly based on his gut intuition, Will followed up with his final line of questioning.

"Did Colonel Marlowe at any time tell you that he was privy to matters of national security regarding this information?"

"Sir, well…this is what the colonel said—I asked whether we were chasing four bad guys—and he said yes, but then added, 'four plus.' And I asked the colonel what the 'plus' was—and he just shook his head and said he couldn't share anything more—it was a need-to-know basis—and these were matters of national security."

Stickton snapped to his feet and fired off an objection.

"Sir, the use of a national-security defense is inappropriate—there are no facts to support this attempt by Master Sergeant Rockwell to defend his commanding officer. That issue is not before this hearing—the defense is trying to sanitize Colonel Marlowe's reckless intent under the guise of his being in possession of national-security information."

Colonel Rogers looked down from the bench at Will. He was not happy. After a few seconds of thought he addressed the defense table.

"Gentlemen, you are making reference to a matter of possible national security. Are you trying to persuade me that a commanding officer of a Marine Expeditionary Unit ordered fire into a little house at the edge of Chacmool, Mexico, because of some matter of national security—is that what you're really asking me to accept?"

Will looked over at Colonel Marlowe. Their gazes met and he knew only his client had the remaining information. He had been kept in the dark by his own client regarding the most important elements of the case—what Marlowe knew, and why he had acted as he did— why he had made a reference to 'collateral damage'—and why he was willing to assume the risk of injury or even death to civilians in the house.

But the attorney also knew what he had *not* been told. Marlowe had been abrupt and absolute in his refusal to talk about the configuration of his unit. DOD had stood fast on the order that there was to be no reference to the military identity of the team that the colonel had led.

To Will, then, that left only one conclusion. And to the extent that he could draw a logical deduction, he was about to try to explain it to Colonel Rogers, the presiding investigating officer.

"What I am asking Colonel Rogers to note and accept is the fact that *no one* has identified the actual mission unit that Colonel Marlowe was commanding. There is no proof that it was a part of a Marine Expeditionary Unit. *No one* has testified to that. And, in fact, I *don't* believe it was an MEU detachment that Colonel Marlowe was leading that day.

"Mr. Investigating Officer, the record in this case will reflect that DOD has placed restrictions on certain evidence, including any reference to the military configuration of Colonel Marlowe's unit. It is classified information. That fact alone is a corroboration of what Master Sergeant Rockwell recalls being discussed in that helicopter before it reached the drop zone. The DOD directive instructing all of us to refrain from speaking openly about the type of unit being led by Colonel Marlowe is supportive proof that there were national-security interests involved that night—and that the colonel was the only one on the ground who actually knew it."

Colonel Rogers leaned back in his chair, but did not take long to deliberate.

"Here is my ruling on this matter—I am *not* going to admonish Master Sergeant Rockwell and am going to leave his answer on the record—for whatever value it has. On the other hand, I'm instructing you, defense counsel, not to pursue any further questions on this matter. Am I understood?"

"Yes, sir," Will responded. "With that, the defense rests."

As Will sat back at the counsel table, neither he or Major Hanover, nor trial counsel Stickton or his associate, knew exactly how to assess what had just happened.

But Stickton was experienced enough to know a field laden with land mines when he saw it. He would not venture into this area with redirect examination. And pursuant to Colonel Rogers' directive, Will Chambers was forbidden from going any further.

"Is the case now submitted?"

Counsel from both tables rose and agreed.

"I declare testimony closed. I will issue findings and recommendations based on this Article 32 hearing. Until that time, this matter is adjourned."

As Colonel Rogers retired through the door behind the bench, Will turned to his client. But there was something in Marlowe's look, in his manner, that told the attorney that his mind was in another place. That his client had not viewed this crucial hearing in a potential capital murder case as the most important thing—that, in fact, to Caleb Marlowe, there was something much more important. The colonel's mind was somewhere else—and wherever it was, Will Chambers was not invited.

29

THE KITCHEN TABLE WAS LITTERED with files, calendars, and Palm Pilots. Will and Fiona were working out the final details of scheduling Fiona's three-week concert tour.

She was sipping a cup of tea and scratching down a few notes. Her eyes were dancing, and her face was radiant with a big, dimpled smile.

Will, sitting next to her, finished his cup of coffee, put the mug down, and then, with a smile, nudged her.

"So what do you think?" he asked. "Don't you think we can work it out? If we rendezvous at these points, I can be with you most of the three weeks."

Fiona laughed, and grabbed his hand and kissed it. "I am so looking forward to our time together. You know, it gets lonely on the road. Now, are you sure this is going to work out with your practice? What about Colonel Marlowe's case? What happens with that?"

"Well, first of all, your tour is scheduled far enough in advance so we can work around that. Secondly, who knows what's going to happen? If the case should get dismissed, then that's probably the end of it. If it goes to a general court-martial, I'll just make sure that we get it on the docket either before or after those three weeks."

"Well, on the other hand," Fiona said, her face suddenly growing more serious, "if you're going to be in a court-martial and it looks like it's going to drag on for some time, then maybe...you'll actually want to schedule the trial—if it works out that way—while I'm on the road. That way, you can dive into the case with your full attention—I know how you get when you go into trial. And I'll be lonely for you, of course...but at least I'll be busy. Anyway, think about it."

Will put his hand on the side of his wife's face and smiled.

"I really am blessed—you know that? You're beautiful, tender, and you're so very tuned in to my life. I know I'm not easy to live with sometimes…"

"Oh, Will," she said, beaming, "even at your hardest, you're easy to live with! You're easy to love—you really are. I do think you have to get off your own back. I know you're still dealing with a lot…with Audra…some things simply take time. But just look at what's happened. When we first met, think about where you were: alcohol problems—despair—your career was teetering on the brink. But God reached down to where you were. He found you because he loved you. And now just think about everything that's changed for the better since then."

Will nodded. He was about to reply, but the telephone rang.

After hurriedly pushing aside some files, he located the portable phone. It was Hilda on the line.

"Sorry to bother you at home, Will. I know you said you were going to come in late today. But Major Hanover just called, and he said it was very important. He has received a decision on the Article 32 hearing, and he wanted to tell you about it right away."

Will thanked her, and then immediately dialed the major at Quantico.

Hanover was in his office. Will could tell by the sound of his voice that it was serious.

"First of all, the IO has filed his recommendations and findings as a result of the Article 32 hearing. That's the bad news," Hanover said.

"Bad—you mean he's recommending that it be referred to a general court-martial?"

"Right. But bear with me. This is just his recommendation. And I'll get to the decision by the commanding general in a minute."

"You mean the general has already reviewed the IO's report?"

"Exactly," Hanover replied. "But in terms of the IO's recommendation—Colonel Rogers is recommending a general court-martial on all the charges. His findings are really interesting—and somewhat contradictory. He makes the standard observation that command judgments made during combat can be flawed, or mistaken, without being criminal. And all of that sounds very good and would seem to dictate a decision to dismiss the charges. But then, at the end he does an about-face and says, because the defense raised the national-security issue, he feels that a decision by a superior officer—namely the commanding general—is advisable."

"In other words—this may be a matter of passing the buck?" Will asked.

"Speaking unofficially, you're probably correct," Hanover replied.

But then his voice changed and rose in restrained excitement.

"But here's the good news—Brigadier General Landon has already reviewed the recommendations and findings, and he indicated to me—in very strong language—that it is his decision that this matter is not going to be referred to a court-martial. He is going to stop this case in its tracks."

"That's terrific news," Will exclaimed. "So what happens now?"

"Now—the standard drill is this. In order to keep this matter from raising its ugly head again—or any of the other brass overruling this decision—Marlowe needs to resign his commission immediately, and the marines will retire him honorably. I've already talked to the colonel—and the matter is already in the works. We think we can get this done by the end of business today. If that happens, he is no longer under the jurisdiction of the United States Marine Corps—or the American military—and the decision becomes res adjudicata. It should prevent him from being collaterally prosecuted by any jurisdiction within the United States."

"It sounds like you've been moving fast on this," Will noted. "And Marlowe was okay with leaving the Marine Corps? I mean, that surprises me."

"I think he probably knew this was coming all along. Win or lose, he knew this was the end of his Marine Corps career."

"So is there anything else you need me to do?"

"Not a thing—we're taking care of all of it at our end."

"Do me a favor, will you?" Will asked.

"Sure—anything."

"Have Colonel Marlowe give me a call. I'd just like to wish him well personally."

"Sure, I will certainly pass that on to him. And Will?"

"Yes?"

"Fine job on this case. It was great working with you."

Even after clicking off the phone Will was still trying to process the information Major Hanover had given him. They had won, despite

Lieutenant Colonel Rogers' reluctance to dismiss the case at the Article 32 stage. General Landon's decision would be full and final, particularly because Marlowe would be released from the marines administratively within twenty-four hours. For all practical purposes, that would deprive the military of any further jurisdiction over him—including the ability to bring further criminal charges.

Will turned to Fiona and smiled and kissed her.

"Good news?" she asked expectantly.

"We won. It looks like that's the end of the charges against Colonel Caleb Marlowe. So let's celebrate! Where do you want to go to dinner tonight?"

"Churchill's," she replied. But then she shook her head. "No—even better—let's go up to Baltimore to Luigi's."

Will chuckled. That was the restaurant where the two of them had had their first dinner together.

"Luigi's—that's perfect."

But the trial lawyer in Will still needed some resolution on Marlowe's case. He wanted to talk to his client and hear everything directly from the soon-to-be-retired marine colonel.

He also wondered, though, why he had the lingering feeling that the incident at Chacmool was not finished...the distinct impression that what happened there had long, choking tendrils—like a jungle vine growing and strangling everything in its path with unnatural strength. And with hideous purpose.

30

SENATOR WAYNE O'BRIEN'S WIFE was standing in the front door of their Bethesda, Maryland, townhouse while she spoke to the two men in suits.

"We're sorry to bother you, Mrs. O'Brien. We're wondering if the senator is available."

Mrs. O'Brien nodded and beckoned to her husband, who was helping the maid carry the dishes to the kitchen after dinner.

The senator greeted the two plainclothes detectives.

"We're sorry to disturb you, Senator. But we have some information that we have to check out. It concerns some allegations about conduct in your home. We're wondering if we might be able to come in and do a very limited search of the premises. We don't have a warrant, so you're entitled to deny our request, of course. And, if you wish us to come at another time...when your attorney can be present, we'll be glad to accommodate you."

O'Brien looked startled, and after a momentary pause he invited the two detectives into the library and closed the sliding oak-paneled doors behind him.

"Now, can you tell me what all this is about?"

The men displayed their IDs. "Senator, you have a private computer here in your residence?"

"Of course I do. Why do you ask?"

"We're wondering if you might consent for us to check your computer. You have privacy rights—of course—and you need not agree to our inspection at this time. But you're free to consent, and if so, it would just take us a few minutes to check your computer. We would like to see if we can clear you regarding our investigation."

"Well…can you tell me what your investigation is about?" the senator asked.

"Unfortunately, we can't. The decision is entirely yours."

O'Brien momentarily entertained the thought of getting his private legal counsel on the line.

On the other hand, he knew he had nothing to hide—and he was well aware of the increased suspicion that usually accompanies a demand for legal counsel at the early stages of an investigation.

"All right," the senator said. "But my consent is based on what you just told me—this is a limited search, and you just want to check out my computer, is that right?"

The detectives both nodded.

O'Brien walked over to an oak-paneled cabinet, opened the doors, and then swung out a retractable computer desk with his equipment.

"I'd like to stay in the room and watch while you check the computer," he said.

The senior detective agreed, and then his partner sat down at the keyboard, booted up, and typed in a series of commands. Then he pulled out of his suitcoat a small USB/flashdrive and hooked it up. After two clicks on the mouse the screen-saver disappeared, and the monitor screen flashed an image.

The senator stepped closer to the monitor and stared at it in disbelief.

The image on the screen depicted a horrifying and violent sex act between an adult male and a small child. Both detectives turned and stared at the older man.

"I don't know what you did—or what command you just gave my computer—but I have never seen this disgusting, vile, degrading image on my computer before. You have to believe me when I tell you that…" O'Brien said, his voice trembling with rage.

"Does anyone have access to the computer other than you?" one of the detectives asked.

O'Brien shook his head vigorously. "No—absolutely not. My wife never touches a computer. The only one in this house besides my wife and me is our maid. And I keep the door to my library locked. And my wife and I are the only ones who have the key. I do that because I keep a lot of my Senate papers and information here when I'm working at night."

"Senator O'Brien," the senior detective said, "I suggest you contact your attorney and speak to him about this matter. There could be a number of explanations. But we're going to want to impound the computer and take it with us so we can let some of our cyber experts take a look at the hard drive. So call your attorney, and we'd like to—if we may—start analyzing the entire computer tomorrow in our lab."

The senator nodded somberly.

There was a knock at the library door. He walked over and slid it open. His wife was in the front foyer with the maid.

"Wayne, I'm letting Juanita go for the night. Is that okay?"

O'Brien nodded and then quickly closed the door behind him. "Officers," he said with passion in his voice, "my attorney is going to be in contact with you tomorrow. But I'm telling you right now—I am going to tell him I want this computer analyzed by you so we can get to the bottom of this. I am innocent—it is clear that somebody is trying to sabotage me. Either that or…well, or else there is some other explanation."

"We prefer to impound this computer tonight. We will do no further testing or analysis on it without the consent of you or your lawyer."

O'Brien agreed. After unplugging the computer and removing it from his library, the two detectives carted it out to the squad car on the street.

The senator and his wife watched from the front porch. O'Brien looked around the neighborhood nervously. He noticed one of his neighbors walking his dog directly past the front of his house as the officers loaded everything into the trunk of their car.

He and his wife quickly retreated into the sanctuary of their townhouse, closing and locking the door behind them.

The senator was still clutching the card from the senior detective in his right hand. He glanced down at it, and then at his wife. She had tears in her eyes, and was clasping her hands together. In her husband's anguished face, she was looking for an explanation.

"This is a nightmare—an absolute nightmare," he said.

31

In THE SECOND-STORY CONFERENCE ROOM of the restored palace in Bern, Switzerland, Warren Mullburn was seated at the head of the ornate marble-topped conference table. He was listening to the last of the presentations by his in-house economists.

Mullburn leaned forward to make a point, and the participants, with their neatly indexed and tabbed financial reports, grew silent.

"I'm disappointed. I told you, and I will repeat myself—a practice, by the way, in which I rarely indulge, and never enjoy—that I wanted two-, five-, and seven-year projections of the impact of the Mexico project on the prices of *non*-OPEC as well as OPEC producing sources. Further, I can appreciate your desire to hedge your forecasting regarding oil prices within the OPEC nations after we begin full-scale production from the Mexico site, given the geopolitical complexities. But then again, that's why I'm paying each of you enormous sums of money—to figure that out.

"Now, do I need to take this little assignment from you and do it myself? And do I need to send you ladies and gentlemen back to your miserable teaching posts at obscure universities—or back to the bottom-shelf corporations you were working for before you came here? I'm giving you seven days—*seven days*—to give me your best picture on what the price response from OPEC will be if we decide to flood the market, based on our new oil venture down in Mexico."

The nine advisors rose quietly and respectfully and filed out of the conference room.

A subtle chime sounded, and Mullburn reached for his personal video pager.

On the screen was the face of his scheduler. "Mr. Mullburn, your special projects manager is here. Would you like to speak to him?"

"Absolutely," Mullburn rapped out.

Within seconds a tall, square-shouldered man with black horn-rimmed glasses and a look about him of all business entered the room, carrying a small metal briefcase. He nodded respectfully toward Mullburn, then took a position behind a chair at the conference table.

"Sit down, Himlet, and tell me where we stand."

The billionaire rose and walked to the other end of the conference room, where he poured some herbal tea into a cup and saucer of Austrian crystal.

Himlet adjusted his glasses and began.

"Mr. Mullburn, the Justice Department and the DC U.S. Attorney's office feel you definitely breached your agreement with them. The word within those agencies is that you were expected to *personally* divulge everything you knew about the scandal involving former Undersecretary of State Sharptin—his suicide, alleged influence-peddling, illegal payoffs, and any conspiracy involving OPEC. And so forth."

"I sent my attorneys to be debriefed," Mullburn barked. "My attorneys are my legal agents. They speak for me. That should have been sufficient."

"It wasn't."

"They are imbeciles. Government morons."

"Perhaps," Himlet replied, "but the government prosecutors wanted to personally debrief you—to interview you, not your lawyers. It appears that their agreement not to extradite you back to the U.S. will be withdrawn. They will probably be impaneling a grand jury to investigate you."

"Let them. Let them," Mullburn sneered. "I have bigger concerns than a bunch of puny-brained federal bureaucrats who want to prosecute a rich man so they can all get a promotion and a pay raise."

"Of course," Himlet replied.

"Tell me about the software."

"We've finished the program, Mr. Mullburn. You can access it anytime—anywhere in the world. It will give you daily global positions on every facet of the oil markets, even those still in R and D."

"Including the Mexico project?"

"That too. It will give you every factor—industrial, technological, geopolitical, legal—that may have an impact on your Mexico activity and your expected revenues. With an emphasis on the American markets."

Mullburn sipped his tea and reflected. "You're positive I will have absolutely complete data on every contingency impacting our Mexico oil project?" he asked.

"Yes, sir—I would bet my life on it."

Mullburn turned and smiled at the man with the black horn-rimmed glasses, and then he spoke.

"Be careful, Mr. Himlet. I take bets like that very seriously."

32

DURING THE LUNCH BREAK IN THE deposition of Dr. Ibrahim
Agabba, the conference room in the Raleigh, North Carolina, law
office was empty, except for Will Chambers. The North Carolina firm
representing Dr. Agabba—and all of the other attorneys involved—
had decided that this would be the most convenient location to conduct his deposition. The Sudanese government had already threatened
to hit Agabba with a suit for libel, slander, and defamation regarding
his anticipated testimony in the deposition. As a precautionary mea-
sure, he had hired the Raleigh law firm—a firm that Will had worked
with on prior cases.

General Nuban and the Sudanese government had already lost
their two original law firms from Washington, DC. Both offices had
quietly withdrawn as defense counsel a few weeks before the deposition and had been replaced by a large international law office from
Miami, Florida.

No reason had been given for the substitution of law firms—but
Will had his theories. He speculated that, as the atrocities of the
Sudanese government had become more and more clear, the two original firms had felt increasingly uncomfortable in their relationship with
their clients. Will also theorized that Nuban and his government had
been lying to their lawyers about their lack of complicity in the missionary murders. When the lawyers had finally discovered, shortly
before Agabba's deposition, the extent of their clients' lies to them,
they had bailed out immediately, Will guessed.

He had not planned on taking lunch but on working through the
noon hour to get ready for the afternoon's session.

He snapped open the flaps of his second large briefcase to retrieve
some papers. When he did, he noticed a small brown bag inside. He

opened it and found a peanut-butter-and-jelly sandwich, carrots, and a small note, all prepared by Fiona. The note read,

> Hope your deposition goes well—I know you don't take lunch, so I made one for you. Hope you like it! I love you truly, madly, forever!
>
> All my love,
> Fiona

Will smiled and chuckled loudly. He walked to the end of the conference room and fished a cold can of soda out of the ice bucket, popped it open, and sat down at the table with his sandwich.

But his mind drifted back to Colonel Marlowe's case. It had been several weeks since the military criminal charges had been formally dropped against Marlowe, but he had never received a call back from the now-retired marine colonel.

The lack of disclosure from his client was one thing. But something else haunted Will. He recalled Marlowe's repeated references to the fact that he still had to complete his "mission"—whatever that was.

As he finished his sandwich, Will was still thinking about Marlowe when the lawyers, followed by Dr. Agabba and the court reporter, started filing back into the conference room.

Will wasted no time firing off the final category of questions, which related to the militantly anti-Christian terrorist groups that Nuban and his government had permitted to flourish within Sudan's borders.

With little effort Will was able to establish, through Dr. Agabba, that Nuban had charged the terrorist groups a monthly fee to establish and maintain their training camps. Nuban would also attempt to skim off a portion of the illegal income of the terrorist groups—income from gun-running, drugs, illegal immigration trade, and some limited piracy along the African coast.

The new defense attorney for Nuban and the Sudan, Cesar Linton, was objecting to nearly every question—on every conceivable grounds.

"Dr. Agabba, would you tell me the names, if you know them," Will asked, "out of the various groups involved in international illegal activity that were sponsored by General Nuban within the Sudan—out of them, which groups openly articulated hostilities against Christian missionaries?"

"Objection," Linton shouted. "Your lawsuit is not about a collective of terrorist groups within Sudan. Dr. Agabba has already given his opinion—which, of course, I consider to be outlandish, unsupported, and defamatory—that a specific group known as the 'Arm of Allah' was involved in the death of these missionaries. What he has to say about any other groups is totally irrelevant and immaterial."

Will turned to Agabba—a handsome, dark-skinned man with short hair and glasses—who was unperturbed.

"I'll be glad to answer that—there were several such groups."

"Would you list them for me?"

"I object—on the same grounds—this is getting us nowhere. Mr. Chambers, you are insisting on polluting this record with nonsense, and false and irrelevant accusations," Linton argued.

Will calmly turned toward the witness and repeated his question.

"Doctor, would you list those groups for me?"

"Certainly. Hezbollah. Al-Qaeda. Asia Islama. And the AAJ."

"Objection! You must stop this, Mr. Chambers. There is no connection between any of these groups—even if they do exist within the Sudan borders, which I believe is an entirely false allegation—and the issues in this case."

Turning back to Agabba, Will glanced down at the notes he had just been taking. He looked up briefly. Then the switch was turned on.

"You said the AAJ. Do you mean the al-Aqsa Jihad?"

"Yes, that organization—most certainly."

"Do you have knowledge about a man purporting to be the head of al-Aqsa Jihad by the name of Abu Adis?"

"Oh, yes, I saw him meet with General Nuban. I believe they were discussing Nuban's demand for royalties from the AAJ's drug operation in Mexico and Central America."

Cesar Linton peppered the room with more objections.

"Was there anybody else in that meeting between General Nuban and Abu Adis on the drug-running issue?"

More objections from attorney Linton.

"There was a man—I believe he was an American—at least it sounded like he had an American accent."

Objection upon objection from Linton.

"Do you remember his name? Anything about his identity?"

"Well," Agabba continued thoughtfully, "as I recall—I believe his name was Black...Mr. Rusty Black, I think."

Linton was now leaning across the conference table, waving his solid gold pen in the direction of Will Chambers, folding objections into a speech and then a diatribe.

Will waited quietly until the other attorney had finished. Then he turned back to Dr. Agabba.

"Anything else you remember about this American?"

"Well, he was working on this drug thing down in Mexico. I don't think he was part of the AAJ—but he was working with them in some capacity, on drug sales. There was something that really struck me about him, though."

"What was that?"

"He had a tattoo on the side of his neck—you couldn't see it all that well unless he turned his head. Then you could see it."

"A tattoo?" Will asked. "What kind of a tattoo?"

"It looked like an eagle...I think that's what it was."

"An American eagle?"

"Not exactly."

"Then what kind of an eagle?"

Agabba shook his head and indicated he didn't recall—it simply did not look like any type of eagle you would see on American currency or American insignias.

Cesar Linton took what was left of the afternoon trying to disassemble and rebut the answers Agabba had given to Will. All in all, however, Linton's effort was fruitless, and his examination was full of sound and fury, but it established very little.

Driving back to Virginia on I-95, Will felt good about the deposition. But he was also thinking about something else.

About the AAJ...and about an American drug dealer whose activities centered in Mexico attending a meeting with the leader of the AAJ. A dealer named Rusty Black. And Will was also thinking about Colonel Marlowe...wherever he was...and whatever he was doing. And whether Marlowe's uncompleted "mission" had to do with Mexico—with finding those who had set the trap for his commando operation and wreaking vengeance on the ones who had put Carlos and his family in the line of fire.

The attorney then called his office from his cell phone and went through the usual litany of office issues and client calls with Hilda. His secretary also said that Captain Jenkins from the DC police department had phoned.

Will told himself that, even though he was going to return the call to Jenkins, he was also going to keep this matter of Audra's murder in perspective. There would be more phone calls from Jenkins in the future, more facts coming out, more leads that turned down blind alleys, more waiting—and all of that had to be secondary to his marriage to Fiona. That was the truly important thing now.

He put the call through to the police captain, and after the exchange of a few pleasantries Jenkins got right to the point.

"The fact is," he said, "we now feel we have an identity for the second perpetrator involved in the death of Audra."

Will was stunned.

"Who is it?" he blurted out.

"He is a man named Damon Lynch. Also a member of that same neo-Nazi group up in Brooklyn. Whereabouts unknown. Did some time both in county jail and in state prison on a variety of charges. But he's been out of prison for about two years. Shortly after being released on parole, he disappeared. Obviously there's a warrant out for him for parole violation. But now we've got a warrant on him as a possible accessory to the murder. I say 'possible,' because we have no evidence that he was actively involved in the commission of the crime. We only have his presence at the scene."

"What else do we know about this guy?"

"We're collecting as much information as we can, trying to get some current data on where he's been last sighted. Of course we'll keep you updated. So that's all I've got for now."

Will thanked the captain and turned off his phone.

On the rest of the drive back to Monroeville, Will tried not to obsess over this newest piece of information. Over the fact that the other demon at the vicious murder of his first wife now had a name. He had an identity. He was *Damon Lynch*. Will tried not to let all of that consume him and control his every thought.

But he failed.

33

CALEB MARLOWE OPENED THE TALL, weathered doors of the old San Bernardino Church in Valladolid in the Yucatán. He walked slowly down the middle aisle of the aged structure. In the fourth row from the front, at the right, there was a woman dressed in black kneeling and praying.

On the left-hand side there was a man—a Mayan—paging through a missal. Marlowe walked up the aisle and scooted down the pew to his side.

"I'm looking for the bird of paradise."

The Indian man smiled.

"You Americans—always big on code words and code names. Yes. I'm the man you're looking for."

"You have some information for me?"

"Yes. But I need something from you first."

"What's that?"

"When all of this goes down, I want the Mayan people to benefit. I want the Independent Revolutionary Party to be punished for the mistreatment of the Indians. And I want the United States government to help us with that."

"I'm afraid we can't promise anything like that," Marlowe replied.

"Then why am I talking to you, my friend?" the man answered. "Do you know who I am?"

"Yes, I do," Marlowe said. "You're Juan Oxla Tulum. You are a leader of the Mayan insurgents who are trying to overthrow the IRP. You're tired of the Indian people getting kicked around, persecuted, and killed."

"So you've done your homework. You know that the Indians have been fighting for their survival for more than a thousand years. And it's still going on. I've spent my whole life fighting for my people. This is not a game. This is my life."

Marlowe nodded understandingly.

"Juan, if there were promises I could make, I would do it. If I could get the American government to back you people down here, I would do it. All I can tell you is this—by helping us with our snake hunt down here, you will be doing yourself and your people a long-term favor. If you think it's been bad for the Mayan people for the last thousand years, think what's going to happen to Mexico—and to your people—if terrorists start taking over."

Tulum gazed forward at the altar and the large crucifix that hung over it. "Did you see anything ironic in my choice of this as the place where we were going to meet?" he asked with a chuckle.

"I'm assuming that, as a Mayan, you still follow the old religion?"

Tulum nodded.

"Someday I'd like to talk to you about that," Marlowe said with a smile. "But about your information—I would appreciate it if you could share with us what you know about the American drug dealer."

The Indian man studied Marlowe for a minute, then he reached into his faded short-sleeved shirt and pulled out a small piece of paper.

"Mr. Marlowe, these are all the names—aliases—that this man has used. And here's his present location, as best as I can determine. I think he'll lead you to what you're looking for."

Marlowe thanked the man, and shook hands with him, then they walked out of the church together.

"This information is going to help me settle a score with someone," the American said as they squinted in the sun outside.

"You better watch yourself, Marlowe," Tulum warned. "You may have been followed. If you aren't careful you're going to get yourself arrested."

"Oh, I'm not worried about that," he responded. Then he gave a smile and a wave to his informant and walked over to his car.

34

WHEN FIONA STOPPED BY HER father's modest apartment near Georgetown, she was greatly burdened. Reverend Angus Mac-Cameron had just returned from a short trip in Israel. Fiona was increasingly concerned about his health, particularly because in the last few years he had survived a heart attack, a stroke, and the death of his wife. But there were also other buried fears that she was struggling with—about Will…and their marriage.

As she sat next to her father on the couch, he looked so much older—even though it had only been two weeks since she had seen him last.

"Da," she said, "I'm concerned about you traveling alone on these trips. The next time you want to travel back to Israel, work it out with Will and me so we can accompany you. Or perhaps have the new editor of your magazine go with you."

"Are you saying that I'm in need of a baby-sitter? Is that what you're saying?" Angus replied brusquely in his Scottish brogue. "I'm as strong as a Highland steer. I've got energy to spare. Don't be treating me like an invalid."

"No, that's not what I'm saying," his daughter replied. "I'm simply saying you have to pace yourself. I want you around for a long time."

"And I plan on being around a long time—exactly as long as the Lord has planned for me. Not a minute sooner or a minute later," Angus declared, waving an index finger at her.

"So you feel like it was a successful trip?" Fiona asked. Her mind had been drifting.

Angus cocked his head and raised an eyebrow. He stared at his daughter for a few seconds before he spoke.

"Fiona, darling, I don't think you have heard a word I've said! I just explained how I was trying to chase down this rumor about a recently discovered fragment from the book of Deuteronomy—and how every antiquity dealer and archaeologist I spoke to led me down a blind alley. Everybody's gossiping about it, but no one has any information about it. It was the most frustrating trip I can remember. I feel that this might be another archaeological hoax, and I want to get to the bottom of it and then expose it in *Digging for Truth*. You do remember my magazine? Honestly, Fiona, I don't think you've been listening to a thing I've said all this time."

His daughter took a deep breath and then shook her head. "I'm sorry, Da. I guess my mind has been wandering a little."

"So what is it?" Angus asked, softening. "Besides worrying about your father."

"Well—in addition to worrying about you," she said with a smile, "things between Will and me have been…rough."

Angus leaned back against the couch, taking his walking stick and laying it across his lap. He smiled at Fiona and waited for her to continue. Beneath his ruddy complexion and lined, life-worn face, the old Scot knew how to use silence to unwrap the secrets of his daughter's heart.

"It's not that we don't love each other, because that's not the problem," she continued. "We are passionately in love. Crazy for each other. But it's…it's just that life, and who he is, and everything else, seems to get in the way of our marriage."

"How is he doing?"

"He's a good husband. He now recognizes he's dragged this business with Audra into our marriage. He thought he had put it all behind him. And now it seems like every couple days something intrudes—something brings back all of the old memories."

"Do you have any idea how difficult I was to live with when I married your mother?"

Fiona laughed and then shook her head. "Da, I'm sure you weren't that bad." Then she looked at her father with an expression that yearned for answers—practical solutions. "So what do I do, Da? How do we fix this? I feel like I'm out in the ocean, swimming without a life vest…and my arms are getting so tired."

"First of all, my darling Fiona, there are some things you are not meant to fix. There are some things God will heal…in his own time. You simply need to be a faithful, loving friend to your good husband. There are some valleys we have to walk alone. You always want to fix things yourself, and the quicker the better! Sometimes, like I said, there are things you simply aren't meant to fix yourself. And sometimes…sometimes the lessons of mercy are the hardest things to learn."

"What do you mean?"

"Just think about Peter denying the Lord Jesus three times and then having to live with that memory. Think about the apostle Paul, who persecuted the believers and participated in the death of Jesus' disciples. Just because he met the Lord on the road to Damascus and God turned his life around—well, that doesn't mean he didn't struggle with those demons—those memories of how he had treated the followers of Jesus so brutally.

"Then there's David—just think about that, little girl. 'A man after God's own heart.' That's what the Bible calls him. And yet he arranged for the death of his friend so that he could take his friend's wife, Bathsheba, into his palace just to satisfy his own lust. The memory of that, and the death of his infant son as God's judgment—all that must have broken David's heart. That's why I love the psalms so much. Because that is where I read about God's mercy from the pen of a man who had to learn to forgive himself just as God had forgiven him."

"Then you think that's what's going on with Will?"

"I'm not sure," Angus replied softly. "But I do know this—just because God saved his soul, that doesn't mean that God won't continue doing surgery on his life. There's nothing more frightening, more challenging, or more necessary than to visit that place where our innermost fears, and pains, and wrongs are laid bare on the operating table of the Lord."

"It's just that this certainly doesn't seem the way I thought marriage was going to be," Fiona said. " I knew there would be struggles. I wasn't naïve. And I know Will loves me. But it seems like his mind is only half with me—even when we're together. We seem to be stuck in this dry, lonely valley. I sure didn't think that marriage would be so much desert…and so little oasis."

Angus smiled. "No, I would expect not," he said. "It usually always ends up both just a little bit worse—and a whole lot better—than we ever expected. We think it's going to be all walks in the heather in the sunshine. Sometimes it is. But sometimes it's also a lot like slogging through the peat bogs in a rainstorm!"

Fiona laughed a little and reached over, giving her father a warm hug.

She had wanted reassurance—and had received some. But she had also known she would not be given any quick, formulaic answers. That was not Angus's style. He always pointed her in the right direction— and then had the unnerving habit of stepping back so she could work it out herself with God.

Fiona was glad that she had visited him. But she had an underlying fear that there were dark passages still ahead for her husband—and perhaps even herself—that she could not predict, and that they could not avoid. It was those events that lay ahead—those things that were totally beyond their control, like cataclysms of nature—that bothered her most. She knew, as she motored back to their log house nestled in the shadow of the Blue Ridge Mountains, that her choices about the future were brutally simple. She could either proceed by faith…or be conquered by fear. As much as she wished it was otherwise—that there could be more options than that—she knew it was not so.

35

PROSECUTOR FRANCINE LES FORGES had assembled two law clerks and her deputy prosecutor, Atavar Strinsky, in one of the conference rooms of the International Criminal Court building in The Hague, Netherlands.

On top of the long, blond-wood conference table, each person had a thick file.

Les Forges was talking quickly—in the staccato that typified her speech when she felt that a case was beginning to roll in her direction.

"So there's no question," she said, addressing Strinsky, "that Mexico has Caleb Marlowe, and that they have him securely detained pending our decision?"

Strinsky nodded soberly. "He was arrested by the federal security police. They have him in lockup in Mexico City. They are ready to fly him out under secure guard, but they're waiting for the word from you."

"Well, that's not going to be a problem," Les Forges answered. "I can get an extradition order. Immediately if necessary. We can have him on a plane headed here within forty-eight hours. But I had asked you to double-check the formal referral from Mexico for prosecution. Are you satisfied that we have a formal request for prosecution from the state party of Mexico—for the prosecution of Colonel Caleb Marlowe of the United States Marine Corps, special unit designation unknown, for war crimes or crimes against humanity or both?"

"I've looked over the referral from the Mexican president's office. Everything's in order. I don't see any problems on that count."

But then Strinsky wrinkled his brow, tapped his pen on the file in front of him, and spoke up again. "However, we do still have the two issues that we discussed previously—first, whether the substantive criminal provisions of the ICC truly fit the alleged crime he would be charged with. And second—the jurisdictional issue still has to be resolved."

Les Forges rose to her feet, thrusting her hands into the pockets of her pinstriped pantsuit.

"Well, let's take the easy question first. I gave all of you a memo on what I think the clear substantive crime is under the ICC article that applies here. It's crystal clear. There is, to me, no ambiguity. A beautiful fit, don't you think? Look at Article 8, Section 2 (b)(iv)—'War Crime of Excessive Incidental Death to Civilians.' Just look. Ladies and gentlemen, there it is. A beautiful and elegant correlation between Colonel Marlowe's conduct as the superior officer, and the ICC Criminal Code."

The female law clerk chimed in. "Yes, certainly on the first element, no question—'the accused launched an attack' as part of a military operation. Here we certainly have an attack on the house in Chacmool, Mexico, as part of a general military operation by the United States. And if I may say so, Ms. Les Forges, I believe that we have the second element of the crime also proven. I've pointed that out in my memo to you, do you recall?"

"Yes, yes. Wonderful work," the prosecutor said effusively. "I had already reached the same conclusion, but your memo corroborated that. The second element is that the attack must cause death to civilians to such an extent as to be clearly excessive in relationship to 'the concrete and direct overall military advantage anticipated.' Now, this is where I think we have them…"

"Yes, because it was a covert operation, pursuing just a handful of terrorists…" the clerk added.

"Exactly," the male law clerk said, joining in. "They expected only four terrorists or so, at best."

"But what is the result?" Les Forges asked, her arms outstretched as she stood, holding court at the conference table. "The result is four dead civilians—an entire family—mother, father, and two little children. And here is where we can put that issue on trial—an issue that has international ramifications. Don't you see? Don't you see the implications of this?"

"Well," Strinsky noted, "I do see some rather complicated implications, Francine. For instance, if you apply this standard to Colonel

Marlowe's mission, even though it obviously went wrong—tragically wrong—but if you say that the death of four civilians as a result of an attempt to kill four terrorists is excessive and disproportionate under Article 8 of the ICC Criminal Code, then aren't you really placing under suspicion every similar attack in every war-torn nation? What about the Israeli Defense Force when they go into the Palestinian Authority chasing would-be terrorists?"

Les Forges smiled, placing her hands on the conference table and leaning toward Strinsky.

"It is time, Atavar, that universal norms of decency, and the international rule of law, must be brought to bear in these violent, bloodthirsty skirmishes around the world. People must be brought to account. Even great—even large, powerful bully nations like America. Even small bully nations like Israel."

The room grew quiet, and the two law clerks shifted uncomfortably in their chairs.

"But enough of my speech-making," Les Forges said with a laugh and brushed the hair from her eyes. "What about the third element— the crime of excessive civilian death—any thoughts?"

The female law clerk spoke up again. "This is clearly the most difficult element for us to prove."

The other law clerk nodded in agreement as the female law clerk continued. "However, the third element is basically one of *scienter*— requiring proof that the accused would have had knowledge that civilian death was inevitable, and that it would be excessive compared to the anticipated benefits of the mission. Here, I think, we can adopt some other useful legal standards to make our point."

"My thinking exactly," the prosecutor responded. "This is an excellent test case. Can't we argue to the trial tribunal that this is really a recklessness standard? We don't have to prove that Marlowe actually *knew* how many civilians he was going to end up killing—or that those civilians would outnumber the terrorists likely to be killed. Rather, can we not simply show that he had a *reckless* disregard for how many civilians might die in the melee?"

The two law clerks nodded, but Strinsky was unconvinced. "Of course," he pointed out, "no ICC case has adopted that recklessness standard."

"But we have the taped communications between Marlowe and his unit—'collateral damage'—remember?" She smiled and then sat back down at the conference table.

"So then, that brings us to the jurisdictional issue."

"And of course, that's an issue with a great deal of controversy around it," Strinsky began. "As we all know, the Rome Statute only permits the ICC to prosecute Marlowe..."

As he spoke Strinsky fished into his thick file and pulled a section of Article I of the Rome Statute in front of him.

"The Rome Statute would only permit the ICC to prosecute him if we can show that the United States, after investigating Marlowe, decided not to prosecute him—"

"And we can clearly show that," the female law clerk added. "The military court-martial was never convened. The convening authority at Quantico, after reviewing the preliminary hearing testimony, unilaterally dismissed the prosecution."

"But we have to show something else," Strinsky continued. "We have to show that the decision by the United States military not to prosecute resulted from the 'unwillingness or inability to do what was required.' So in other words, we have to show that the United States Marine Corps, in declining to prosecute Colonel Marlowe, was really not making an honest, genuine effort to consider the evidence regarding his actions."

Francine Les Forges did not respond immediately. But she broke into a broad smile and folded her hands calmly in front of her on the conference table. Then she cocked her head and, looking at Atavar Strinsky, finally spoke.

"And what do you think the response will be from the ICC judges on that issue? They will believe—as I do—that an American military court that exonerates its own decorated military hero without even referring the matter to a general court-martial—that such actions do not represent a serious consideration of prosecution."

Les Forges paused and then added one final thought.

"Foxes may be allowed to guard the chicken coop in the United States—but not here at the ICC."

36

"SENATOR O'BRIEN, JUST SO THAT you understand, no one's rushing to issue charges against you. In fact, we're looking right now at the possibility that your computer was sabotaged."

Before the Assistant United States Attorney could continue, however, Senator O'Brien's lawyer jumped in. "And of course we believe that your investigation is going to show exactly that. After all, a high-profile person of influence and power such as my client, Senator O'Brien, is a perfect target for cyber-slander—someone feeding this filth into his computer."

O'Brien, who was sitting next to his attorney and had been uncharacteristically quiet, nodded vehemently.

"Well," the U.S. attorney continued, "our computer experts took a look at something they call the meta-data of this computer and have concluded there is a chance that the child pornography image on your computer screen was a result of surreptitious entry through a pop-up. How that entry was made into your computer, we're not quite sure. But we have some theories."

"I'd appreciate it if you could share those with us," the senator's lawyer said.

"Well, we normally do not bring defense counsel into the loop at this early stage of the investigation—not until we've arrived at our final conclusions."

"Let me just tell you," the lawyer stated emphatically, "what our investigators and cyber-experts tell us. They believe that the illegal images were transmitted from international sources. Perhaps one of the Russian crime syndicates that deal in international pornography."

The U.S. attorney gave a little nod and then responded. "I'm not saying that we are one-hundred-percent convinced of that—but let me just say we are seriously considering that theory. Our people are aware of that possible source and are considering those kinds of groups as one of the likely scenarios."

"Look," Senator O'Brien broke in, "I'm innocent. I know that—and anybody who knows me would know that. But I've got enemies. You know what the media is going to do with this if they find out? How are you going to guarantee that there are going to be no leaks in your investigation?"

"I wish I could give you a hundred-percent assurance on that," the U.S. attorney said sympathetically, "but I can't. I can guarantee that no one under my charge in this office, or in the FBI, with whom I am working, is going to leak this information to anybody. Now I cannot control, on the other hand, the Maryland police, the Maryland prosecutor, or anybody else from the state agencies who know about this."

And then he looked the senator in the eye.

"Nor can I guarantee that anyone in your house may not leak this information. Didn't you say you had a housekeeper who was present when the police came in and conducted the voluntary search?"

Senator O'Brien grimaced slightly and shook his head.

"Yes, I did tell you that," he replied. "But we've had her for years. She's very faithful. We've asked her not to tell anyone about this. I don't believe she will."

But no sooner had he uttered the words than he was struck with the recollection that, ultimately, there are no secrets in Washington. Capitol Hill was not only the political center of the free world, it was also the capital of instant information—particularly when it came to matters of low, degrading, or illegal conduct concerning high, influential people.

Senator O'Brien realized that now all he could do was sit, and wait, to see if the pond scum of rumors and gossip, innuendo and intrigue, would float to the surface.

37

SENATOR WAYNE O'BRIEN HAD NEVER attended a meeting like this before. But then, the recent turn of events in his life had defied all usual political protocol. O'Brien stood at the base of the Washington Monument and scanned the horizon. He looked down toward the Lincoln Memorial and the Potomac, and then he cast his eyes along Constitution Avenue and the usual bumper-to-bumper traffic crawling its way to Capitol Hill and the hundreds of government buildings in that part of Washington, DC.

He was looking for the other member of that meeting—Senator Jason Bell Purdy.

Purdy had called O'Brien's office, vaguely making reference to a need for an an emergency meeting with the older senator. But he could not come to his office, he explained. It had to be somewhere else— Purdy suggested they meet under the shadow of the tall, white obelisk that had been erected to the memory of America's first president.

O'Brien glanced nervously at his watch, and then, from around the corner of the monument, Purdy strolled into sight. He smiled broadly and extended an eager hand. The older man shook it cautiously. "Okay, Jason," he snapped, "what's all the cloak-and-dagger stuff? What's this about?"

"Look, Wayne," Purdy explained with a veneer of empathy in his voice, "I'm not here for me—not entirely—I'm also here for you. I didn't like the way we had that falling out. We've got to look out for each other in this dog-eat-dog political environment. I figure it this way—what's good for you is good for me, and vice versa."

"So? Let's cut to the chase here, Jason. What's up?"

"A phone call I received. A man on the other end—he didn't give me his name—it sounded like he had a Spanish accent. He told me he had some information about you. He said it was some down-and-dirty stuff. Some kind of police investigation. It involved your computer. I told him I didn't appreciate someone trying to spread scandal against a fellow senator, particularly one from my own party and my own home state."

O'Brien studied the other man. "Jason, what else did this man tell you?"

"Well," Purdy continued, "that was it. He suggested that he had a lot more detail—but it would cost me some money."

O'Brien eyed him suspiciously, and then he asked, "Why would this man have called you? Why would he think you would be interested in that information?"

"Well now, that is exactly what I wondered. But this guy knew somehow that you and I had had a falling out. An argument. He had heard that—and he thought maybe I would like to use this information against you. Now you know, Wayne, I would never do that. I play hard—and I may land a few kidney punches now and then—but that kind of stuff is not my style."

"And why did you have to tell me this *here?* Why couldn't you have spoken to me in my office?"

"Hey," Purdy replied quickly, "I don't want anybody hearing this stuff. I am really trying to do you a favor, Wayne."

O'Brien smiled politely. But he was waiting.

"Look, I will be glad to do what I can to try to find out who is spreading this stuff. If it is of interest to you, when the guy calls me back I could play along and maybe we can locate the source of this smear campaign." And then Purdy looked the older man in the eye and added, "Of course, there is nothing going on, right? You are not in any kind of trouble, are you, Wayne?"

O'Brien did not respond. Somehow, he knew what was going to come next. He would not be disappointed.

"Well, and hey—anyway," Purdy continued, "I am willing to do you a favor. That's why I am here—you know, back-scratching time. I do want you to reconsider giving me the chair of an ad hoc subcommittee to take a look at this Chacmool incident. There may not be anything to it—but I need some visibility and name recognition between now and election time."

"And you think I am going to change my mind," the other senator countered, "just because you told me this information about some anonymous Hispanic caller who says he's got something on me?"

"No, of course not," Purdy replied with a smile. "I expect you to do this for me because it is the right thing. Besides, we all need friends. And I am willing to be your friend—and your best advocate. And this business about the phone call—this is going to stay strictly between you and me."

"You wouldn't be trying to blackmail me, would you, Jason?" O'Brien asked, glaring at him.

Purdy laughed out loud, but when his laughter died down, he noticed that O'Brien was not joining in the mirth.

"Wayne, you aren't serious, are you?" he said nonchalantly.

"You ought to know me by now," the older man said soberly. "I may be able to tell a good joke, but that does not make me a joker. Right now, Jason, I'm just as serious as a heart attack."

Purdy's face fell and his mouth tightened. Then he clicked his teeth together—a little mannerism that he exhibited when the stress was getting high.

But his eyes were unblinking as he stared at O'Brien.

"Wayne, I am shocked. I mean, really shocked. I guess we have nothing more to discuss. I met with you as a friend—I felt we still could do some reconnoitering together. But maybe not. Hey, you keep yourself out of trouble now." Purdy turned and started to leave.

For O'Brien, he knew this was the go–no go point. He didn't want to trust a snake like Jason Bell Purdy. On the other hand, he wondered what choice he had. The story certainly made sense. He was beginning to think that his housekeeper was trying to generate some extortion income.

He had made up his mind.

"Even though you will chair the committee, I want the ability to pull the strings behind the scenes. You understand?" O'Brien said, calling after the other man.

Jason Bell Purdy stopped, turned, and faced him with a smile.

"Anything you say, Senator."

"And you swear what you are telling me is the truth?"

"Oh, absolutely," Purdy said soothingly. "I wouldn't lie to you—particularly here. George Washington could not tell a lie. And George Washington is my hero."

He extended his right hand and the two senators shook on it.

At that moment O'Brien couldn't help but think that it was all wrong that their agreement had been reached in the shadow of the Washington Monument.

It occurred to him that the handshake with Jason Bell Purdy ought rather to have taken place under a more appropriate monument—if perhaps the nation's capital had constructed one to the memory of Benedict Arnold.

38

QUESTION: Was there anybody else in that meeting between General Nuban and Abu Adis on the drug-running issue?

ANSWER: There was a man—I believe he was an American—at least it sounded like he had an American accent.

QUESTION: Do you remember his name? Anything about his identity?

ANSWER: Well, as I recall—I believe his name was Black...Mr. Rusty Black, I think.

WILL CHAMBERS WAS STUDYING SOME questions and answers in the transcript of Dr. Agabba's deposition. He glanced at the blinking light on his telephone. He had attorney Cesar Linton from Miami holding on the other end.

The deposition transcript had arrived only the day before, and reviewing it would not have been the first thing Will would have planned for the day. But Linton's phone call had prompted him to quickly scan some of his questions—and some of Agabba's answers—concerning the connection between an American drug dealer, al-Aqsa Jihad, and government officials in Sudan.

Just now, Linton had spoken vaguely, and very generally, about wanting to "strike certain portions of the transcript from use at the trial" and then put the remaining portions of the transcript "under seal." That's when Will had asked him if he could hold for a minute.

He had quickly grabbed the transcript and located the testimony he'd just been studying.

He put a marker on that page of the transcript and then picked up the phone.

"Cesar, sorry to keep you on hold. Now," he continued, "what parts of the deposition were you concerned about—and more importantly, why are you concerned about them?"

"'Concerned'—that's really not the right word," Linton replied. "You know I play tough—I play hard—but I'm not just blowing smoke here. You've got some scandalous—defamatory—frivolously false garbage in this deposition of Dr. Agabba."

"Well, then answer my question. What are the parts of the deposition you think should be stricken?"

"Oh, come on, you know exactly what I'm talking about—all of that trash about the other so-called terrorist groups that had dealings with Sudan. You know what I'm referring to."

"No, I don't. I'm not a mind reader," Will replied. "Cesar, you're going to have to be specific—page and line number. Do you have the deposition in front of you?"

"Yes, I do."

"Well, I've got mine in front of me also. Cite me the sections you think we ought to consider striking."

"Everything from pages one-hundred-nine to one-hundred-twenty-one."

Will glanced at the transcript and noted that the testimony regarding Rusty Black and the AAJ was found on pages one-hundred-twenty and one-hundred-twenty-one.

"I don't think I can agree to that—under any circumstances," he replied. "The fact of other terrorist organizations operating freely with the support and encouragement of Sudan is relevant. It shows a pattern of practice and has bearing on the intent issue. I explained all that at the deposition."

There was a moment of silence. Then Linton spoke up.

"Look—I'm a reasonable man. You're a reasonable man. We can work something out. Okay, maybe you can convince the court about the relevance of all this jazz about the other terrorist groups—and that it somehow creates a pattern that's relevant to the issues. Okay. Let's assume that. But—I mean—some of this stuff, you're allowing people's names to be smeared—Americans—you can't verify this information—Dr. Agabba is just shooting blind on some of that stuff."

Will could hear, in Linton's rhetorical ramblings, the evidence of a curious, even bizarre, reality. There was something in this deposition that the other attorney wanted to cover up and remove from the record. Something more than just the mere fact of terrorism running rampant in Sudan. It was something specific. It was a name. It was a person.

"Try to get focused here, Cesar," he said. "Tell me exactly what you're referring to. What is it that you think—bottom line—we ought to agree should be stricken from the transcript?"

"Well, take pages one-hundred-twenty to one-hundred-twenty-one, as an example," Linton replied. "You've got this stuff from Agabba talking about some supposed American drug dealer by the name of Rusty Black. I don't know who this guy is. Maybe he's imaginary—maybe he's a cartoon character—maybe he's a real guy that Agabba wants to pay back—and he's an innocent American. Whatever the fact, the business about this Rusty Black guy is absolutely irrelevant and immaterial, even under your own theory about a pattern of terrorism. There's simply no need to be talking about some American citizen dealing drugs. That has nothing to do with this case."

Will reflected on the other man's comment for a few seconds. Then he came to two conclusions.

First, Linton was probably correct. The questions and answers about Rusty Black, his connection with the AAJ, and his ties to Mexico as well as Sudan could probably not be justified under any of the issues of the lawsuit.

And Will had also come to a second conclusion. Linton's concern about the Rusty Black testimony was being driven by something. It didn't seem likely that the government of Sudan had any real interest in an American drug dealer—although Will could not be positive about that. But assuming that was true, why did Linton want to protect the Rusty Black–AAJ–Mexico connection?

"Okay, Cesar, I'll tell you what I will do," Will said. "I will *consider* striking pages one-twenty and one-twenty-one, *if*—and only if—you agree we can use the other pages of the deposition that relate to terrorist organizations in general operating within Sudan, and you will not object."

"You drive a hard bargain, Will," Linton replied. "I'll think about it. You think about it. I'll get back to you in a couple days and we'll see if we can do business. Okay?"

By the time Will hung up the phone Hilda had opened the door to his office and was waving frantically to him.

"Something important, Will—somebody out here in the lobby…"

Will held up his hand to Hilda as he called Todd Furgeson, his junior associate, to do a quick research matter for him.

"This is Will. Do me a favor, will you? Check in Martindale-Hubbell for the listing of Cesar Linton's law firm down in Miami. Give me a printout of their list of representative clients. I'd like that right away, if you could."

He turned off the intercom and turned to Hilda.

"Okay, what's the emergency?"

"There's a man out in the lobby—he's from the U.S. Marshal's Service—he's serving a subpoena on you."

"A subpoena? On me?"

She nodded vigorously.

He stepped out into the lobby, where the process server handed him a folded piece of paper with one hand and held out the original in the other.

"Mr. Chambers, as agent and attorney for Colonel Caleb Marlowe, United States Marine Corps, you are hereby served with a subpoena to appear at the time and place indicated to give testimony before a subcommittee of the United States Congress, the Senate Select Subcommittee on the American Response to Terrorism in Mexico."

The process server placed the folded paper in Will's hand, turned, and left the office.

The attorney opened the subpoena and quickly scanned the subject matter of his testimony. It involved all aspects of the incident at Chacmool, Mexico, "including, but not limited to, the activities of the American military, and the involvement of Colonel Caleb Marlowe and members of his commando unit."

Hilda must have noticed his stunned look because she quickly asked whether he was all right.

He nodded and glanced back at the subpoena. Then he noticed the name of the chairman of the subcommittee—and gave a wry chuckle, shaking his head in disbelief.

There it was, as clear as day—Senator Jason Bell Purdy, Chairman of the Senate Select Subcommittee.

He passed the subpoena over to his secretary.

"Take a look at this—notice any names that look familiar? Look at the bottom, at the name of the chairman."

"Jason Bell Purdy—we know this guy, don't we?" Hilda asked. "What was that case where he was involved…sort of indirectly, I think. At least his name came up. Wait a minute—it was that custody case you handled down in Georgia, right?"

Will smiled and nodded.

With the subpoena in his hand he stepped into his office, closed the door, and quickly dialed legal counsel for the senate subcommittee at the number indicated at the bottom of the document.

One of the lawyers answered the phone, and he referred Will to the chief legal counsel—an attorney by the name of Ralph Vetter. After a few minutes attorney Vetter answered the phone.

"Don't you guys usually give a letter of introduction and a few phone calls as a way of getting a witness for one of your subcommittees—rather than just dropping a subpoena on a private attorney?" Will asked.

"I do apologize for that," Vetter said. "Yes, normally we do that— use the informal route—but we're really pressed for time. We're cranking up the subcommittee rather quickly, and the exigencies of the schedule made that impractical. But I was planning on giving you a call. I'm sorry the subpoena reached you before I could contact you informally."

"Well, courtesy aside, I have some vehement objections to the scope of the subpoena."

"Like?"

"Well, let's begin with the attorney–client privilege. Most of what you're asking about—the basis of my knowledge of what went on down in Chacmool, Mexico—is based on my representation of Colonel Caleb Marlowe. I will not respond to questions that pierce the attorney–client relationship."

"I certainly understand that," Vetter said reassuringly. "I'm sure we can work out some middle ground on this."

The subcommittee counsel then suggested that Will submit himself to questioning on everything except direct conversations between him and his client concerning the Chacmool incident. But Will felt that was too broad. He argued for a much more restrictive focus in his testimony.

After fifteen minutes of wrangling, the subcommittee attorney conceded the point.

Will and Vetter finally agreed that the scope of his testimony would pertain *only* to matters contained in the transcript of the Article 32 hearing. Will asked the subcommittee counsel to draft a letter documenting their agreement on the very limited scope of his testimony.

After he hung up with Vetter, he buzzed Hilda and asked her to get Major Hanover at Quantico on the line for him. Will wanted to find out if his co-counsel in the Marlowe case had been served with a subpoena himself—or whether he had any information on what the subcommittee might be looking for.

Todd, Will's junior associate, breezed into the room with a printout from Martindale-Hubbell.

"Here's the listing of representative clients for Cesar Linton's law firm."

Will glanced down the list of corporate and institutional clients. Then his eyes fixed on two entries. He circled one of them.

Todd bent down and took a look at the circled name.

"Global Petroleum—is that an important name?"

Will nodded. "Yes it is—it's owned by someone that I've met in the past."

"Who?"

"A renegade billionaire by the name of Warren Mullburn."

"Yeah. He's the guy who was in the news a couple of months ago. He's over in Switzerland. I think they're asking him to come to the United States for some investigation. Right?"

Will nodded again. He glanced back at the list and circled a second name. It was Nuevo Petróleo Nacional de México—subsidiary of New Century Oil.

The younger attorney glanced down at the name that Will had just circled.

"And what's the deal with that company?"

Will was silent for a moment as he studied the name, and then he answered quietly.

"I'm really not sure. Let's just call it a hunch."

39

WILL WAS SITTING AT THE KITCHEN TABLE, his hands clasped around his coffee cup, his eyes looking at some indistinct, distant point on the horizon. Fiona's left hand was on his shoulder, and with her right hand she was filling his cup from the pot.

"So you were telling me," she said, "that a name surfaced in this Sudan case—someone connected with the case you handled for Da?"

"Right. Mullburn. Warren Mullburn."

"The billionaire? The one you met face-to-face?"

Will nodded and took a swig of his coffee.

"Yes. Out at his mansion in the Nevada desert outside of Las Vegas."

"That place with the strange name, right?"

"Yes—'Utopia,'" Will noted. "Anyway, his name came up—well, not exactly his name. The Miami lawyer who's on the other side of our Sudan case also happens to represent one of Mullburn's companies."

Fiona sat down across the table and studied Will carefully.

"So, what does this mean?" she asked.

"Probably nothing. It's just that Mullburn is a very dangerous man."

"You still see him as a danger to *you?*" Fiona asked with a tinge of incredulity in her voice.

"You want me to be honest?" her husband responded. Then he motioned with both hands to the kitchen around them.

"Look around," he said, not able to keep from going over the ground they'd covered before. "I love this place. We built it together. But remember what was here before this house was built? An antebellum Southern mansion. A house that was burnt to the ground. The police know it was arson. I know it was arson. And I will believe, until my dying day, that Warren Mullburn was connected to that. During

169

your father's case I got too close to some of Mullburn's dealings...and somebody wanted to put me away."

"Look," Fiona said gingerly, but with some skepticism, "if I had gone through some of the things that you did, I'd probably feel the same. But they never found any proof it was Mullburn—right?"

Her husband nodded.

Then Fiona's expression changed. Her lips tightened slightly and she rested her cheek in her hand as she spoke.

"You know what I think? I think Mullburn's name took you back to when the old mansion stood on this hill. And then you thought about the years you spent in that house—the years you spent with Audra. And then you thought about her death. And it put you back into the same emotional nosedive. Am I right?"

Will shook his head.

"No...not at all. Really, darling—you're wrong about that. It's a practical issue. Mullburn's name...the name of his company comes up. I think about him. I think about what it might mean to the case. I think about his power, his money, and his twisted motives. The guy is evil. We've talked about it before. Why can't you see that?"

At first Fiona flushed with hurt and anger. But she took a deep breath, reached over the table, grabbed her husband's hand, and squeezed it.

"All right. Let's talk plainly here. You were up in the middle of the night again, weren't you?"

Will eyed her a little sheepishly.

"I was hoping I didn't wake you up."

"So...three-thirty in the morning you get up and you walk out into the great room. And you pace—you look out the window. You don't think I know what's going on? So tell me—what were you thinking about?"

Will shook his head and gave her the kind of look that passersby give as they drive by a car wreck on the highway.

"Nothing specific. Indistinct. My mind races...I guess I keep hanging on to this—digging my fingers into it. It's as if there's this other guy, somebody out there walking around on the streets...somebody named Damon Lynch. It's as if I need to get to this guy before he can get to Audra. But...we both know that to think things like that is just crazy. Audra's dead. I've moved on, and the Lord has led me to you. You're the best thing, Fiona darling, that ever happened in my life. When I committed my life to Christ—when everything turned around—I thought all the ghosts were gone. But that's not the case…not entirely. It's like I have this road I've got to walk—I've got to walk through the valley of the dead. As if there's something out there that needs to be overcome. Something that needs to be conquered."

"Something…like what?" she asked quietly.

"I've spent my whole life as a trial lawyer. I like my adversaries across the table from me, where I can see them…on the other side of the courtroom—where I can size them up and take them on. But I'm beginning to think there's an enemy that isn't like that. Something else I need to vanquish. But I'm not quite sure what…it's like God is sitting there looking at me from his throne room. He's saying, *You can choose to win this struggle—you can shake this business about Audra's murder—and your feelings about the men who did it. I've given you the power to do it. Now it's up to you, though. You don't have to make the choice. But it begins in the quiet center of your will. And that's where it gets tough.*"

Fiona smiled. Her eyes brightened.

"Will, sweetheart, it's so good to hear you talking about this. So much of the time I feel as if you've got an iron door with a lock. And you keep me closed out of parts of your life. I love it when we can talk like this."

Will stretched his hands out on the kitchen table and happened to catch, in a glance, the time on his watch. He took a second look, then looked up at his wife.

Fiona eyed him. He didn't have to say a thing. He was already shutting down the communication…his mind was now halfway to his office.

"I'm a mind reader," she said with a sigh. "You know what Will Chambers' mind is now saying? It's saying, *Okay, where are my keys? Don't forget to take your briefcase. I wonder how many pink slips are waiting for me at the office. Let's see—what do I need to do on that case today?* Am I right? Tell me I'm not right."

"That's what I get for marrying a woman who's smarter than I am," he said with a smirk.

"That kind of flattery won't get you anywhere," Fiona said, but she was not smiling back. Then she added, "Will, maybe you ought to talk to somebody about what you're going through."

Her husband stood up from the kitchen table but then stopped and bent over, looking her in the eye. His expression was stern.

"Like who? A psychiatrist? A psychologist? You think I need that?"

"No—not you. Not the invincible *Will Chambers*. You're made out of steel and concrete," she bulleted out angrily, with hurt in her face.

Will struggled to respond. But there was nothing to say...or at least, nothing that fit. He had always been good at articulating facts that were able to fit into logical, analytical categories. But this was something different...this smothering, suffocating feeling about Audra's murder. He had thought it was over, but now he knew that it wasn't. But he also knew he had to let his wife know where his heart was.

He walked over to Fiona and wrapped his arms around her. Then he kissed her fully on the lips. She pulled back slightly and eyed her husband.

"When was the last time you met with Len Redgrove?" she asked, trying to open up the way to a suggestion. She knew that her husband's spiritual and professional mentor might be able to unlock something she couldn't.

"Last couple months our schedules have both been bad. Maybe I'll give him a call. We'll catch up for a cup of coffee or something," he said, glancing at his watch.

Fiona's eyes narrowed, and she said sarcastically, "So—session's over for the day? Everything's all fixed—and Will Chambers is off and running again."

Will gave her a befuddled look. She added, "Go ahead, dear. Get to your office. Topic to be continued..."

After the attorney had grabbed his briefcase and was heading to the front door he remembered something. Whirling around, he called out to his wife.

"Say, Fiona—what about that fund-raising gala in DC? Did we both agree that we can make it—and are we going?"

Fiona poked her head out of the bathroom where she was brushing her hair.

"You mean the one for the monument...to honor the veterans from the Gulf war and the Afghanistan war?"

Will nodded, and then he continued. "I thought we both said we could make it—right?"

"Yes. In fact—I think I have the invitation in the kitchen. Don't worry about it," she added. "I'll RSVP for us."

As he reached the door Fiona called out after him—with a reluctant smile on her face.

"Romans eight thirty-eight and thirty-nine. Remember?" And then she blew him a quick kiss.

Will smiled back and nodded. The passage was a favorite of Angus, Fiona's father. It expressed the profound, nearly incomprehensible reality for those who were "in" Jesus Christ—that nothing, for them, could separate them from the love of God. Nothing.

As Will climbed into his Corvette and started it up, he had a fleeting thought. That passage in Romans had been penned by the apostle Paul—former persecutor and torturer of Christians, later turned into a death-defying missionary after his encounter with the risen Christ on the Damascus road.

As he cruised down the long tree-lined driveway from Generals' Hill to the road below, he was struck with a further thought.

Maybe the most formidable enemy was not pain, or the threat of death, or devils, or catastrophes—perhaps, really, it was nothing out there in the world that forged the most sinister lie that God's grace was insufficient. Perhaps it was something else altogether.

As Will wheeled his convertible onto the county trunk road and accelerated quickly, the idea grew.

What if—among all of those enemies—what if the most dangerous one of all is really me?

40

WILL WAS STILL IMMERSED DEEPLY in thought when he parked his car in his space at the law office. He took a moment to survey the grime on the chrome trim and the dirty whitewalls. He could always tell when life was getting out of control—for that was when his beloved Corvette was neglected.

When he walked in, Hilda was at the reception desk with an excited expression.

"You just missed him!" she cried out.

"Who?"

"Colonel Marlowe. He just called. Collect."

"What did he want?"

"I'm not sure. He didn't say. But he needed to talk to you right away."

"Well, where was he calling from?"

"Oh! Yes. That's right. He was calling from Mexico City. It sounded like he was at a pay phone or something. A lot of noise in the background. Something about the people in charge not letting him make another phone call—but he would try again in a few minutes, hoping to catch you."

Will's mind starting racing. *Mexico City. What was Marlowe doing down there?* The attorney had speculated that his client's "unfinished business" had something to do with tracking down and wiping out the perpetrators of the Chacmool catastrophe. His own private vendetta. Now it seemed like exactly what Will had feared was happening.

"Hilda, if he calls again, I don't care what I'm doing—interrupt me and put him through."

Hilda nodded dutifully as Will walked into his office and tossed his briefcase on the black leather couch. He had just started reviewing his schedule for the day when Hilda buzzed him and let him know that Colonel Marlowe was on the line again.

"Caleb, what are you doing down in Mexico City?"

"Listen, Will, I've got a problem down here. I need to give you the short order on it because I'm not quite sure how long they'll let me talk. I'm in custody. The facility is called the Special Confinement Center of the Federal Police."

"What were you arrested for?"

"It's complicated. But the papers I was given were not issued by the federal police down here in Mexico. These are charges for war crimes, Will."

"Who issued the paperwork?" Will asked, grabbing a yellow notepad and a pen and scribbling notes down furiously.

"The International Criminal Tribunal."

"Say again?"

"The ICC—the International Criminal Court in The Hague, Netherlands. You know, the new criminal court the UN created a few years ago."

Will tapped his pen on the notepad and thought for a second.

"Right. I remember reading about it in some of the law journals. It began hearing cases back in 2002."

"Will, I need your help on this thing. And I mean now. I think you better start brushing up on your international law."

"I've already got some ideas. I'm going to bring someone in on this with me. Say—the charges you received, and the paperwork. Do any of them show there's going to be a move for extradition?"

"I read them pretty quick, but I don't think so."

"Well," Will said, trying to make use of the precious minutes on the phone with his client, "I have a feeling that will be their next move. They're not going to let you sit down there in Mexico. They're going to try to ship you over to The Hague. And that's going to make my immediate work much more difficult."

The attorney heard some noise at the other end—someone yelling in Spanish, in the background. Marlowe apparently turned away from the phone, but Will still overheard his client speak what seemed to be some remarkably fluent Spanish. Then he got back to the phone.

"That's my zookeeper. He said that's it. Listen, step up to the plate on this one. This could be pretty important. For me. And for a lot of other people."

"Caleb, I'll do my best. But I've got a question for you."

"Hey, I've got to go."

More Spanish yelling in the background.

"Just tell me one thing—what were you doing down in Mexico City?"

"Can't talk. Long story. Don't forget me down here."

A few more words shouted in Spanish, and then the connection was broken.

Will leaned back in his chair, trying to process what he just heard. Then he punched the button on his intercom and connected with his junior associate.

"Todd, I've got a research project. This has to be top priority. The International Criminal Court was created back in 2002. There was an enabling statute..."

He thought for a moment before he continued.

"I think it was called the 'Rome Statute.' Pull that. And pull the full text of the code of procedure for the court, as well as all the substantive offenses. Three-hole punch it and put it in a notebook for me. I need that right away. Then get the Office of Legal Counsel for the State Department on the line. In fact, get the guy I've been dealing with on our Sudan case, Randy Walford."

Then Will sprang out of his chair and stepped quickly into the lobby.

"Hilda, please get Len Redgrove on the line."

She nodded, punched the number up in her database, and clicked to make the connection.

Will had taken several classes from Len Redgrove during law school. In the years after that, however, Redgrove had become a close personal friend, and a spiritual mentor of sorts. Not only did he possess several advanced law degrees, he also had an MDiv and PhD in theology, and he occasionally wrote and taught on the interrelationship between religion and law at colleges and seminaries around the country. The University of Virginia law professor would be an invaluable co-counsel to Will on this case. But where was he now?

Will and his mentor had been meeting on a regular basis for years. But for the last few months the professor had been out of circulation. Thinking back, he thought he remembered Redgrove indicating he would be doing a lot of traveling while on sabbatical for a semester.

While waiting for Hilda to track down the professor, Will went back to his desk and quickly phoned Major Hanover, who had not yet returned his call about the subpoena Will had received from Jason Bell Purdy's subcommittee.

On the third ring, the major answered the phone.

The Marine Corps lawyer apologized for not getting back to Will sooner, but he had been involved in a multiday court-martial case. To answer the prior question, he said he had heard nothing about Purdy's subcommittee. The whole thing was as much of a surprise to him as it had been to Will.

But when the civilian lawyer opened up the issue of the ICC war-crimes charges, Hanover was quiet and somber, but apparently not surprised.

"There's been a lot of talk," he finally replied, "among the top brass, and the rest of us, that this was going to happen some day. It was just a matter of time. There's been concern about the scope of ICC authority—how far it'll reach—and what it's going to mean to the American military out there in a variety of combat situations. So here we are. Now, thinking back, I'm also wondering if there's something else that now fits in."

"What's that?" Will asked.

"When Colonel Marlowe was first apprehended down in Mexico, you will recall that Lieutenant General Cal Tucker went down personally. Well, afterwards, when the case first started cranking up for the court-martial—and after you and I had met for the first time—I ran into him here at Quantico. He asked a little about the case and said he was glad to see that I was on the case as detailed military defense counsel—but he also said he was equally happy that Marlowe had hired you and had good civilian defense counsel as well. And then he said...I can't remember exactly...but something like this was the kind of case that could mushroom far beyond just military jurisdiction. Or words to that effect."

Concluding the call, Will promised to keep the major posted on the progress of the ICC case.

There was a knock at his door, and Hilda poked her head in.

"Dr. Redgrove has been traveling during his sabbatical. But he is going to be back in town tonight. He is flying in to give a lecture over at the University of Richmond. You may want to try to reach him there."

Just seconds after Hilda had disappeared from the doorway, Will's intercom buzzed. Todd had State Department legal counsel Randy Walford on the line.

Walford confirmed that the State Department already had gotten the heads up on the ICC charges. He indicated that the department was preparing to lodge a protest through formal diplomatic channels with both the UN and Mexico.

"What about formal representation of Colonel Marlowe?" Will asked the State Department lawyer. "Doesn't the United States government have a vested interest in defending him before the International Criminal Court in The Hague?"

"Difficult question," Walford responded cautiously. "A very complicated issue. We're sorting that through. We're not quite sure, at this point, how extensive the U.S. government's involvement is going to be in the actual case."

"Why not?" Will asked with a note of irritation in his voice. "This man was operating as part of the United States military in an American-sanctioned combat situation in Chacmool, Mexico. Why wouldn't our government intervene in this case? At least as amicus curiae in support of our defense, if nothing else?"

"That's certainly a possibility," Walford said, still vague in his response. "But Will, you have to remember that Marlowe is now retired from the Marine Corps. As I understand it, that's the deal that was worked out. When the charges were not referred up to court-martial, he immediately resigned his commission. I know that's somewhat standard in the military. It keeps any further charges from being lodged and makes the whole thing res adjudicata. The point is, he is not active military right now."

"I see that as a distinction without a difference," Will shot back. "What else is there?"

On the other end the lawyer from State shifted the phone a little and cleared his throat.

"Other considerations. I don't have the whole story on it. This is classified stuff. I'm really not privy to everything. That's all I can tell you right now. We're looking at it. We're pursuing the diplomatic angle. Just hang in there for Colonel Marlowe. We'll do everything we can."

After Will hung up he felt that he had just entered another maze. Like an ancient labyrinth out of some long-forgotten mythological tale. And if he took the wrong turn in his strategy, in the procedure he pursued or his defense of the case, he would encounter—rather than victory—a fierce, bloodthirsty creature with an insatiable appetite for destruction.

41

On his way to Richmond, Will phoned Fiona to tell her he wouldn't be home for dinner. He hoped to catch Len Redgrove at the tail end of his lecture and set a little time with him to try to convince him he should assist Will in the defense of Colonel Caleb Marlowe before the International Criminal Court. But he couldn't get Fiona on her cell phone or at home. So he left a voice mail at both places.

The attorney pulled into the wooded parking lot of the University of Richmond, parked his car, and then walked quickly across the plaza toward the law school building. Reaching the lecture hall, he slipped into the back and sat down.

On the dais for the symposium were several scholars and law professors, along with a moderator. Len Redgrove was at the podium. He was the final speaker.

The professor was sixty, with short, pure-white hair and bifocals perched on the end of his nose. He was dressed casually in a tweed jacket, but with a plaid shirt that clashed with his tie. He had a familiar, almost folksy way about him as he spoke, though his content was erudite, even lofty. Typical Len Redgrove. He was just ending his talk.

"...No matter how elegantly these global institutions of justice, like the International Criminal Court, are constructed—and no matter how eloquently they may articulate the international standards of law—without restraints, or competing checks and balances, they will succumb to the natural principles that apply to any political institution. If not restrained, they will become unrestrained. Though they may wear the respectable robes of jurisprudence, beneath those robes lie the same old straining, muscular ambitions of a brute—and if not soundly limited by national sovereignty, those ambitions will become unstoppable."

The audience gave Redgrove mild applause, and then the dais was surrounded by members of the audience.

Will stayed at the back of the room until the milling audience thinned out. A few college students who passed by were deriding Redgrove's "right-wing supernationalism." The professor was ambling out of the lecture hall when he caught sight of Will and gave him a hearty wave.

The two clasped hands warmly.

"Will, my friend, I certainly didn't expect to see you down here. How have you been?"

As they left the law school building and headed for the parking lot, as always, Redgrove wanted to find out how the younger man was enjoying marriage, and he asked to be brought up to speed on Fiona's singing career.

As the two approached the professor's Land Rover, Will finally got to the point.

As they stood at the car, he described the International Criminal Court charges against Colonel Marlowe, and the Chacmool incident, and then led Redgrove through a quick summary of the Article 32 hearing that had been conducted at Quantico. His friend listened intently and asked a few pointed questions. Then he responded.

"I have to tell you, Will, honestly—this is an amazing case you've got. For some time I've been predicting a major clash—a confrontation between the ICC's grab for global power and American sovereignty. And now—here it is. Do you realize what you've got here?"

But Will wasn't really interested in Len Redgrove's imaginative criticisms of international law. Though he greatly respected his friend's brilliant mind, he did consider him a bit over the top in some of his jurisprudential theories.

"Len, listen. I appreciate all that. But what we really need to do is focus on an aggressive defense of Caleb Marlowe. Let the diplomats and politicians argue about the rest."

Redgrove, however, was not really listening. His mind was on his schedule—and on how he could fit in this remarkable opportunity to strike at the ICC's audacious claim to world jurisdiction.

"You know I'm on sabbatical—I'm supposed to be finishing my book."

Will nodded. "I was hoping you could fit this case in—helping me as co-counsel. You'd still be able to make the deadline for your manuscript, don't you think?"

"You know the editors—taskmasters to the end!" the professor said with a chuckle. Then he grew solemn, and his eyes drifted downward as he thought over the timing.

Then he straightened up and put his hand on Will's shoulder.

"I wouldn't pass up this case for the world."

He suggested that Will follow him over to a late-night diner where they could catch some pie and coffee and lay out an agenda for immediate preparation of the defense.

Will was about to turn toward his own car when Redgrove spoke up again.

"You know, Will," he said thoughtfully, "I can imagine only one reason why the prosecution is pushing a case like this—a unique, small-impact combat-type case. Where you're *not* talking about hundreds or thousands of people being butchered—the typical war-crimes situation. Really, I can think of only one reason why your client has been charged before the ICC."

Will eyed him expectantly and waited for the punch line.

"Not to be too hasty, of course," the professor interjected. "But I think this is a test of strength—of the superiority of ICC jurisdiction. The elegant, eloquent brute is flexing its muscles."

42

THE BALLROOM IN CONSTITUTION HALL was crowded with military officers, members of Congress, Capitol Hill staff, diplomats, a few foreign dignitaries, representatives of military organizations and veterans groups, many spouses of the foregoing, and a handful of reporters and television news anchors.

Fiona was sipping a glass of punch. Then she noticed something. Reaching over, she delicately adjusted her husband's bow tie and tugged gently on his black tuxedo to straighten it. Will looked at her and smiled. She was dazzling. Her raven-colored hair was swept back expertly, and her eyes sparkled like the diamonds on her ears and around her neck. She cocked her head a little and smiled broadly enough to show both of her dimples.

By now Will was staring at her...grinning like a high-school kid.

Earlier that night the two of them had agreed to a peace treaty—to end the little border skirmish brewing between them. Fiona had said she just loved Will too much not to cut him a healthy slice of grace. He, in turn, had pledged to put his *whole* mind and heart into communicating his feelings.

"What?" she asked as she noticed the lovestruck look in his eyes.

"You're absolutely stunning tonight," her husband said. He discreetly slipped his hand around her waist, and pulling her slightly toward him, whispered in her ear, "You're absolutely dazzling—brighter than the light on the Capitol dome—and you're all mine. Am I blessed or what?"

Amid the noise of the crowd she bent over and whispered in his ear, "Keep dishing out the compliments, big boy—you still have a lot of territory to make up!"

Will chuckled. Then he spotted an officer striding toward them in full dress uniform. He introduced himself as Lieutenant General Cal Tucker, United States Marine Corps.

He nodded politely to Fiona, and then he turned to Will and extended a big right hand.

"Counselor, I appreciate what you did for Colonel Marlowe. And what you're going to do."

As Will clasped the general's hand firmly and studied him, he had the distinct impression that this terse comment was not just idle conversation. In a strange way, Will felt as if he had just received a direct order.

"Thank you, General. I'm going to do everything I can for the colonel. You can count on that."

"About this ICC thing," Tucker continued, "have you tried back-channeling this to the administration?"

"I've been in touch with the State Department. They're playing it coy. I'm really not sure what their position is going to be in terms of joining us in the defense…as strange as that seems to me."

The general nodded. "Yes—that sounds just about right. Well, keep up the good effort."

Then he turned to Fiona and said, "Mrs. Chambers, I haven't had the pleasure of listening to your music. But I want you to know that my daughter's a big fan of yours. She's got a number of your CDs, and I believe she's caught at least one of your concerts. She wanted to make sure that I said hello."

Fiona smiled warmly. "I'm so pleased that she appreciates my music ministry. Please give her my warmest regards. And thank you, General, for your service to our country."

Tucker smiled and turned to leave.

"And thank you also, General, for the invitation," Will added.

The general gave a quick wave as he strode away and disappeared into the crowd.

Will led Fiona over to the long table of hors d'oeuvres in the middle of the hall. She waved it away, but her husband picked off several Swedish meatballs and a few shrimp. Munching on his booty, Will glanced vaguely at the sea of faces around the room. Then something caught his eye. A familiar face.

Will's riveted expression caught Fiona's awareness. She tugged at his sleeve and gave him a quizzical look.

But his attention was not diverted. He was staring across the room…into the eyes of Senator Jason Bell Purdy. Surrounded by a small group, Purdy had stopped talking in mid-conversation and was staring back at Will. The senator lifted his glass and tipped it toward the attorney.

Will half raised his glass of ginger ale and tipped it in Purdy's direction.

There was a broad, confident smile on the other man's face. Then he turned back to his small group of well-wishers and continued his conversation.

"Who is that?" Fiona asked. "He looks familiar. Who is he?"

"Senator Jason Bell Purdy. From Georgia."

"Oh, so that is Jason Bell Purdy," she remarked. "You met him during that custody case in Georgia."

Will nodded.

"And he's the one with the young niece. The one who reminded you of Audra," she added. "You also met her, didn't you?"

Her husband nooded again and was about to change the subject when Fiona continued.

"The pretty, young, blond niece. The one who flirted with you in Purdy's mansion?"

Will did not reply diplomatically. "Fiona, you're not jealous, are you?"

He smiled and studied his wife's face, which was now in full blush.

"You know, my dear," he said, whispering in her ear again, "you're always beautiful. But when you blush like that, you're absolutely indescribable."

Fiona's eyes narrowed. Her lips twisted a bit into an odd little smile.

"I am *not* jealous. I am…okay, yes. That was a hurtful time. I remember that phone call, and how you told me about spending time with his niece. How you were so attracted to her—"

"Whoa—stop," Will broke in. "First, let the record reflect that Purdy set up that meeting with his niece. He was trying to tool me around. I think he was playing some kind of mind game with me. He knew my background with Audra. And I will believe to my dying day that he was planning on using his niece to manipulate me because I was about to expose his financial misdealings down there in Georgia. I caught on to his little game, and I called his bluff."

"Will, just listen to you," Fiona replied. "You make it sound like this was just some high-stakes game of wits. When you told me about that meeting you had with her, I was really wounded."

"Fiona, darling, that was just a one-time encounter with that girl. Orchestrated by Purdy. I've never seen her since. Besides, it was before we were even engaged."

"So you were playing the field?"

"Of course not," Will responded. "Purdy was trying to play me."

Then he took her slender hand in his, squeezed it, and looked into her eyes.

"You know how much I love you? Don't ever forget how much I love you."

Fiona's expression started to change. She looked down and then looked up again. Her eyes were tearing up. She managed to smile at him, then she grabbed both of his hands and squeezed them.

"Can we go home now?"

Will nodded. He popped one of the Swedish meatballs into his mouth, gave his plate to one of the waiters, and took his beautiful bride arm in arm out to the vestibule, where they hailed a cab.

Fiona was holding on to his arm tightly, but she was pensive, deep in thought. Struggling to achieve some objectivity—and mask her hurt—she asked him about Purdy.

"Isn't he the senator who issued the subpoena for you? The one who's having you testify before a subcommittee—that Senator Purdy?"

Will nodded.

"So you have a real history with this man...and yet he wants to bring you up before his subcommittee—before the whole world—and have you testify. That's seems odd, doesn't it?"

As the two stood by the cabstand, Will considered her comment. Just one more example of how she could, at the most unexpected times, display her unique perception.

"You're right on the money," he replied. "That's exactly what I've been wondering. Of course, we've got an agreement in writing, narrowly limiting the scope of my testimony. So maybe Purdy and his staff feel they can keep me pigeon-holed so I can't bring out any of the dirt that I know about him. Besides, all that stuff back in Georgia—his information-launderers and spin doctors did an excellent job of explaining all that away before he was selected to fill the term of the senator who died. But you're absolutely right. Our prior relationship does put this in a curious light. And then there's also something else—something else that's been weighing on my mind."

Will thrust his hand out and a cab pulled over.

As he opened the door for his wife he added, "I also wonder how much Purdy knows about the International Criminal Court charges against Marlowe. I'm sure he must."

He closed the door, walked to the other side of the cab, and scooted into the backseat next to Fiona.

"So, what do you think?" she said, pursuing the issue. "How is the international case going to affect what you say in your testimony?"

"Good question," he replied. "Let's just say that the subcommittee hearing is going to take me back to my college days."

"Why do you say that?"

"Because I'm going to feel like I'm back in a boxing ring again. The only difference is that up in Congress they allow kidney punches."

43

THE SENATE HEARING ROOM WAS already jammed, even though it was still thirty minutes before the select subcommittee was scheduled to convene. Leather-covered chairs behind a high bench would seat the members of the subcommittee. Jason Bell Purdy's chair, in the middle, was empty. In a row behind the leather chairs, against the wall, were the smaller chairs, where the assistant legal counsel and legislative aides would sit. A few had already taken their positions and were exchanging comments.

Some of the crowd in the room consisted of the usual political devotees and curious members of the public. There were numerous representatives of interest groups with a stake in the hearings: a variety of conservative, pro-defense, and pro-military associations. A handful of liberal groups opposing human rights violations and concerned about what they perceived as the never-ending expansion of war on terrorism. Some representatives from the Pentagon, from the Antidefamation League for Mexico, and from the League for Civil Rights for the Americas. And a bevy of reporters.

A battery of news cameras had already been set up on tripods in the far corner of the hearing room. Along one wall there were two long tables filled with background papers and prepared comments from some of the witnesses.

On the level below the committee dais, there was a long table for the witnesses. It was covered with a green felt tablecloth, with several microphones on top. The seats at the witness table were empty—for now. One of them would soon be occupied by Will Chambers.

A handful of reporters were in the front of the room, kibitzing. One of them—Jack Hornby—was a newspaper institution in Washington, DC. He was now bureau chief for one of the large wire services.

"So what's the focus here? Purdy's going to do a rain dance about the incident involving the Marines down in Chacmool, Mexico, right?" one of the reporters queried.

"Yeah. Purdy's got a short Senate term to fill—and the need for a long reputation," another reporter quipped to the amusement of his colleagues.

"Gentlemen," Jack Hornby commented, "you are about to see—I truly believe—a performance of epic proportions."

"Yeah, but what kind of performance?" another reporter chimed in. "Is this going to be tragedy or comedy?"

"Well," Hornby continued, "I'm not quite sure. I'm a little confused about Senator Purdy's timing."

"Timing? What do you mean?" One reporter was making the mistake of taking Hornby's comment too seriously.

"Well," the bureau chief brought out his punch line, "Purdy's late— the circus already left town some time ago."

"Look, we need to get serious about what the tag line's going to be on this," another man broke in after the chuckles subsided. "He's looking at this shoot-'em-up down in Mexico. You got some marines. You got war on terrorism. You got bad relations between the U.S. and Mexico. And I hear there's an economic development bonanza going on down there."

"So—we've got to *gate* this story," another responded. "You know— Watergate. Iran-gate."

"So, how about this—Murder-gate—what do you think?"

"I like Mexi-gate," one of them chimed in.

"Well," Hornby said, weighing in sarcastically, "by the end of these hearings, I think we're all going to agree on the new hook for this—for Purdy's congressional investigation."

"What's that?" one of the others asked.

"*Regurgi-gate*," Hornby quipped, igniting an explosion of cackles from his news cronies.

That was when Will Chambers, briefcase in hand, opened the tall, thick wooden doors to the hearing room. He was immediately hit with a welter of noise from the mingling crowd and the packed rows of seats in the chamber.

He turned and gestured to Fiona, who had come along with him, to stick close.

They shouldered their way through the crowd toward the front row, just behind the witness table. Jack Hornby caught sight of Will, and he pushed his way through.

"Well, if it isn't Will Chambers—the inimitable—the indefatigable—the lawyer's lawyer in a profession where it's hard to find an honest man. Will, how have you been?" Hornby said, giving Will a smile and a firm handshake.

"Fine, Jack. It's been a while—I think the last time you and I chatted was the Reichstad versus MacCameron case. In fact, the 'MacCameron' was Fiona's dad, whom I represented." With that Will turned to his wife. "Jack, this is my wife, Fiona Chambers."

"Yes, I guessed that it was you—the gracious and beautiful Mrs. Chambers. I think you're the singer. Right? The voice of the heavenly choir, I hear."

"You're very kind," Fiona said with a cautious smile.

"Mrs. Chambers, you're about to see a classic sword fight—between a superb trial lawyer and a senator who's got the worst case of Potomac fever I've ever seen," Hornby said with a wry smile.

"Sword fight?" Fiona responded. "Then I think that means, as the reporter, you're the one who'll actually come out on top."

Hornby studied her for a second, arched his eyebrows, and then asked, "And why would you say that?"

"Because I always heard that the pen was mightier than the sword."

Hornby laughed out loud and then turned to Will.

"Not only a wonderful singer, but smart. I wonder...possibly smarter than you, Will. Because you always seem to get yourself in the middle of these legal and political cyclones. And let me tell you, I know you've got a background with this Jason Bell Purdy—I've done my research."

"You always do," Will commented. "What do you think?"

"I think that Senator Jason Bell Purdy is the biggest glutton for political power since Huey Long."

"Interesting. Wasn't Long assassinated?"

"Exactly!" Hornby snapped out, and then added a guttural chuckle.

One of the legislative aides interrupted their conversation and introduced himself to Will. He had the attorney sign in on the witness roster and then led him to the front row of chairs next to the witness table.

After he was seated in the front row, Will turned around and saw Fiona making her way to a seat in the back of the room. She caught his attention, and then she mouthed the words, *I love you—I'm praying for you.*

A few minutes later, several of the aides and the committee legal counsel scurried in and filled the rest of the seats on the back wall behind the dais.

Then the door to the anteroom swung open and the members of the senate select subcommittee entered—smiling, casual, confident, and ever mindful of the cameras that poised at the rear corner of the room.

The last to enter was Jason Bell Purdy. He was walking in with long strides, carrying a small, thin notebook under his arm. He greeted several members of the subcommittee with handshakes, a few words, and an effervescent smile. Then, as he took the chairman's seat at the middle of the dais, his smile faded into a serious, almost stern, expression. His gaze stretched out over the crowd, the reporters, the interest groups, and finally the witnesses, including Will. The noise in the room settled down quickly.

Purdy grasped the gavel with his right his hand and banged it triumphantly on its wooden square.

Silence swept through the room, except for the quiet beeping tones and whirring of cameras and the shuffling of a few papers in the audience.

Senator Jason Bell Purdy was about to begin his opening statements. This would be his finest hour.

44

THE FRONT ROW OF WITNESSES, including Will, were up on their feet, facing the panel of senators, with their right hands raised. As a group they were sworn to tell the truth, the whole truth, and nothing but the truth, so help them God. To the right of Will were the Assistant White House Legal Counsel and the Assistant Secretary of Defense for Special Projects. Those two witnesses were slated to testify first, with Will then finishing up the morning session.

To Will's left were the two witnesses for the afternoon session—the National Director for the Hispanic League for Civil Rights, and Fernando Fuego, the brother of Carlos Fuego, the CIA agent shot to death at Chacmool.

The first two witnesses took their seats at the witness table and adjusted the microphones.

Jason Bell Purdy cocked an eyebrow, and with all the solemnity that his short senatorial experience could muster, he reminded all of those present of the profound importance of the subcommittee's task—to investigate the manner in which the United States government had responded to the *perceived* threat of terrorism from within Mexico—and to investigate the murder of innocent Mexican nationals at Chacmool, Mexico, including an agent of the Central Intelligence Agency. Purdy described the "slaughter" that had taken place there as one of the "most troubling aspects of America's war on terrorism."

"The incident at Chacmool," Purdy continued, "should give us all pause about the scope, breadth, and unrestricted nature of the military action that the United States government has brought to bear abroad, even against nations that have been our friends."

As the senator concluded his opening statement, Will was listening intently. It was becoming clear where Purdy was heading—and why he had subpoenaed attorney Will Chambers.

The chairman talked about the unfettered right of special operations military personnel, in conjunction with the CIA, to assassinate perceived terrorists at will in any country of the world. This, he pointed out, was a direct result of, and an expansion from, the directive issued a few years before from the White House—an executive order lifting the prior ban against foreign assassinations.

Further, Purdy emphasized the point that special operations units were being developed without full disclosure to the subcommittees in Congress that had jurisdiction and oversight regarding military spending.

But it was his final comment that pushed all the buttons, rang all the bells, and sounded all the alarms of Will's mental detector system.

"The threat, I believe, that these hearings will reveal is the development by the American military, with the assistance of the United States Marine Corps and the Central Intelligence Agency, of a new and startling breed of warrior. America has developed an experimental model of soldier–spies—killing specialists who can metamorphose like chameleons from full military combat status into civilian intelligence status at the blink of an eye. We will see that the shocking incident down in Chacmool, Mexico, may be just the beginning of murders, assassinations, and political coups orchestrated with American tax-payer money, and armed with the near-limitless power of the American government."

Purdy turned his head ever so slightly toward the cameras.

"As citizens of the twenty-first century, perhaps it's time not only to harbor fears for our homeland's security, but also to reflect faith in universal standards of human rights as well."

The first witness was Assistant White House Counsel Larry Bracken.

Purdy began by sparring on a procedural point—that his letter had requested that Chief White House Legal Counsel Harold Birnbaum attend the hearing and give testimony, not his assistant. Bracken explained that Birnbaum had a conflict, but if there were any questions he could not answer, his superior would probably be happy to answer them in writing at a later date.

Then the chairman moved into the real substance—the fact that the White House was following the new rule vacating the prohibition against foreign assassinations. The ban on political assassinations had been arguably reversed by President George W. Bush in the war on terrorism, at least regarding enumerated enemy combatants. Purdy pushed the point—demanding that Bracken admit that the order permitting foreign assassinations made the incident at Chacmool possible. The witness saw the risk in that admission—but couldn't avoid making the concession.

"Yes, Senator," Bracken answered, "that executive order—in an indirect sense—did permit the attempt to kill the cell of terrorists at Chacmool."

The next witness was Major General Harlan Koeptke—Assistant Secretary of Defense for Special Projects. Purdy questioned Koeptke about the most recent budget document approved as a result of the work of the Senate Military Oversight Committee during the previous October.

The senator wanted to know whether the military budget document revealed any appropriations for experimental special operation units that included features of both military special ops and CIA-type covert operations.

Koeptke straightened his shoulders and answered sharply, "Your office delineated the scope of my testimony in advance—and this is not an area we agreed to discuss in this hearing."

But Purdy kept pushing—demanding information about budget allocations for a "unique paramilitary assassination group funded by American taxpayer money."

Finally, the general drew the line in the sand. Refusing to answer any further questions on the grounds that Purdy's committee lacked the usual safeguards utilized in Senate intelligence committees, Koeptke said that he would answer no further questions until he had consulted with the Secretary of Defense.

When General Koeptke was released, he stood up quickly, wheeled around, and walked straight out of the hearing room, disregarding a few raised hands from reporters who wished to get a statement from him outside.

The table was void of witnesses when Purdy called Will Chambers to the front.

The attorney removed his file from his briefcase, placed it on the green felt tablecloth, and sat down in his chair. He folded his hands in front of him, smiling directly at Senator Jason Bell Purdy.

"Ladies and gentlemen," the chairman began, glancing at his watch, "this next witness is attorney Will Chambers from Monroeville, Virginia. Mr. Chambers has been called to this hearing because he was civilian legal counsel to Colonel Caleb Marlowe, who was investigated by the United States military relating to the incident at Chacmool, Mexico. But before we begin with attorney Chambers, I do have an important announcement."

The other members of the committee turned and studied Purdy intently. The room fell silent.

"My staff…" Purdy continued—and as he spoke, his staff rose from their seats behind him with large stacks of paper in their hands—"my staff is going to place on the information table a press release from my office announcing the news we have just received. This is very troubling news. Matters of great importance—that I think all Americans should know about. The International Criminal Court in The Hague—the permanent war-crimes tribunal of the United Nations—has formally charged Colonel Caleb Marlowe, United States Marine Corps, retired, with war crimes in connection with the operation in Chacmool."

The hearing room erupted in confusion. The journalists—and several members of the public—began elbowing their way—rushing over to the information table, where Senator Purdy's staff was stacking copies of the press release. The senator glanced again at his watch. His office had given an informal assurance to the White House that there would be no release of information about the ICC charges until after the White House had issued a statement. That statement was to come in fifteen minutes. But Purdy had decided to beat them to the punch.

As Will studied the contrived theatrics of the moment, he knew there would be no referees in this match. No rules of proper procedure. And he also knew one other thing.

This was no longer just an unrefereed boxing match. Purdy clearly had the intent of turning it into something fit for the World Wrestling Federation.

45

"MR. CHAMBERS, YOU WERE CIVILIAN defense counsel for Colonel Caleb Marlowe, United States Marine Corps, now retired, regarding his military defense at the Quantico proceeding, is that correct?"

"Senator Purdy, that's correct."

"Now, Colonel Marlowe never did testify at that Article 32 hearing. Is that correct?"

"He did not testify—as was his legal right. He relied on that right."

"So it appears that you—as his defense counsel, Mr. Chambers— you may be one of the few people who really knows what was going on in Colonel Marlowe's mind at the time he gave the order to his unit to fire upon a small, civilian house outside the village of Chacmool, which resulted in the death of a mother, her two small children, and the father of those children—who was also an agent with the Central Intelligence Agency."

"Is that a question, Senator?"

The chairman straightened up a bit and clicked his teeth together slightly, then dug in.

"Is it a fact that you may be one of the few people who really knows Colonel Marlowe's version of that tragic slaughter of four individuals down in Chacmool?"

"I find it difficult to respond to a question that attaches the word 'slaughter' to what happened there."

"Well—now let's just look at it this way, Mr. Attorney. If you and your wife had two little children and you were sitting at the kitchen table having dinner, and an officer from the United States military ordered his troops to surround your house and fire on it until all four of you were dead—wouldn't you call that a slaughter?"

"Well," Will said with a smile, "if I were dead, I don't think I'd be calling it anything. But yes, your hypothetical certainly sounds like a slaughter. The difference between your scenario and what happened at Chacmool is that I wouldn't be harboring terrorists. Nor would I have been kidnapped by terrorists, tied to a chair, and used as bait in a trap set for the military."

"Is that what Colonel Marlowe told you happened?"

Purdy studied Will and saw the ire flashing in his eyes.

The attorney clenched his jaw and took a second to regain his composure before he answered.

"Senator Purdy, I do believe that you understand exactly why that question is entirely objectionable. Why I can't answer it. And why it directly violates the understanding I had with your office—"

· "Mr. Chambers, do you realize that we have contempt powers in this subcommittee hearing?"

"I'm sure you have that authority, Senator," Will responded calmly. "But the real question is whether I am in contempt of Congress for failing to answer your question. And the answer to that is—I am *not*. As I was trying to say before you cut me off—"

"Mr. Chambers," Purdy said, interrupting him again, "I just want to make sure I'm hearing correctly. You're refusing to answer the question about what you do or do not know about your client's case."

"That was not the question. You wanted to know what my client told me. That's attorney–client privileged. That is *exactly* why it violates our letter of understanding."

And with that Will pulled out of his file the letter from Senator Purdy's office, signed by the legal counsel for the subcommittee, and setting forth the scope, and limitations, of the questions that would be asked during the hearing.

He lifted the letter up—high enough so the reporters and the audience could see it in his right hand.

"This letter that your office issued to me—pursuant to the specific understanding we reached—said this, and I quote—"

"Mr. Chambers, I'm the one asking the questions here—"

"First bullet point," Will said, plowing ahead, 'your attorney–client privilege with your client, Colonel Marlowe, will be protected, and no questions will be asked regarding confidential attorney–client communications.'"

"Mr. Chambers, no one on this panel disputes the right of you, and your client, to demand…to insist on relying on the technical legal rules—the legal loopholes, if you will—of attorney–client privilege. And we have agreed to honor that. But I want to hear from you what you think went on down there at Chacmool."

"It is my belief, Senator, that Colonel Marlowe and his small unit were led into a trap—that AAJ terrorists, possibly in connection with other individuals—possibly Mexican nationals—set up this incident so that four innocent people would be killed. And so that the United States military would be embarrassed. That's where I believe the truth lies here."

"An experienced, seasoned combat veteran like Colonel Marlowe. And his band of highly trained special operations combat veterans." Purdy's tone was sarcastic. "Those folks were just plumb tricked—led into a deadly trap by a ragtag band of Islamic extremists. That's what you want us to believe? Do you have one shred of evidence that backs that up—one that you can share with us today?"

That was when Will understood, better than anyone else in that room, that Jason Bell Purdy had him in a stranglehold. The senator was quietly gloating, like a schoolyard bully.

After an interminable silence, the attorney answered.

"Senator, I cannot share Colonel Marlowe's version of the events that day—because it was given to me in the course of attorney–client communication. And if I were to share that with you, which I earnestly wish I could, it would—as you and your legal staff well know—open up the door…it would entirely waive the attorney–client privilege as to everything else in this case. And that I am not prepared to do."

"So your answer is—you cannot give us one shred of evidence. Right? Is that right?"

"I'm afraid that's correct," Will said reluctantly.

He could see Purdy's game now, with crystal clarity. The Senator was asking the most damaging questions possible, couched deliberately in terms such that Will could not answer them without violating the agreement as to the scope of his testimony. Purdy was hoping that the lawyer's inability to answer the questions would create a deceptive impression that the Chacmool incident had been a military debacle, and that Colonel Marlowe was a military officer out of control—fueled by an administration's executive order permitting the indiscriminate killing of terrorists on an ad hoc basis.

"Now, Mr. Chambers," the chairman continued. "We have agreed to try to limit your testimony to the matters in the Article 32 hearing. And a record was made of that hearing, right?"

"Yes, a transcript was made of the testimony in that hearing."

"Do you have a copy of that transcript with you?"

"I do," Will responded, setting the thick set of papers in front of him.

One of Purdy's staffers, from behind him, quickly handed the chairman a copy also.

"Now, Mr. Chambers, we know that a near-tragic kidnapping of the Secretary of Commerce, Secretary Kilmer, took place down in the Yucatán. We're all very pleased—overjoyed—that his release was secured, and a few of the kidnappers were killed. And we can also thank the Mexican police—the federal police—and the Mexican government for their cooperation in assisting us in that successful operation.

"But then we have this Chacmool incident not long after. In another part of the Yucatán many, many miles away. Here's my question, Mr. Chambers. Is there one shred of evidence—one little, teeny-tiny piece of evidence of any kind, in this very thick hearing transcript, from any witness who testified—that shows that the men in that little house in Chacmool could be conclusively tied back to the kidnapping of Secretary Kilmer?"

Will saw the avenue of response closing before him. The senator was, again, asking questions he knew the attorney could not answer. The Department of Defense had required him not to go into any matters involving the kidnapping of the secretary. That had been deemed classified information, and he had been unable to solicit information even from his own client. Purdy had walked Will out on a gangplank. He now would begin sawing it off.

46

WILL WAS STRUGGLING TO EXPLAIN the DOD restrictions. "Senator Purdy, I think it would be useful if I explained the restrictions placed on the lawyers in the Article 32 hearing. Because of classified information—"

"Well now, Mr. Chambers, I'm very sorry that you can't answer. You don't seem to be responding to the questions that are being asked of you. Now please answer this question. Is there anything in this transcript of the Article 32 hearing—any shred of evidence at all—that anybody in that house in Chacmool had anything to do with the kidnapping of Secretary Kilmer?"

"As I was trying to explain, Senator, the Department of Defense imposed a gag order on all the attorneys in the Article 32 hearing. We were prohibited—"

"Mr. Chambers, you are not answering this question—"

"Senator Purdy, your question doesn't make any sense because it presumes this transcript—this Article 32 hearing—dealt in some way with what went on before the Chacmool shootings. But we were *prohibited* by the Department of Defense from going into the connection between Chacmool and the kidnapping of Secretary Kilmer because that connection was deemed to be classified information."

Will had managed to finally get it out, and on the record. But he wasn't at all confident it would make any difference. This subcommittee hearing, he was convinced, was not searching for truth. It was merely a platform for Senator Purdy to bluff, bellow, and grandstand.

"Mr. Chambers," the chairman continued with a smirk, "I will take that as an answer of *no* to my question."

Purdy then flipped to a page in the transcript, studied it for a second, and looked up and smiled. Then he continued.

"Tell us about BATCOM, Mr. Chambers."

"I'm sorry. Could you repeat that question?" Will asked.

"Certainly." Now the senator's voice had become slow, deliberate, and self-confident.

"Here is my question," he continued. "Would you tell this committee everything you know about BATCOM?"

Will thought for a few seconds. He knew the name. Back in Marlowe's case—where was the reference…who had mentioned it?

"The name is familiar. If you could be more specific…"

"I'll be glad to accommodate you, Mr. Chambers. Turn to page 179 of the transcript. This is the testimony of one of the members of Colonel Marlowe's unit. A combat soldier by the name of Thompson. Right there, in the course of his testimony, he gives the name of this small, select special operations unit that the colonel was leading as 'BATCOM.' My question is this—what can you tell this subcommittee about BATCOM? Because it's a military designation unknown to me. And I would imagine it's unknown to almost every other senator who has any responsibility in any of the military oversight committees. What is BATCOM, Mr. Chambers? Is this a specialized, covert, paramilitary assassination group?"

"I'm afraid I can't answer your question," Will responded. "I don't know what BATCOM is—or any of the details surrounding that designation. I only know that the information happened to slip out in the testimony of one witness. It probably should have been stricken from the record—"

"But it wasn't stricken. It was not," Purdy said, his voice rising. "It's right there in the record. And I believe that the United States Senate has the jurisdiction and the authority to demand answers about a new, experimental, controversial special operations group being formed. Don't you agree that the United States Senate—and the American people—ought to know about this?"

"That's a decision that this subcommittee, the Congress, and perhaps even the courts will ultimately have to iron out," Will answered. "That is not my decision to make."

"But I am right, am I not, in saying that your client, Colonel Caleb Marlowe, knows, perhaps better than any other potential witness, what BATCOM is—when it was created—who gave the order for its creation—and what its mission is. Am I not correct?"

"Senator, again you're asking me to reveal attorney–client communications. Which I cannot—and will not—do."

"Oh no," the senator said, raising his finger and wagging it in the direction of Will. "This is not privileged communication. This is a matter having to do with an answer given by a witness in the Article 32 hearing. The letter of understanding we sent to your office clearly indicates that any matter within the Article 32 hearing record was fair game for questioning. Now, I'm going to ask you again—in your opinion, what do you think Colonel Caleb Marlowe knows about BATCOM?"

"I'm not able to speculate about what my client's knowledge may be. And even if I were, I'd be speculating based on information he provided to me and inferences I have drawn from that information. That's attorney–client privileged—and I will not budge on that."

"Mr. Chambers, a little while ago I had to remind you about the power this body possesses, the power of contempt of Congress. I will not hesitate to use the authority vested in this deliberative body."

There was quiet for a few seconds. And then Will answered.

"Senator Purdy, respectfully, I understand the authority for contempt. And it does not intimidate me. And it does not change my mind. And you, of all people, should know I do not fear the possibility of contempt charges—as long as I am confident I am correct. And, Senator—I know that I am correct."

Purdy glared at the attorney, sizing up his resolve.

But Senator Jason Bell Purdy knew something about the lawyer from Monroeville, Virginia, that most of the audience, and all the other senators on the subcommittee, did not.

The more abusive he might become, the more fixed and intractable Will Chambers' devotion to his cause would become.

In the end, the senator knew he would gain no advantage by using the contempt powers of Congress against Will. Instead, Purdy would resort to the age-old strategy of a senator in a subcommittee—under the guise of asking a question, make a speech—and preferably one at the expense of the witness.

"Well, Mr. Chambers, this subcommittee will have to consider its awesome power of contempt—and whether we are going to use it in response to your defiance this morning. But until that day, let me conclude my questioning with this."

With that, Purdy took the papers in front of him, tapping them briskly on the surface in front of him to square the corners as he prepared his final volley.

"Your client—Colonel Caleb Marlowe—has been charged with war crimes by the International Criminal Court—the judicial arm of the UN—for the killings that took place in Chacmool, Mexico, is that correct?"

Will agreed. But he knew that this was not the chairman's real question.

"And do you think that the reputation of the United States of America—a reputation that has been so tarnished and torn abroad, among the nations of the world—our reputation, which, for reasons that go beyond the scope of this hearing, has been held in contempt by too many nations for too long—do you believe that the good will and the honor of America is well served—do you think that it will help our American citizens hold their heads high—when we realize that the International Criminal Court has charged one of our highly decorated military officers with unspeakable crimes of brutality and murder?"

As Purdy finished his remarks his voice had risen to such a level that it filled the subcommittee hearing room and caused the microphone to shriek with feedback for a moment. He was wagging his finger directly at Will Chambers.

The attorney gathered his thoughts for a moment and then attempted to answer.

"Senator, first let me say, I'm not quite sure how to answer your question," he began. But he paused slightly, and that was all Purdy needed.

"I'm sure you're not. I'm sure you don't know how to answer that question," Purdy bellowed. "But I'm sure the American people know how to answer it—I'm sure that the other members of this subcommittee know how to answer it. And as we investigate the murders that took place in that little village in Mexico—and the abuse resulting from an ill-conceived administration policy of allowing foreign assassinations—I believe that we, here in Congress, will have the courage to do a better job of policing the actions of our military forces in these secret, covert special operations attacks in otherwise peaceful nations like Mexico—attacks that look more like the shoot-'em-up at the OK

Corral than a restrained response in protection of our national interests."

The questioning then shifted to the ranking member of the subcommittee. He glanced over at Purdy, who avoided his look. The senator looked down for a second, then looked up at Will Chambers.

"Mr. Chairman, I'm sure that you did not mean to cut Mr. Chambers off in his answer to your question. I'm sure that was not your intent. So in the interest of fairness, perhaps I could offer our witness an opportunity to answer the question. Mr. Chambers, would you like an opportunity to finish your responses—if you have anything else to say?"

And so the attorney began his full response—arguing that Senator Purdy had committed the same mistake that flawed human nature is so prone to—he had already assumed Colonel Marlowe's guilt and had then wondered at the effect it might have on America's reputation around the world.

Will argued that the protection of our national honor—and fear of slander in the eyes of the world—should never justify a betrayal of our pursuit of justice, fairness, and truth.

The only alternative to that, he noted, would be to allow America to be blackmailed by international courts and global institutions whenever they might bring unfounded—and politically motivated—charges against our military officers, or even our political leaders and ordinary American citizens as well.

"Thank you for those exceptional remarks," the ranking senator said to Will after he had concluded.

But the reporters were no longer there to listen. The cameramen and the newspeople had already gathered up their notepads, laptops, and video cameras and had fled the hearing room en route to their deadlines.

As Will had been giving his response, Senator Purdy had already turned to his staff in the row behind him and was engaged in a conversation with them—giving all the appearance of being oblivious to the attorney's answer to his inflated question.

The photos in the next morning's newspapers, and the image clips of the television news services, would all display some version of Purdy's final question—complete with finger-wagging in the direction of a stone-faced Will Chambers.

47

THE MEETING WAS CONVENED IN the Situation Room at 10 A.M. sharp. In attendance was the Vice President of the United States, who chaired the meeting—along with Charles Keaton, White House Chief of Staff; John McCarthy, the Assistant Secretary of Defense; Chief White House Legal Counsel, Harold Birnbaum; and National Security Advisor Eloise Lorton.

The vice president seemed calm. But to those who knew him, he was clearly perturbed and anxious for answers. His hands were folded in front of him but his thumbs were opening and closing.

"How did we find ourselves in this kind of a position? That's really where I want to start," he asked. Then he turned to the chief of staff. "Charlie, as congressional liaison you normally keep a very tight rein on what's going on in your office. Why didn't your people see this thing coming?"

"Mr. Vice President, we had one small blip on the radar. My congressional people assured me this thing was never going to raise its head. We had spoken to Senator O'Brien's office directly, and he had given me the same assurance some time ago. That was the end of it. But you know, we cannot be put in the position where we have to run down every rabbit trail when a rumor starts forming. I really do believe, Mr. Vice President, that we ran this one down, found it was a dry hole, and that's where things were left."

"You see, this is the thing that baffles me," Assistant Secretary McCarthy noted. "O'Brien has always played ball. He has always been a team player. On budget matters, new military programs, defense spending—whatever the issue has been—from the Pentagon's standpoint, the senator has always been there when we needed him. So what's driving this? What's pushing this thing? Has anybody talked directly to Senator Purdy since his subcommittee hearing yesterday?"

"That's being handled as we speak," the vice president responded. "All right. Let's focus. How much damage was done yesterday in Purdy's subcommittee hearing, taking into consideration the coverage it had and some of the early op-eds we think are coming down? Charlie, I'm going to start with you."

The White House Chief of Staff, a short, gruff man, shifted slightly in his chair and laid both hands flat on the conference table.

"I really think this is about a five-point-five on the ten scale. And I believe that's about as bad as it's going to get, as long as we don't let it get away from us."

The vice president looked at Chief White House Legal Counsel Birnbaum and nodded at him.

"Well, we did a rush on the transcript of yesterday's testimony late last night," he said. "I looked at it myself. I had Bracken, the assistant legal counsel who testified, also look at it. I think there was a lot of bluster—but I don't think there were a lot of ballistics."

The vice president then directed his attention to the National Security Advisor.

"Ellie, you read the bullet points, the summary of the testimony?"

"That's right," Lorton said. "Harry is sending me a copy of the full testimony. I'll take a look at it. I mean, I trust your evaluation, Harry, from your standpoint. My main concern was how much it might have compromised our work on *the project*. I don't think it has. Of course, optimum is always no information, no inquiries—that all four corners of the project are sealed off. That's not always possible—but that's always the best-case scenario from a national security standpoint. Are we in jeopardy? No. Is it going to compromise the strategy? Probably not."

The chair recognized Secretary McCarthy again.

"The only thing that troubles me is the fact that somehow the transcript of that Article 32 hearing, in its unedited and unredacted form, got into the hands of Senator Purdy's office. That shouldn't have happened. And I will confess that I am talking to my folks at Quantico about that. I'm not quite sure why there was even a reference to BATCOM at all in that hearing. If we had given a clear directive to all counsel, both trial counsel and the defense should have avoided any reference to matters that preceded the Chacmool incident, as well as anything having to do with the configuration—or the identity, including the name—of the unit actually involved."

"We did look at that Article 32 testimony," Birnbaum noted, "and, Mr. Vice President, it was a bit of a quirk. Yes, there was a Defense Department directive that all that information the assistant secretary indicated would be confidential. It would be treated as classified and would not be referenced.

"Somehow, though, one of the special ops guys blurted it out on the stand—mentioned the name. That's really as far as it went. The problem lies in the fact that trial counsel, who should have known better, should have moved to redact that immediately. I think, probably for some strategic trial-lawyer reasons, he did not. Maybe the guy wanted to win a referral to a court-martial more than he wanted to follow a Defense Department directive—I don't know. But the point is, he didn't object. In fact, nobody raised an objection, and it got left in the transcript.

"But that's only part of it. Then when the transcript got shipped over to Capitol Hill at the request of Senator Purdy, someone should have flyspecked that thing carefully and removed the offending reference. So that's where we are."

"If I may," Chief of Staff Keaton said, receiving an approving nod from the chair, "what we are hearing, in any event, is that this is as much bang as there's going to be over this. This Senator Purdy, we are told, is about to implode."

"Implode?" Assistant Secretary McCarthy asked. "Let's hope it's not the other way around—the shrapnel from the other scenario would guillotine a whole lot of folks—and that would do a tremendous amount of damage. And now I'm talking about national-security damage. I'm talking about the physical safety of our most basic national and political institutions."

"All right, John—Charlie and I can talk a little bit more, between the two of us, on the political angle of this," the vice president said, "but I think the next thing that has to be addressed is the status of the International Criminal Court charges that were filed. Harry, why don't you take it?"

"Each of you has received a summary memo from my office on the nature of the charges, the background, and some of the legal issues we are addressing," Birnbaum explained. "And of course, ultimately, the decision—and we're talking with the Solicitor General's office about this—on the extent to which the United States government is going to formally participate in the proceedings. And in what way we would participate."

"Just one question that I've got," McCarthy spoke up again. "You do describe a little, in your memo, the status of Colonel Marlowe's legal representation. I'm concerned about that. Could you elaborate?"

"Certainly," Birnbaum said. "His chief legal counsel is the same attorney who represented him in the military tribunal—Will Chambers, a lawyer from Monroeville, Virginia. I've included some information on Mr. Chambers attached to my memo. He's also being assisted by Dr. Len Redgrove, a University of Virginia law professor. A little eccentric—quirky even—but a brilliant man. Certainly lines up with our view of things in terms of the supremacy conflict between the ICC and American law. I think, when it comes to the actual trial, this Will Chambers is the guy who's going to be doing the heavy lifting."

"So we've got a lawyer from a three-person law firm in—where was it—Monroeville, Virginia?" Keaton growled. "*This* is the guy who's going to be protecting the interests and the integrity of the United States government in the face of the first truly direct jurisdictional clash with the ICC? Excuse me while I up the dosage on my ulcer medication." And with that the chief of staff rolled his eyes.

"What about that, Harry?" the vice president asked. "Are we going to formally appear of counsel for Marlowe in this thing? Are we going to file an amicus brief? Are we going to intervene in some way?"

"We're looking into that. We're researching that," Birnbaum noted. "There are a number of complexities here. Unique. These are issues of first impression. We've been anticipating this kind of a challenge from the ICC for some time, but not exactly in this context. We were expecting a challenge in regard to some of our peacekeeping troops. Or a challenge to major combat decisions involving big troop movement—large combat attack—large loss of civilian life—that sort of thing. We really didn't think the prosecutor's office in the ICC would try to pick a small, covert operation involving four civilians—one of whom was a CIA agent. That did surprise us."

"Well, what about the involvement of the U.S. government in Marlowe's defense?" the vice president asked again. "What's the answer on that?"

"Well...we haven't resolved this yet," Birnbaum answered, hedging. "I'm getting the opinion from the Solicitor General's office. We're talking to the Attorney General. The State Department is weighing in. In fact, I've already been on the phone to the Office of Legal Counsel from State. They've had some contact with this Will Chambers on another case he has going, some civil-rights case against Sudan.

"But it's not an easy answer about our involvement. The reason is severalfold. First of all, Colonel Marlowe is no longer an active-duty officer with the United States Marine Corps. He resigned his commission immediately after the decision came down that the convening authority would not be referring his case to a court-martial. So the military charges against him were dismissed, and his resignation was pretty pro forma—you know that's the way it's done, so that it's completely res judicata, from the standpoint of American law, on the potential for further charges being brought. Now if he were an active-duty officer out there in the field, there's no question the United States government would see this as a case where the government was being directly attacked by the ICC. So—that's point number one.

"Point number two is, we have a unique legal relationship with Mexico. For reasons I can explain if you want—but are very, long, detailed, and historical—we do *not* have a status of forces agreement in force with Mexico. That would have limited, for all practical purposes, Mexico's ability to bring any charges, including referral to the ICC.

"And the third issue is really foreign relations—a little bit out of my bailiwick. But there are some unique factors in our relationship with Mexico—and the situation occurring down there."

The vice president nodded. "Thank you, Harry. That last point is correct. The president has asked me to be directly involved with the unstable terrain in our relationship, diplomatically, with Mexico. I'm working very closely with our person down there—Ambassador Hurtado, a good man—but I agree with Harry. It's a very troubling situation geopolitically. There's a lot at stake, and the question is whether or not we want to send a message to Mexico that the United States government is formally aligned against them in this ICC case. The other option is to intervene in the case, but not as a direct party—so we don't offend Mexico, maintain some neutrality, but ensure a just result for American interests."

"So, where do we stand on the legal defense issue for Colonel Marlowe? That's my main concern," McCarthy reiterated.

"For what it's worth," Keaton added, "you've sure got my concerns on that too. Myself, I would try to get to Colonel Marlowe and put together a dream team for him, under the radar."

"Monroeville," the vice president mused. "What do you think about Monroeville?"

The attendees at the meeting fell silent and looked curiously at the vice president, who continued.

"Harry—what's your feeling about this Will Chambers as defense counsel?"

"Well, we've looked at his background. He's a wild card, there's no question about that. Too much a maverick for a lot of people's taste. But he did an exemplary job in the Article 32 hearing. My assistant legal counsel, Larry Bracken, testified with him yesterday."

"So—what's your feeling?" the vice president pressed.

"I think of all the concerns we've got in this case, that's not one that's going to trouble me."

And then Birnbaum stated his own question.

"Just out of curiosity—why did you ask about Monroeville?"

"Oh, nothing, really," the vice president replied with a smile. "Just remembering my history. I think a bunch of the Founding Fathers came from Monroeville—and practiced law down there."

And after a pause, he added, "I think a few of them were mavericks—but they still rallied to the cause of the Union pretty well."

After another moment of reflection, the vice president went on. "All right. Let's move on to the next agenda item."

48

JACKI JOHNSON WALKED INTO WILL CHAMBERS' OFFICE displaying the front page of the morning paper.

Just below the fold, on the right side, was a picture of a glum-faced Will seated at the witness table—and across from that, on the left, was a photo of Senator Jason Bell Purdy, in an orchestrated moment of self-righteousness, wagging an accusing finger in the lawyer's direction.

The headline read,

U.S. ASSASSINATION SQUAD EXPOSED

Jacki smiled and pointed a manicured finger at Will's picture.

"You know, Will," she said, "what my mama would call that kind of a look? The look on your face in that photo?"

Will struggled to return a smile. "I suppose I'm going to hear this whether I like it or not," he said ruefully.

"My mama would say that's the look of a goose stewing in his own juice!"

Will shook his head. "The power of the press. At least the camera caught me in one of my brighter moments."

"So, media spin aside," Jacki went on, "and I hate to ask this, but I will anyway—do you think your testimony damaged your defense of Colonel Marlowe?"

"I'm not sure. I know that the people in The Hague at the ICC read the newspapers. Particularly the esteemed dailies out of Washington, DC."

"Well, and don't forget the New York papers," she said, brandishing the front page of the *New York Daily Tribune:*

PANEL PROBES USMC HIT MEN

blared the headline. The subheading read, "Senator Purdy Questions Assassination Policy of Soldier–Spies."

"The Marine Corps is going to be thrilled with that one," Will commented gloomily.

"Oh, by the way, Hilda gave me this runout that Dr. Redgrove just e-mailed. This is for you."

And with that Jacki handed him a ten-page document from his co-counsel and friend.

As his associate started to leave, she turned and tossed a final comment over her shoulder. "Keep marching, General. And keep your powder dry."

So Will buzzed Hilda and asked her to start working with his travel agency to check flight plans to The Hague. The International Criminal Court had set a date for a plea hearing for the following week. Will would be required to be present then, standing next to his client.

He also asked her to contact Tiny Heftland and put him on the alert that his help would be needed on the war-crimes case. Then after further reflection, the attorney buzzed Hilda again and also instructed her to have the travel agency check into an immediate flight for him down to Mexico. Will needed a chance to confer with his client before the court appearance overseas. Topping the list of his many questions would be a thorough inquiry into why Caleb Marlowe was back in Mexico—and why he had been arrested.

Will grabbed a cup of coffee in one hand and Len Redgrove's memo in the other and sat down on the couch in his office to start absorbing some of the history of the International Criminal Court.

In his research paper, Redgrove explained that the concept of an international criminal tribunal had been long in the making. The UN had created ad hoc war-crimes bodies to investigate and try offenses against humanity in Rwanda and the former Yugoslavia. But those proceedings had been limited to specific conflicts that occurred in specific nation–states. And in those cases, the nation–states that were victims of the atrocities had requested the assistance of the UN in manning a war-crimes judicial body to administer justice within their borders.

By contrast, the International Criminal Court was a free-standing, and permanent, judicial body. Its jurisdiction extended arguably around the world—even, under some circumstances, to nations, like the United States, that had neither ratified the enabling statute nor formally agreed to be bound by its terms.

However, in July of 2002 a sufficient number of nation–states had become signatories to the Rome Statute, and the ICC was created. President Bill Clinton, in the waning hours of his presidency, had signed his name in approval. President George W. Bush and an outraged Congress had quickly vacated America's consent. Then they had gone even further. Congress had passed a law authorizing the president to use military force, if necessary, to counteract any attempted intervention of the ICC into American military affairs overseas. President Bush had threatened to cease American participation in UN peacekeeping missions around the world unless United States military personnel received formal immunity from prosecution under the ICC. Clearly, the U.S. stood against the court.

But as Will discovered, while the nation of Mexico had not been one of the original signing parties to the Rome Statute, it had later ratified it—bringing Mexico within the direct jurisdiction of the ICC.

Deep in thought, Will let the memo fall to his lap. Then there was a knock at his door.

Hilda swept in and handed him a fax. At the top it had the seal of the ICC and the introductory paragraphs on the fax cover sheet were printed alternately in Dutch, French, Spanish, and English.

He flipped to the next page and saw an order, signed by the International Criminal Court, providing for the immediate extradition of Caleb Marlowe.

Will quickly fished through his file to locate the telephone number of the prison in Mexico City where Marlowe was being held. After connecting and wading through several jailers who spoke only broken English, he was connected to a federal police captain who was second in command for the jail. His English was good, but his information was disheartening.

"Señor Chambers," he reported nonchalantly, "your client—Mr. Caleb Marlowe, prisoner number X34T2—was transferred from this facility late last night. Mr. Marlowe, as an international war-crimes accused, is being transported to a detention facility in The Hague, Netherlands."

The attorney thanked the police captain and hung up the phone. Then he told Hilda not to bother with the flight to Mexico.

So, Will thought to himself, *this is it. The battle has been joined.*

49

WARREN MULLBURN PUSHED HIMSELF away from the Louis XIV desk and turned to the ornate table in this, his "small" study. He walked over to the floor-to-ceiling French doors that opened onto a third story balcony. Through the windows, he took in the view of the snow-capped Alps of Switzerland.

There was a discreet tap at his door. He gave the servants leave to enter, and a butler and serving maid brought in his lunch on a silver tray. They placed it on the table, bowed deferentially, and left.

Mullburn strolled over to the table, lifted the silver tray cover, and beheld his chef's creation for the day—a seafood salad, with fruits picked earlier that week on the island of Bali, and giant lobster caught off the tip of South Africa and flown in to his palace the day before. Also on the tray was a large china bowl of soup—a special bisque made from fresh tomatoes grown in the dry heat of Sicily.

Seating himself and spreading the linen-and-silk napkin across his lap, the billionaire pushed a button under the table, and a computer screen rose slowly from the tabletop. He pushed another button, and a panel retracted, displaying a keyboard with a smaller screen above it that showed a constant readout of oil prices in every market on the globe. Touching the keyboard, he booted up his link with a global geo-logical map. As he scrolled down on the screen, the map holographically displayed, in concentric array, areas in the world where petroleum explo-ration was underway—not only Mullburn's, but that of every competing enterprise. In fact, it displayed any kind of survey project with any oil potential at all, going on anywhere in the world.

Mullburn tapped the keyboard again, and a small subscreen popped up that read:

LAST ENTRY UPDATED 1.24 HOURS BEFORE DATA RETRIEVAL

The billionaire employed dozens of scientists and technology spotters who performed covert surveillance on each area of oil exploration in the world. Using his newly developed software, they would report back several times each day, updating his global screen—usually with satellite photography of production sites, confidential information on production volumes, and intelligence on contract negotiations and joint-venture agreements, both existing and in process, for each site.

The oil magnate paused, and then tapped the keys until the holographic globe spun slowly. He stopped the projection at North and South America and then zoomed in on the Mexico project. When he clicked on "view," an image of the offshore oil project gradually came into view. He tapped down for a closer look, and the image enlarged to a close-up on the deep-water drilling structure. Today, Warren Mullburn would spend the afternoon assessing each of his competitors' projects and then comparing them to the golden egg—Global Petroleum/Nuevo Petróleo Nacional de México—a subsidiary of New Century Oil.

He minimized his global survey map and brought up a small screen that said:

SOCIOLOGICAL AND GEOPOLITICAL FACTORS IMPACTING THE PROJECT—

- Senate Select Subcommittee on the American Response to Terrorism in Mexico/Chairman—Senator Jason Bell Purdy (first term—Georgia)

- Economic Summit of the Americas (date pending—was rescheduled)

- Federal Elections (National) within Mexico

- International Criminal Court—in Re: The Matter of Caleb Marlowe, Accused

He clicked on the International Criminal Court bullet point. A display of the specifics of the case appeared on the screen. He then clicked on the category "Defense Counsel."

The information flashed on his screen.

WILL CHAMBERS, ESQ./MONROEVILLE, VIRGINIA

Co-counsel: Dr. Len Redgrove, University of Virginia
Law School, Charlottesville, VA

Mullburn eyed the screen. Then, from his solid-silver spoon, he took a sip of the tomato bisque.

"Mr. Chambers," he muttered after he had swallowed, "you continue to be a fly in my soup."

50

It was late. The grandfather clock had chimed the quarter-hour several times since Will had climbed quietly out of bed and padded into the large front room with its high, timbered ceilings, exposed log walls, and massive stone fireplace. But he didn't bother to look at the time on the face of the clock. He knew it was now just a few hours before dawn would start showing up over the distant Blue Ridge Mountains. When the gray of first light would filter, dimly, through the windows of the big log house.

He and Fiona had had a good evening together. Because Will would be a flying to The Hague the next day, they had both left for home early—he from the office, and she from a meeting with her business agent about concert contracts.

At home Fiona cooked a magnificent beef Wellington. Then after dinner they watched some of the news on television, then took a stroll in the full moonlight along the path that wound its way through the woods toward the hills in back of their house.

They talked again about how God had brought them together—and laughed about their first awkward dinner together in Baltimore at Luigi's. The dinner had followed one of Fiona's concerts, where she had invited Will to listen backstage. He had often recalled this memory of her lilting, passionate voice—and how, even though separated from the thousands in the audience before her, Fiona had seemed to embrace them personally with a sense of warmth and authenticity. That was the first time she had come alive as a person to him—dazzled him.

On their walk through the woods, which were illuminated so brightly by the moon that the trees cast shadows, he recalled to his wife another concert—one that she had ended with an a cappella rendition of "Amazing Grace." He related how hearing her sing the words of that hymn—the idea of once being lost but then being found—had moved him in a way he had found surprising, even overwhelming. Fiona had never heard that story before—at least not about "Amazing Grace."

After their walk the two went to bed early because of Will's flight the next day.

But then something startled Will out of his sleep. In his mind there had been an attacker who was pursuing a woman. The woman had been walking calmly, not seeing her pursuer rushing at her from behind. It had not been Audra. He thought deeply about the meaning of the face of the woman in his dream. No, this time the nightmare had not been about his murdered first wife. This time the face of the woman had been very different.

This time, the woman had been Fiona.

Will had bolted up from bed so quickly that he didn't have time to catch his breath. Fiona was still sound asleep next to him, so he had walked quietly into the great room and sat down in the leather chair that looked out over their front acreage and the long driveway down the hill. He decided he would sit there and pray quietly, and wait for the dawn.

Then he felt a hand touch his left shoulder gently.

He turned and saw his wife's face, still sleepy, but concerned.

"What is it?" she asked, putting her hands on both of his shoulders.

"A dream. You were being pursued by someone. You were being threatened. So I woke up—and couldn't get back to sleep," Will explained. "I'm okay now. It's nothing, I guess."

Fiona brushed the hair back from his forehead and put her hands on both sides of his face.

"Talk to me. Tell me everything. Don't minimize this. Don't brush it aside."

"Okay. So—you know me pretty well by now. I try not to let my emotions rule my judgment. But I can't shake this feeling of fore-boding…this feeling there's some kind of catastrophe approaching. I can't pinpoint it. I can't even put a name to it. I don't know whether it's you…or us…or something beyond our marriage and our life together. It's just this feeling I can't shake. I'm sorry. I didn't want to wake you up."

She shook her head and smiled.

"You and I are split from the same atom," Fiona said. "Things that you're dealing with—they're important to me."

Will tried to cover up a big yawn, and they both laughed.

After a few minutes of chatting about his flight, whether he had packed everything, and when they would next connect by telephone, they both rose to go back to bed.

"You know, maybe you should move in with your father while I'm gone," Will suggested. "Just to be safe."

"Safe from what?" Fiona replied casually. "I'll be perfectly all right. Absolutely safe."

"It's just that…thinking about you alone in the house. I just don't feel real easy about that."

"And what about the trip you took down to Mexico?" she asked. "You didn't give it a second thought then. And I was fine. Please don't worry about me."

They slipped under the cool sheets of the feather bed. The darkness outside was now fading, giving way to a gray light. Fiona rolled over next to Will, tenderly wrapped her arms around him, and then kissed him sweetly and gently on the lips. The moment was fleeting, but perfect—the mingling of best friends, lovers, and kindred souls.

51

IT HAD BEEN SEVERAL DAYS SINCE the first session of subcommittee hearings chaired by Senator Jason Bell Purdy. Today, the subcommittee would reconvene. The senator had only one witness slated for the morning. He had recalled Major General Harlan Koeptke—Assistant Secretary of Defense for Special Projects. Koeptke had testified on the first day, but Purdy had recalled him to address a number of areas that he had delineated in a letter to the Department of Defense. The assistant secretary was seated, unmoving, at the witness table. His gaze, focused and intense, was fastened on Purdy.

Purdy had spent time questioning Koeptke on the basis of military budgets and then emphasizing—as he had on the first day of hearings—the fact that neither the Pentagon nor the Department of Defense had revealed any expenditures for the experimental BATCOM program.

"General Koeptke, I would ask you again," Purdy then said, "whether you find any disclosure of expenditures for the development of a BATCOM special operations military unit in this budget document?"

"Actually, I do, sir," Koeptke answered matter-of-factly.

Jack Hornby and a few other members of the press corps sat up a little straighter in their chairs.

Purdy parted his lips, but said nothing. His eyes were wide and unblinking. After a few seconds of reflection, he pressed on.

"Did you say, General Koeptke, that the BATCOM expenditure item is somehow reflected in this budget document?"

The witness nodded nonchalantly.

"Yes, Senator, that's exactly what I said."

"Well, first of all, General, let's make one thing clear. At your last testimony before this subcommittee, I referred you to your testimony before an oversight committee last October concerning the budget for special operations activities. Do you remember your testimony? I pointed out that, at page 146 of your testimony before the oversight committee, you had indicated there were no specific allocations in that budget for special operations activities involving the possible assassination of terrorist cell groups within the borders of friendly nation states. Do you recall that?"

The general nodded confidently.

"Yes, I certainly do."

"Well," the senator said, lifting both hands in the air dramatically, "I don't see how you can explain the contradiction. Are you telling us something different now from when you were in this hearing before the oversight committee?"

"No—not at all, sir."

There was a manufactured smirk on Purdy's face—but it hid the sinking feeling that things were not going his way—that his name-recognition voyage was heading for the reefs.

At this point, Senator Wayne O'Brien slipped into the back of the hearing room and seated himself in the last row. Purdy caught sight of him, and then quickly tried to refocus.

"Well then, General, maybe you can explain the mystery. How could an allocation for BATCOM both be in this budget—and not be in the budget—at the same time? Back in Georgia—my home state—folks would say that you're shucking shells with no peanuts inside."

There were a few titters from the audience.

Koeptke waited for the response to die down. After that he responded.

"Senator—over at the DOD the kind of shells we shuck, I assure you, are fully loaded. If you would direct your attention," he continued, "to page 79—line item 24. See the words 'Iron Point'?"

Purdy quickly leafed through the budget document and located the line the witness was referring to.

"Yes," he responded, "I see it. Now what's the point? What is that, General?"

"Well, Senator, I believe the answer should be apparent to you—because the letters S–A–P appear right next to the words 'Iron Point.' Do you see that, sir?"

Purdy nodded, but looked up with a slightly bewildered expression.
"Senator—are you familiar with an unacknowledged SAP?"

The Georgia politician now knew he had ventured into territory with which he was not intimately familiar. With all of the briefing and research made available to him by his staff, something had slipped through. He was heading for the rocks, and it was time to take a dramatic turn back to deep water.

"Well, General, let me go into something else—"

But the assistant secretary wouldn't let him go.

"Senator, I'm sorry for interrupting," Koeptke said, his voice now resounding, "but we have to straighten this out so the record is clear. You have implied that I may have changed my testimony about whether or not a special operations unit, referred to as BATCOM, was part of this budget document. Or that we, somehow, failed to adequately acknowledge the existence of this program to the oversight committee—an oversight committee, I don't need to remind you, that is *not this subcommittee*. So I think I should have a right to explain myself."

With that Purdy gave him a wave to proceed, but at the same time he looked back, furtively, to his staff for help.

But each of his staff members was stone-faced.

"So to continue," Koeptke said, "do you know what an unacknowledged SAP is, Senator?"

Purdy moved himself slowly toward the microphone.

"I really don't think it's appropriate for me to be answering the questions—I'm the one asking the questions in this hearing."

"Then let me assume that your answer is—that you don't know what it is. So let me give you a primer. An unacknowledged SAP is a special access program, which is, from a traditional budget standpoint, extra-documentational. It does not appear in the traditional budget documents. The reference here is to 'Iron Point.' That is an unclassified code reference to a program of which BATCOM was a part. Now there are further delineations—there are classified code names for the project, but those cannot be disclosed. 'Iron Point' was mentioned because it was designated for decision by the SAPOC. Now, Senator, are you familiar with the SAPOC?"

Purdy again cautiously approached the microphone and said, "Well, as I explained, I should be asking the questions—"

But the witness plowed ahead.

"Again, Senator, I will presume that you have no idea what it is. So let me tell you—it stands for Special Access Programs Oversight Committee. There are approximately 150 special access programs that involve what federal regulations refer to as a 'core secret'—the compromise of which could result in an 'unrecoverable failure.' In other words, it would undermine, directly, the military value of such a project if its details were made public."

"Right there, now, I see a problem," Purdy leaped in, hoping to recover some of the offensive in the session. "More than a hundred of these programs kept from the public eye—I see a real danger in that."

"The only danger," Koeptke countered, "is releasing the information about these sensitive programs so that our enemies—so that terrorists—so that those barbarians and thugs who mean to do us harm—could use that information against us. That's the only real threat, Senator."

"And yet—you still haven't answered my question," Purdy pointed out, struggling for some kind of control over the testimony. "You said that the expenditures for the BATCOM project were part of the budget. And yet all you've pointed to is a code word for the program. There are no allocation amounts—there's no evidence that this oversight committee was ever informed of the money that would be expended or the manner in which that money would be put to use—for possible assassinations around the world."

"Judging by your statements today, Senator," Koeptke replied, his posture now ramrod-straight in the chair, "perhaps it's time to explain something that will shed some light on why this particular subcommittee is—if I may be so blunt—starting to take on some of the characteristics of a misguided missile. Full of firepower, but liable to do damage to innocent parties—and never hit the target."

Purdy's face flushed with anger, and he was ready for a volley of political finger-pointing, but the witness beat him to the punch.

"So here it is, Senator. Here's the reason why this subcommittee—and your questions, I believe—are aimed at the wrong target."

Now Jack Hornby was leaning forward over the chair in front of him, madly scribbling in his notebook, his eyes fixed on the interchange. The reporter smelled blood. And he was going to sponge up all of it for his news service.

"Here is the bottom line, Senator," Koeptke continued, readying the final stroke. "Shortly after my testimony before the oversight committee, the Special Access Programs Oversight Committee met in secret session. Such a procedure is allowed by existing regulations—you may not realize that, but that is the fact. Under those provisions, at the direction of the Secretary of Defense, a full reporting to Congress may be waived by oral disclosure to the full SAPOC and the chairmen and ranking minority members of the four congressional oversight committees.

"That was exactly what was done in the situation involving BATCOM. You will not find it in the Congressional Record. You will not find it in the traditional research material that I'm sure your staff dutifully prepared for you. But those who are intimately involved in the process of overseeing military expenditures, and the development of military programs, know this procedure well. And they will tell you—as I've just told you—that this budget item was approved using that established secret procedure. The Secretary of Defense himself gave the verbal waiver and disclosure."

There were a few chuckles that broke out among the press corps as the full realization of Koeptke's disclosure sunk in.

Purdy stared blankly at the witness and tried to manage a smile, but was unsuccessful.

Koeptke had time for one final thrust.

"And also, Senator," he added, "I come from North Carolina. And down there we also have a saying. Senator, it looks like you've bought yourself a dog that won't hunt."

Now the laughter filled the hearing room. Purdy's face flushed, and he tried to regain his composure and his control over the hearing. But the laughter continued. Senator O'Brien stood up in the back of the room and caught the glance of his fellow Georgian. O'Brien narrowed his eyes, smiled slightly, and turned and left the hearing room.

The ranking member of the subcommittee turned to Senator Purdy.

"Senator, I hope you'll excuse me, but I have business in another hearing right now."

As the ranking member stood to leave, so did all of the other members of the subcommittee. After a few moments, Purdy was left alone before the microphone—in a Senate hearing room that was now alive with reporters jumping to their feet and exiting, members of the public laughing, and onlookers shaking their heads in disbelief.

Washington insiders were used to seeing politicians make mountains out of molehills. But this was the first time that they had ever seen a fledgling senator take a mountain and—after discovering it was actually a volcano—throw himself in.

In the corridor, Jack Hornby was already on his cell phone.

"All right, here's the headline," he said, and then paused for a second. Then he barked it out:

SENATE FLAP OVER BATCOM TURNS BATTY

52

ONCE WILL HAD SETTLED IN ON the international flight over to the Netherlands, he had a chance to review the rest of the research that Professor Redgrove had prepared for him on the International Criminal Court, and on the substantive criminal offenses with which Caleb Marlowe had been charged. Because the Court was still relatively new, it was clear that this case had the potential of cutting a pattern for cases yet to come.

On the flight over he could also prepare for his jail interview with Caleb Marlowe. Will was intimately acquainted with *some* of the facts of the Chacmool incident—but only those that his client had permitted him to know, and that the Department of Defense had not restricted as classified information.

Now it was time to begin unraveling the mystery. What was it about Caleb Marlowe's mission, and the nature of his military unit, that required such secrecy? And why had Marlowe traveled back to Mexico immediately after resigning his commission from the marines? To Will, it seemed too much like his client was engaged in a one-man vendetta.

Will had an aisle seat on the plane, with no one in the seat to his left. But there was a businessman in the window seat. He was a well-dressed, polite man with a vague, almost indistinguishable accent. He struck up conversation with Will from time to time, telling him he had guessed he was a lawyer. The man said he was a business representative for an international investment firm.

The attorney found the conversation to be a pleasant break from his work on the case. The gentleman shared that he made frequent trips from the EU countries to New York and Washington. Will noticed that he had a copy of *Roll Call*—the official Capitol Hill newspaper—

227

tucked under his copies of the *Wall Street Journal* and the *International Financial Times.*

"You follow American politics?" Will asked.

The man shrugged and laughed politely.

"In these days," he noted, "politics and economics are inseparable bedfellows."

His fellow passenger noted that he was married but had no children. He inquired a little into Will's background and seemed genuinely interested in Fiona, her singing career, her upcoming concert schedule, and their first year of marriage together.

Will closed off the conversation and went back to work. But his mind wandered. He thought of his dream about Fiona...the vague, undefined sense of danger.

And then there was his client. Marlowe's self-described "mission" might be nothing more than a bloody plan for revenge.

But even if that was the case—then would that make him much different from anyone else? Different, say, from Will himself?

He knew, after all, that he had pushed Damon Lynch further and further to the back of his mind. But the thought was still there— merely less articulated, perhaps.

Will still knew that, somewhere, he was privately—tenaciously— clinging to a sense of rage.

And it was being reserved for one man.

How does one forgive such a man? he wondered. Even though God surely commanded such forgiveness...there seemed to be no practical way for Will to ever achieve that. Or even, at best, get beyond the grudging acceptance that Damon Lynch's complicity in the brutality could not be undone or erased. So it must be left at that.

At least Marlowe's sense of revenge had some shade of official government sanction to it. So what was Will's justification?

The next time the attorney glanced at his watch he found that he had only another hour before landing.

When they landed, Will said goodbye to his fellow traveler and then caught a cab to his hotel. Checking in, he left a quick message for Fiona, letting her know that he had arrived safely and on time. Then he showered, shaved, changed, and hurried down to the lobby. From outside it he hailed a cab to the detention center where Caleb Marlowe was jailed.

It took an hour-and-a-half for Will to pass through the security system which was manned by guards in drab gray uniforms and black-brimmed hats. Eventually he was led to a small room with windows on three sides and seated at a table with two blond wooden chairs. After a few more minutes Caleb Marlowe, dressed in his street clothes and wearing a big grin, strode into the room.

Will extended his hand, but Caleb grabbed him and gave him a bear hug.

At first they caught up on small things—how Will had been doing since the last contact—then they moved into some of the preliminary research on the case and the thoughts that Redgrove and Will had about his defense. Marlowe also wanted to know, in great detail, what had transpired in Senator Purdy's subcommittee hearings. The colonel had only been able to get bits and pieces on the news.

The easiest decision attorney and client had to make was the nature of the plea Will would enter the next day before the pretrial chambers judge.

But after agreeing on a not-guilty plea and a demand for trial, Marlowe was vehement about another point, which made Will reel with shock.

"You've got to make a demand for the speediest trial possible," his client insisted. "I'm talking no more than a few weeks, maybe. If we can do it in less than that—even better," he said firmly, and then added, "And don't ask me why—I've got my reasons, and I can't share them with you yet."

"Caleb, that's not what we want," Will pleaded. "As much as I know about your case, there's a lot I still don't know. And we don't know the evidence they've got. I've got to obtain that in discovery. This is an incredibly complex case. I am strongly against a quick trial. You're really putting my back against the wall."

Marlowe nodded and said he appreciated Will's dilemma. But he wouldn't budge.

"I have the feeling," he continued, "that the other side is going to think that, if we want a quick trial, they'll be glad to accommodate us—because they figure they've got the jump on us. If they won't object, don't you think the court will give it to us?"

Will pressed in again, trying to convince his client that putting the trial on a fast track was a disastrous idea. He went over the preparation necessary for the case, the unresolved legal issues, the legal briefing for the court, as well as the political angle—he was still hoping for assistance from the Solicitor General's office or the Attorney General's office, as well as the State Department.

But Marlowe was utterly unmovable. Reluctantly, the attorney agreed to ask for a speedy trial. But inside he felt like he had just booked a quick passage on the *Titanic*.

Then he dug into one of the "mysteries" he had been thinking about. He asked his client—point-blank—what he had been doing in Mexico at the time of his arrest. Marlowe explained that he had been doing "unofficial reconnaissance." He wouldn't share any more details about what he meant by that, except to say he had hoped to obtain some information that would be helpful to the United States government in its ongoing war on terrorism. When Will tried to remind him of something a former colonel in the marines should not have needed to be reminded of—that he was a civilian now and no longer in the military—he gave a strange little smile.

"We all have our jobs to do for God and country," Marlowe said.

"So what was your job down there?" Will asked.

"I was trying to locate one of the linchpins in that whole Chacmool situation. He's an American drug dealer who has been a mediator between the Mexican government and the AAJ."

Will paused for a minute, and then, after retrieving a name from his memory, he put it to Marlowe.

"Are you talking about a guy by the name of Rusty Black?"

His client nodded.

"Yes—and he's got some other aliases—"

"Like Victor Viper?"

Marlowe nodded again, and then added, "Yeah—that one's really tacky, huh?"

"I know something about this guy."

"I know you do." The other man paused. And then he said, "That's why you're going to meet with him personally."

Will sat back, surprised, and studied his client.

"Oh? And what is it I'm supposed to find out from this creep?"

"I believe he knows who set me up at that Chacmool site. I have a very strong reason to believe there is an official in the Mexican government who worked with the AAJ. They were in on the kidnapping of Carlos and his family. This Mexican official would have known, in advance, about the kidnapping of Secretary Kilmer. And the AAJ would have led us right to that safe house."

"What was their motivation?"

"A number of things, I suppose," Marlowe continued. "But high on the list would be international embarrassment for the United States and a potential condemnation from other nations for our new experimental model in the war on terrorism."

"And what's the benefit for Mexico?"

"Our information is that the country is on the verge of an economic renaissance. Mexico believes it is on the brink of moving from the position of a third-rate nation plagued by an economy constantly in collapse, to the status of a nation that can demand global respect."

"What's going on down there—did they strike gold?"

"No, but close. They struck oil. Big time. They have tapped into some oil deposits, in deep water just off their coast, that promise to make Mexico the second Saudi Arabia."

Will thought for a moment about the implications of what Marlowe had said.

"So why does Mexico want to try the stick approach, rather than the carrot approach, in their relationship with the United States?"

"Oh, I'm not talking about Mexico as a nation. I'm talking about the small group of terrorists within the Mexican government. Perhaps only one person. But frankly, there are some who believe that, because of America's world dominance, the only way to deal with us is by embarrassing us, or by tarnishing our reputation in the eyes of the world community."

"So, you know where this Rusty Black is?"

"Yes, I did locate him. You don't think that the federal police really masterminded my arrest, do you?" his client noted with a smile. "I had heard that he was in jail somewhere in Mexico, and the rumors were that he was in the correctional center down in Mexico City. The best way to get the scoop on someone like that is from the inside out." And with that Marlowe gave a big grin.

"So you got yourself arrested?" Will asked.

"I knew that Mexico was thinking about charging me down there. I knew if they did, we wouldn't have much of a problem beating that case and getting the U.S. government to help in my defense. On the other hand, what I didn't count on was that Mexico would field the case to the ICC. Which is exactly what they did."

"Did you ever talk to this guy—this Rusty Black?"

"No, I never did. But I did verify that he's in jail, in the central correctional center down in Mexico City. He is finishing out a short sentence. He's due to be released any day. You need to get to him immediately before he disappears."

"And why should he talk to me? What's in it for him?"

Marlowe leaned back in his chair and eyed Will. It was a different kind of look this time, not just friendship, or camaraderie, or even respect. It was the expression of a man who knew he was sending a foot soldier on a mission, the implications of which could not be fully shared.

"Let me just say this. And I want you to hear me very clearly, Will. This mission—contacting Black and finding out from him as much as you can about the Mexican contact, who he is, what his position is in the Mexican government—this is more important than you can possibly imagine. It's not just about my case. It's also about getting my hands on the human slug who set me up to kill my best friend and his family. And then there's the mission goal—a threat I can't discuss with you right now. There may be a time when I can brief you in more detail. But contacting Rusty Black and getting the information on the Mexican official—that's going to give us an interdiction of something—something of catastrophic proportions."

"Interdiction?"

"There's something coming down the pipeline. Like a monster in the sewer system. Ready to crawl up into the city and start chewing flesh. You need to do this thing, not just as my lawyer—but as a loyal American."

"How am I supposed to know what I'm looking for or listening for? Unless you can give me some guidance..."

"Will, you're smart. You have a lot of background information about me, the Chacmool mission, and some international issues. I'm sure that when the time is right, the pieces will fall together. But you need to be careful. And you need to have your game face on. And no matter what happens, just promise you won't bail out on me."

"What are you talking about?" Will asked with some hesitation.

"When you're dealing with this Rusty Black guy, you need to remember two things."

The attorney waited expectantly.

"First, this guy's vicious. Very dangerous—not only because of what he can do, but because of what he knows, and his connections."

"And what's the second thing?" Will asked.

"Let me tell you straight," Marlowe said with a flinty look, "I think you're about to face the bogeyman, my friend."

And then, after a few seconds, he added, "So it's time to finally decide who's bigger and tougher—God, or the bogeyman?"

Will chuckled a little at that. He didn't want to take Marlowe seriously. But then the thought struck him. Perhaps the bogeyman wasn't just some American drug dealer. Maybe it was something monstrously darker...darker even than that.

53

THE PLEA HEARING BEFORE THE International Criminal Court was set for nine o'clock in the morning. Will arrived early and sat down in the sparsely furnished blond-wood-and-chrome courtroom. There were three armed bailiffs in their drab gray uniforms and brimmed caps—in three of the corners of the room. They stood politely, with their hands crossed in front of them. At the defense counsel table there was an earpiece resting to the right of the microphone. On the right-hand side of the courtroom, two interpreters were seated behind a large glass window.

Will's eyes surveyed the courtroom and finally came to rest on the blue United Nations emblem that was prominently displayed on the wall over the judge's bench.

Then the doors swung open in the back of the courtroom, and prosecutor Francine Les Forges entered, with a law clerk on each side. She proceeded directly over to Will and thrust her hand out in front of her.

Will rose, shook her hand, and introduced himself.

"Ms. Les Forges, has the U.S. State Department been in touch with you, or the Solicitor General's office?" he asked.

"Yes. Legal counsel for your State Department."

"Did they indicate to you whether the United States would be intervening formally in this case?"

"No. They were actually calling to ask me to suspend the indictment for a period of time. But I said no. I see no reason to stay prosecution of Colonel Marlowe."

"And your position on release of Colonel Marlowe from custody? Are you going to be arguing for continued detention pending trial?"

"Most certainly," she replied curtly. "This man is an international menace. He has global connections. The ability to travel from country to country at will. He could disappear easily if he is released from custody before trial."

"Try to see it our way," Will said. "Colonel Marlowe is going to be severely handicapped in his ability to assist me in his defense if he has to sit in your detention facility here at The Hague."

"You know," Les Forges replied with some level of amusement, "I always am entertained by those arguments. I've heard them before. So often. Defense lawyers say they need their clients released from prison to aid in their defense. And yet, all the defense work—you and I know this—takes place with defense counsel, and *your* investigators, and *your* legal research. The only thing you need your client for is to glean the facts—which you can do in the safety and comfort of our detention center. As you can see, I am not moved by your arguments. And I don't believe the Pretrial Chambers Judge will be either."

She excused herself, turned, and quickly unpacked her briefcase at the prosecution table.

Hans Junger, the permanent judge with the ICC who would take the plea, entered the courtroom. He was a light-haired, middle-aged man who spoke fluent English with a strong Norwegian accent.

"Ms. Les Forges," he began, "I know you speak English quite well—you are bilingual. And as I understand it, Mr. Chambers here, from the United States, represents Colonel Marlowe. So we can dispense with the interpreters and handle the plea hearing in English. Agreed?"

Les Forges and Will both nodded in agreement and indicated their approval on the record.

Judge Junger asked that the accused be brought into the courtroom. A few minutes later, Caleb Marlowe entered the room, in his street clothes, with his hands manacled and a guard on each side. Marlowe smiled confidently at Will and then sat down at the counsel table to his right.

Junger proceeded to read the lengthy criminal indictment, and each of the charges.

After that, Will strode over to the podium in the middle of the courtroom.

"And have you had an opportunity to consult with your client, Mr. Chambers?"

"I have," the attorney responded. "Your Honor, we are waiving the thirty days under Rule 62. We are prepared to enter a plea today."

"And what plea do you enter?" Judge Junger asked.

"The accused enters a not-guilty plea and demands a trial."

"Very well," Junger replied. "This case will be transferred to the trial chamber for the setting of a trial date. As Madame Les Forges knows, although I'm not sure if you're acquainted with the procedure," the judge said to Will, "the three-judge panel will be selected at random prior to trial. Therefore, I do not know who those judges will be. But you will be informed at the same time Ms. Les Forges is. Discovery matters can still be referred to the pretrial chamber if an issue arises regarding the production of information. Mr. Chambers, do you have any matters to record?"

"I do," Will responded. "I'd like to address the issue of the release of Colonel Marlowe pending trial. And I also would like to make a demand…" and with that, Will glanced over at Marlowe, whose eyes locked on his.

"I'd like to make a demand," he continued, "for a speedy and expedited trial. For a trial at the first possible opportunity."

Judge Junger glanced at the prosecutor, who rose to her feet and smiled. She took a moment to tap a painted nail on the tabletop, and then she responded.

"Your Honor, this is the first I have heard of this demand. I received no written motion in this regard. But I'm willing to waive the requirement of a written motion at this time. I would simply ask that Mr. Chambers follow up by filing his request in writing. But as to the merits…," she said, and gazed down for a moment—but then continued, "we would have no objection to a trial handled on an expedited basis. It has long been my practice, and Your Honor may appreciate this, that I prepare my cases before the first appearance. I don't work on my cases as they go along. Frankly, we are prepared now. We would like to see—as Mr. Chambers does—this matter handled expeditiously."

"Of course," the judge noted in a quiet voice, "I cannot vouch for the schedule of the trial chambers to be able to accommodate this request. But for what it's worth, we will pass it on. Both of you will be required to contact trial chambers with a mutually convenient date, and to try to confirm it with the clerk."

After some short reflection, Junger added, "Of course, Madame Les Forges, you will need—if you are to have an expedited trial—to immediately disclose all of your evidence discovery to Mr. Chambers—"

"Already prepared," she responded in a chipper, rapid-fire reply. "We have a complete copy of all our discovery—several boxes—in my office, ready to be picked up by Mr. Chambers today. As well as a set for his co-counsel. We can comply with Rule 66 forthwith."

Junger nodded with satifaction.

"Now, Mr. Chambers," the judge continued, "as to your motion for release of the accused pending trial, this tribunal will hear your arguments on that."

As Will began his presentation, a man in a tan raincoat in the back of the courtroom rose and left. He walked quickly through the corridor, down the stairs, through security, and out onto the street. On the sidewalk he glanced at a parked limousine approximately half a block away and gestured toward it. The limo pulled up to the curb, and the man got in the backseat. Seated in the back of the limo was Will's fellow passenger on the flight to The Hague. He pushed a button, and a sliding glass divider sealed off the passenger compartment from the chauffeur.

"Not guilty. They want an expedited trial," the man said to the passenger in the limo. "Chambers is asking for release of the accused on bail."

"Very good," the other man said. "Now go back in and monitor the rest of the hearing."

The man in the tan raincoat exited the car and headed back toward the courthouse.

The limo passenger took out his cell phone and made a call to Bern, Switzerland.

At the other end Warren Mullburn picked up his private direct line.

"We're monitoring the hearing right now. Our information is that Marlowe stands little chance of being released before trial. They are asking for an expedited trial schedule."

"And how was your flight over?"

"Rewarding," the man replied. "I met an American attorney. Will Chambers. He lives in Virginia, has a beautiful wife. She is a Christian singing and recording artist. We had a delightful chat."

"Yes. It is interesting, the people you run into on international flights. Small world," Mullburn replied facetiously.

"The American government has not weighed in yet as to whether or not they'll be intervening in this case with a formal appearance. Mr. Chambers was in court alone."

"Now, as to the expedited trial issue," the billionaire mused, "that does not exactly comport with the strategy I've got for our project. I need more time for the United States to twist in the wind—more world criticism—while oil prices go up."

"I'm sure," the other man said, "that a delay can be arranged."

"Oh?"

"Yes. Unfortunate, really. Another family tragedy for attorney Chambers. I'm sure it will result in a delay of the trial date. It is sad that Mr. Chambers doesn't seem to be able to keep a wife."

"On the other hand," Mullburn said blandly, "no one said that life is fair. It's not like a chess game with fixed rules. For the mass of mankind it just means they have to learn to absorb the endless blows to the head. The stake to the heart."

Upon further reflection, he added one final thought.

"But when you can make the rules, then it is different—then you can drive the stake."

And at that, he chuckled a bit.

54

ANNOUNCEMENTS WERE DRONING OVER the loudspeaker and echoing throughout the airport building. But Will wasn't paying any attention. As he slouched into the fake-leather upholstery at the airplane gate, he was feeling weary—down to his soul. After a quick flight over to The Hague to interview Marlowe, enter an appearance, and argue motions for bail and an expedited trial, he was now ready to take in another flight—this time to Mexico City. He had had only two short phone conversations with Fiona, trying to update her in the small snatches of time he had. She had given him her love, said she was fine, and assured him that he need not worry about her.

What Will really wanted to do was to close his eyes and take a nap. He had an hour before they would start boarding his flight on Aeroméxico. But he couldn't do that. He needed to call Len Redgrove and connect with him on strategy—and update the law professor on what had transpired at Marlowe's hearing before the ICC magistrate.

He caught Redgrove in his office as he was preparing for a lecture to some foreign dignitaries visiting the University of Virginia.

"Len, I know you don't have a lot of time," Will began, "so let me give you the headlines. Marlowe is insisting—for reasons that are very murky—that he receive the quickest and most expedited trial possible. Which is insane, given the fact that this is a war-crimes trial. I tried to talk him out of it. He was absolutely unmovable. Like a rock. Which, of course, is oh-so-untypical for him."

Redgrove saw the humor in that and laughed heartily at the other end.

"So," Will continued, "I argued for the expedited trial. Not surprisingly, the prosecutor—a French lawyer by the name of Francine Les

Forges—didn't object. We went down to the trial chambers and consulted with the clerk there. He actually set a preliminary date for the commencement of trial eighteen days from now—*eighteen days!*" Will's voice was so loud and agitated that a few other travelers, reading or gazing off into space around him, began staring.

"Yes, that's a very bad situation," the professor responded, trying to quickly sort it out in his mind. "I know that you've already gone through the Article 32 hearing in the military proceeding, but still—eighteen days is nearly impossible. You wanted me to start preparing some motions and doing the research on the jurisdictional objections and a motion to dismiss."

"Well, can you get them done on a compressed timescale?" Will asked hopefully.

"I think…" Redgrove's voice trailed off as he considered his options. "I think I'm going to have to call my editor and tell him I need an extension for my book deadline. That's not going to be a pleasant conversation. I'm not going to be able to do this round-the-clock and still keep up with my writing project. Listen, don't worry. We'll get it done. But what is it that's driving Marlowe on this expedited trial? I don't get it."

"Neither do I—at least, not entirely. Although I think that he expects an acquittal. He expects to be released. And there's something in the works. He's still acting and talking like he's on a mission—I get the feeling that he wants to get back to Mexico to mop up the terrorists down there. He promises he's going to make some of this clear to me later on. But like you, I'm very much in the dark."

"Speaking of getting out of jail—how did you do on your motion to get him released from detention?"

"Well, at the same time we were arguing for an expedited trial I was also shooting myself in the foot for my argument for bail release. The judge took the position that because we were likely to get a quick trial, the burden of keeping Marlow in prison pending the trial itself was going to be less than the typical case. Furthermore, he was concerned about Marlowe's international connections and his ability to disappear instantaneously. So, all of that goaded the judge to deny our motion for release. My client's going to sit in the detention center in The Hague until trial."

"So where does that leave you?" Redgrove asked.

"I'm sitting here in the airport, waiting to take off for Mexico City."

"What's up? Factual investigation?"

"Look, Len, call me paranoid. But I don't want to go into a lot of details on a cell phone. Let's just say that I have an appointment to interview someone whom Marlowe gave me as a possible lead. To help us prove that the incident at Chacmool was a setup orchestrated by a combination of foreign terrorists and federal nationals within the government down there."

"You be careful. This sounds risky."

"Yes, that's what Marlowe told me. I have a very uneasy feeling about this. I can't put my finger on it. Call it a premonition…"

"Why don't you send your private investigator down there? What's his name…Heftland? I know from your other cases that Mr. Heftland knows how to take care of himself. He has a military and police background, doesn't he?"

"Yes. But I've got another job for him to do, so he's going to be out of circulation. Besides, if this person is as important as Marlowe believes he is, he may be the link to our entire factual defense before the ICC."

"Got to go," Redgrove said. "May God be with you. Be careful, my friend."

Will rubbed his eyes and then yawned. He pulled a legal pad out of his notebook on which he had begun listing some of the questions that were going to be critical for Rusty Black to answer. He was still uncertain whether the interview would even take place. He had asked Jacki, back at his office, to make the arrangements with the federal police in Mexico City. But he had wondered why Black—who was serving a short sentence for theft—would even give him the time of day. However, when Jacki had contacted the jailers, and they, in turn, had spoken with Black about the interview, he had apparently agreed.

Why an American drug dealer would be interested in talking with someone else's lawyer about issues that were totally unrelated to his own case was something Will couldn't yet understand.

Before continuing with his interview questions for Rusty Black, he dialed one more number—for Tiny Heftland's cell phone. The big private investigator was bench-pressing in the gym when the ringer went off.

"Hey, Will boy," Tiny said, out of breath, "you caught me pumping iron."

"In other words," the lawyer retorted with a chuckle, "you're lifting triple cheeseburgers in each hand?"

"Ow—a blow to the heart. But listen up, law boy, I'm down another ten pounds over the last six weeks."

"Seriously, I'm proud of you, Tiny," Will said. "I should talk. It seems like I'm on a permanent diet of airport fast-food, lack of sleep, and too much coffee. This Marlowe case is driving me crazy."

"Well, the big doctor is here to help. What do you want me to do?"

"Are you still licensed to carry a concealed weapon?"

"That's an intriguing way to start off our discussion. The answer is yes. Now it's my turn to ask a question. What kind of trouble have you gotten yourself into this time?"

"I need your help between now and the time of trial for this war crimes case, which is now only about eighteen days away. But it's going to take all your time. Can you prioritize this?"

"Hey, Will—who are you talking to here? Of course I can."

"Can you get to a land-line phone in the next twenty minutes or so?"

"Yep."

"Okay. My flight is going to start boarding in about an hour. I'm going to get off my cell phone and call you from a pay phone here. You want me to call you at your apartment?"

"Sure," Tiny replied. "It's only about ten minutes from here. I was almost through with my routine anyway."

"Fine. I'll give you all the details of what I want you to do in about fifteen minutes."

As Will turned off his cell phone, put it in his coat pocket, and stood to stretch at the airplane gate, an observer who was looking over books at a nearby newspaper stand turned and began walking quickly in the opposite direction. He left the terminal and, once outside, quickly punched a number on his cell phone to Bern, Switzerland.

Warren Mullburn was in the middle of a meeting with several of his advisors when a call came in on his private line. He excused himself and turned to take it.

"The lawyer's on his way to an international flight."

"Where to?" Mullburn asked.

"Mexico City."

"Fine," he replied, and then hung up.

He turned to his three consultants and resumed the conversation. "All right, continue."

One of the men went back to his notes.

"As I was saying, Mr. Mullburn, OPEC will be announcing their temporary embargo of oil exports to the United States at noon tomorrow. The information they are going to relay to the United States—through diplomatic channels—is that the OPEC nations have grave concerns on three fronts. First, they accuse the United States of breaking its promises regarding postwar Iraq. Secondly, the reports of an attempted, but failed, American-backed effort to topple the current regime in Iran are now hitting the international press. A wire service article is going to break today in *L'Agence Presse Française*. And Iran, backed by Syria and Egypt, is applying tremendous pressure on the OPEC nations—particularly those in the Middle East—to shut down oil exports to the United States as punishment. And thirdly, there is the ongoing concern over American sympathies for Israel, and their failure to condemn some of Israel's recent aggression against Syria, Egypt, and Jordan. So that's the formal diplomatic explanation that's going to be given."

One of the other consultants raised a finger.

"Mr. Mullburn, we also need to decide, perhaps as early as today, about what we are going to tell OPEC about having the Mexico project join their cartel."

"Run the clock on that," Mullburn snapped. "Delay. Keep them at bay. But keep them thinking we're interested in becoming full partners in OPEC."

The third advisor jumped in.

"Mr. Mullburn, if I may. I do have some concern about our ability to keep this information confidential—I mean about the full scope of the Mexico discovery. The fact that your joint venture is going to be one of the world leaders in oil production."

"Oh, I'm not worried," the oil magnate said with a smile. "I understand that the rumors are already surfacing. We've had flyover surveillance of our project. I know that. Let the gossip begin. Let them wonder. Let the speculation take flight and soar."

The three consultants nodded. And then one spoke up.

"Just let us know when you want to start working on a public relations campaign. The fact that we can soon start pumping eight-and-one-half million barrels per day—exceeding even Saudi Arabia—is going to rock the world. Until then, you can count on us—of course—to keep this information absolutely confidential and secure."

"Oh, I don't worry about that," the billionaire said, smiling. "I know that you gentlemen will honor my request for complete secrecy."

And as he rose to dismiss the three, he added his closing comment.

"Because—if you breach our little understanding—I would have all of your eyes plucked out, and your families tortured."

The three of them broke into a nervous titter, but the laughter quickly subsided as they noted the lack of expression on Mullburn's face.

They knew him well enough to know that no comment of his was ever idle. And no threat should ever be dismissed.

55

THERE WAS AN UNCOMFORTABLE PAUSE in the three-way telephone conversation between Chief White House Legal Counsel Birnbaum, the Deputy Solicitor General, and the Chief Counsel for the Secretary of State.

"I know this is a sensitive issue—very touchy and very volatile—but I think we have to bring it up. What's the president's approach going to be on implementing the American Serviceman's Protection Act?" the State Department counsel asked.

There was another pregnant pause, and Birnbaum cleared his throat. Then he started in.

"Okay. Let's address the ASPA. I think..." he cleared his throat again. "I think the president is of the mind *not* to use the full authority he has under the ASPA. At least not yet."

"In other words, what you're telling us is, the president is not going to send troops into The Hague to shoot up the prison and effect the rescue of Colonel Marlowe?" the Deputy Solicitor General said sardonically.

"Let me assure both of you," Birnbaum continued, "that the president believes that he has the authority to do exactly that under the specific provisions of the American Serviceman's Protection Act. The language is very clear in the supplemental appropriations bill that was signed into law in August 2002. And we believe that it provides the president with all the authority he needs to, and I quote from the language of the act, 'free any citizen of the U.S....being held' by the ICC in The Hague. The language is clear. Direct. And unambiguous."

"But of course, there are national political and geopolitical problems he has to deal with in using that authority," the State Department legal counsel said.

"Exactly," Birnbaum replied.

"How about the president's authority under the ASPA for a less drastic remedy? The Act also provides that the United States may withdraw military assistance from Mexico because of their participation in the ICC."

"Well, let me just tell you State's position on that," the legal counsel from the State Department said. "There's been a political sea change down there. First, there's the protest Mexico made back in 2003 over our executing three Mexican citizens convicted of murder. But then there's the fact that the Independent Revolutionary Party may well beat the sitting president in the next election. And they are vehemently anti-American. They don't care about military assistance from the United States. As a matter of fact, they want to kick all our DEA agents out."

"Not only that," Birnbaum added, "but there's also the whole oil bonanza issue down there."

"Oil bonanza?" the Deputy Solicitor General asked.

"Well, let me put it to you this way," the White House counsel continued. "Our intelligence has substantiated a massive deep-water oil discovery off the shore of Mexico. Our neighbor to the south is about to become the second Saudi Arabia. And I'm sure each of you received the briefing memo yesterday, indicating how this case might be impacted by the OPEC oil embargo. The American public is going to freak. And here we have a potential oil partner in Mexico, one who could rescue us, in terms of oil supply, over the next few years. So, just exactly how hostile are we going to get against Mexico over one United States Marine Corps colonel?"

"Well, that's more than a rhetorical question," the Deputy Solicitor General noted. "Do we want to sacrifice our potential oil-trading relationship with Mexico over one American colonel who is on trial for war crimes because he was hunting down terrorists—terrorists, I might add, that tried to kidnap our Secretary of Commerce? I didn't hear anybody venture an answer on how that equation is going to play out."

There was another pause in the conference call. Finally, Birnbaum broke the silence.

"My friends, I just give legal advice to the president. That is both the limitation, and the consolation, of my job. Ultimately, this may be a matter for the president—and the president alone—to decide."

The three government lawyers had all heard the same thing, though it was never said in so many words. As the diplomats, the lawyers, and the bureaucrats scrambled to make the best of a difficult situation, the granite-hard reality of politics—with its inexorable gravitational force—would ultimately take over.

And when that happened, despite all the head-shaking, regretting, and lamenting, the irresistible temptation would be to find the ultimate political antidote.

A sacrificial lamb. Perhaps even one that used to wear a uniform.

56

WILL ARRIVED AT THE MEXICO CITY airport on time. He was still confused as to exactly what his mission in interviewing Rusty Black was supposed to be. Of course he knew what Marlowe had told him—that he was to interrogate Black to find out the identity of the Mexican official who had helped orchestrate the AAJ trap that had been set for Marlowe and his unit at Chacmool. But what could his client have possibly meant by his reference to the "bogeyman"?

The attorney was traveling light, and had only one small piece of carry-on luggage in addition to his briefcase. As he scurried through the airport, a man with dark glasses, a Panama hat, and a white short-sleeved shirt strode up to him quickly—so quickly that Will was taken aback, and eyed him cautiously as he approached.

"Mr. Chambers," the man in the hat and sunglasses began, "I'm a friend. I've got a car waiting for you. We've cleared the way for your interview at the federal correction center."

"Who are you?" Will asked, taking a step back.

"I'm here to help you and Colonel Marlowe."

"Actually, I appreciate your help, but I don't think I need it. I've already made arrangements for the interview..."

"Sure you did," the man said, stone-faced. "And the Mexican jailers were prepared to make sure that you never connected with Rusty Black. And they were also prepared to make sure you had a nasty accident. Now, you can trust me—or you can not trust me. But if I were you, I'd be looking for a friendly face down here in the midst of unfriendly territory."

"How do I know I can trust you?" Will took a step toward the man and peering into his sunglasses.

The man took off his sunglasses, beads of sweat collected under his eyes in the Mexican heat. The din of the airport, of passengers retrieving their baggage, of announcements overhead, all faded into the background when Will heard what he had to say next.

"Will," he said calmly, "I'm here to make sure you don't miss your appointment with the bogeyman."

Will's eyes widened and he took a step back. He stared at the man, clearly an American and—as Will then surmised—an agent with the United States government.

"I suppose it would be stupid of me to ask for some identification…"

The man smiled. "Yes, real stupid."

The two walked out of the airport together to where the man had a cab waiting.

"This guy's going to be your cabbie. Don't use any other taxi drivers except him. Do you understand?"

The attorney nodded.

"Will, he's going to take you over to the de la Gruta hotel. You're going to have to stay there for forty-eight hours. I'm sure you've got some things to do on your case. Then he will pick you up at 8:30 sharp on the morning of the day after that and take you over to the correctional facility. He will give you the name of the jailer to ask for. You will ask for that jailer—and nobody else—when you present yourself at the prison. Do you understand everything I've told you?"

Will acknowledged that he had.

The man opened the door of the dark blue taxicab and motioned for his companion to step in.

After he had closed the door behind Will, the man stuck his head through the window and gave him one last piece of advice.

"Will, stay focused. Keep on task. And watch your back."

The cab jolted forward, picking up speed rapidly, and exiting the airport so fast that Will was thrown from one side of the seat to the other, as the driver made abrupt turns, accelerating as he went. Finally, the car came to a stop sign. The driver, a Mexican man, slowly turned around to face Will. He smiled, showing several missing teeth, and began to laugh.

Suddenly, the attorney realized he knew this man. It was Pancho, his taxicab driver down in the Yucatán during his investigation of Marlowe's case before the Article 32 hearing.

"I suppose you're flabbergasted to see old Pancho again? I'm glad to be of service…"

Will was astonished at Pancho's sudden fluency in English, and then he chuckled to himself as he realized the obvious—Pancho had been assigned to keep an eye on him during his first trip to Mexico. And he had been assigned to Will again—on this trip as well.

After about an hour the cab pulled up in front of a drab hotel on the outskirts of Mexico City. There were a few palm trees outside. The hotel was a four-story affair, and when Will checked in, he would discover it had few amenities—and terrible service. But then, as he finally concluded, this was not a hotel that was in the business of making money—not exactly. Most of the persons checking in and out were English-speaking businessmen—nondescript—who spoke confidently and casually, but kept their distance. No families. No married couples. No tourists. The "bellhop" who escorted him up to his room was a thick-necked man in his thirties…who looked more like a bodyguard than a hotel staffer.

As the attorney was about to close the door to his room, the man told him, "I'll be outside your door, in the hall. Keeping an eye out on things. If you need anything just talk to me."

As Will closed the door, then locked and bolted it, it was now very clear—he had been recruited for a task that transcended any legal case—or any jailhouse interview he had ever performed.

He quickly telephoned Fiona and caught her as she was leaving to visit her father.

"I'm aching for you," she said mournfully on the other end. "This bed is so big and so empty without you."

Will smiled and then replied, "You save up all those kisses for me— because I'm going to need them when I finally get home."

He decided not to share with his wife his dawning realization that he had suddenly been thrust into the role of a covert operative—on a mission whose breadth and scope was still unknown, but with implications and dangers he could only imagine. Besides, he wasn't totally convinced the telephone was secure. And he didn't want to use his cell phone.

They exchanged a few tender words, and then Fiona said she had to get going.

"I'm making dinner for Da tonight. You know how he's just been feeling so tired lately. Well, I'm going to go over and cheer him up!"

"Be careful," he urged her.

After assuring each other of their undying love, they hung up. Will worked for a while, plowing through the first pile of evidentiary discovery he had picked up at Les Forges' office before heading to the airport.

It had been organized, indexed, and summarized by the prosecutor's office. The report from the Mexican federal police who had investigated the shootings also had attached to it a word-for-word translation into English, provided by Les Forges' office.

It was very apparent to the attorney that the prosecutor was making every effort to comply with the discovery demands made necessary by an expedited trial. It was also clear that she could not be accused of delaying or obstructing his access to the evidence they planned to present at trial.

After a while his eyes started closing involuntarily out of exhaustion.

He stacked the file on the desk, got himself ready, and turned out the lights as he climbed into the sagging metal-framed bed.

Out on the street below, he heard the sound of music and of sirens off in the distance. Someone was yelling down in the street.

As the sirens wailed in the streets of the city that housed ten million people, Will sank into a deep, almost medicated, sleep.

The next morning he woke and ordered room service. It took an hour for his breakfast to arrive—a lackluster affair with fruit that was fairly fresh, but a rubbery egg and orange juice that was room temperature. The only thing that was truly good was the dark coffee. At least it was hot.

He spent the day taking notes on the hundreds of pages of discovery documents from Les Forges. He made one phone call to his office to check in with Hilda, as well as with Jacki. He was hoping that the State Department had called and left a message that the United States government would be formally joining his defense of Colonel Marlowe. But according to both of them, no such call had come in.

The attorney lost track of time as he immersed himself, first in finishing a review of all of the Mexican police reports, then in a review of a forty-page report by a Dr. Michael Zagblundt. Zagblundt was clearly going to be used as an expert witness by the prosecution. He was a retired army colonel, a former instructor at the War College, and an expert in international military affairs. His conclusion at the end of the report was devastating.

> It is clear, based on my review of the evidence in this case, that the death of the four individuals at Chacmool, Mexico, was so clearly excessive in relation to any military advantage Colonel Marlowe could have anticipated, that Colonel Marlowe's conduct satisfied element number two of the "War Crime of Excessive Incidental Death to Civilians" under Article 8(2) (b)(iv) of the International Criminal Code.

As Will settled down for his second night of sleep in the indifferently serviced hotel, he was feeling overwhelmed by the immensity of the case against his client. And he wondered how he was going to be ready for trial in just over two weeks.

The next morning, Will woke and dressed for his jail interview with Rusty Black. Before he was able to load up his briefcase, there was a loud pounding on the door.

He opened up. It was Pancho, his missing teeth displayed in a broad smile, and the "bellhop" standing behind him.

He followed them down to a waiting taxicab. Pancho climbed into the front, and the hotel man climbed into the back with Will. There was little conversation as they drove an hour and twenty minutes through snarled Mexico City traffic down to the federal correctional center.

The building was an ugly cement-block edifice, three stories high. Pancho handed Will a slip of paper. The name on it read "Juan Vila."

"Ask for that jailer—only that jailer," he said with a smile.

The man sitting next to Will thrust out a thick hand and gave Will a bone-crushing handshake, then added, "Good luck."

Will slipped out of the taxicab, dodging fast-moving traffic, and entered the main lobby of the jail.

He asked for Juan Vila and was told to have a seat. He waited in the lobby for about half-an-hour before a brown-uniformed Mexican jailer greeted him. He followed the man down the corridor, down a stairwell two flights, to a cell in the basement unit.

The jailer brought Will up to the cell. The attorney peered through the barred window and saw a man with shaven head, sitting on the edge of his bunk and smoking a cigarette. He had on a sleeveless T-shirt, with jeans and black boots. Muscular and heavily built, he was a little shorter than Will, and as he was smoking his head was bobbing, as if he were listening to an inaudible tune from somewhere else. The eyes in his stubbly, unshaved face were staring at the cement floor.

The jailer unlocked the door and swung it open, waving for the visitor to enter. Will walked into the cell and jumped slightly as the metal door slammed behind him and he heard it lock.

The man on the bunk took a deep drag on his cigarette and then slowly exhaled as he lifted his head and stared at his visitor.

Will had never met this man before...at least he didn't think so. But there was a cold, animal look to his eyes. And something vague...some connection. But he couldn't even begin to describe it. He sat down on the bunk across from him.

The prisoner sucked on his cigarette and exhaled slowly again. Then he spoke.

"Okay. Let's get this on. Let's go. This is your show..."

THE EVENING THAT FIONA HAD spent with her father, Angus Mac-
Cameron, had been warm and nostalgic. She had traveled to Angus's
sparse little apartment between DC proper and Georgetown and had
spent the evening making supper for him and catching up on things.

Angus's health—after the heart attack and stroke—kept Fiona in
constant contact with him. She called him every other day and would
visit him once, sometimes twice a week. Since the death of her mother,
Helen, Fiona had tried to tailor her concert tours around the need to
be close to her widowed father—and, of course, to be close to Will as
well.

After dinner and the dishes, she played a few songs for Angus on
his out-of-tune piano and sang one of his favorite ballads, "Dark
Island," in her lilting, ethereal voice.

Then her father, leaning on his cane, made his way over to the
closet and, after a few minutes of fishing and hunting through odds
and ends, produced an old scrapbook of photographs.

The two of them sat down on the couch together and laughed, and
teared up, over the family album. Particularly when it came to pictures
of the two of them with Helen—who had died of cancer several years
before.

Angus talked a little about how his archaeological magazine was
doing now that he had designated a younger man to take over as editor
and publisher. He was still keeping busy, however. He had requests
now and then to speak at churches and conferences on issues of Bible
prophecy.

And, at his daughter's urging, Angus had been working on the
rough draft of a book based on his trial on charges of defamation
against fellow Bible scholar Dr. Albert Reichstad—the case in which

he had first met a lawyer by the name of Will Chambers, the man who had successfully defended him.

The two of them reminisced a little about their first meetings with Will. The searching but agnostic former ACLU lawyer had seemed so skeptical of Angus's claims about the resurrection of Christ and the fraudulent nature of Reichstad's claimed proof of the nonresurrection of Jesus. As they talked, Angus grew quiet, and then he turned to his daughter.

"You know that young man is like a son to me," he said with a catch in this throat. "What a revolutionary change has taken place in him since he gave his heart to the Lord Jesus Christ!"

Fiona updated her father with a little of what she knew about the Caleb Marlowe case. Angus—forever the student of current events and a Bible scholar with the big picture of life—asked for detail after detail about the case that would soon be tried before the international court. He would listen carefully to each response from his daughter, adding only short replies like "amazing...unbelievable...incredible."

When Fiona had exhausted everything she knew about the case, her father said thoughtfully, "Fiona, dear, I love the way your husband has a love for God and a dedication for justice." But then he added something that took her by surprise.

Angus gazed off in the distance somewhere and after a moment looked back at his daughter.

"I do believe, some day, that Will Chambers will stand trial, himself, before the principalities and powers of this world...like the apostle Paul before King Agrippa."

Fiona gave him a puzzled look. Over the years she had become accustomed to his obscure, sometimes even eccentric, comments. But that remark, even for Angus, was over the top.

She took his hands and gently asked him, "Da, what do you mean by that?"

But her father looked tired. He turned to look at her with a puzzled expression, as if he had forgotten what he had said. *Perhaps it was his stroke...a loss of memory,* Fiona thought. She kissed him good night and drove home.

At the house, finishing up the details of the night, she followed her usual routine. She checked all the doors to make sure they were locked and secure. She set the alarm system. And she walked into her bedroom, washed up, brushed her hair. Then she climbed into the big bed…a bed that, without Will, seemed more empty than ever that night.

Reaching over to the nightstand, she took some lotion and rubbed it on her hands. Then she folded them in front of her, closed her eyes, and prayed for Will's safety. For justice to be done in his case before the ICC. For their marriage. She also prayed that the two of them might soon be able to start a family. Very soon.

Glancing over at the photo of the two of them on the opposite nightstand, she said a quiet good night to her husband's picture and then turned out the lights.

She did not see the man walking up along the winding driveway that led to their log home on the hill—nor could she have—because he was dressed all in black. He stopped behind one of the large, spreading trees, took out a pen flashlight, and flashed it inside the black bag he was carrying, double-checking his equipment. The cutting tools, screwdrivers, needle-nosed pliers. And then he removed and fingered a large, tempered-steel knife with a serrated edge. Placing it back in the bag, he closed it and continued walking up toward the house where Fiona had just turned off the light.

58

IN THE MEXICAN JAIL, WILL BEGAN LOGICALLY, methodically describing the fact that he represented Colonel Marlowe. That he wanted to get to the bottom of what had happened at Chacmool, Mexico. He described a little about the military operation—Marlowe's involvement—and the charges now pending against his client. Then he indicated to the prisoner that he needed to find out everything he knew about the incident and the involvement of any Mexican officials in setting up the trap for the colonel and his unit.

The man's head continued bobbing slightly as the attorney spoke. And when he finished, the prisoner flicked his cigarette to the floor and crushed it with his black boot.

As he stretched and straightened his back, Will caught sight of the tattoo on the left side of his neck. A black eagle.

"So, Mr. Black, I need to get this information from you, and I need to get it today. What can you tell me?"

The man tilted his head slightly and stared at Will for a few seconds with a blank look. Then he began giggling. He giggled, then laughed, staring up at the ceiling and shaking his head back and forth.

"What's so funny?" Will asked, his irritation growing.

"Oh man, oh man, this is something...you are really something else," the prisoner said, sitting up straight in the bunk with a hand on each knee and his feet spread in front of him.

"What are you talking about?" Will asked, starting to flush with anger.

"You—you I'm talking about!" he said. "You're talking about all this stuff—your client—your law case—what kind of a man are you? Are you a man? Or are you a little girl?"

Now Will was incensed.

"Is your name Rusty Black? Were you told that I was going to be coming to interview you?"

"Oh, yeah. That's right. I'm Rusty Black," he said, giggling some more. "That, and a lot more. Oh, yeah. A lot more…what's the matter with you?" the man asked, pointing both of his index fingers at the lawyer's face.

"There's something I'm missing here," Will said, standing up but not knowing why.

Suddenly, Black leaned back on his bunk and stroked his shaven head. Studying his face more closely, Will saw that his nose was bent, obviously broken in the past. The man was smiling and showing his stained teeth as he continued to laugh and just shake his head at his questioner. Finally he stopped laughing. And then he spoke.

"Oh, man. I think I see…I get it now. Chambers, Will Chambers, lawyer. Doesn't get it. And nobody told you. You jerk!" he laughed again. "You really don't know who I am, do you?"

As the man leaned forward on the bunk, he pulled his T-shirt down slightly to scratch his neck. As he did, more of the black eagle tattoo on the left side of his neck was displayed. It caught Will's attention, and he looked at it more closely. The black eagle—it was a symbol he had seen somewhere. Documentary film perhaps. A historical symbol…of hatred…where had he seen it?

Then he remembered. It was the same eagle that had stood atop the Reichstag building during the reign of the Nazis in Germany.

As Black continued to scratch his neck, tugging slightly at his T-shirt, the attorney could see more of the tattoo. He looked at it in horror. A sense of nausea, dread, and fury rose up—an electric convergence of emotion that flashed through his brain and clouded his reasoning.

Now there was only visceral, blind reaction. Will stood and stared. Then he shot his hand, unthinking, toward the man, grabbed his T-shirt, and yanked it down even farther. There, at the base of the eagle tattoo—there it was.

A Nazi swastika.

Black jumped to his feet, slapping Will's hand away, and began screaming profanities at him.

But Will was numb. It was all starting to make sense—it was all beginning to become clear…in its irrational, horrifying reality.

"So...now you understand. Yes, I'm Rusty Black. And a lot of other names. Like Victor Viper. You know that one?" he asked, pushing at Will's chest and knocking him back slightly.

"And I'm also a lot of other people..." he said, shoving the other man back again.

"You know my name. Don't you?" he demanded, pushing Will a third time, this time down onto the bunk.

"Say my name. Say it!" he yelled.

Will jumped to his feet so he was only inches away from the man's face. But he wouldn't say the name...he couldn't say it.

"So, let me make this short. Sweet. So even a stupid lawyer like you can understand...I'll give you a statement. I'll give you any statement you want about this Chacmool incident. And believe me, I can name names. And I know exactly who it was in the government who was playing ball with the AAJ to set up Marlowe and his military goons. I know it all. And I'll tell it to you on one condition..."

Will was struggling to understand...to comprehend how he could be conversing with this animal in the jail cell. The man with the Nazi tattoo. Will didn't want to admit who he was. And yet he knew—he knew the awful truth.

"I'll give you the statement," the prisoner continued. "My sentence is almost up, and you've got to promise me that, when I'm done, I'm walking out of here. No calls to the cops. No calls to the FBI. I disappear into the night. You call the cops on me and they nab me here for what happened up there in Georgetown, and I give you no statement. Nothing."

The man was standing nose to nose with the lawyer, waiting for his reply.

Finally, Will uttered the name. A name he didn't think he could speak aloud. But he said it.

"You're Damon Lynch, aren't you?" he asked almost inaudibly.

"Hey, you guessed right, moron," Lynch sneered. "I'm the guy who was there. I'm the guy who was watching when your wife—what was her name—Audra Chambers—that's it. I was there when she got it. I know exactly *how* she got it. I know what she said when she was pleading for her life. I know it all because I was there."

And then he started to giggle again. Will stepped closer to him and the man took a step back.

"So we got a deal or what?" Lynch asked. "Hey, gutless—you leave your tongue in the briefcase on the floor there? You gonna talk or what?"

Every sinew and muscle in Will's body was tensed. He felt as if his brain was on fire.

"I don't deal with scum like you," he said through gritted teeth. "Not now, not ever."

Will grabbed his briefcase and headed to the metal door of the cell. Then he turned to Damon Lynch, who was standing with his mouth open and a serious look on his face.

"And now I'm going to walk out of this cell, and I'm going to call the authorities. And they're going to drag you up to a jail cell in the United States. And I'm going to make sure you get tried for murder. And I'm going to make sure you get the death penalty."

"Wow, suddenly you grow a spine, Mr. Moron!" Lynch jeered as he followed Will to the door and shoved him from behind.

"You wanna to know what happened right at the end?" Lynch taunted in a whining, tittering voice. "You wanna know what we did to your precious wife before we killed her? You wanna know how we did it—and how she screamed when we were doing it?"

Something clicked. Like a switch. In one motion, Will dropped his briefcase and whirled around.

His fist flew in an arc into Lynch's face, connecting with his nose in a crunch that sent the man spinning in a half-circle against the wall of the cell. He tried to maintain his balance, but slowly collapsed like a rag doll to the floor, leaving a bloody smear on the cement surface. He was bleeding from his nose and mouth, his eyes were unfocused, and he was trying to hang on to consciousness, reaching out weakly in a directionless attempt to grab onto something.

Will leaped on Lynch and wrapped two hands around the other man's throat. He struggled weakly, trying to fight back, but Will began pressing on his voice box, and as he closed his hands around Lynch's throat, he felt the cartilage of the airway begin to collapse. The other man was starting to lose consciousness again, and he was no longer able to gasp for air. Will tightened his grip—and as he did, he stared at the Nazi tattoo on the neck of the man who had helped to torture and murder Audra.

And as he continued to squeeze, he closed his eyes...not caring, not thinking.

59

THE MAN IN BLACK CLOTHING, WITH the little bag, was at a side window of the log house on Generals' Hill. Quickly retrieving a small pair of cutters, he cut through the alarm system telephone wire. Then he moved rapidly over to another side window, pulled out some tape, and covered the entire pane. With a small hammer he tapped the window. The tape kept the broken glass in place. He removed the shards carefully, without a sound. After reaching through, unlatching the window, and raising the sash, he climbed into the kitchen. He had left his bag on the outside of the house, taking only one thing with him.

The military-style knife with the long stiff blade and serrated edge. Such a weapon was capable of gutting a human being in a matter of seconds.

The scene would be violent—messy—with an excess of blood. He would have to be careful not to leave any DNA—no footprints, no evidence. But he did want to leave plenty of gore. That was the point.

He knew that Will Chambers would have to see the photographs—the lawyer would insist on that—and he would see his precious bride slaughtered—disfigured.

In rubber-soled shoes, the intruder deftly stepped through the kitchen, through the great room toward the bedroom. Fiona had tossed and turned for a while. But now she was asleep. She was breathing easily.

The man had the military knife in his right hand.

With his other hand he reached out and turned the doorknob. The door swung open quietly, gently. He saw Fiona in bed, sleeping on her side with her back to him.

Just a few more seconds now.

"Stop right there, slime bag!"

The intruder whirled around.

Tiny Heftland was poised near the front door, revolver in both hands, pointing it at the man's chest.

He froze for a second, considering his options, and then he sprinted, like a leopard in the night, out of the great room, through the kitchen, and dove through the open window.

Tiny bolted through the front door, down the steps, and around the side of the house.

As the detective rounded the corner of the house at full charge, the other was waiting for him. With a pistol from his bag, he fired two shots.

The first missed, but the second caught Tiny in his left bicep.

But the detective needed only one shot. Pointing at the intruder's chest, he squeezed the trigger. The bullet tore into the man's heart, dropping him immediately.

Tiny stumbled over and made sure the attacker was dead.

Then he heard Fiona screaming. Grabbing his arm, he made his way to the porch, where she was standing in her robe, steadying herself on the railing.

"What...oh, please, Tiny...what's going on?" she cried.

But then she saw that his left arm was bleeding. She took him inside and grabbing some towels, wrapped a pressure bandage around his arm.

"Fiona, you'd better call the police. Tell them an intruder's been killed by a licensed private investigator. Tell them the investigator is waiting here for them and that the area appears to be secure—and no other shooters are involved."

Fiona's hand was trembling so much, her mind so shocked that she hit 4-1-1 instead of 9-1-1. An information operator answered. She hung up, pushed her hair back, took a deep breath, and then punched 9-1-1.

She dutifully relayed all of the information, as Tiny had told her. And then she added one more thing.

"And make sure you bring an ambulance. A man has been injured. A very good man."

60

THE JAILERS WERE RUNNING DOWN THE corridor toward Damon Lynch's cell.

Will was at the barred window of the metal door, yelling for the them to come immediately.

They unlocked the door and swung it open.

The attorney pointed at Damon Lynch's body slumped on the floor.

"Your prisoner—he's having a hard time breathing."

The two jailers glanced down at Lynch and then looked at Will suspiciously. Slumped against the wall, Lynch was slowly raising his head with one hand stanching the blood from his nose, with the other rubbing his neck, choking and coughing.

"Stop him...he tried to choke me...tried to kill me," he croaked.

Will pushed his way past the two jailers and then said, "Excuse me, I have a plane to catch."

As the attorney walked away, Damon Lynch was struggling to his feet. And then the yelling began.

"You punk...you wimp...that was nothing but a sucker punch... come back here and try that again...you really blew it, man, blew it big-time. You'll be so sorry. You're a dead man!"

Lynch's hoarse, screamed threats were reverberating down the corridor as Will walked grimly, stone-faced, toward the stairwell and out of the building.

Pancho was waiting half a block away, and he quickly pulled his blue taxicab up when he saw the lawyer. The other man was still seated in the back.

"Get me to the airport," Will said in a low voice.

Pancho turned around and smiled, but his smile faded as he studied his passenger's expression.

The man next to Will leaned over.

"How did it go? Did you get the information? Have you got it set up?"

Will didn't turn to look at him, but stared out the window of the cab as it threaded its way through the jammed traffic of Mexico City. It was hot—actually sweltering—but Will didn't feel the heat. He didn't care about where he was or where he was going.

There was only one thing that he did care about right now.

He fished his cell phone out of his briefcase and dialed the number to connect with the Washington, DC, police department.

"Is Captain Jenkins in?" he asked.

The man sitting next to him in the taxicab breathed in heavily and shook his head. Whatever hopes he and his agency had had for the retrieval of information from Damon Lynch, aka Rusty Black, now appeared to be dashed.

The agent knew, as did Pancho, the other intelligence operative, that they could simply wait for the drug dealer's release from the Mexican jail, kidnap him, and secretly remove him to the United States for interrogation. But that would take days, even weeks. And Lynch would play games, legal and otherwise, before releasing any valuable data. Even then, coercive interrogation techniques might not retrieve information that was reliable.

They had pinned their hopes on Will cutting a deal—offering not to report Lynch to the authorities for his involvement in Audra's murder—in return for a full statement about the Mexican connection to the Chacmool incident, hopefully in the context of a sworn deposition. In the small scope of things, that would assist Colonel Marlowe in his defense before the ICC—and on the big scale, it would provide substantial information about a potentially catastrophic threat.

But as Will's fellow passenger watched the lawyer on his cell phone, waiting to talk to Captain Jenkins—and ready to announce Damon Lynch's location and availability for extradition to the U.S. on murder charges in the District of Columbia—he knew that Plan A was definitely collapsing.

"Mr. Chambers?" The special assistant to Captain Jenkins came on the line. "I'm sorry to keep you holding. The captain is out in the field. I don't expect him back for the rest of the day. Is there a message I can give him?"

Will fell silent and considered his options. Then he replied, "No. I'll get ahold of him later myself."

He clicked off the phone. Then he noticed that the man in the backseat was staring at him.

"Sorry," Will said. And that was all he said.

"Which airline?" Pancho asked over his shoulder as he was driving.

"Just get me to the airport," the attorney answered. "I'm going to find the quickest flight I can back to Dulles airport, and to my home. And my wife."

The occupants of the taxicab were all quiet until they pulled up to the terminal. Before Will climbed out, the man in the backseat reached out a big hand, thrust it into Will's, and squeezed hard.

"Just remember something, Will. It's not too late. We can still turn this thing around—if you're willing to play ball with us." Then he handed him a white card. It bore only one item—a telephone number with an international exchange for Mexico City.

"Only one thing, Will. If you ever call this number, in order that I know it's you and that you're in a safe environment when you're speaking—secure surroundings—you've got to use a word, the code word. And I don't want you to share this with anybody. Not your wife. Nobody."

Will fingered the card in his hand.

"Why should I keep this? Tell me why I ought to get this code word from you. Why should I have anything to do with you people?"

"Because," the man said quietly, "there are lives at stake in this. Something really bad is being planned. That's all I can tell you. Something evil is going to come down unless you keep working with us."

Will had the door open and was halfway out, mulling over what the agent had just told him.

"Okay," he said, putting the card in his top pocket, "what's the code word?"

"Coral."

"That's all?"

The man nodded.

Will slid out of the taxicab, closed the door, and then hurried into the building to try to find the quickest flight back to the Washington, DC.

As he disappeared into the busy terminal Pancho and his passenger looked at each other, but said nothing. Now, all they could do was wait.

61

WILL WAS DRIVING HOME FROM DULLES airport, having made an urgent call to Len Redgrove, when his cell phone flashed a reminder that he had three messages.

He cut short the conversation—they had covered as much as they could. The issue, as Will had explained to his friend, was his dilemma involving Damon Lynch. There was no question that Lynch would be crucial to Marlowe's defense—but Will simply couldn't continue representing the colonel under those circumstances. He would not compromise his desire to have the man charged, convicted, and punished for Audra's death. The drug dealer had wanted to cut a deal allowing him to give a statement and then disappear. That the attorney was not willing to do.

"Bottom line, Len," Will had said to Redgrove, "is that you're going to have to handle the defense of Marlowe yourself. I will sit down with you and go over everything I have done up to now. But you're going to have to do this without me. I am withdrawing as Marlowe's attorney."

His friend and co-counsel told him he certainly understood and said he felt candidly that his younger colleague would be irreplaceable.

Then Will accessed the messages that had popped up on his screen. All three were from Fiona. She didn't explain anything, but said there was an emergency and he needed to come home immediately. The first call sounded frantic—it sounded as if she were crying. The second message was calmer, as was the third.

Chilled, he called her immediately.

"Fiona, dear, I'm about twenty minutes from home. I don't want to wait. Tell me right now what happened."

"An intruder. A man. He got into the house."

"Dear God!" Will whispered.

"Tiny was here. He chased him out. There were some shots fired. Tiny got hit, but he's all right. The other man was killed. The sheriff's department has already been here a couple times. They're taking Tiny in for questioning. He's very calm about the whole thing. His arm is going to be all right. I just praise God that you asked him to stand guard. But why didn't you tell me you had him on surveillance? And that you had given him a key to the house?"

"I guess I should have. I thought about it as I was heading over to The Hague. I really don't know how to explain it. I just had this fear. I know who we're dealing with…and I know I don't think I could live if anything happened to you."

Fiona started crying softly and told him she loved him.

"Honestly, darling, I had Tiny watch over you as a precaution. Because there was a risk…even though I thought it was a slight risk Mullburn would try to do something. But I never really believed…I somehow couldn't believe it would really happen."

Will's voice tightened as he began to choke back tears.

He raced home. Parking his car right at the door, he forgot to turn off the ignition before he took his foot off the clutch, and the car lurched forward, killing the engine. Not bothering to pull out the keys, he ran into the house. He and Fiona embraced—and stayed locked together for a long time.

The sheriff's department arrived again shortly afterwards and took statements from both of them. They assured Will that the investigation into Tiny was a formality, and that he would be restored to normal status.

Will and Fiona spent that day, and the next, within inches of each other's side. Will said he didn't want to talk much about what had happened down in Mexico but would discuss it with her later. He was just glad she was safe. Then he started telling her that he was feeling it was perhaps time to get out of law practice. That handling cases involving threats to his family was just more than he could tolerate. He loved his wife too much to sacrifice her for *any* case—no matter what the stakes, no matter what the issues.

Fiona was a willing listener, but offered little comment in reaction to her husband. She just shared with him how violated she felt to have had an intruder in the house—and how frightening it was to feel so vulnerable.

They both took the next day off from work and spent it together. In the early afternoon, after a quiet lunch, Will asked Fiona if she wanted to take a walk. The two of them strolled up into the surrounding foothills of the Blue Ridge Mountains. When they got to a high point—in a clearing they would often pick as a hiking destination, they turned around and looked northeast at the vista of mountains off in the distance. There was a mild breeze blowing, so Fiona took out her baseball cap, swept her hair under it, and placed it firmly on her head. She was quiet, waiting for her husband. She knew he had something he had to tell her.

He began describing his meeting with Caleb Marlowe. And the hearing, and the flight over to Mexico City. And his interview with the man he thought was Rusty Black…and how he had turned out to be one of the specters in the nightmare that had been haunting Will since Audra's murder.

And then he walked Fiona through his reaction—his physical attack on Lynch. And how, with that single blow, he had made an irrevocable decision that he would not be using the man as a source of information to help his client's defense. And how his withdrawal as legal counsel for Marlowe was now a foregone conclusion.

When her husband had finished talking, Fiona slipped her arm around his waist and put her head on his chest. The two said nothing for several minutes.

Then she looked up and asked Will a question.

"Have you connected yet with Captain Jenkins? Have you told him that you've located Damon Lynch?"

He shook his head.

"No, I tried to call him down in Mexico, but he was out in the field on some investigation. He's probably back in the office by now. But I didn't want to try to get ahold of him again until you and I had a chance to discuss this."

Fiona turned to him, not saying anything at first. Then she spoke.

"This has to be done the right way," she said thoughtfully. "We need to pray about it. But you've got to make this more than just a decision about a legal case."

"What do you mean?" Will said, grasping at her meaning.

"Audra. Damon Lynch. You and me," she said. "Your ability to let God take the chains off—the chains of the past. Maybe this is the decisive moment for you. For both of us..."

After a pause and some further deliberation, Fiona offered a suggestion.

"Will, I want to suggest something to you. Let's go over and talk to my Da about this."

"Any particular reason?"

She shook her head. "I can't tell you exactly. I just think we need to get his wisdom on this."

That night they drove to Angus's apartment and surprised him for dinner. He was overjoyed to see both of them at one time. He hugged his daughter, getting tears in his wrinkled eyes, and told her how shocked he was about the attempted attack.

As Fiona was fixing dinner Will sat down with Angus in the living room and discussed the background of Marlowe's case, Damon Lynch's connection to Audra's brutal murder, and his own moral and spiritual dilemma—over withdrawing from defending Marlowe in the ICC trial, in light of the fact he could not honor his client's wishes to cut a deal with Lynch in exchange for information.

The elderly man asked several probing questions but listened quietly through most of Will's explanation.

Fiona was busy setting the table for the mutton stew she had prepared. After scratching his chin, Angus threw a smile at Will, who asked him what he was thinking.

His father-in-law broke his uncharacteristic silence.

"Will, my boy, I was actually thinking about Romans chapter twelve, verses nineteen to twenty-one. Lately, I've gone back to read it."

Will chuckled. That was just like Angus—a walking Bible.

"Okay, what's the connection?"

Then the elderly preacher recited the passage from memory:

> Beloved, do not avenge yourselves, but rather give place to wrath: for it is written, *"Vengeance is Mine, I will repay,"* says the Lord. Therefore, *"If your enemy is hungry, feed him; If he is thirsty, give him a drink; For in so doing you will heap coals of fire on his head."* Do not be overcome by evil, but overcome evil with good.

After a few moments of reflection, Will asked, "So let me ask again—what's the connection? I'm supposed to forgive this animal? I'm supposed to let him walk absolutely free, when he was there, participating in Audra's murder? Is that what you would do if that intruder had gotten to Fiona?"

Angus shook his head.

"No, my boy, I'm not saying that. But I'm saying that any right *decision* has to start from a *heart* that's right before the Lord. And if your heart's going to be right before the Lord, you need to lay down any thought, any motivation of personal vengeance. And then you need to ask yourself one important question—how can I overcome evil with good?"

"And what if I were to tell you," Will responded quietly, "that I just don't know what the answer is to that question. Nor am I sure I even want to ask it."

"That would make you an honest man. Which is one of the reasons I like you," Angus said, reaching out and patting his son-in-law's shoulder.

"When you said Romans chapter twelve," Will began again, "I thought you were going to go to verse one. That's the one I know. You know—'present your bodies a living sacrifice, holy, acceptable to God...'"

"Yes, that's a great verse. But it's all related. It's all connected, you know."

"What do you mean?"

"Sacrifice—forgiveness. Those two eternal principles are closely related."

After a moment of reflection, Will asked, "You mean Christ dying for us—his forgiveness for our sins?"

"Yes," Angus replied. "But it's part of God's eternal way of dealing with things. There can be no forgiveness unless there's a sacrifice. And the need for a sacrifice comes because there's sin in the world."

And then Angus leveled his gaze at Will, looking him in the eye.

"Forgiveness of this Damon Lynch doesn't require that he *not* suffer the punishment for his dastardly, terrible deeds. But it does require a right attitude—and a sacrifice. You were the person wronged. You are the only person who can make the sacrifice. I can't do it—and your precious wife, Fiona, can't do it either. There is something you need to lay on the altar—once and for all. And only you can do it."

Then Fiona called them to the table. Will was quiet and contemplative throughout the dinner and on the drive home.

"Thanks for suggesting that I talk to your dad," he finally remarked. Fiona smiled and scooted closer to him.

As the two of them motored up the long, winding driveway to their log house on the hill, Fiona knew that inside her husband's brain there was a high-speed race going on. It would now just be a matter of time before she found out which of his decisions would hit the finish line first.

62

THE OFFICIAL THREE-MAN ENTOURAGE was striding quickly down the corridor of the Senate office building. In the lead was the Chairman of the Senate Ethics Committee. Next to him was Senator Wayne O'Brien.

Behind them was a congressional sergeant at arms.

As the trio of officials entered Senator Jason Bell Purdy's office, the receptionist smiled at first. Then, when they identified themselves and asked for Senator Purdy, she gave them a startled look, opening her mouth, but unable to speak for a few seconds.

"Please, ma'am, get the senator out here immediately."

The receptionist closed her mouth, punched Purdy's intercom, and told him he was needed in the lobby right away.

When Purdy strode out into the lobby, the Chairman of the Senate Ethics Committee handed him a packet of papers.

"Senator Jason Bell Purdy, it is my unfortunate duty to deliver formal ethics charges to you relating to your conduct in the United States Senate. Each of the details and specifications of your ethics violations, including but not limited to coercion and blackmail against a colleague, namely, Senator Wayne O'Brien, is enclosed."

Purdy reached out a limp hand to receive the papers.

Glancing back toward his office, he noticed Linda, his press secretary, approaching him.

"Linda, hey—help me out here, will you? Start making some calls immediately. Round up the troops for me here," he whispered.

Linda gazed at him, shook her head, and then handed him an envelope.

"My resignation," she said. "I've been hired by the majority leader's office. Sorry."

Purdy glumly inched his way up to O'Brien.

"Wayne, friend. Let's talk. You've got to help me out of this deal."

Senator Wayne O'Brien fixed his fellow Georgian with a stone-cold stare.

"Jason, let me just say this," he replied. "I can't say I'm happy about this. I would rather have seen you charged with a federal crime. But I can say I'm satisfied. And that will have to do."

After the threesome had left, Purdy stood, clutching the packet with the ethics charges.

He wanted to say something clever to his receptionist, something bold and confident. But as he glanced over at her, she looked down at the papers on her desk, making herself look busy.

Purdy clicked his teeth together—and wondered how long he would have to wait till he could get himself a stiff drink.

63

THE NEXT MORNING WHEN FIONA awoke, even though it was very early, she noticed that Will was not in bed.

She threw on her bathrobe and scurried into the great room. She heard his voice on the telephone. Next to him, on the end table by the fireplace, was his Bible.

He was leaving a message on the voice mail at work for Hilda and Jacki.

"Hilda, please tell Jacki that I want her to send a notice of deposition immediately to Francine Les Forges, the prosecutor in the ICC case. Ask her to schedule a deposition for Damon Lynch—to take place at the Federal Police Correctional Center in Mexico City. And ask her to make sure that we fax the notice of deposition to Les Forges today so she has at least seven days' notice. Lynch is due to be released the day after that, so we have to have the deposition taken on the seventh day. Then arrange for a court reporter we can trust to fly down there with me to transcribe Lynch's testimony."

"What's going on?" Fiona asked as her husband hung up the phone. "Did I hear right? You're going back down there to get Lynch's testimony? So you're staying on the case?"

Will nodded. Then he walked over to his wife and gathered her up in his arms.

"They've already cleared Tiny in the investigation. I want him here in the house with you while I'm down to Mexico. Are you okay with that?"

She smiled and nodded.

"I'm also asking for the sheriff's department to provide some protection as well," Will said.

"So, my darling husband," Fiona asked, "tell me—what changed your mind?"

Will pursed his lips as he thought. And then he answered.

"I'm trying it…to lay something on the altar. And then I'm trying to walk away from it. Once and for all."

Still in her husband's arms, Fiona put her hands on both sides of his face. "You're the man of God's choosing for my life. I'm absolutely certain of that. And so I want you to know, my precious husband, that I am with you on this decision—with you all the way." And with that she planted a kiss on his lips.

Fiona fixed a big breakfast for both of them. After that, Will connected with Tiny. He had had some emergency-room surgery on his arm, but otherwise was doing fine, and said he'd be glad to house-sit with Fiona for the few days the attorney had to be in Mexico.

Then Will walked to the bedroom, and after closing the door, retrieved the white card with the telephone number and called the government agent.

"Give me the code word,"said the voice at the other end.

"Coral."

"What's up?"

"I've scheduled a deposition for Damon Lynch. I'll give you the date and the time. I've got a court reporter who's going to go down there with me. I have no idea what this guy's response is going to be when he sees me—I think I broke his nose—again."

"Oh, man, that breaks my heart," the agent said, chuckling. "Listen, Will, thanks for the information. Thanks for coming back on board."

Then the attorney arranged to have Jacki send out all the files from his office relating to the Caleb Marlowe case. Even though Fiona objected, he insisted on continuing his work on the case from their home, so he could be physically present with his wife.

While he worked in the study for the next few days, analyzing the discovery produced by the prosecution and trying to map out his preliminary strategy for the trial, Fiona was in the great room at the grand piano, plunking out a few new songs she was working on.

A few days after Will's office had faxed the notice of Damon Lynch's deposition to Francine Les Forges, the prosecutor sent back a scathing fax.

Hilda read it over the phone to Will when it came in.

I am in receipt of what purports to be a notice of deposition for a witness—to wit, a Mr. Damon Lynch—in the Federal Police Correctional Facility in Mexico City, regarding the above entitled war-crimes case presently pending before the International Criminal Court. Neither the identity of this witness nor your intent to take his deposition was disclosed to me at the time that we set out our discovery and trial-preparation plan with the trial chambers in The Hague.

Accordingly, and for several other reasons, I *will not* consent to your taking this deposition, and I *will object* to the admission of the transcript of any such purported deposition at the time of the trial. I will fight the admissibility of any deposition testimony of Mr. Damon Lynch coming into evidence at the time of the ICC trial.

Should you be unclear, for any reason, as to my position on this outrageous development, please feel free to contact me.

Les Forges' response did not surprise Will in the least. He also knew that she would not be sending a representative to attend the deposition—because that would undercut any objection she might later make at the trial that she didn't have a fair opportunity to cross-examine the witness. And in fact, in her closing remarks in the letter, the prosecutor indicated that her schedule, and that of her associates, could not be changed in order to attend the deposition on such short notice in any event.

Will had contacted Len Redgrove and advised him of his changed decision—that he would continue as lead counsel in the defense, and that he was going to agree to Lynch's proposal—that in return for his testimony under oath in the deposition, the attorney would not alert the police authorities to the drug dealer's whereabouts upon his scheduled release from the Mexican jail the day after his deposition.

As Will prepared for his flight back down to Mexico City, from where he would again fly directly to The Hague, he mapped out his deposition questions. But two unresolved issues still plagued him.

First, what information did Lynch really have about the inside connection between the AAJ and a high-ranking Mexican official, in regard to the kidnapping of Carlos Fuego and his family, and the setting of the trap at Chacmool?

And the second issue was equally bothersome, but for different reasons.

He wondered about the reaction of Damon Lynch—a man seemingly possessed with the instincts and savagery of a wild animal—toward his deposition being conducted by an attorney who had just broken his nose and whose wife he may have helped to murder.

Will had never faced a quandary like this before. When he thought it over, he could only shrug.

There's always a first for everything, he thought to himself the next morning as he sat down next to his court reporter and buckled himself in on the airplane bound for Mexico City.

64

DAMON LYNCH HAD LARGE AREAS OF black-and-blue under his eyes and on his left cheek, and a large swath of blood-stained bandage on his nose.

Elbows on knees, he was sitting forward in his metal folding chair, and staring at Will Chambers.

The court reporter was positioned about four feet off to the side. She was eyeing the prisoner nervously. The two Mexican jail guards stood behind him with their arms crossed.

The attorney leaned forward and returned Lynch's stare, eye-to-eye.

"Let me repeat the question—in case you have some problem answering it. I know it's a complicated one for you."

He then paused and asked the question again.

"What is your full name?"

The prisoner sneered, looked around the room, and scratched the growth on his chin. He put his lips together as if he were going to speak, but nothing came out.

One of the Mexican jailers looked at the other and smiled.

"Your name?" Will asked again, this time with his voice raised.

Lynch's head bobbed a little as he looked from one side of the room to the other. Then he stopped the bobbing and looked back toward Will.

"You want my birth certificate name? Is that what you want?"

"Yes."

"The name on my birth certificate is Damon Lynch. That's what it says."

As the attorney carefully and cautiously led the drug dealer through his questioning, first going over his connection to the AAJ through drug-dealing networks, and then over his connection with officials within the Mexican government, he was waiting for the man to pull the plug at any moment.

He was waiting for Lynch to say that that was it. No more talking. That he wanted an ironclad guarantee that, upon his release from the Mexican jail the following day, nothing would be done to apprehend or interfere with him. But he made no such demand. His answers were brief, coated in sarcasm, but generally responsive.

After about an hour of background questioning, Lynch wanted to take a break to smoke and stretch.

During the break he lit up a cigarette and then made several inappropriate comments toward the court reporter.

"Mr. Lynch—I would imagine that if someone were to punch you in the face, right on your broken nose, that would hurt, don't you think? So please be more polite to my reporter."

Lynch threw his cigarette down to the ground and took a few threatening steps toward Will. The two guards quickly intervened.

Before they settled back to the questioning, Lynch moved over toward Will a little, and in a low voice he said, "How do I know you're going to keep your word? How do I know you haven't already called the American cops to come get me?"

"You're just going to have to trust me."

The prisoner laughed and looked up at the ceiling.

"Yeah, right. I'm really going to do that. I'll tell you what. If something happens to me—if they arrest me when I'm walking out of this jail tomorrow, I'm going to make sure everything I say in this deposition gets retracted. You understand me?"

Will didn't respond.

The two of them sat down, cautiously eyeing each other.

Then the attorney led him into the final two areas in his questioning. The first was the extent to which he knew about a planned incident involving the safe house in the village of Chacmool. Lynch indicated that he dealt on a regular basis with the cell members of the AAJ, and they said they had a contact within the Mexican government. The plan had been to kidnap Carlos Fuego along with his family and set them up as sitting ducks in the house. The American commandos would be led to the site and prompted to shoot at the building, injuring or killing the hostages. The AAJ members were to escape through an underground tunnel leading out to the jungle. Three of them made it safely out. The fourth—the lookout—was killed on the front steps in the shootout.

As Lynch explained it, the AAJ had an inside source. This Mexican official had been able to find out about the movements of the American commandos, following the kidnapping attempt against Secretary Kilmer, from the high levels of the government. The plan, of course, had been to have Kilmer killed—but that plan had been foiled. Kilmer had been released unharmed, and two of their cell members had been killed.

"Do you have any direct evidence," the attorney asked, "that the four cell members of the AAJ who were to be present at the safe house that night were the same AAJ members who had participated in the attempted kidnapping of Secretary Kilmer?"

Lynch squinted and laughed contemptuously.

"Of course I don't know that. Gimme a break. I have no idea."

Will knew that this was a problem. He anticipated that the French prosecutor would try to show that, while the commandos might have been justified in using deadly force to free the kidnapped secretary, the privilege of deadly force could not be properly extended if they could not connect the AAJ cell group at Chacmool with the kidnapping.

Now the attorney was ready for his final line of questions. They would all revolve around one key piece of information—the identity of the Mexican official who had collaborated with the AAJ to set up the Chacmool trap.

"Do you know the identity of the Mexican official who conspired and participated with the AAJ to orchestrate the kidnapping of Carlos Fuego and his family, and draw the attention of American special operations forces to the safe house?"

Lynch paused for a second, then sat up straight in the metal folding chair. He stretched both arms and yawned. Then he lifted one muscular arm and, flexing his bicep, he pointed to it and smiled at the court reporter.

"You want some of this?" he asked her.

He was toying with them, but Will knew he had to keep his cool.

"Mr. Lynch, I'd like to ask you the question again. Do you know the identity of the Mexican official who was involved in setting up the Chacmool incident?"

Now Lynch had both of his arms raised in a bodybuilder's pose and was flexing both of his biceps and admiring them.

"Your answer, Mr. Lynch?"

The drug dealer turned back toward Will and shook his head in disgust.

"You know," he began, "if I were you, there's no way I would let me out of this jail alive. Do you know that? So that means you're no real man at all."

"Mr. Lynch, are you going to answer the question? Or do I pack up and leave this room and get myself to the nearest telephone?"

Lynch's head was bobbing again, but he was studying Will carefully.

"Yeah—I know who it was. I know the guy."

"Do you know what part of the Mexican government he works in?"

"Yeah. I know that."

"What department of the government?

"He works in the Ministry of Tourism. That's a laugh, ain't it?" the prisoner said with a cackle.

"And what is his name?" Will asked.

He was looking the man in the eye. Neither attorney nor prisoner flinched or moved.

Lynch swallowed and then coughed, putting his hand to his still-painful neck and rubbing it. He fingered the red marks that were still on his throat as a result of Will's near-strangling of him.

"You know, I'm a little confused. I had an injury here in the jail cell a couple days ago. I got sucker-punched. So as a result, I'm a little foggy about things. Could you ask that question again?"

"Yes. Here's the question—who was the Mexican official who conspired with the AAJ to set up the Chacmool incident?"

After a few minutes of reflection, Lynch answered.

"You know, I'm not real sure. I'm not real sure about that…"

"Mr. Lynch?"

"Yeah? What?"

Will asked the court reporter to go off the record.

"Would you like to smoke your cigarettes in the open air of the outside world? Would you like to go do your dirty business—whatever it is—without having to check in with jail guards? Want to use the toilet without asking permission first? Or do you want to continue living in a cement cage until you finally get old—until you get really old…and get sick. And then, if you're lucky, they take you to the infirmary—when they get the time.

"Or maybe you cough yourself to death. Or you get cancer. Or you simply start dying from bad hygiene. Or maybe, a lot sooner, some other guy just puts a knife in your back. Then they take you out in a box and drop you in the ground. That's what happens when a guy spends the rest of his life in jail."

Will stared Lynch straight in the eye.

"Now perhaps your memory's been refreshed about the Mexican official who conspired with the AAJ." He nodded to the reporter.

The other man tried to manage a smile, but unsuccessfully. His eyes searched the room for something, anything—but whatever it was he didn't find it.

"Okay. So here's the name. Here it is. Manuel Abdal Vega. That's the guy's name."

"Are you sure?"

"Yeah, I'm sure. That's it."

Will stood up so abruptly that Lynch almost fell back in his chair. The guards stood up straight.

The attorney turned to his court reporter.

"You and I are going to go back to the airport together. And then I would like you to get me an immediate transcript. If you can, e-mail an advance copy to me tomorrow in The Hague."

He packed up his briefcase and escorted the reporter to the door as she gave Damon Lynch a wide berth.

As Will reached the metal door frame of the cell, the other man called out to him.

He turned—and Lynch said under his breath, "You and I got unfinished business. Just remember that."

"You know, Damon, I'm trying to forgive you. For what you did—for what happened that day with Audra—because Jesus Christ died in my place and forgave me. I want you to know that. I really do. But know this also—just because I've forgiven you, that doesn't mean that if you ever come against my family, or anybody I love, or anybody else for that matter—that doesn't mean I won't turn you into a grease spot on the sidewalk."

Lynch was still staring, slack-jawed, at Will as he disappeared down the corridor and made his way to the outside of the prison building—on his way to catch his flight to the Netherlands.

65

IN THE FINAL WEEK OF PREPARATION before the trial of Colonel Caleb Marlowe, Will Chambers had, in all, only two hours and thirty-five minutes of free time. He spent it by leaving the suite of rooms that had been reserved for him at the Embassy Hotel in The Hague, and then walking the twenty minutes down to the beach and taking in the view of the North Sea for a few minutes. Then he sauntered over to a museum, where he took in some of the paintings of Vermeer and Rembrandt. As his open time ran out, he walked back to the hotel, which was within view of the tall clock-tower spires of the Peace Palace—the home of the World Court, which handled civil matters brought to it between competing nations. The International Criminal Court was not within view of his hotel, but it was not far away—just a few minutes' walk away from the Peace Palace.

Every day he spoke exactly thirty minutes on the phone with Fiona. He would remind her of his love for her. And he would double-check to make sure Tiny was still on guard. Fiona said that the big detective was falling in love with her cooking—which struck them both as immensely funny.

The remaining time, some nineteen hours a day, Will worked feverishly with Professor Redgrove, as well as with his senior associate, Jacki, whom he had flown over to the Netherlands to assist him.

Four days before trial he got a knock on his hotel room door.

When he opened it, two United States Marine Corps escorts stepped inside, and a small entourage entered and marched through to the large conference room of the suite.

The U.S. government had sent a briefing group to assist in the defense of the case. For the next three days, Will, Redgrove, and Jacki were briefed by the Assistant Director of the Military Foreign Affairs

Office, legal counsel for the Central Intelligence Agency, and legal counsel for the Defense Intelligence Agency. On the fourth day, just twenty-four hours before the opening of the first trial session, a senior lawyer from the Office of the Solicitor General of the United States arrived and went over the international law implications of the case, and discussed the defense's planned argument by Professor Redgrove, which related to jurisdictional objections. Will didn't stay for that, as he was delegating it to his co-counsel. Instead, he spent the day preparing Caleb Marlowe for the trial and his expected testimony.

After ten hours, Will and Marlowe finished the formal business of his criminal defense. Marlowe stretched and leaned back in his chair in the detention center, and then he asked the attorney about his life and his marriage to Fiona.

Then, for the first time, the retired colonel shared some of the details of his own life. How his first and only marriage had started with such promise. But soon, his wife had grown tired of the grueling schedule of a special operations warrior.

Tensions began developing in their marriage. He went to a chaplain for advice. But in the counseling session he discovered he had an emptiness and a hunger in his soul that went deeper even than the profound issues of his marital troubles. The chaplain then explained something to him. How sin not only for Caleb Marlowe, but for everyone, would be an insurmountable barrier in our desire to connect with God were it not for one, irrefutable fact—that God had sent His own Son, Jesus Christ, to be the sacrifice for those sins. All it took, the chaplain told him, was to acknowledge that Jesus Christ was both his Savior and his Lord and let him come into his heart by faith.

The message was so stunningly simple, and his choice was so clear. But he wondered to the chaplain how his role as a military man would fit into that. He had committed himself mind, body, and soul to fight for his country—and to kill whenever necessary.

The man smiled and told the story of Jesus' encounter with the centurion.

"The centurions," he explained, "were not only highly trained officers of the Roman government, they would also often be called upon to execute brutal punishment and death. They were the marines, if you will, of the Roman Empire. Yet when one certain commander wanted Jesus to heal his servant, the military officer sent the message that Jesus should not personally come to his home, for he was not worthy to have him within his four walls. Rather, the man asked Jesus to merely say the word, wherever he was, and he knew that the powers of heaven would obey his command. Jesus remarked that he had rarely seen such an example of faith.

"So, you see," the chaplain continued, "Jesus picked a soldier as an example of the greatest faith he had encountered in his time on earth. Faith—and service to your country in the military—are not mutually exclusive."

That got to Marlowe, and unashamed, he knelt on his knees with the chaplain, to welcome Jesus Christ into his heart by faith.

Unfortunately, his wife was less than excited about his spiritual awakening. She was not interested in going to church, reading the Bible, or praying with him. She seemed more and more distant the more he grew in his newfound spiritual life.

"But let me tell you something, Will," Marlowe said with a half-smile that reflected sadness and a reluctant recognition. "I was gung-ho in the military—and I was gung-ho for Jesus Christ. I came on too strong, frankly. I probably pushed too hard. I wanted to move her to the same point I had arrived at. I wanted her to have the same kind of spiritual rejuvenation I was experiencing. You know, you just can't force a wife to do that. She's got to see it in your boots before she's willing to listen to it come out of your mouth. I guess I didn't realize that."

He nodded his head a little, affirming what he'd just said. "So I take some responsibility for what finally happened, I guess."

Marlowe explained that, finally, one day he had returned to his small apartment on base several days earlier than planned. He had found his wife in bed with another marine. He did not retaliate—though he wanted to—and he described the fact that he had let the other man live as the greatest exercise of restraint in his life.

Some time after their divorce, Marlowe had decided he would remain single—particularly in light of the fact that he was accepting more and more specialized and challenging assignments—most of them very hazardous—in special operations work for the American government.

Wrapping up his story, Marlowe switched gears to the present.

"Will, do your best—remember, I need a quick decision by the court. I've got to get out as soon as possible."

Then the two of them folded their hands, bowed their heads, and spent a long time in prayer.

As Will walked back to his hotel room along the seven-hundred-and-fifty-year-old cobblestone streets of The Hague, the immensity of his legal task began settling in.

He really wondered how a lawyer from Monroeville, Virginia, had found himself in the precarious and dizzying situation of defending the autonomy of the American military in the controversial global criminal court of the United Nations.

For a fleeting moment he even wondered, as he entered the lobby of the hotel, whether he had done the right thing regarding Damon Lynch. By now, Will surmised, Lynch had hidden himself deep in the barrios of Mexico or Central America, or perhaps had even fled across the ocean.

But it was now too late for second-guessing. The die was cast. And the next day the Trial Chamber of the International Criminal Court would convene and commence the first day of his client's war-crimes trial. Will knew that, now, he had to set his face, sternly and unwaveringly, toward that task.

66

"ALL RISE FOR THE SOLEMN PROCEEDINGS of the International Criminal Court, which is now in session. The trial session in the matter of Colonel Caleb Marlowe, United States of America, accused, shall commence. His Honor Alexei Korlov, of the member nation of Russia, shall sit as the Presiding Judge."

A heavy-set man in his late fifties with curly gray hair and bushy eyebrows, Korlov ambled into the courtroom in red judicial robes. He nodded to the members of the court. The next judge who was announced was Hans Brucker of Germany, Associate Judge. Last was Associate Judge Jean René Ponti of France. As the judges sat down simultaneously, so did the lawyers and spectators.

Counsel on both sides were introduced to the court, and each of the lawyers hooked on earpieces.

The first order of business was a consent agreement between the prosecution and the defense for the case to be tried in closed session due to the specialized intelligence concerns of the issues involved. Judge Korlov instructed all onlookers, members of the media, and non-court personnel to leave the courtroom.

When the courtroom had emptied, the guards locked the doors, and the Presiding Judge administered a "Solemn Declaration" to all of the court personnel, including the court reporters and the interpreters behind the glass wall, by which they promised to maintain absolute secrecy regarding the conduct of the proceedings.

Korlov noted one preliminary matter that needed to be argued—the defense motion to dismiss—on the grounds that the ICC lacked jurisdiction to try Caleb Marlowe.

Len Redgrove strode up to the podium and opened his blue notebook containing an outline of his arguments and applicable sections of international law.

However, it did not surprise Will that, during his co-counsel's brilliant argument, he never looked down at his notes, but spoke directly and eloquently to the three judges.

Redgrove's argument went to the heart of the alleged jurisdiction of the ICC in matters where a UN member state, like the United States, had already determined that an accused should not be prosecuted.

"The issue," he noted, "revolves primarily around Article 17(1)(b). That section indicates that where a case has been investigated by a state—like the United States—which has jurisdiction over the matter, and the state has decided *not* to prosecute the person concerned—here Colonel Caleb Marlowe, who was investigated at Quantico Marine Base in Virginia by the United States military—in that event such a case, before this tribunal, is to be determined 'inadmissible,' and this tribunal is to have *no* jurisdiction. There is only one exception that pertains to this case."

Redgrove stepped to the side from the podium and gestured, stretching his arms out toward the three judges.

"That exception has two parts," he continued. "This court can proceed *only* if it can show that the decision by the United States military not to refer Colonel Marlowe to a full court-martial trial was a decision that resulted, for the first reason, from the *unwillingness* of the United States to genuinely prosecute Caleb Marlowe—" and with that Redgrove raised the index finger of his right hand into the air.

"And the second reason for exception," he noted, "is that the United States' failure to genuinely prosecute Caleb Marlowe was a result of its *inability* to do so under American law," and with that, he raised the index finger of his left hand.

With both fingers pointed in front of him like the horns of a steer, Redgrove declared, "This court finds itself on the horns of that dilemma. Because it can neither prove that the United States was *unwilling* to prosecute—indeed, the United States went through a full Article 32 hearing and fully investigated the potential crime of murder against Colonel Marlowe. Nor can this court find that the United States was *unable* to put forth a genuine effort of prosecution. The United States made an able, competent, and vigorous prosecution of

Colonel Marlowe. The mere fact that a defendant is acquitted, or the charges are dismissed, or prosecution does not continue—does not mean that the state is 'unwilling' or 'unable' to genuinely prosecute."

Returning to the podium, Redgrove closed his notebook and glanced up at the three judges.

"Your Honors, shall the world believe that this court has arrogated to itself such power that it will overrule, at will, any decision of any nation simply because the internal decision of that nation's court does not mirror the legal philosophy of this body? I trust and hope not."

Judge Ponti of France was the first to respond.

"Monsieur Redgrove, I have read your law-review articles and some of your speeches in which you bitterly criticize the founding and the creation of the ICC. It seems to me that your argument implies that the legitimacy of this court is still a matter to be debated. Do you concede that this court, and the provisions of the Rome Statute, are a matter of legitimate, binding international law?"

Redgrove paused—but only for a second.

"Your Honor, this tribunal exists. This building, and its personnel, and the armed bailiffs in this courtroom, are not fantasy, but reality. I do not question the existence of this court or its legitimacy—at least in the eyes of those nation–states that have signed the Rome Statute. I simply wish to remind you that some nations—like the United States of America—have not signed on to the Rome Statute and do not formally recognize the ICC. That also is a reality as firm as the stones of this building, and as real as the armed bailiffs in this courtroom."

Judge Brucker of Germany drew Redgrove's attention to Rule 12, which stated that "determinations of courts of any state are not binding on the Tribunal."

"Doesn't that tell you, Professor Redgrove, that the decision of the United States military not to prosecute Colonel Marlowe is not necessarily binding on this tribunal? That we are free to disregard the investigation by the American military?"

Redgrove agreed, but suggested that Rule 12 had to be interpreted in conjunction with the principle of complementarity outlined in the preamble of the Rome Statute.

After the professor had concluded his presentation, prosecutor Les Forges made her argument short and to the point.

"Can we trust the military of a nation to effectively pass judgment on soldiers of its own military when innocent civilians have been slain, but the military chooses not to act?"

Les Forges likened the United States military deciding not to court-martial Colonel Marlowe to the Nazi judges during World War II Germany, whose allegiance to the regime transcended allegiance to international norms of humanity, decency, or justice.

At this, the lawyer from the U.S. Solicitor General's office sat up straight in his seat—and Redgrove strode boldly to the podium, waving his hands.

"I exercise the right to object—to move to strike that scurrilous and obscene argument by the prosecution that likens the United States of America to Nazi Germany. That argument has no place in any judicial setting without proof…which this prosecutor, I submit, has none!" he thundered.

Judge Korlov slapped both hands down on the bench and barked a command in Russian, which, after a few seconds' lapse for translation, became clear to the American team. Korlov was threatening Redgrove with contempt of tribunal if he interrupted any further portion of the prosecution's argument on the motion to dismiss. The professor shook his head and resumed his seat next to Will.

Les Forges smiled coyly and made her last appeal. It was a clever one.

She suggested that the American government would actually be better served by a full prosecution under the ICC so that—in the eyes of the world, one way or the other—the world community would feel confident justice had been done, and the Chacmool incident could be, at last, put to rest.

"If the Americans believe in the innocence of their United States Marine Corps colonel, then they have nothing to fear from this impartial tribunal. For we all seek the truth—and we all revere the blessings of justice," Les Forges concluded.

Then she politely bowed toward the bench and took her seat.

The microphones of the three judges were turned off, and they spoke quietly among themselves for a few minutes.

Then the microphones were turned back on, and Judge Korlov announced they would defer decision on the jurisdictional issue until at least the end of the prosecution's case.

Les Forges once again walked to the podium. Delivering her opening statement, she was poised, cool, and confident.

She explained she would call, as a witness, the chief of police in Mexico. He would share his investigation of the scene, the incriminating evidence the police had found, and what they had deduced about the circumstances of the attack. His testimony would, she noted, decimate any potential defense of Colonel Marlowe that this was a "setup" or a "trap" for his unit. In fact, the prosecutor explained, the presence of CIA agent Carlos Fuego and his family in that little house in Chacmool would be explained in a way that would leave no question—no doubt—that he was not a hostage and was in no bodily danger that night, except from the machine guns of the American commandos.

Les Forges then promised a "bombshell" in terms of surveillance evidence regarding the malicious and murderous intent of Colonel Marlowe.

When she said that, Will turned to Marlowe, who wrinkled his brow but shook his head.

The prosecutor also promised "devastating" evidence from another Mexican police official, who had had actual contact with Carlos Fuego a few days before his death. Such evidence, she assured the court, would leave no doubt that Fuego had disagreed with his prior activities with the CIA and wanted to get out, but feared for his life—and actually believed that the American government might plan to exterminate him rather than allow him to leave its service.

Reporter Philippe Luc Cartier would be called as a witness, the prosecutor explained, with reference to his investigative work for a prominent French newspaper. Cartier had come into possession of information and documents showing the creation of BATCOM as an illegal assassination unit that broke with the traditional military hierarchy established under American law. His testimony would also show that the amorphous structure and lack of accountability of the BATCOM unit was an invitation for the kind of reckless and murderous event that had taken place at Chacmool.

Lastly, the prosecutor previewed the testimony of Dr. Michael Zagblundt—a retired colonel in the United States Army and a military expert. He would testify that the structure of BATCOM was a threat to freedom and to the civil liberties of citizens in other nations, and further, that the Chacmool mission, in its execution, constituted a clear violation of Article 8(2)(b)(iv) of the ICC war-crimes code—namely, that Marlowe had committed the war crime of excessive incidental death to civilians.

Will Chambers walked deliberately to the podium after Les Forges had finished.

"Your Honors," he began, "I reserve my opening statement until after the close of the prosecution's case. But I would urge this tribunal to remember what it knows full well—that this profoundly important, seminal case is ultimately going to be decided on credible facts and trustworthy evidence—not on empty promises or political arguments from the office of the prosecutor. Until I address this court at the close of the prosecution's case, may your ears hear only the evidence, and may your eyes see only the truth."

When Will sat down at the counsel table, Jacki, who was seated in the row behind him, leaned over and whispered in his ear, "Is it just me, Will—or are we a long way from Monroeville?"

67

THE FIRST WITNESS CALLED BY THE prosecution was Jorge Martinez, Deputy Secretary of the Foreign Ministry of Mexico. Martinez would lay the background and foundation for Les Forges' case.

He testified that, at the time of the Chacmool incident, there was no status of forces agreement between Mexico and the United States. He explained the background of such agreements. Their purpose was to establish a legal protocol of liability and jurisdiction concerning the activity of troops of one country within the borders of another.

"However, in the absence of a status of forces agreement," the secretary explained, "then, under international law, Mexico certainly has the sovereignty and international legal authority to prosecute Colonel Marlowe—or any other United States agent or soldier—for alleged criminal conduct within Mexico."

Les Forges asked whether there had been any negotiation between the two countries relative to the presence of American troops.

"There had been," Martinez noted, "but those negotiations broke down. There had been some tension developing between Mexico and the United States over a long period—very regrettable—we find this a sad thing—but a reality nevertheless. Mexico was very interested in our integrity as a nation—our individual sovereignty—and we were concerned about American military control."

"Can you expand on that, Secretary Martinez?" Les Forges casually put the question.

Oh, yes," the witness replied. "As an example, back in the year 2003, a well-known polling organization in Mexico, Mundo Americas, did a poll of the Mexican people. Seventy-seven percent of our citizens saw the United States as a force that is trying to dominate the world. Only twenty-three percent of our citizens saw the U.S. as a nation that really wants to play a constructive role in world affairs.

"We have, several times, gone to the International Court of Justice—the World Court here in The Hague—to complain about the death penalty in the United States being administered to Mexican citizens without giving deference to their rights as such.

"Further, we've had several instances where we have grown weary of Drug Enforcement Agency personnel of the United States conducting raids within our borders that we do not agree with.

"So you see, there is a very extensive background that led to our decision not to enter into a status of forces agreement. Also, Mexico rejected the United States' overtures—they wanted us to enter into a written agreement under which, if their troops came into Mexico, the U.S. would be immune from any prosecution under the ICC. We refused to sign that agreement also."

"Was there any permission for the United States to bring any of its military personnel into the nation of Mexico—except in regard to the attempted kidnapping of Secretary of Commerce Kilmer?"

"No, no permission whatsoever. The only permission we gave the United Statees was *very limited*—we told them they could bring in a small, limited military or paramilitary operation to help secure Secretary of Commerce Kilmer's release."

The prosecutor stepped away from the podium and situated herself directly in front of the three-judge panel.

"Did Mexico have information about the identity of the group that had attempted to kidnap Secretary of Commerce Kilmer?"

"Most certainly," Martinez answered. "We had very reliable information that the group was an element of FARC, a rebel group that has operated in the Central and South American regions for many years."

"Did you relay this information to the United States?"

"Yes, in our conversations with the United States State Department and their Department of Defense we explained this. But they rejected that information. America claims superior intelligence, and they kept insisting that the group had something to do with the al-Aqsa Jihad—AAJ—a Middle Eastern group."

"Did the nation of Mexico, through any of its agencies, grant permission to the United States to expand its military mission from its original limited scope of rescuing Secretary Kilmer in the Cancún,

Yucatán, area to a wider mission of chasing and trying to kill persons suspected by the United States to be terrorists?"

"The nation of Mexico gave no such permission whatsoever."

"And did the nation of Mexico grant any permission for the attack by American commandos at Chacmool, Mexico?"

"No, we did not authorize that attack."

"Last question—did the United States agree to cooperate with Mexican police in the Cancún attack on the kidnappers?"

"That was the agreement—that the United States' units would cooperate fully with, and be subject to, the Mexican police. Regrettably, the U.S. did not honor its agreement. Our federal police officers were left very much in the dark during the entire rescue effort."

Les Forges smiled, gestured toward Will Chambers, and sat down with her head slightly raised—as if she were a monarch ready to wave to the masses.

The American attorney strode to the podium, adjusted his earpiece, and glanced over at the interpreters behind the glass. Then he turned to the witness.

"Regarding the Mexican opinion that the group kidnapping our Secretary of Commerce was FARC, rather than AAJ—Mr. Martinez, do you know whether Mexico had access to any satellite intelligence on that issue?"

Martinez paused, looked down at his hands, and then answered.

"No, I do not believe so."

"So then," Will continued, "if the United States had credible, timely evidence from its satellite surveillance that verified the presence of AAJ terrorists among the group actually present at the kidnapping site of Secretary Kilmer, you would not be in a position to either admit or deny that—is that correct?"

Martinez nodded reluctantly.

"That's correct. I have no satellite information. I have no way to respond to that."

"And as to the issue of the United States having permission to expand its mission to include the Chacmool attack—did Mexico ever *expressly forbid* the U.S. from expanding its mission to include tracking down the kidnappers all the way to Chacmool and attacking them there?"

"No, we did not."

"Are you familiar with Manuel Abdal Vega—a chief administrator in the Ministry of Tourism?"

"Yes, I have had dealings with him within our federal government."

"Is he a practicing Muslim?"

Les Forges rose quickly to her feet and objected on the grounds that such a line of questioning had no probative value whatsoever.

To Will, the objection should have been quickly overruled. Judge Korlov seemed overconcerned about the issue, but then overruled it and permitted him to proceed.

"Yes, I believe he is. Although I'm not positive."

"Let me refresh your memory—isn't it correct that, about two months ago, you requested that Manuel Abdal Vega attend a meeting at your office, and he indicated by e-mail that he would be unable to attend because he was observing an Islamic holy day?"

Martinez shifted in the chair.

"Yes…I do remember something along those lines."

"And Vega, an officer in the Mexican military before he was transferred to the Ministry of Tourism, had extensive personal contacts with rebel groups in the Yucatán Peninsula where he had been stationed—is that correct?"

The secretary shifted again.

"Some contacts. I do not know what you mean by extensive."

Will knew that he could reap only limited benefits from this witness, so he concluded his cross-examination.

Les Forges' redirect examination was pointed and direct.

"Did the United States bother to share its alleged satellite surveillance information about the AAJ with any representatives of Mexico?"

"Not at all. We would have been most happy to have seen such information."

"And Mr. Chambers asked whether Mexico expressly prohibited the United States from expanding its mission to include chasing down and trying to kill the suspected terrorists. Was there a reason why Mexico did not *expressly* prohibit that expansion of America's original limited mission?"

"Yes, there was." Martinez turned in the witness stand to face the three judges. "Mexico made the mistake of believing that the United States—out of all the nations of the earth—would certainly understand the need for us to have national sovereignty. We assumed the

U.S. would respect our sovereignty and make a formal request before it would surround a house outside one of our villages and shoot up our citizens. Tragically, our trust was apparently betrayed."

The prosecutor smiled, bowed politely, and resumed her seat at her counsel table. Will knew he could have made some hay out of Martinez's last statement—but chose not to. This was certainly not an array of judges who would be sympathetic to that kind of questioning, in any event.

His only hope—and that of Colonel Caleb Marlowe's—was that these judges would blow away the anti-American geopolitical smoke and rest their decision solely on the credible facts.

That, however, remained to be seen.

68

Salvador García, chief of the Mexican federal police, stood rigidly next to the witness stand, as if he had a pool cue down the back of his jacket. He was in full-dress uniform with gold-braided epaulets and a chest full of ribbons. He held his tiny patent-leather-brimmed cap over his heart, and his right hand was thrust straight up, as he took the Solemn Declaration to tell the truth. Will had noticed the conspicuous absence of any reference to God in these declarations, already administered numerous times during the proceedings.

The chief first testified that his office had received an anonymous tip that American commandos were about to strike, and possibly kill, innocent Mexican citizens at a house near Chacmool that night.

Anticipating her opponent's potential cross-examination on that point, Les Forges exhaustively examined the witness on the circumstances of the anonymous tip. He said he did not know where the call had originated from. It had not been called into their emergency line, which recorded all calls. It had been called in on the nonemergency line. It had been a man, and he had given only the sparsest details and then hung up. García had questioned the dispatcher who had taken the message, and she had been unable to provide any further information.

As a result, several squad cars of Mexican federal police had been dispatched to the Chacmool area. García further explained that because of the attempted kidnapping of Secretary Kilmer at Cancún, the Mexican police had taken one of their most sophisticated pieces of surveillance equipment—a long-range listening dish—to the Chacmool area. This was in case the dish might be needed to track any of the FARC kidnappers, who—it was surmised—might be heading in the direction of Chacmool after the aborted kidnapping.

The chief said he had personally inspected the tragic scene inside the house—after noticing what appeared to be American commandos fleeing the area. One of his squads headed over to the area of Chichén Itzá, the Mayan ruins, and arrived just as a U.S. Navy helicopter was picking up the commandos.

García then gave, in excruciating detail, a description of Carlos, his wife, and their two small children. He described the injuries, the blood, and the position of the bodies.

Again, trying to close off an area of cross-examination in advance, Les Forges asked the witness if any of the victims had appeared to be restrained or tied in any way.

"In no way whatsoever," García replied confidently. "They were lying—the bodies—in disarray on the floor. In various positions. There were no ropes. Or chains. No restraints. Just the terribly mutilated, bullet-torn bodies. In fact, the horror of the scene actually reminded me of something else."

"And what did it remind you of?" the prosecutor asked, her brow wrinkling in sympathy.

"It reminded me of a scene of human sacrifice. Horrible. Chilling."

Then Les Forges moved in, focusing like a prowling jaguar.

"And on the listening device that was manned by your police officials, what, if anything, was heard?"

"We had detailed to the dish Sergeant Orlando Lidos, who speaks some English. As I drove up to the scene, he was positioned about a hundred feet from the house, with the dish pointed directly toward where the commandos had been firing from. The sergeant reported that someone who had identified himself as the 'number-one man' said he would accept the 'collateral damage' and had given the order to open fire."

Will had expected that evidence to come out. The prosecution's office had the entire text of the Article 32 hearing, and the whole transcript had been received into evidence as part of the prosecution's case. There was very little he could do about that piece of evidence...except to ride out the storm.

"And did this 'number-one man' say anything else that was picked up by the sergeant—that the sergeant heard?"

"Yes," García recounted, "the sergeant was very excited and upset, and the minute I arrived he yelled out to me that he had heard the man who sounded like he was in charge of the commandos say, 'I know there may be civilian loss here—,' and the sergeant heard that right before the gunfire began."

At counsel table Will leaned over to Caleb Marlowe and whispered, "Do you remember saying *anything* about 'civilian loss' to the other members of your unit before giving the order to fire?"

Marlowe shrugged, wrinkled his brow, and then whispered back, "I don't know. Honestly, Will, I may have said something like that. I'm not sure."

The attorney straightened up slightly and stared at his client in disbelief.

"Tell me you're kidding," he said in a hushed, tense voice.

"I just told you—I *may* have said it," Marlowe snapped back in a hoarse whisper.

Jacki had leaned forward from her seat behind and had heard the entire conversation between the two.

Will turned slightly and his eyes locked with Jacki's. They both had the same thought at the same instant.

Both lawyers were wondering if their defense was starting to resemble the Chacmool incident itself—a mission with the best of motives, carefully planned—but disastrous in execution.

When Les Forges concluded her direct examination Will asked for a five-minute recess, which was granted. He quickly huddled with his legal team and the lawyers from the CIA and the DIA. Turning to the two government attorneys, Will requested that they do some instantaneous research while he commenced with the cross-examination of García.

The two quickly exited the courtroom, cell phones in hand.

"Chief García," Will began slowly, buying time, "let me go over, first of all, the photographs of the scene of the incident."

With that Will retrieved the photos that the chief had identified and walked him through each of them.

Under the attorney's questioning, the witness admitted that none of the photos showed any close-ups of the wrists or hands of any of the victims.

"So, if we assume for the moment—just for the sake of a hypothetical—that the wrists of the four victims bore marks, abrasions, or cuts as a result of being tied tightly to their chairs—if that were correct, since none of these photographs include a close-up of the hands or wrists, they would not show that—is that correct?"

García professed confusion at the question, and Will asked it again, breaking it down into separate questions.

After a moment's reflection, the chief answered.

"Well, yes...the photographs were not close-ups of the wrists and hands. But there's a reason for that. There was no reason for close-ups of the hands or wrists because we did not find the victims tied or bound in any way. Thus there was no reason to focus on those parts of their bodies. They appeared to have been hit with a heavy volley of shots—large-caliber bullets—their bodies were ripped apart—and they had fallen in a random way onto the floor."

"And you had the bodies autopsied, did you not?"

"Yes, what was left of them," García answered with a subtle sneer.

"I don't see the pathologist who did the autopsy in court today. I do not see him on the list of the prosecution's potential witnesses. And, in fact, when my office tried to locate him in Mexico, he could not be found. Where is that pathologist?"

"Our medical examiner is presently unavailable—I believe he is traveling to take part in a medical conference in Venezuela. If your office had asked me how to locate him, I'm sure we could have accommodated you—and allowed you to talk to him personally."

"No doubt. I'm sure you would have been most accommodating," Will replied. "But I did look at his pathology report. On the autopsy protocol."

And with that, he presented a copy of the autopsy report to the chief.

"Yes, I have seen this," the witness said. "And I believe this was in the documents that everyone has."

"And there were no marks noted on the wrists or hands, is that correct?"

"That's exactly right."

"Did you bother to look at the section under 'physical examination'?"

"Oh, I suppose I did," García said with a shrug.

"Well, the purpose of the physical examination section is to give a detailed, exacting description of each part of the body that was examined—and the results of that examination. There is no reference in this autopsy report to an examination of the hands, wrists, or arms of the victims, is that correct?"

García took several minutes to look over the report, painstakingly reviewing each page. When he was finished, he looked up with a smile.

"There were extensive injuries for our medical examiner to account for. Amid all of the physical damage caused by the bullets, I'm sure he examined the wrists, hands, and arms, but perhaps it was an oversight—perhaps he simply neglected to indicate that in his report."

Then Will eyed the police chief and wondered if he should take a gamble. There was a question he wanted to ask. But should he ask it? He decided to wade in and hope there weren't any sharks in the shallows.

"Chief García, you say that your medical examiner is available to talk to me?"

"Most assuredly. We could have you connected with him."

"And if I were to ask him this question, tell me how he would honestly answer it—'Mr. Medical Examiner, was Chief of Police García present, standing next to you, during the entire autopsy?'"

The chief squinted a little, half-smiled, and then answered.

"I suppose he would answer that I was. Because, in fact, I was present. That's not unusual."

"No, I suppose it's not. But if I were to ask the medical examiner this question—and he answered truthfully—what would he say? If I were to ask him—'Mr. Medical Examiner, was Chief of Police García at your side while you typed every word of your autopsy report, talking to you about its contents as you typed it?'—would he say yes? Is that how it happened?"

Les Forges rose to her feet and objected to the form of the question as confusing and asking for the state of mind of the medical examiner.

But Will brushed aside the objection and indicated he would immediately rephrase it.

"True or false—did you stand next to the medical examiner as he typed his report, talking to him about the contents of his report as he typed each page, each sentence, each word?"

García's head snapped to the side, and after pursing his lips as if he were chewing a small seed, he replied.

"I was present during the typing of the report. I resent your implications. I resent your derogatory tone."

"And I resent, sir," the attorney responded, his anger rising, "an autopsy protocol that misses a critical element and that is typed in the presence of a coercive police chief, and the fact that the medical examiner is conveniently absent from court. That's what I resent!"

Judge Korlov slammed the gavel down and rebuked Will firmly.

He gathered his thoughts and nodded and apologized to the bench.

Will then noticed that the lawyers from the CIA and DIA had reentered the courtroom. He asked for a sixty-second opportunity to speak with some of his team.

After conferring with them quietly behind the counsel table, Will returned to the podium.

"About that listening device," he said, bringing to a close his cross-examination of the witness, "this is one of the most sophisticated such devices in the world, isn't that correct?"

Chief García broke into a broad smile and nodded proudly.

"That is absolutely true."

"And did you buy this listening device through a covert surveillance organization located in Egypt?"

"Ah...I'm not sure about that...perhaps."

"And this device was designed and built by the Russians, is that correct? In fact, designed by the..." and with that Will glanced down at the small piece of paper the two government lawyers had handed him—"...by the 'Glavnoye Razvedyvatelnoye Upravleniye'—the military counterpart to the KGB?"

García squinted and moved his lips nervously before he answered.

"This is...yes, I've heard of that...I'm not sure why that is significant."

"Only this. That the Russian black market has sold a handful of these—only a few—and two of them ended up in Egypt in the hands of the AAJ—and one of those ended up in the hands of the Mexican police. Can you contradict or deny what I've just told you?"

"I deny it. I deny it absolutely."

"Then if you did not buy this from intermediaries in the AAJ, tell me exactly who you did buy it from, and the name of the person or persons involved in that transaction."

"I can't remember that. I have a very high position as chief of the Federal Police. I attend to many details...complicated matters of police work. I can't recall that."

"One of the most advanced pieces of surveillance equipment in the world, one which you are apparently very proud of—but you can't recall the circumstances of its purchase. Is that what you're saying?"

García twisted in his chair, straightening his uniform and a few of his medals.

"I'm saying I cannot recall. That is it. That is the end of it."

Francine Les Forges jumped to her feet.

"Your Honors, I note that Mr. Chambers has not listed any names on his list of potential witnesses who could likely give information about this listening device. Thus, am I to presume, Mr. Chambers, that you are making speculative and wild accusations that you are not prepared to prove during this trial?"

"What I am saying," Will said, addressing the tribunal, but focusing his eyes on Les Forges, "is that the United States government does not want to risk the lives of Egyptian informants who provided this information to the Central Intelligence Agency and Defense Intelligence Agency. It is enough that an honored and decorated member of the United States Marine Corps should find himself on trial for war crimes before this tribunal—but to cause the death of informants who are courageously assisting the United States in stamping out terrorism—that is a price we do not wish to pay."

At the bench, Korlov looked at Judge Ponti, who was shaking his head and seemed to be chuckling under his breath. Judge Brucker remained expressionless but was listening intently to the ensuing off-mike conversation between the other two.

Then Korlov glanced at his watch, looked up at the clock on the wall, and indicated that the tribunal would adjourn for the day.

Len Redgrove scooted over next to Will and whispered, "What in the world are we going to do about this 'civilian loss' reference they got into evidence?"

The younger attorney wanted to give a snappy, brilliant reply, but he had none.

"Len, I'm not sure. I'm working on it."

As Will and his team packed up their briefcases and prepared to head out of the courtroom, they knew they would be met by an international army of reporters and cameras. But because the tribunal had placed a gag order on them, at least that task would be easy—"We are prohibited from commenting by order of the court."

Approaching the exit from the courtroom and the armed ICC bailiffs, who swung the doors open, Will now had only one daunting task.

To put on a confident smile and hide his profound anxiety over the case he was defending.

69

UNLIKE CHIEF GARCÍA, THE NEXT representative from the Mexican federal police—José Ortega, a lieutenant—was absent much of the spit and polish of his superior officer—or more accurately, he showed more spit than polish.

His tie was skewed slightly to the left, and his paunch was straining the buttons of his jacket. His entire uniform seemed slightly rumpled.

Les Forges' purpose in calling Ortega quickly became apparent. She paced him quickly through the preliminaries and got right to the point.

The witness testified that he was familiar with Carlos Fuego and had known his family for many years. And Fuego had confided in him that he had been, for many years, a CIA operative. But more recently he had begun to regret many of his "immoral" and violent activities on behalf of the American government. Even further, the lieutenant described how, just two days before the shooting at Chacmool, Fuego had confessed to him, in a private meeting, that he wanted to leave the CIA—but he was fearful that his agency was aware of this and was targeting him for assassination.

"And two days later," the prosecutor asked, "is it correct that Carlos Fuego was shot to death by American commandos, along with his family, while meeting with, not members of the FARC, but members of the AAJ?"

"Yes. Oh, yes—that is correct," Ortega answered vehemently.

Will objected on multiple grounds—that the testimony was clear hearsay, and that because Fuego was dead, it would fall under the dead man's rule recognized under American and English common law, as well as other national jurisdictions.

Judge Korlov, however, wasted no time in brushing aside those objections and allowing Les Forges to proceed with her questioning on Fuego's alleged statements to Lieutenant Ortega.

"And do you know why Carlos Fuego was meeting with members of the AAJ that night?"

"Yes, I do," the lieutenant answered, bobbing his head up and down. "He told me, in the same meeting we had, that he wanted to arrange a conversation with an Abu Adis, a member of the AAJ. He knew that some members of the AAJ were in Mexico. But they were there for nonviolent reasons—trying to raise funds for the humanitarian projects they were doing back in the Middle East. Fuego told me that he was going to urge them to leave because he knew the CIA was tracking down all Muslim extremists in Mexico—and would be shooting them and killing them if they didn't flee. He suggested that they relocate to Guatemala for their own safety."

"And so Fuego indicated he was setting up a voluntary meeting with Abu Adis and a small group of AAJ members. Do you know where the meeting was going to be held?"

"Oh, of course," Ortega answered, "it was in the little house outside Chacmool where the shooting took place."

Les Forges rested, and smiled at Will as their paths crossed.

Will took a moment at the podium to reflect before he began his examination.

"Are you able to give me the details, today, of all of the allegedly 'immoral' activities you say Carlos Fuego regretted? All of the supposedly immoral things he did for the CIA? Did he tell you the details?"

"No. I do not think so. I can't remember those."

"Now, Lieutenant Ortega, where was this meeting that you say took place between you and Carlos Fuego?"

"In a café."

"What was the name of the café?"

"Can't recall."

"Was it a café where other people were dining?"

"Yes. I believe there were people dining."

"Was it a nice day that day?"

Ortega laughed a little and then answered.

"Yes. Sure. It was a nice day."

"And so you were outside—in an outside café?"

"Oh, perhaps. I suppose so."

"And what was the city?"

Ortega took a few seconds to think and then shook his head.

"Can't remember, really. But I do remember the conversation. Just can't remember the city."

"Would it refresh your recollection if I were to tell you that it may have been in Nanchital?"

Ortega looked over at Les Forges, glanced over to the judges, and then looked back at Will.

"Yes. Now that you mention it, that's probably where it was."

"Lieutenant Ortega, I do not believe that you met with Carlos Fuego. But I do know that you are familiar with Nanchital. Because that's a city run by the labor union for oil workers. It is a city known for corruption—and it is a city that you frequent often. And I say that because you are currently under investigation, are you not, on charges of bribery and assisting kidnapping in your association with the People's Oil Union of Mexico down in Nanchital?"

Les Forges pranced up to the podium and shot out several objections.

Will countered by rephrasing the question, but still laying the accusation of an investigation of Lieutenant Ortega clearly at his feet.

At that point Judge Korlov stopped the proceedings, turned off his microphone, and conferred with the other two judges. Their discussion was prolonged—longer than Will would have expected. Ortega's credibility was clearly a key element now. Why in the world would the judges not permit him to cross-examine Ortega in regard to his dishonesty or willingness to lie so as to gain some benefit?

After a full ten minutes, Korlov flicked the switch at his microphone and leaned forward.

"The tribunal has voted, two to one..." Then he paused, looked down at the desk, and rubbed his hands together. Looking up again, he continued.

"...Two to one, to permit this line of questioning. Continue, Mr. Chambers."

Ortega glumly responded that he was under investigation—but he suspected the charges had been trumped up by criminals—by the criminal element he was investigating. He indicated he believed he would be fully cleared of all of those charges.

"In fact, you believe that those charges against you are going to be dismissed by Chief García, is that correct?"

Ortega took the bait and nodded vigorously.

"Yes, sir. Yes, that is correct. I am told by Chief García that the charges against me will all be dismissed."

"And there's a reason for that, isn't there?" Will asked, raising his voice.

"What do you mean?"

"I mean that the reason that the charges will be dismissed against you is because you have fabricated your testimony about meeting with Carlos Fuego—and fabricated statements, allegedly made by Carlos Fuego, that were never made. And you did this because you knew that, if you provided the testimony the Mexican government wanted, you would be cleared of all of the charges relating to your own misconduct—isn't that true, Lieutenant?"

Ortega almost stood up from the witness chair as he waved his hands back and forth wildly.

"No, no, no—do not say this."

"Lieutenant, do you know what the penalty is for lying after making a solemn declaration before this tribunal? Do you know that you could be sent to prison by this tribunal if you are found to have deliberately lied?"

Ortega squirmed and resumed his seat, but rose again slightly, as if realizing that there were several tacks on his chair. Then he sat down fully.

"I have said what I have said. And I do not believe I should speak anymore...if there is trouble for me here—then I want to talk to the Chief—Chief García. I want to know my rights..."

"Lieutenant Ortega, I'm not half as concerned about your rights as I am about my client's rights," Will said firmly, concluding his cross-examination and glancing over at Caleb Marlowe, who gave him a quick nod of approval.

70

PHILIPPE LUC CARTIER, AN INVESTIGATIVE reporter from *Le Monde*, the Paris newspaper, had spent his career specializing in coverage of terrorism and military-related issues. He was no slouch. As Francine Les Forges covered his qualifications in her direct examination, he acknowledged having been a recent winner of the Fullerton International Prize for Investigative Journalism.

"And what was the subject matter of the investigative article that caused you to win that award?"

"I was covering the supersecret United States Air Force base—flight test center—at Groom Lake, Nevada," Cartier responded. "It's more popularly known as 'Area 51'—and has been kept closed by virtue of consecutive presidential orders for many years."

Cartier then described how he had spent more than a year investigating the background and formation of the BATCOM unit. He described how it had been assigned "Top Secret Special Access" status within the American government and the Pentagon. That meant, he explained, that documents relating to internal decision-making, missions, and logistics of the unit were probably kept in secured areas, protected by armed guards.

"I first tried to dislodge information regarding BATCOM by making an FOIA request—a freedom-of-information request under American federal law. However, after months of legal wrangling, the government refused access, and an American court upheld that."

Thus, Cartier explained how he had had to use every investigative technique he had ever learned to try to gain access to the papers and records relating to the decision to initiate BATCOM as a weapon against terrorism.

"What I learned, after months and months of investigation," the reporter continued, "is that BATCOM was created by the United States government to operate, and I quote, 'outside the defined operational control of the United States combat forces within the traditional Unified Combatant Commands.'"

"Did you ultimately obtain this information through internal documents of the Defense Intelligence Agency that related to the creation of BATCOM?" Les Forges asked.

"I did. Actually, to be precise," Cartier explained, "I wasn't sure where the documents had come from. I had received a message from a person who simply identified himself as 'Deep Source.' He said he had a memo that laid out the philosophy and strategy for the BATCOM unit."

"And did you ultimately obtain a copy of that internal memorandum from the Defense Intelligence Agency in the United States government Department of Defense, that outlined what BATCOM was and what it was supposed to do?"

"I did."

"And let me just ask you this," the prosecutor said, clearly hoping to ward off preliminary objections, "at the time you received this memo, did you know you were receiving a document that was protected as top secret? In other words, did you intentionally violate any secrecy laws of the United States, that you know of, in receiving this document?"

"Honestly," the reporter continued, "when I received this memorandum, I was not told that the man giving it to me had any connection at all with the American government. I do not know where he got it. It appears to be authentic. But there are no markings or stamps on this memorandum indicating that it is top secret—or even confidential."

Will's cross-examination of Cartier focused on establishing only one fact—that the investigative reporter had been put on the BATCOM scent by prosecutor Les Forges herself. Though this point was not critical legally, it did prove one thing. Les Forges wanted the United States squarely in the dock. And wasn't too reticent about how she did it.

71

"I AM DR. MICHAEL ZAGBLUNDT. I am a colonel—retired—from the United States Army. I have a PhD in history—primary area of emphasis is military history, with a particular focus in military strategy. I've taught extensively, in the past, at the U.S. Army War College. I've taught military history and logistics at the South Carolina Military Institute and the Academy of Arts and Technology in Alabama. I am also a founding member of the Capital Foundation of International Affairs. I've testified numerous times before the United States Congress on matters of military intervention and issues pertaining to joint UN peacekeeping efforts. I consulted with the United States government regarding inspections for weapons of mass destruction, both in Iraq I and Iraq II."

"Dr. Zagblundt," Les Forges continued, "have you authored any books dealing with subjects that are within the scope of your expertise?"

"Yes—one of my books, used as a standard textbook in military academies, is *Logistics in Low-Intensity Combat: Theory and Practice.*"

Under the prosecutor's questioning, Zagblundt explained that, in preparation for his testimony, he had reviewed the full transcript of the testimony at the Article 32 hearing held at the Quantico Marine base and had read all of the police reports from the Mexican federal police, as well as the report of Philippe Luc Cartier—the investigative reporter for *Le Monde.*

"Dr. Zagblundt, let's address, for a moment, the information you relied on from the award-winning journalist Philippe Luc Cartier. Specifically, how would you characterize the configuration of BATCOM?"

"This is a very troubling development for the United States."

Les Forges glanced at the panel. Judge Brucker had a bland expression, but Korlov and Ponti seemed to be riveted by the witness's testimony.

"And why do you say this is a troubling development?"

"Well, let's take the big picture. Historically, special operations have been divided between the military on the one side and the Central Intelligence Agency on the other. Each approach has strengths and considerable weaknesses. The CIA can slip in and out, relatively unnoticed, from a hostile area and execute its task covertly, with little bureaucracy and great rapidity. But that's also a problem. It means there's a lower level of accountability and visibility—which means that human-rights violations can occur under the radar quite often. The military has greater firepower, and better discipline, but it's slow-moving. On the other hand, it has a higher level of accountability—to congressional oversight committees and the executive branch, and ultimately, to the American people."

With that, Zagblundt got up from the witness stand and moved over to a large easel, where he took a laser pointer and began indicating various areas on a large world map.

"Today, American special operations forces have been deployed to thirty-five different countries around the world, in thirty-two separate deployments. Eight in Central America, nine in Africa, two in Europe, and some thirteen in the Middle East and the Far East. There are some forty-four-thousand American special operations personnel. The military branch with the smallest number—the United States Marine Corps—was likely picked for the experimental development of BATCOM for that reason. It was probably easier to keep BATCOM under the radar in the Marines than in one of the other branches. And then, of course, we have no idea how many CIA agents have been deployed as special operatives around the world to fight terrorism as well."

"And considering the configuration of BATCOM," Les Forges followed up, "what threat does it pose to human rights of citizens in other nation states?"

"Oh—there is a considerable threat. As I have studied it, BATCOM seems to possess the worst of both the CIA and the military special operations units. It has the covert nature and low accountability of the CIA, matched with the ferocious firepower and huge support network of the American military. In short, it is a strike force with the potential of doing great harm to civilians with limited oversight by the government."

The prosecutor joined Zagblundt at the world map, took the laser pointer, and indicated several of the spots where special operations forces were presently deployed.

"Yet, Dr. Zagblundt, how do we know whether such harm is likely—do we have any historical models?"

"Oh, yes," the witness answered affirmatively. "Just look at the history of the CIA and special operations forces. The Bay of Pigs failure in Cuba was a special operations catastrophe of enormous proportions. The increasing use of the CIA in assassinations and the destabilizing of foreign governments led to a ban, under President Gerald Ford, against CIA assassinations. Under President George W. Bush that assassination ban was rolled back. And then, in February of 2002—as a result of the rollback, I believe—a CIA-launched Predator missile struck a truck in Afghanistan, killing three local citizens. There is strong evidence that those killed were not terrorists, but merely petty smugglers."

"Do you have any similar concerns for special operations abuses within the American military?"

"I do have concerns," Zagblundt continued, now back in the witness stand and folding his hands in front of him at the witness table. "I would direct this tribunal's attention to a tragic series of events back in 2002—several American special operations soldiers at Fort Bragg, North Carolina, killed their spouses and themselves, all within a short period of time. The psychological and psychosocial factors that led to those deaths are still not entirely clear—but it *is* clear that without strict constraints, a rigid chain of command, and high accountability, these special operations troops can become rogue and violently dysfunctional very easily."

"With what result?" the prosecutor asked, spreading her arms before the three judges.

"Well, let's be very specific," Zagblundt answered. "I believe that the slaughter of innocent civilians, including an American CIA officer, at Chacmool, Mexico, was a result of two things. The first factor is the irresponsible design of the BATCOM unit from a strategic standpoint. Lack of accountability. The 'train as you fight and fight as you train' philosophy they use for these special operations forces. The very nature of BATCOM predicted that, very quickly after it started being deployed, a tragic loss of civilian life would likely ensue. And that's exactly what happened."

"Now, Dr. Zagblundt, you say that the structure of BATCOM predetermined the tragic outcome here—the reckless and unnecessary taking of civilian lives. But you also said there was a second factor. What did you mean?"

"Well, what I was referring to was the way in which the military operation was actually carried out," the witness replied. "And here I relied primarily on the Article 32 hearing transcript from the military tribunal. In the hearing at Quantico, Master Sergeant Rockwell suggested to Colonel Marlowe that, before commencing a massive attack on the house, they take out the lookout with a single, noise-suppressed round, and then do a close-up reconnaissance of the house to see who was inside. Had they done that, they would have discovered there were civilians in the house, and this occurrence could have been avoided."

"Well, let me just argue from the devil's advocate position," Les Forges said, pacing a little before the judges. "What if the defense in this case says that this is merely a negligent command decision from Colonel Marlowe—that it was certainly not done intentionally?"

"The problem I have with that," Zagblundt answered, "is the fact that there are two very condemning pieces of evidence that show us that Colonel Marlowe knew there was a high risk, even likelihood, of civilians being in the house. First was his reference to his taking responsibility for 'collateral damage.' And then there's the very disturbing reference Marlowe made, one that was documented by the prosecution's prior witness, Chief Salvador Garciá. To me that means Marlowe knew, or at least should have known, that the attack would cause incidental death to civilians, as Article 8 requires the prosecution to show."

The prosecutor returned to her notes, and then prepared for her final volley of questions, which were tailored to address the element of Marlowe's offense requiring evidence that incidental loss of civilians would be of such an extent as to be "clearly excessive" compared to the concrete military advantage being anticipated.

"Dr. Zagblundt, would you tell this tribunal, from an objective military strategy standpoint, what concrete and direct military advantage should have been anticipated by the American government from this attack in Chacmool?"

"I must be very honest here," the witness said, leaning forward and spreading his hands out before him, palms down. His voice was intense and disciplined.

"Frankly, I do not think the American military could have anticipated much, if any, concrete military advantage from the attack they launched against the individuals in the house. There was scant evidence that actually connected to persons there with the kidnapping attempt on Secretary Kilmer.

"Even further, if we assume they knew Abu Adis was present, I believe the American government knew only that Mr. Adis had *political* affiliations with the group that was led by the late Abdul el Alibahd. In other words, the American government knew only that Mr. Adis *associated* with known terrorists. I do not believe there is any evidence based on which the American government could have anticipated that Adis himself was a terrorist, or was engaged in any conspiracy to commit a terrorist act. Merely being associated with groups of persons who have a terrorist background should not cause one to pay the price of execution for that association."

With that statement by the witness, Francine Les Forges rested her direct examination and strode confidently back to the counsel table.

72

MICHAEL ZAGBLUNDT WAS A DOUBLE-BARRELED witness, and Will knew it. First, he was an expert witness for the prosecution—and he had been left as their final witness so as to produce the greatest impact on the judges.

But beyond even that, the attorney understood that a former American military officer who had published a book on military strategy—and who was criticizing not only the execution of the military operation at Chacmool, but also the very existence of the BATCOM unit in the first place—could be pivotal in the judges' deliberations.

Zagblundt was confident, at ease, and unperturbed as he watched Will approach the podium for his cross-examination.

"Are you assuming here today, Dr. Zagblundt, that the nation of Mexico is a friendly nation–state in its relationships with the United States—friendly from the standpoint of there being no antagonistic military relationship between the two countries?"

The military expert studied Will for a moment, then smiled.

"Yes, I suppose I am. Though I do not believe that is a critical assumption to my ultimate opinions here."

"Not critical?"

"That's what I said," Zagblundt replied casually.

"Are you saying that it would make no difference if Mexico had been harboring anti-American terrorists—who were planning to attack American citizens and institutions of the American government?"

Zagblundt leaned forward and then back again in his chair, clearing his throat.

"No, I'm not saying that. That would make a difference."

Now Will thought it was time to direct a blow to Zagblundt's soft underbelly.

"You have testified that there was little or no tactical advantage to the United States of America, in relation to its war on terrorism, in the attack on the house at Chacmool—which was purportedly for the purpose of killing Abu Adis and his AAJ cell group. Is that right?"

"Not exactly. I think you're twisting my words, Mr. Chambers. What I said is that there was very little concrete advantage for the American government in the attack—and even if Abu Adis was there at the time, there was no proof he was engaged in acts of terrorism against the United States. Thus, there was no justification—no real military advantage—for the slaughter at Chacmool."

"And when you say there was no proof of Abu Adis having plans to launch a terrorist attack against the United States—do you base that on your vast access to American intelligence?"

Zagblundt chuckled a bit and then, with a superior look, rebuffed Will.

"Mr. Chambers, let me be clear about this. For many years I taught at the United States Army War College—and for many years, I have had access to American intelligence, much of it dealing with Mexico, and Central and South America. I was, as you recall, also an advisor to the United States government on weapons inspections going on in Iraq, both in the 1991 post–Gulf War inspections, and those back in 2001 and 2002. Yes—I've had access to high-level intelligence on terrorism, and that's what I draw from in forming the opinions I'm stating here today."

Will stepped over to the podium and retrieved something from his file—then covered it up under a notebook. He looked at Zagblundt and smiled.

"Let's talk about your access to American intelligence. In fact, let's address your role as an advisor to the United States government regarding arms inspections in Iraq. You are no longer an advisor to the United States on Iraq or Middle Eastern weapons inspections, is that correct?"

"That's correct. I've retired from that role. I am now a consultant to other entities in other capacities."

"Is that another way of saying that you spend most of your time now in testifying for attorneys in personal injury lawsuits where harm or loss was caused by actions of the American government?"

Zagblundt paused. But seeing a window of escape, he came back aggressively.

"I would deny that's my primary source of income, so that's not true."

Will pulled from his file a listing of legal cases.

"Dr. Zagblundt, I have here a multipage list of case after case in federal and state courts around the United States, and even some in other countries. In these cases, in the last few years, you have testified almost exclusively for persons who sought to sue the American government, or other American agencies, relating to claimed misdeeds by the American military. Will it be necessary for us to itemize each of these cases and ask you how much you received as a testifying expert in each of them?"

But Will's concentration was suddenly broken by an outburst from Judge Korlov.

"Mr. Chambers...I'm not sure we will find much value in this line of questioning. What possible difference does it make whether this man makes money from being paid as an expert witness in various cases? We have certified him as an expert—we will receive his testimony as an expert—and I don't think adding up the amount of money he gets paid for his expert opinions will have any influence on the deliberations of this tribunal. You are instructed to change your line of questioning to another subject. You are required to do so now."

"I will respectfully defer to the opinion of this tribunal. If this court feels it is not important to know that this man gives expert opinions as his primary source of income, and that in almost every single case, for the last few years he has criticized the American government—if you do not feel that has bearing on his potential bias against the actions of the American military—then I do not believe there is any way I can enlighten you to agree with my position, and abandon yours."

Korlov burst out in anger.

"Mr. Counselor Chambers, if you argue with this tribunal again after it has made a ruling, I will consider that to be contemptuous and a disregard for the authority of this tribunal!"

Will took a second to refocus and disregard the Russian judge's seemingly complete immunity from understanding the issue of witness credibility.

"Dr. Zagblundt, let me continue. You indicated that you no longer are an advisor for the United States government regarding arms inspections in Middle Eastern countries, including Iraq—correct?"

Zagblundt nodded with a broad grin, clearly feeling the support of the court as he testified.

"Yes. That's exactly what I said."

"Isn't the reason you're no longer a paid consultant for the American government on arms inspection—isn't the real reason that it was discovered you had a serious conflict of interest—that you had, in fact, received seventy-five-thousand dollars from a pro-Iraq organization within Saudi Arabia at the very same time you were purporting to act as an independent consultant for the United States government?"

Zagblundt exploded.

"That is preposterous! You are twisting and distorting the truth, Mr. Chambers!"

Korlov, this time joined by Ponti, raised his hands in objection and shouted at Will.

It took a few seconds for the translation to come through. Judge Ponti was of the opinion that Will Chambers had insulted the witness and had also insulted the integrity of the tribunal with what he called a "scurrilous and defamatory attack." Korlov was adding his objection that Will had disregarded his prior admonition not to go into the background of the expert witness.

"With all due deference," Will argued, looking directly at Judge Ponti, "charges are only scurrilous or defamatory when they are false. I have not been allowed to continue. If I am, I will show they are true."

Then the attorney turned to Judge Korlov.

"And, Your Honor—with all due respect—the issue of witness bias is always relevant. It's always probative. Under Rule 89 this tribunal is bound to apply those rules of evidence that best favor a fair determination of the matter before it—and that are consistent with not only the spirit of the ICC law but also the general principles of law as well. Not only is examining witness bias consistent with American principles of law, it is also cited throughout the Queen's cases in English common law."

Finally, Will turned back to the French judge.

"And, Judge Ponti, in your country took place one of the world's most notorious cases of a person wrongfully convicted of a crime even though he was innocent—the infamous Dreyfus case, where a French officer was charged with a crime he did not commit. What would have been the result back then if the French tribunal had permitted more interrogation about the biased motives of those who wrongly accused Officer Dreyfus?"

Ponti glared at Will. Then bent over and whispered something to Korlov. Korlov turned to Brucker, who was watching passively and without expression. Then after switching off their microphones, the three engaged in a short conversation, which the interpreters raced to keep up with.

Korlov then flicked on his switch and bent to the microphone.

"Mr. Chambers…"

"Yes, Your Honor?"

"Continue with your examination."

Will nodded and turned to Dr. Zagblundt.

"Do you deny the accuracy of the charges I've made against you— of conflict of interest as the reason for the American government no longer using your services?"

"Absolutely. That was not the reason."

"But it is true—it is correct that at the same time you were advising the American government on inspections relating to Iraq's weapons of mass destruction, you were receiving seventy-five-thousand dollars from a pro-Iraqi group in Saudi Arabia? Is that true?"

"The timing…" the witness, narrowing his eyes and pausing to tug an ear, "the timing was unfortunate. It was not a conflict of interest. And furthermore—the group in Saudi Arabia was absolutely *not* pro-Iraqi."

"Dr. Zagblundt—did you do an interview with the *New York Times* approximately seven months ago regarding that incident?" And with that, Will pulled a copy of the *New York Times* from his file and held it high.

"Yes, I recall it. I can't remember everything I said there…"

"You talked about the payment from the Saudi group?"

"Yes…the payment…and a lot of other things…many other things…"

"And the *New York Times* article records you as saying that, and I quote, 'While the group had some sympathy for Saddam Hussein's regime, I was not aware of that at the time I received the payment.' Is that what the article reported you had said?"

"Misquoted!" Zagblundt shouted. "I was absolutely misquoted—my remarks were taken out of context!"

"Well, that does happen," Will remarked quietly. "Which is why we have listed the reporter from the *New York Times* as one of our witnesses. He recorded that interview. And you do recall that, don't you, Dr. Zagblundt? The fact that you consented to a recording—word for word?"

The military expert took a few deep breaths, his lips parting but emitting no words. Finally, he spoke.

"And is there a question?"

"Yes—should I bring in the *New York Times* reporter, with his recording, and play for the court your statement to the reporter in which you admit that the group had pro-Iraqi sympathies, but simply claimed you didn't know about it at the time?"

Zagblundt paused, glanced up at the ceiling, and replied.

"No. Not necessary. I may have said it…and forgotten it."

"Finally," Will said, concluding his cross-examination, "let's talk about what you contend was Colonel Marlowe's knowledge of the likelihood of innocent civilians being in the house when he ordered the attack."

The attorney stepped away from the podium so that he stood directly in front of the witness. His arms were at his sides, and his eyes were locked with Zagblundt's.

"Now, in addition to your private consulting work with personal-injury lawyers who are suing the American military, are you also a member of an organization called World Without War?"

"Yes, I'm a charter member. I'm not ashamed of that. The purpose of that foundation is to minimize the risk of global warfare. I think that's a laudable enterprise, don't you?"

"Most certainly," Will replied. "But it is an organization that consistently criticizes American military policy. Would you agree with that?"

"Oh, I don't know about that. That characterization is far too broad."

"How about an article in last month's issue of *World Economy and Policy* magazine, in which the present executive director of World Without War described America's war on terrorism as 'typical of the American military philosophy—using a blunt axe when a mere butter knife would do.' You do acknowledge that your organization made that statement?"

The witness's eyes searched the courtroom for an escape from the question. He lifted his hands aimlessly—as if he hoped to be able to construct an answer with his fingers when his brain was unable to do so.

"I do not deny that such a statement was made by another person in our organization. But I can't vouch for everything our organization says or writes about American military policy. But I will tell you this, Mr. Chambers...I have looked at the photographs of the Chacmool incident. I've seen the bodies of those children ripped apart by American bullets. That, to me, resembles a policy that uses a blunt axe."

Zagblundt's final grasping effort paid off. His response registered with the three judges. Will could see that on their faces. The attorney had only one remaining line of questioning left to turn things around.

"By looking at the bodies of victims, can you tell the intent of an official who ordered that attack that caused the deaths?"

The witness shook his head and smiled.

"Of course not."

"And by looking at the photographs of these poor unfortunate victims—Carlos Fuego, his wife, and his two little children—by merely looking at the photographs, are you able to exclude the possibility that a high-ranking Mexican official conspired with the AAJ to lead Colonel Marlowe and his unit to that house, and to cause a lookout to shoot in their direction, knowing they would fire back and likely hit Carlos, his wife, and children, all of whom were strapped to chairs inside that house? Can you exclude that possibility merely by looking at the photographs of the victims?"

Zagblundt's hands were outstretched again, groping, reaching for a response. But this time they found none. Finally, he drew them back, folded them politely in front of him, and gave a half-smile.

"Of course not, Mr. Chambers. It would be unreasonable to jump to any such conclusions based only on the photographs."

Zagblundt was not willing to stretch his testimony any further.

Nor was Will Chambers willing to venture into any more fields laden with legal landmines.

Whether it could be characterized as a truce or not, Will did not know. But the result of his cross-examination of Zagblundt—at the very best, perhaps—might only have been a draw.

73

ALONE IN THE ELEVATOR, WILL was oblivious to the fact that it had reached the floor of the courtroom in the International Criminal Court Building and that the doors were open. In fact, they were beginning to close when Will snapped out of his cogitation and thrust his hand out to catch them and exit.

He had been deep in thought about the testimony he would present that day. The defense case would be compact, even slim. It would consist of only two bodies of evidence. First, the testimony of Caleb Marlowe himself.

And secondly, Will would have to rely on the deposition testimony of Damon Lynch. Will knew the prosecutor's office had filed an objection to its admissibility, and that was yet to be argued. Of course, he was also relying, in part, on the Article 32 hearing testimony, which the prosecution had moved into evidence in its case. Will considered that a two-edged sword, actually helping the defense slightly more than the prosecution—though prosecutor Les Forges obviously didn't see it that way. But he would rely on Sergeant Rockwell's testimony that Marlowe had been in possession of intelligence information that linked the group in the house at Chacmool to the terrorists who had attempted to kidnap Secretary Kilmer.

Will, Jacki, and Professor Redgrove had spent the previous evening framing and analyzing the questions that he would put to his client during direct examination.

And now, as Caleb Marlowe sat in the witness stand in a simple civilian suit and tie, Will knew he would have to strenuously confine his questions to the game plan.

Marlowe described the authorization he had received from the highest levels of the United States government for the attack. But under Will's questioning he also laid the foundation for its preparation.

The operation had really begun at the Economic Summit of the Americas, which had been convened at a lavish hotel in Cancún. Three Secret Service agents had been killed, and a fourth injured, when Kilmer was abducted. Eight terrorists in all had been involved in the operation. The USS *Nathan Hale*, which was in the area, had been dispatched to a point just off the Yucatán Peninsula and would provide a launching platform. Marlowe's BATCOM unit was aided by other special operations forces and a squad of United States Marines. In the ensuing rescue four of the terrorists had been killed and Kilmer had been released unharmed, but the other four terrorists had fled.

Marlowe then explained the hastily arranged meeting aboard the *Hale* between himself, the Deputy Director of the CIA, the Deputy Secretary of Defense, and a representative of the Defense Intelligence Agency. He was told that the Mexican government had authorized the deployment of American troops to secure the release of Secretary Kilmer.

"Colonel Marlowe, were you given authorization by those in attendance at that meeting aboard the USS *Nathan Hale* to pursue and eliminate any members of an AAJ cell group believed to be involved in the kidnapping incident?"

"Yes, sir, I received that authorization in our meeting. If I was able to verify linkage between Abu Adis or his AAJ cell unit and the kidnappers, I had the authority to use deadly force and eliminate them."

"During that meeting, were you given top secret information regarding a threat posed to American national security by Abu Adis and his AAJ cell group?

"Yes, sir, I received such information," Marlowe answered. "I was bound—and am bound now—not to disclose the details of that information. But yes, there was information of a serious threat to the safety and security of the United States of America from Abu Adis and his AAJ cell group, who were in Mexico at the time."

"Now, at the time of the Chacmool incident, had you come into the possession of intelligence information that actually linked Abu Adis with the aborted kidnapping of Secretary Kilmer?"

Out of the corner of his eye, Will noticed that Les Forges was sitting steel-spine straight at her counsel table, her body angled forward, her eyes riveted on Marlowe.

"I had received intelligence information linking Abu Adis and his AAJ cell group to the kidnapping of Secretary Kilmer."

"And what was the source of that information?"

"Ultimately—the origin of that information was our CIA operative, Carlos Fuego. Fuego had disclosed to me, personally, as we were planning our rescue of Secretary Kilmer, that he had the cell-phone number of Abu Adis. He had gone to great lengths to develop that information. That cell-phone number, as it turned out, would provide two separate corroborations—of the AAJ involvement in the kidnapping and of their final location at Chacmool."

"Let me just step aside for a minute from this line of questioning and ask you a few things about Carlos Fuego. First of all, he was a good friend of yours?"

Marlowe paused and looked down. Will could see that he was struggling a bit as he recalled his friend.

After he had composed himself, he answered.

"Carlos Fuego...I was the best man at his wedding. He and I fought and trained together. He was a good friend and a brave, loyal American"

"So that the record can be entirely clear on this matter, did you have any information—any knowledge—any suspicion or inkling—that Carlos Fuego might have been in that house in Chacmool when you ordered your men to commence firing?"

Marlowe paused, clenched his jaw slightly, and began to answer— but there was a catch in his voice. He cleared his throat...took a drink of water. Then he answered.

"I had absolutely no suspicion—I had no information whatsoever—that my friend Carlos, or his wife, or his children were in that house when I gave that order. That is the absolute truth. I know it to be the truth. And God—who searches all minds and hearts and souls—knows that it's true."

"In any of your conversations with Mr. Fuego, did he ever indicate to you any regret over his work with the CIA?"

Marlowe shook his head sternly.

"Carlos Fuego never made any such statement to me. I never heard any information that he had made any statement like that to anyone in the world. In all of my dealings with him, I found him to be enthusiastic and courageous about his work with the CIA. Of course he had concerns for his safety, and the safety of his family, from time to time. But the assertions I've heard in this courtroom in this case—that he wanted out of the CIA, that he regretted his work with that agency, and that he feared retaliation by the United States government against him—are shameful, cowardly lies."

Now Will turned to one of the central issues of the case—the connection between the occupants of the house at Chacmool and the group of terrorists involved in the kidnapping.

"Would you explain to this tribunal," the attorney asked, "how you received verification that the terrorist cell—at or in the house at Chacmool—was part of the same terrorist group involved in the kidnapping of Secretary Kilmer?"

Marlowe described, in only general terms, his access to American surveillance intelligence through the SIGINT satellite.

"Did you receive confirmation that the SIGINT satellite was able to lock in on the cell-phone number of Abu Adis?"

"Yes, sir, I did. SIGINT locked in on Abu Adis' cell-phone signal at the exact location where, a short time later, we assaulted the terrorists and rescued Secretary Kilmer—it was at Puerto Juarez, slightly up the coast from the Cancún hotel. It appeared they were planning on faking an escape by boat from Puerto Juarez while actually taking the Secretary of Commerce inland, toward the jungle. Of course we got to them first and secured the Secretary's release."

"Within the next forty-eight hours, were you able to also locate Abu Adis' cell-phone signal at another location?"

"SIGINT again confirmed a lock-in on Adis' cell-phone signal—this time at the safe house, which we shortly thereafter attacked."

Marlowe then described the logistics of the nighttime attack itself—their landing point near Chichén Itzá, and the positioning of his unit at the house in the traditional L-shaped surround—with Master Sergeant Rockwell, Staff Sergeant Baker, and him covering the side of the house; Sergeant Thompson in sniper position covering the front entrance; and Chief Dorfman covering the road and any possible escape of the terrorists from the side or back.

As the colonel described his entrance into the small house and his discovery of the bound bodies of Carlos and his family, he paused several times.

"Colonel Marlowe, is there any possibility—even if we assume you are completely incorrect that Mr. Fuego and his family were tied to chairs as hostages—is there any reason to believe that Carlos Fuego would have identified himself as a CIA agent in his negotiations with the AAJ?"

"Mr. Chambers, sir, that is an outlandish and ridiculous scenario. Mr. Fuego was a seasoned, experienced CIA operative. He knew that the AAJ simply would not have trusted him—no matter what he said. His revealing a direct agency relationship to the United States, Mr. Fuego would have known, would have resulted in his immediate execution."

"And would such a CIA agent, even if he had wanted to negotiate with the AAJ, ever have considered bringing his wife and children along for the ride?"

"Not only is that a prohibited scenario, but knowing Mr. Fuego's love for his family—it simply never would have happened."

"Did you review the reports of the Mexican federal police?"

"Yes, sir, you provided those reports to me. And I read them over exhaustively."

"Did you find anything unusual about the description of Mr. Fuego's body?"

Marlowe hesitated for a moment and searched Will's face. Though they had discussed this in pretrial preparation, somehow the question had taken him by surprise. After a moment's reflection, he gathered his thoughts.

"Yes, sir, I think I know what you are referring to. The police report—I think it was on page 3—mentions that Mr. Fuego's body was found with his CIA ID tag hanging from his neck. It is impossible to conceive of any explanation for that except one."

"And what explanation is that?"

"That when he was captured and tied up by the AAJ, they put it on him as a message to me and to anyone else who might find him."

Les Forges rose and politely objected, assuring the tribunal that she had tried to minimize her technical objections to Marlowe's direct examination, but she could no longer sit by and watch him speculate wildly about the intentions of so-called terrorists who had never been identified and who were not before the tribunal as witnesses.

Korlov rapidly sustained the objection and struck Marlowe's last remark.

"Why did you instruct the members of your unit not to enter the house after you had discovered what had occurred?" Will continued.

"It was clear to me, when I saw that Mr. Fuego and his family had been hit by our weapons fire, that this was going to be a matter of an inquiry—by someone—at some point. I wanted to shoulder the responsibility for the incident myself. Frankly, I didn't want anyone else to be in a position of having to describe what I had seen."

"And why did you instruct your unit to evacuate the scene immediately when you detected Mexican police arriving?"

"It seemed to me more than coincidence that, immediately after our assault on the house, several squad cars of the Mexican police should arrive on the scene. Members of the Mexican military—and the law enforcement personnel whom we had kept informed of our rescue efforts—had been told that an American unit might be moving out, toward the jungle, from the Puerto Juarez area. They had promised complete secrecy. Obviously, that promise was not kept."

The colonel then cleared his throat and leaned forward in the chair. "I felt it was my responsibility to avoid—if at all possible—an international incident between the American military and the Mexican police. Therefore, I thought the safest course was to immediately evacuate and abort the mission."

74

WILL CHAMBERS' FINAL QUESTION to Colonel Marlowe was a technical legal one. In preparing for the defense case, Len Redgrove had urged his younger colleague to zero in on paragraph iv of the "War Crime of Excessive Incidental Death to Civilians" under Article 8(2)(b) of the ICC Criminal Code. That element of the crime required that "the conduct took place in the context of, and was associated with, an international armed conflict." It was the kind of technical element Will felt the tribunal would give short shrift by simply assuming that the incident at Chacmool would qualify as part of an "international armed conflict."

Nevertheless, after Redgrove's insistence upon it, Will figured he should address the question, as there might be some ambiguity about the meaning of the phrase "international armed conflict."

"Colonel Marlowe, lastly, would you tell this tribunal whether or not your mission at Chacmool was, in your understanding, part of an international armed conflict between the United States and the nation of Mexico?"

Prosecutor Les Forges objected, submitting to the tribunal that it was irrelevant whether or not America was at war with Mexico—as Article 8, paragraph iv did not require any proof of that. She submitted that the word "international" was to be taken in its ordinary and plain meaning. That is, a conflict between one or more nations and the territory within another nation—not necessarily conflict *between* nations.

After a short consultation, Judge Brucker of Germany broke his characteristic silence in the trial to pose a question to Will.

"Mr. Chambers," Brucker began, "am I to assume that you are interpreting paragraph iv of Article 8 to require the existence of an international armed conflict in the sense of one nation–state fighting against another nation–state?"

"Your Honor," the attorney replied, "that is exactly what our interpretation is."

"Well," the judge responded, "then isn't the United States government asking for the chance to have it both ways? Hasn't the United States declared war on terrorism?"

"We certainly have."

"Then, can you point out on the globe where the nation–state of terrorism resides?"

Judge Ponti smiled at that, and Judge Korlov nodded in agreement.

"Of course there is no nation–state specifically involved in our war on terrorism. But the concept of a war on terrorism is a legitimate and sovereign right of self-defense of the United States of America. And I would submit that the War Crimes Criminal Code was drafted substantially before September 11, 2001. The drafters had not ever countenanced the possibility that a nation–state, like America, would declare a global war on terrorism out of its sovereign right to defend its own borders."

Judge Brucker was not convinced.

"You have not answered my question," he said. "It appears that the United States wants the best of both arguments. It wants to declare war on terrorism without limitation to borders or nations—and yet it is requiring this tribunal to interpret paragraph iv, with its reference to international armed conflict, in a way that excludes the war on terrorism from any elements of the war-crimes statute. Is that what you're saying?"

"What I am submitting, Your Honor, is that paragraph iv's reference to 'international armed conflict' must be interpreted according to the language of the war crimes code itself, and the Rome Statute, which acts as the preamble. If I may direct the court's attention to the Rome Statute, it says that the jurisdiction of this court, with regard to war crime, extends only—and I quote—'over the most serious crimes of concern to the *international community* as a whole.' In other words, only those war crimes, that have a characteristically *international* aspect. And that means war crimes involving two or more nation–states—or internal civil war between competing factions within a single nation–state.

Now Judge Ponti was joining the fray.

"Mr. Chambers, point out to me—anywhere—proof of your statement that your interpretation is somehow part of the history of the development of this criminal code. I simply reject that. I know of no support, whatsoever, for that statement. Can you enlighten me?"

Will paused for a moment, excused himself, and walked over to defense counsel table. He snatched up a black notebook marked "History of International Criminal Tribunals in the ICC" and then returned to the podium. Flipping open to a page, he looked up at the French judge.

"If I may, Judge Ponti, I would direct your attention to Volume 89 of the *International Law Review*. Within it is an article written in 1995, about the 1994 adoption by the International Law Commission of a draft statute for an international criminal court. That draft served as a basis for what would later be the ICC under the Rome Statute."

"I'm still waiting," Ponti retorted, "for some proof that supports your interpretation of the word 'international' as excluding the situation that occurred in Chacmool, Mexico."

"If I may," Will replied, "let me call your attention to a statement in that *International Law Review* article. It described the initial work of the International Law Commission, and its draft statute, as extending jurisdiction only—and I quote—'over grave crimes of an international character under existing international law and treaties.' So, what is the 'international community'?"

"Isn't that self-evident?" Ponti shot back.

"I certainly think it is self-evident," the attorney replied. "The other day, I looked up in several different dictionaries the definition of the word 'international.' Every primary and secondary definition included the concept of two or more nations. When we talk about crimes that impact the 'international community', we cannot simply mean 'impacting global citizens of the planet Earth,' can we? For if that is the interpretation, then this court is urging the breakdown of sovereign boundaries between nation–states. That certainly is not the intent—is it?"

Judge Brucker saw where Will was heading and tried to redirect him.

"So how do *you* define 'international community'—or 'crimes of an international character'?"

"Respectfully, Judge Brucker, that term does not apply to the circumstances as they existed at the time that the United States made a limited assault on the house outside of the village of Chacmool in pursuit of terrorists who posed a threat to the national security of the United States. That was not an international armed conflict."

Judge Korlov weighed in.

"Can you give us other examples of what would *not* be an international armed conflict?"

After reflecting for a moment Will answered.

"As an example, if a customs agent, or perhaps a state patrol officer, in the United States, were in hot pursuit of a bank robber, who then crossed the American border into Mexico. And just on the other side of the border, a gun battle broke out between the customs agent, or state patrol officer, and the bank robber. Just because it took place on Mexican soil doesn't mean it was part of an international armed conflict. Or, perhaps this—an American naval vessel stops at Cancún, and one of its sailors goes ashore on leave. He's kidnapped by a drug cartel, and the American military attempts to secure his release by the use of force—on Mexican soil. That also is not an international armed conflict."

Will was ready to list a half-dozen more hypotheticals, but Judge Korlov cut him off, raising his hands and waving them.

"Thank you. Thank you. That's enough. I think we see what your argument is. We're going to permit the question to be asked and the answer to be given—for whatever weight it may have."

Will put the question to Colonel Marlowe again, as to whether or not he considered the assault at Chacmool to be part of an international armed conflict.

"Sir, as I understood the situation, I had no reason to believe that it was part of an international armed conflict of any kind. We were not attacking the nation of Mexico. We were defending the security of the United States from a small group of known terrorists."

Will then rested the defense case.

Walking back to his counsel table, the attorney was not entirely sure what might have been accomplished by his dialogue with the judges on an obscure point of international law. Indeed, he could only hope that, as far as obscurity was concerned, his argument had not clouded what he felt were the truly critical issues in the case—issues that were now hanging precariously in the balance.

75

FRANCINE LES FORGES SNATCHED UP her notebook and legal pad and strode rapidly to the podium. Everything in her demeanor and her bearing indicated that she meant business—and she would get right to it.

"Colonel Marlowe, you placed great reliance on the fact that your satellite technologies supposedly traced the signal from the cell phone of Abu Adis to the location of the kidnappers near Cancún, and again, later, to the house where you launched the attack—correct?"

"Yes, ma'am—I have testified that we identified that signal on two separate occasions, tying Abu Adis to the group of kidnappers and then tying him to the house we attacked."

"Correct me if I'm wrong, Colonel, but is a cell phone a small portable item that can be handed from one person to another?"

"Yes, ma'am."

"Thus, Abu Adis—even if he had been the one who owned the cell phone—could have handed it off to someone else, and your sophisticated satellite equipment would have been picking up the location of the cell phone. But it would not necessarily have been registering the location, or even the presence, of Abu Adis himself?"

"Yes, ma'am, that would be true except that—"

"So, it is true. You had no reason to believe you were locating Abu Adis—you were only locating a cell phone that might have been passed off to somebody else?"

"Madame Prosecutor, if I might answer. What I was trying to say is that your question has a wrong assumption in it. Abu Adis was known to have several cell phones—but the cell-phone number in question belonged to the phone he protected with his life. It was his most secure number—and he was known to have killed others who had come into possession of it. The chances that Adis passed off that cell phone, with that number, to someone else during the time of our mission, are infinitesimally small—almost nonexistent as far as I'm concerned."

Les Forges decided to change direction.

"You've listed the high-ranking government officials who participated in the decision to undertake this mission. I know that you did not mention the presence of either the President or the Vice President of the United States in that meeting."

Marlowe smiled.

"Yes, ma'am, that's correct. Neither of them was present during that meeting."

"But because of the high ranking nature of the American government officials present there, you were certainly given the information that the president himself had approved this mission—is that correct?"

Marlowe eyed the prosecutor. He knew something about booby traps. But he also knew they were usually more carefully disguised than this one.

"Ma'am, I had absolutely no information to lead me to believe the president specifically knew of, or specifically authorized, this mission. To this day I have no information that the president himself was involved in authorizing it. The decision to undertake the mission was mine—and mine alone—in consultation with the government representatives I mentioned previously in my testimony. Any fault that may be laid on anyone's shoulders as a result of this incident is to be laid on my shoulders, and mine alone."

"I appreciate the nobility with which you assume responsibility— therefore you accept responsibility for having committed a war crime at Chacmool?"

"No, ma'am. I accept the responsibility for having accidentally caused the death of a close friend, his beautiful bride, and their two little children. To this day I struggle with that tragic loss."

"Is that correct? Do you really?" Les Forges with a tinge of sarcasm.

"Of course I do."

"And do you, today, regret your actions and the decision that you made—and the orders that you gave that night at Chacmool?"

"Madame, I regret that I was led into a trap by devious and evil people. But I did not have sufficient information to have understood that trap, and to have prevented the tragic consequences."

"But you knew there would be civilians—there might be civilians in that house when you ordered the bullets to begin flying into it?"

Marlowe took a second to respond. Will was glued to his seat at the defense table, waiting, holding his breath, for Marlowe's response.

"I knew there might be a civilian presence in the house—that is correct."

"And yet you ordered an assault that was likely to take the lives of everyone in the house, including those civilians?"

"Ma'am, I'm not sure I agree with that."

The prosecutor bulleted her next question, this time moving away from the podium with her hands clasped behind her back, her eyes fixed on the man in the witness chair.

"Did you consider yourself the 'number-one man'—that is, you were man number one in the radio transmissions to your team?"

"That's correct."

"And it was you—man number one—who indicated you knew there might be civilian loss at the very instant you gave the order to shoot. Correct?"

"You're correct in that. I did say those words. The listening device of the Mexican police did pick up my words correctly."

Les Forges handed something to the clerk, who then walked it over to Marlowe at the witness stand.

"Look at these pictures," she said brusquely. "Look at the photographs of the murdered bodies of Carlos Fuego and his wife, Linda, and his two children. Study those pictures, Colonel Marlowe. And then tell me that you regret the loss of civilian life. These are the civilians you killed—these are the civilians you murdered. Were these lives worth the tactical advantage gained by chasing some men through the jungle whom the United States thought might possibly pose a risk to it?"

Marlowe's gaze was locked onto the pictures in front of him. His chin quivered, and he raised his face toward Les Forges. He was silent for almost a minute.

After regaining his composure, he answered.

"Madame Prosecutor, I can imagine nothing in this world that would have been worth taking the life of Carlos Fuego and his family."

Marlowe cleared his throat and took a swallow of water. His expression was controlled, as if etched in stone. But the court personnel could not see the tears that were welling up in his eyes.

As Les Forges sat down, Will knew two things despite the theatrics of her cross-examination. He knew that the prosecutor was moving from her initial theory—that the United States had used Marlowe and his squad to deliberately assassinate Fuego as a potential CIA defector. But he also knew Les Forges had confidently built a convincing fallback position—that proving that a war crime had been committed by Marlowe required her to demonstrate only a high degree of recklessness in the face of very little tactical military advantage. If the tribunal accepted that interpretation of Article 8 of the codes, Colonel Caleb Marlowe might be spending the rest of his life in a prison for war crimes.

The attorney walked slowly to the podium for redirect examination. His task was simple. His questions were going to be concise.

"Colonel Marlowe, this has been a very difficult day for you. My questioning is going to be very limited. You were asked about 'civilian loss'—'collateral damage' was also a phrase that was used by the prosecution. You used both of those phrases in the seconds and minutes prior to giving the command for the assault to begin—and you admit that?"

Marlowe nodded slowly.

"Yes, sir, that is correct."

"What civilians were you referring to?"

"Not civilians. Not plural."

"So, you were considering the possible presence of *one* civilian in the house at the time you ordered the attack?"

"Yes, sir, that is exactly what I intended. There were four terrorists who had escaped. It was clear to me that Abu Adis was one of them, and that he had his cell phone with him in the safe house in Chacmool. When I looked at my thermal-imaging scope, I saw four individuals, seated. There was a lookout out front. That makes five people. Of course, the fifth person could have been another terrorist. But I also considered the possibility it was not. That it was, for all intents and purposes, a Mexican civilian."

"And did you have any reason to believe that it was one civilian in particular?"

"Yes. I did not know his name. But American intelligence knew there was a high-ranking Mexican official who had been collaborating with the AAJ. Our belief was that this Mexican official had given information to the AAJ to aid them in their kidnapping of Secretary Kilmer. That same official was the civilian I anticipated might have been in the house that night."

"I do have a question to ask you—and if I do not ask it, I am certain the prosecutor's office will be sure to ask it. Here it is—why would an influential member of the Mexican government place himself in a safe house together with known terrorists immediately after the aborted kidnapping of the American Secretary of Commerce? Wouldn't that have been a very risky thing for that official to do?"

"Exactly," Marlowe answered quickly. "But there's a reason why I believed this Mexican official, in particular, might have been willing to assume the risk."

"And what reason was that?"

"We had word about the planning of an attack against the United States—that this official had sensitive information that was being delivered to Abu Adis directly. It was such a critical piece of information that I believed this individual would have risked apprehension in order to deliver this information in person to Adis, rather than trying to transmit it through a third party—or via telephone, which can be monitored—or via a cell phone, which can be monitored even more easily."

"So that is why you felt there might be *one* civilian present—one who was a co-conspirator with a terrorist cell group that had intentions to make some sort of strike against the United States?"

"Yes, sir. That's exactly what I thought when I gave the order for the assault to commence."

Will knew there was nothing more he could do. He rested his cross-examination and yielded the podium to Les Forges.

"But," the prosecutor stated quietly, "your assumptions about who was in the house—that it might be a co-conspirator with the AAJ— those assumptions were absolutely incorrect, weren't they?"

Marlowe knew the truth. And he would speak it.

"Yes, ma'am. My assumptions were entirely incorrect."

After Marlowe's testimony, there was only one other item of business for the defense case. Will asked the court to receive into evidence the entire transcript of the deposition of Damon Lynch, taken in the jail in Mexico City.

Les Forges objected vehemently, spitting out her words like an automatic weapon, arguing that Lynch had not been listed originally on the list of witnesses presented by the defense—and that the circumstances of his testimony were inherently unreliable. Then she landed the lowest blow of all.

"Your Honors, to show the unreliability of this testimony, you need only know that Mr. Chambers was so desperate to use Mr. Lynch's lies that he struck a deal with him. Mr. Chambers agreed, as the transcript of the deposition will reveal, to let Lynch escape the consequences of his participation in the murder of Chambers' own first wife, Audra Chambers, in return for his testimony."

The three judges sat bug-eyed, and then Judge Korlov responded.

"This is most outrageous, Mr. Chambers," the presiding judge said, drumming the fingers of both hands on the bench. "This is most troubling. By what darkened logic did you arrive at a decision to bargain with this Mr. Lynch, even though he was apparently involved in the death of your own wife?"

Will had spent his entire adult life in courtrooms around America. He was rarely at a loss for words...but then, at that moment, utterance escaped him After a protracted period of silence, he addressed the tribunal.

"I believe it was the French philosopher Pascal who said that the human heart has reasons which reason cannot know. To answer you, Your Honor, this was not a matter of logic. It was a matter of sacrifice. And perhaps even of forgiveness, as strange as that may sound. My desire for revenge upon and punishment for Damon Lynch needed to be sacrificed in order to overcome evil with good."

"Good?" Judge Ponti exclaimed. "What good could you possibly be talking about?!"

"The good of the truth—that you three judges would know the truth about the identity of the Mexican official who conspired to set a trap for Colonel Marlowe and caused the death of four innocent individuals. The truth I hope will motivate your sense of justice—and your decision to acquit Colonel Marlowe. I have no explanation other than that."

After the three judges quietly conferred, Judge Korlov addressed the lawyers.

"We will allow the transcript of the deposition of Damon Lynch to come into evidence. But with the understanding that we are inclined to view his comments with a high degree of suspicion, if not contempt."

Will made the perfunctory motion for dismissal of the proceedings in favor of acquittal, and Korlov indicated that they would defer decision on that. He was about to make another comment when he saw something that stopped him. A clerk hurriedly approached the bench and passed a letter to him.

Korlov took his time reading the note, and then started urgently whispering to his colleagues. The whispering continued among them, and the faces of all three became animated. Five minutes turned into ten minutes. Then twenty minutes. Whatever it was they were discussing, it seemed to center on the letter.

Finally, the presiding judge clicked his microphone back on. He leaned forward.

"This proceeding is adjourned for five hours. All lawyers and personnel are to be present again in five hours."

The courtroom rose as the judges quickly disappeared through the doors of their chambers.

Les Forges packed up her briefcase with an air of smugness. Will took a few steps toward her and extended his right hand.

"May justice be done."

The prosecutor took his hand limply, offered a half-smile, and then turned and exited the courtroom with her assistants.

76

Aꜰᴛᴇʀ ᴛʜᴇ sᴇssɪᴏɴ ᴡᴀs ᴀᴅᴊᴏᴜʀɴᴇᴅ, the bailiffs permitted Will to spend some time talking with Caleb Marlowe alone in the courtroom.

His client wanted to know, of course, why the judges had so abruptly adjourned for a short period. The attorney could only surmise that an exigency had arisen in another case that would require them to participate in an emergency hearing lasting several hours.

Final closing arguments had yet to be heard. Judging by the lateness of the day, Will assumed that the court, when it reconvened, would schedule closing arguments for the following day. And then it would inform the participants of its schedule for deliberations and for announcing the release of its decision on the case.

Marlowe wanted to know Will's assessment of his testimony. The attorney assured him that no witness had ever performed more truthfully, nor more effectively.

As the two then chatted about a few personal things, the colonel said that the only positive point about his confinement was the quality of the food—which he found surprisingly good.

Will then asked a question, offhandedly.

"So—if we're blessed with an acquittal in this case, what are you going to do with your life?"

His client smiled and thought about it for a minute.

"I expect I'll be traveling. Quite a bit. Maybe I'll revisit Chichén Itzá."

Will looked at him, thunderstruck. Then a wry smile broke out on Marlowe's face.

"For a minute there, I thought you were serious," Will commented.

"Oh, I am. I think that's a fascinating place to visit as a tourist—*el cenote sagrado*—the great sacrificial well where the Mayans threw in human beings to satisfy their gods. You saw that place, didn't you, when you went down to investigate?"

"Yes, though I didn't have too much time to linger. I walked past it with Pancho on the way over to the house."

"It is interesting," Marlowe mused, "how even the pagans who lived hundreds of years ago in the jungles of Mexico understood the necessity of a blood sacrifice to appease a deity whose sense of justice had been offended."

"Yes, I thought about that. Where they went wrong was in the presumption that humans could ever make a sacrifice good enough to cover their own sins. And as we both know, only the sacrificial Lamb was capable of doing that."

Will decided he would walk back to the hotel. His client would have to go back to his jail cell for a few hours. Before the two separated, Marlowe handed a blank white envelope, sealed, to the other man.

"When we win this case—and I believe we will—you can open this and read it. Not until then."

Another mystery from his enigmatic client. Will took it and headed down the street to his hotel room. The air was clear and warm, and the tulips were in bloom, filling big baskets in front of several shops. The horse-drawn taxis were out in full force, clip-clopping down the medieval streets. In spite of all the charm of the old-world atmosphere, though, he was suddenly aware of how homesick he was for the sweet smell of wildflowers at his Virginia home.

Jacki Johnson and Len Redgrove were going to catch an early dinner and they invited Will, but he declined. He would go back to his room and call Fiona so they could catch up a little on their life together. Then he would ask for a wake-up call in a few hours and collapse on the bed for a nap. The prolonged schedule of sleep deprivation was starting to really get to him.

Exactly five hours after the court had adjourned, Will, Professor Redgrove, and Jacki were seated at counsel table. Caleb Marlowe was brought in and seated next to Will. Les Forges and her entourage arrived. The prosecutor looked slightly distracted, and strangely agitated.

A few more minutes went by, and then the door to the chambers opened and the three judges, in their robes, assumed the bench.

Judge Korlov quickly rubbed his eyes, sighed, and then moved closer to the microphone.

"Reconvening now the matter of Colonel Caleb Marlowe, accused. Are all parties present with their legal counsel?"

Les Forges snapped to her feet and acknowledged she was ready to proceed. Will Chambers followed, acknowledging the presence of Caleb Marlowe, and indicated he was ready to proceed as well.

Then Korlov started speaking. It appeared that he had some notes in front of him, and he glanced at them as he spoke.

"There are some preliminary matters that need to be disposed of. First of all, co-counsel for the defense argued, at the beginning of this case, that this court did not have jurisdiction. That the United States had made a genuine effort to prosecute Caleb Marlowe, and for that reason, this court was precluded from hearing this case—and that the case against Colonel Marlowe was therefore inadmissible. We hasten to disagree with that argument, and we deny the motion to dismiss for lack of jurisdiction."

Will was not surprised, though when he turned and gave a reassuring look to Redgrove, the law professor was clearly disappointed.

"Also, we feel that it is an opportune time for us to dispose of defense counsel's arguments in favor of acquittal and dismissal at the end of the evidence. We will not be reciting, in any detail, the factual record or the evidence that has come in throughout this trial."

The presiding judge paused again and rubbed the bushy eyebrow over his right eye. Then he continued.

"We mention only, however, one very small piece of evidence—the testimony of Colonel Caleb Marlowe relating to his opinion—as a military officer, and obviously not as a legal expert—that his mission at Chacmool, Mexico, was *not* part of an 'international armed conflict.' We are not bound by the opinions of laypersons—particularly, that of the accused in a war-crimes case as to whether or not he believes he is engaged in an international armed conflict."

As Korlov halted again for a moment, it seemed to Will he was belaboring the obvious. The court was not going to rely on Marlowe's self-proclaimed defense that he didn't consider the conflict to be of an "international" character under paragraph iv of Article 8, Section 2(b) of the War Crimes Criminal Code.

"So, this tribunal does not rely upon the accused's own proclamation that paragraph iv of the elements of the crime was not satisfied. What is important is *not* what Colonel Marlowe said in his testimony regarding that."

Glancing over at his client, Will could see that he was struggling to figure out where the judge was going in his remarks, but without success.

"What is important, rather," Judge Korlov continued, this time slightly twisting some of the hairs of his bushy eyebrows between his fingers, "is what testimony *did not* occur during the evidence portion of the trial."

Suddenly, it was as if someone spoke...faintly.

Somewhere in the recesses of Will's thinking patterns—that hidden place where law-school professors say they are forming a "lawyer's mind" in their students, something slightly distinct from the thought processes of the rest of the human race—Will could hear a voice.

And that small voice was saying that—somehow—all hope had not been lost. Not yet.

77

After clearing his throat and glancing down at his notes, Judge Korlov continued.

"What we did not hear—nor did we expect to hear—was testimony relating to the international aspects of the armed conflict involved in this case. The basic facts surrounding the actions of the BATCOM unit and Colonel Marlowe, on behalf of the United States of America within the sovereign territory of the nation–state of Mexico, are essentially uncontroverted. They are not contradicted. They seem to be assumed by all parties.

"Colonel Marlowe—indeed, the Solicitor General's Office of the United States in its amicus brief—argues that the BATCOM unit was there because of the U.S. war on terrorism. The office of the esteemed prosecutor seems to agree that was the putative reason, but argues that the occurrence itself at Chacmool clearly exceeded any tactical or military advantage that might have justified the killing of four innocent human beings. Thus, those are the undisputed positions of all of the parties here. That is the framework of this case. That is also, we regret to add, the dilemma facing this tribunal."

As Korlov concluded his remarks, he folded his hands in front of him, and the two other judges—one on each side—stared directly ahead.

"The dilemma is simply this—the actions of the United States government, and Colonel Caleb Marlowe in particular, show a disregard for the human rights of Mexican citizens—indeed, show a disrespect for the sovereignty of Mexico."

It was at that point Will considered rising to object. The court had not even heard the closing arguments from counsel, and it appeared to be issuing its decision of guilt. However, something told the attorney he should hold his peace.

He was glad he did.

"Nevertheless," the judge intoned, glancing over at the bank of interpreters behind the glass wall along the side of the courtroom, and then looking back, directly at Will Chambers, "it is the decision of this tribunal—"

But before he could continue, Judge Ponti reached over and grasped his arm. The two began arguing vigorously. It looked like Ponti was making a last-ditch effort to redirect the tribunal's decision. Korlov was shaking his head. The French judge's hands were now frantically jabbing the air. The Russian judge argued back. Judge Brucker of Germany, expressionless, was leaning into the discussion, but listening only.

Ponti raised his voice one more time, but Korlov had reached his limit. He slammed the palms of both hands down on the bench. And then he raised his voice and gave his final response to his associate— one that could be heard throughout the room and needed no interpreting.

"Nyet!" he said forcefully.

Then he turned back to the courtroom and continued reading the decision.

"The defense motion for acquittal…that motion must be granted."

Will, Redgrove, Jacki, and Marlowe all simultaneously jumped up from their seats. The professor thrust his hand into that of his colleague's and whispered, "Well done, well done!" Will was momentarily numb.

Judge Korloff hammered his gavel to quiet the defense bench and then continued. "There is an ambiguity within an element of the war-crimes offense that is the subject of this case. It is not entirely clear that the episode here, issuing as it does from America's self-proclaimed 'war on terrorism' qualified as a form of 'international armed conflict' within the language or the intent of Article 8, Section 2(b)(iv) of the War Crimes Code. Because this is a criminal case, we must err, under the well-known doctrine of lenity, on the side of disfavoring a conviction based on a criminal code of uncertain interpretation. This case is dismissed. The accused is hereby ordered discharged from custody."

From somewhere Will heard a gasp—he was not sure where. But before he could wrap his thoughts around the immensity of what he had just heard, Les Forges dashed to the podium, her arms outstretched.

"Your Honors, I strenuously object. We do have a right of appeal under ICC procedure. Before I can make a decision on an appeal, I would respectfully request that the accused be detained in custody, rather than released."

Will was halfway to the podium to counter her argument when Judge Korlov signaled for him to sit down.

"The request is denied, Madame Prosecutor. You may make the decision to appeal if you wish, but the accused is released."

Francine Les Forges was stunned—she stood for a moment with her eyes wide open and unblinking. Then she cocked her jaw and tossed her head ever so slightly—like a teenage socialite who suddenly, and quite unexpectedly, found herself without a date for the ball.

She was too immersed in the agony of her own defeat to notice Atavar Strinsky, who was seated at the counsel table struggling not to smile.

Not that it would have made any difference if Strinsky had broken into a grin. He had been out interviewing anyway and had already secured a new position—with a large law firm in Belgium specializing in EU trade law. In a few weeks he would give notice to his superior and the personnel administrator at the ICC.

And so all three judges rose to their feet, and at a quickstep, disappeared from the courtroom through the chambers door, followed by two of the armed bailiffs.

Another took a smiling, relieved Caleb Marlowe down to the detention area to gather his personal effects.

Len Redgrove wrapped his arms around Will in a huge bear hug, and whispered, almost in tears, "God bless you, Will. Magnificent."

Jacki was clapping her hands and laughing, struggling to find an adequate response—but failing.

"You better get outside in the corridor—the press is going to be salivating for a comment on this. This is most incredible!" Redgrove declared.

Will turned to his old law professor. He smiled and put a hand on his friend's shoulder.

"Len," he said with a smile, "I want to go down and escort Marlowe out of the jail myself, and I would greatly appreciate it if you and Jacki could go face the media hounds and give them some good sound bites—what little you can actually say. You know how to do it. You know the routine."

He paused. "And thank you both. From the bottom of my heart."

Will took a side door out, went down to the detention center, and announced to the jailers he was there to escort Marlowe out of the building after his release. They acknowledged they would let him know when his client would be free to go.

Will understood there would be paperwork and a processing procedure that might take some time. But after nearly an hour, Will grew tired of waiting.

"Would you check on the status of Colonel Marlowe? He was discharged by the court more than an hour ago. How are we doing with his release?"

The jailer agreed to check and she disappeared behind a door. Another twenty minutes went by.

Then the jailer returned, shaking her head.

"I'm sorry," she said with a thick accent, "Colonel Marlowe has already been discharged. He's left the detention center."

"Did he leave a message for me? I'm his defense counsel. He was supposed to meet with me."

The jailer simply shook her head. Puzzled, Will left the building and walked out onto the street. Briefcase in his hand, he walked along it toward the harbor on the North Sea. It was good to get some fresh air to clear his head. He wanted to call Fiona immediately and tell her the great news, but he was wondering what to do about his client...and about the strange feeling of foreboding in the pit of his stomach. When he reached the water, he dropped his briefcase at his feet, and leaned against one of the large gray posts with a tourist telescope.

Then he sensed someone's presence and looked up. It was a familiar face, a familiar uniform. Standing next to him at the North Sea harbor was Lieutenant General Cal Tucker.

Tucker extended his big hand and shook Will's firmly.

"Congratulations," he said, smiling.

"You heard the good news about Colonel Marlowe?"

The general nodded.

"You came all the way here to follow the outcome?"

"In a way, I did," Tucker said. "I came in with some of the Navy. Your little case here came close to an international incident."

"How much can you tell me?"

"Just this. Earlier this morning, the President of the United States sent a letter to the President of the International Criminal Court. Putting the ICC on notice that Marlowe's continued detention posed a risk to the national security of the United States."

Will nodded. He now understood what the note had been that Judge Korlov had received during the last day of the trial.

"I suppose you can't tell me what the president would have done if the ICC had found Marlowe guilty?"

"You're right," General Tucker replied. Then he gave Will another handshake and quickly walked back to his waiting aides, who escorted him to a small landing craft. In a few minutes, Will saw the vessel motoring rapidly out of sight.

78

WILL HEADED STRAIGHT TO HIS HOTEL ROOM. He had made plans to rendezvous with Redgrove and Jacki and celebrate at one of the finer restaurants in the old section of The Hague. But first he wanted to call Fiona with the good news, and then access his e-mail on his laptop so he could catch up on things with his office.

After reaching his hotel room, as he tossed his coat on the bed, he caught sight of the envelope that Caleb Marlowe had given him.

He sliced it open and read the note inside. It was typical Caleb Marlowe—direct, but enigmatic—and a little troubling.

Will—

I couldn't have had better legal counsel. A job well done. Now I have to finish the final phase of this mission. This is the reckoning. I do need your help one last time. You have a card with a telephone number on it. Share it with no one, but call the number. May the Lord be your shield.

This was not the kind of message Will wanted from his client. He had successfully navigated Caleb Marlowe through a potential court-martial, a Senate subcommittee hearing, and the International Criminal Court. Whether Marlowe's "mission" was real or imagined, he did not know—and at this point, he was not sure how much he really cared.

Something had happened to him in front of the international tribunal when his personal life and Audra's death had suddenly been interjected into the record. Perhaps the meeting with Damon Lynch, in a strange way, had forced him to confront—and begin to move

353

beyond—the shadow of darkness that still lingered within him over his first wife's death.

But if it had, then Will wanted to move forward. He wanted to get home to Fiona. To think long and hard about exposing his family to any more danger because of the high-risk cases he accepted.

He pulled out his wallet, and flipped to the little snapshot of Fiona he kept there. Staring at his precious wife's face, which was framed by her dark, flowing hair, he remained deeply in thought for a few minutes. Finally, with a sigh, he retrieved the small white card with the telephone number on it. It was not something he wanted to do. Yet at the same time, he felt a tidal pull to make the call. Somehow, Will understood that there was unfinished business for him...business not just his own. Perhaps the completion of something much larger than he had ever imagined.

He lifted the phone and punched in the number from the card.

On the third ring, the agent in Mexico answered.

"This is Will Chambers calling."

"Prove it."

"Coral."

"What's up?"

"I'm supposed to call."

"Oh?" the man at the other end said.

"Look," Will said, "I have to tell you—I'm not in the mood to play twenty questions. Marlowe said I'm supposed to call, so I'm calling. I'm the one who ought to be asking the questions."

"Well, maybe there was something he wanted you to know."

"Like what?"

"Marlowe believes he's on some kind of mission. I'm really not sure what's involved. I would hate to think that a decorated war hero like Caleb Marlowe has gone off the deep end..."

"I'm still not getting any answers."

"You know, Will," the man continued, "Marlowe may need you. I believe he's down here somewhere."

"Where? Mexico?"

"Right. Down here in Mexico. You may be able to do your client a whole lot of good. And maybe even your country at the same time. I'd like you to head over to the commercial-cargo section of the airport there in the Netherlands. We've got a plane that can bring you down to Mexico City. We can talk down here."

The attorney paused. He was tired of riddles. And he was homesick for his wife. The American agent at the other end, it was clear, was being deliberately obscure.

During the silence Will thought about something else. The reason for the intentional ambiguity was now becoming obvious. A collision course was being planned. Something was going to happen. Marlowe was certainly involved...and for some bizarre reason, so was he.

Why did he think that this last, unexpected chapter in the case of Colonel Caleb Marlowe, accused, might be not only bigger than he thought, but more personal as well?

What if this final road led to that unknown ground where the puzzles of forgiveness and vengeance would be resolved? What if he was being called to a place of ultimate sacrifice?

He took a deep breath and cleared his throat. Then he asked one last question.

"On a scale of one to ten—what is the risk here?"

"Well, Will, let me put it to you this way. Life is full of risks. There's a risk when you travel the freeway. Or when you fight for justice. Or when you put yourself in harm's way because you just may have the chance to save the lives of innocent people."

Will was no longer wondering what he had to decide. His only question was how he would tell Fiona.

"Do I need to get to the airport immediately?"

"Yeah—I'd say so."

"What do I look for?"

"There's a red-and-blue jet in the international-cargo section. It's marked 'Liberty Cargo Company.' There's a flight crew waiting for you. They'll land in Mexico City, and we'll have some folks there to meet you."

Will hung up and then took some time to pray. After that, he dialed Fiona. He wasn't quite sure what he was going to tell her. He didn't want to share the feeling of foreboding that he had. He wanted to tell her how much he loved her, and how this first year of marriage had been the greatest time of his life. The two of them had talked about having children, and he wanted that. And he wanted to raise a family and grow old with her. And to spend the next forty years of his life waking up every morning seeing her face on the pillow next to him.

But in his message, he had to settle for something much less. He got voice mail at home and on her cell phone also. So he left a very short message.

> Fiona—this is Will. I have one short side trip before I get home. I'll love you forever, and whatever separates us now—the oceans or the mountains, or anything else—will never change that. I'll see you at home, darling.

On his way out of the hotel with his luggage, he left a message with the front desk for Len Redgrove and Jacki Johnson, letting them know he had had to take an early flight out and would meet with them back in the U.S.

Then he hailed a cab to the airport. He found the small blue-and-red jet on the tarmac. A pilot and copilot were leaning against the small stairway that had already been lowered.

"Mr. Chambers?" the pilot asked.

Will nodded, scampered up the stairway, and settled into one of the seats.

In a few minutes he found himself winging over the medieval spires of The Hague and heading back to Mexico City—not yet knowing exactly why.

But he was unable to shake the distinct and overpowering impression that there was something very final about this journey.

79

MAKING HIS WAY THROUGH THE CROWDED lobby of the airport in Mexico City, Will was not surprised to see Pancho waiting for him. But this time he had a serious expression, and didn't smile. The Mexican shook Will's hand, patted him on the back, and then led him quickly toward the exit.

"How was your flight over?" Pancho asked as they reached the door where his cab was waiting.

"Bumpy," Will replied. "They had to take a wide swing because of the hurricane headed this way."

Pancho opened the glass door, and as the two men stepped outside the airport building they were hit by a stiff breeze that made their jackets flap.

Will climbed into the back of the taxicab, and not surprisingly, the American agent with the bull neck was in the backseat waiting for him.

The agent was blunt.

"I'm going to give it to you straight, Will," the man said. "We need you on something. Colonel Marlowe is waiting for you at a site near that house in Chacmool. He is carrying a briefcase. There's a meeting. You know who Manuel Abdal Vega is?"

"You're kidding, of course," Will replied sardonically. "Of course I do. He's the guy who set up the Chacmool trap with the help of the AAJ. He's a sympathizer with the terrorists. And he works in the Ministry of Tourism for the Mexican government."

"Yeah, all of that's right. There are a couple more things you need to know, though. There are a lot more things you can't know. But since you received a security clearance as part of your defense of Marlowe back at Quantico, the top dogs thought it would be okay to bring you in on this on a limited basis."

Will gave him a befuddled look.

"Here's the deal, Will," the agent continued. "Vega has sent out signals that he is ready to turn, and deliver to us some highly sensitive and invaluable intelligence information—all for a very large price, of course. So Marlowe carries that price inside a briefcase to a meeting. Marlowe gives the briefcase to Vega, and Vega delivers a piece of information."

The attorney was staring at the agent, but it was clear that one large piece of the puzzle was still missing.

"What does this have to do with me? Why did you bring me down to Mexico City? I'm getting the impression that you've volunteered me for something I didn't ask for. I'm a lawyer. I'm not a soldier. What is it you want from me?"

"You're not a lawyer today, Will. And you certainly don't need to be a soldier. But we need you to be something else."

Then the agent paused and gave his fellow passenger a sympathetic look.

"You do much fishing?"

Will didn't respond. But it didn't take him very long to figure out the homespun metaphor.

"I used to do game fishing. Out on the ocean. Blue sky. Blue ocean. Yellowfin tuna. Sailfish. Marlin. Yeah, I used to do some fishing when I was younger."

Inside the car it was quiet. The only sounds were the whining of the tires of Pancho's taxicab as he motored down the federal highway—and the whistling of the wind that was now blowing harder.

"So—" Will broke the silence. "I'm the bait. That's it, isn't it?"

"Your friend—Damon Lynch—has been told you're back in Mexico. We made sure he got the word that you're going to be there with Marlowe. We are hoping that Lynch shows up—and that he has the AAJ with him. In short, you're the raw meat, and they are the flies."

"Sounds lovely," Will commented, staring out the window and watching the trees and underbrush sway wildly in the mounting wind.

"So what do you think?" the agent asked after a long period of quiet in the taxi. He could see the anguish on his companion's face. "If it helps, we've got a Kevlar vest for you. And we've got folks who'll be looking after your backside."

None of that was of any great comfort to Will. He opened his wallet and looked at the photo of Fiona once more. It was a picture he had taken of her on their honeymoon. She was at the railing of their hotel room, the azure blue of the ocean behind her. The sun was on her face, on which there was a look of bliss and beauty.

He slipped the snapshot out of his wallet and put it in his top pocket, just over his heart. He had the sinking feeling he must surely do this mission—but that, just as surely, it might come with an enormous price to pay.

"Just tell me one thing," he said quietly. "Is this just about capturing or killing some terrorists? Or is it about saving some lives?"

The agent leaned toward Will with a look of unrehearsed candor.

"You're going to be saving the lives of some Americans."

"That's what I was afraid of."

After another moment, he added something.

"All right. Count me in."

After more than an hour of driving, Pancho turned down a small dirt road that led to a private airstrip. A small jet was on the landing strip—the stairs down, the pilot waiting.

As Will mounted the stairs, he noticed that Pancho and the agent were still standing on the tarmac.

"This is where we say goodbye," the man said, and he reached out and shook the attorney's hand.

Not smiling, Pancho gave a last, solemn wave to Will as he ducked into the small jet. Debris was starting to blow across the airstrip with the approaching storm front.

Taking a seat, Will shouted up to the pilot.

"I've had some flying experience in bad weather before. On a small plane. Just give me a guarantee you're going to get me down safely—without any fancy stunts."

The pilot laughed and told Will to buckle in.

"There's a strong crosswind, but we'll get you down before that hurricane gets too close to shore," he said.

As the plane winged down toward the Yucatán, and the canopy of the jungle became thicker and greener, Will could see the treetops tossing with the high wind like a blue-green sea. The jet was buffeted considerably, but the pilots were handling it with poise.

Will wasn't really worried about the flight, or the hurricane, or much of anything else—except surviving. And getting back to Fiona, and gathering her in his arms. And finding a way, somehow, to make sure they could enjoy a long life together and die of old age.

The jet dropped down so dramatically that Will almost became sick. Then it touched down roughly on a small airstrip in the middle of the jungle.

As they taxied down the strip, branches and leaves and dust were blowing wildly across their field of vision. He heard the pilot comment to his copilot about wind shear as they brought the plane to a stop.

The men quickly lowered the stairs, and gripping the handrails tightly, Will slowly descended onto the broken concrete below. Now the wind was blowing so hard that there was a high, whining whistle everywhere. The pilot pointed to a car that was waiting about two hundred feet away. There was someone sitting behind the wheel.

Will closed the front of his raincoat, hiding the bulletproof vest that had been given to him. As he walked to the car, fighting the mounting tempest, his eyes were searching for a glimpse of who was inside—and as he drew nearer, the driver's features became clear.

The man behind the wheel rolled down the window.

"Hurry up, Counselor," shouted Caleb Marlowe. "We've got a very tight schedule."

80

WILL CHAMBERS RAN THE LAST FEW FEET to the car, clutching his jacket together, and jumped into the front seat next to Caleb Marlowe.

"Let me start off by saying that I'm really not glad to be here," he shouted over the noise of the wind.

Marlowe smiled and nodded. Then he reached over and patted Will's shoulder.

"Don't worry, Private Chambers, you'll be okay."

They drove through the storm that was now ripping through the jungle. They were on their way to Chichén Itzá, Marlow told him, and a rendezvous point by the Sacred Well of Sacrifice. Here and there they noticed the Mayan locals boarding up their windows against the approaching hurricane. Occasionally, small flocks of pink flamingos and white herons flew past them, a startling contrast to the darkening sky as they winged their way inland toward safety.

His companion explained as many of the details as he could of the planned meeting with Manuel Abdal Vega. Much of it made no sense to Will. And worse than that, it sounded as if he and Marlowe would be meeting with Vega in the open, at the rim of the huge gaping well, with no supporting military to defend them. Even to the lawyer's non-military understanding of logistics, it sounded as if the two of them would be sitting ducks.

"Can I just point out some flaws in this plan?" he asked. "You're giving a briefcase with money to Vega in return for some intelligence information. But I'm coming along to attract Damon Lynch and—hopefully—armed members of AAJ. Maybe even Abu Adis himself. So what happens if they are watching, and waiting for us? What happens when they come up to us and surround us—and start shooting?"

"You're going to have to trust me on this," Marlowe replied. "Whatever information I give you, you might be tempted to share with someone else if this thing goes bad and you get captured."

"So what am I supposed to do?"

"Just be visible. Just be there with me."

None of that was reassuring. Will patted his top pocket to make sure the photo of Fiona was still there.

The two men were silent. The wind noise had now reached a low moan, and occasionally, a gust would buffet the car, pushing it sideways. The tops of the jungle trees on both sides of the road were flattening out almost to forty-five degrees under the power of the massive air currents sweeping in from the ocean.

"There was this commander…" Marlowe said loudly, finally breaking the silence, "this commander, Joshua," he continued. "He had orders to advance, take all of Canaan. The first hostilities were at Jericho. It was a flat, open place on the edge of the desert. An oasis with palm trees. Vegetation. Springs. Surrounded by mountains. Joshua and his army had to take that place first."

Will was silent. Listening, as the whining, roaring wall of the hurricane closed in on them.

"You know the rest," his companion said, his voice raised so he could be heard over the storm. "The city fell, and Joshua marched on to the battle of Ai."

Will had heard the Old Testament story, and he nodded.

"But before the fighting began, Joshua had this encounter," the other man continued. "He sees this big warrior standing off in the distance. The warrior has a huge sword drawn in his hand. So Joshua says, Hey—are you for us—or are you for our enemies?"

And then Marlowe paused, and swallowed, and stared ahead for a moment. Then he cleared his throat and went on. But in a voice more passionate than Will had ever heard before.

"But the warrior says, 'I am the Captain of the Host…'" he drew a long breath—"'I am the Captain of the Host of the Lord! And where you're standing is holy ground.'"

He glanced over at Will and kept talking—almost shouting—with the moaning tempest rocking their car

"The Captain of the Host is going to be there with us today, Will," he said. "I know you think that maybe this has all been about my getting revenge—the big payback. I'd be lying if I said this wasn't personal. But it's much more than that. And no matter what happens...*no matter what*...because the Captain of the Lord is there with us—we're going to be on holy ground."

Then they spotted the top of the tall Mayan pyramid off in the distance, over the waving jungle treetops.

Marlowe bulleted out a quick spoken prayer, ending it by saying, "As in the battle of Ai, Lord..."

As they pulled up to the grounds of Chichén Itzá, a green Ministry of Tourism emergency vehicle blocked their path. Two uniformed officers, who were standing behind a temporary barricade across the entrance to the Mayan archaeological site, ran to the car, holding their hats on. Marlowe rolled down the window, greeted the men and seemed to be explaining something to them in rapidly spoken Spanish. After a moment they waved the two Americans through. Marlowe pulled in and parked the car just out of sight of the entrance. He grabbed a briefcase out of the trunk of the car—the trunk lid almost blowing out of his hand—and signaled for Will to follow him—past the towering stairs of El Castillo, past the Temple of the Warriors, down the path that led to the mammoth, gaping hole in the jungle floor, *El Cenote Sagrado*—the Sacred Well of Sacrifice.

A man stood alone at the rim of the abyss.

He was a Mexican with a neatly trimmed beard and short black hair, which was blowing wildly in the mounting storm.

When the two Americans were about a hundred feet away, Marlowe turned to Will.

"You stay here."

He strode through the wind over to Vega, who had his hands thrust into his wildly flapping raincoat. The Mexican was nervously glancing from Marlowe to Will, then back to Marlowe again as the colonel approached.

"I want to see the contents of your briefcase first," Vega snapped loudly.

Marlowe laid the briefcase on the ground, unsnapped it, opened it slightly, and showed the contents to the other man, being careful not to let the wild winds catch the contents.

"You have some information for me?" he shouted out.

The Mexican said nothing at first. He chuckled, and then spoke.

"You think you really know who I am?"

"I know who you are," Marlowe said, now shouting above the roaring wind of the storm. "You're a Muslim sympathizer with the AAJ. And before that, you were a bloodthirsty member of the military who killed and persecuted the Mayan population down here in the Yucatán. I know who you are. And I know *what* you are. But worse than any of that—you are the gutless snake that planned the death of my friend Carlos Fuego and his family."

Vega laughed, and shook his head.

"Do you have no sense of history?" he bellowed with amusement. "My ancestors can be traced all the way back to the Spanish *conquistadores* who came and slaughtered the Mayan chiefs. So you see—history does repeat itself!" And with that, he began to laugh again.

"The information," Marlowe snapped. "I want it now."

"Is this what you're looking for?" Vega asked, taking his hand out of his raincoat pocket and lifting a small card in the air, which vibrated in the wind. His motion, as he raised the card over his head, was obvious enough for Will to see.

It was also obvious enough to be seen by another set of eyes. Vega had just given the signal. An armed band quickly burst out from the edge of the jungle, into the clearing—running toward Will, Marlowe, and Vega. There were three Middle Eastern–looking men, each carrying an automatic weapon. In the lead, however, was a Caucasian man with a bald head. The three Middle Eastern men scurried over toward Marlowe and Vega. But the man with the shaved head strode directly toward Will. It was Damon Lynch. He lifted his weapon and pointed it directly at Will's face, and then screamed out an order.

"Over there! Over there!" Lynch screamed, motioning with his weapon for the other man to join Marlowe and Vega at the edge of the well. As Will walked over, the wind was whining and whistling through the jungle, blowing with such force that it was difficult for Will to go in a straight line over to Marlowe's position.

Through the roar of the storm he could hear Lynch screaming profanities at him as he walked. Will had a momentary thought that this was how it would end—a bullet in his back from the man who had watched his first wife die. But he knew he couldn't dwell on that. He couldn't think about it.

"You are such a gutless wimp!" the man behind him screamed. "You could have had me—turned me over to the feds. Now look at you! So here it is—this is my payday. I helped do your wife. Now I get to do you. Man, oh, man. This is so sweet!"

Will's eyes searched the surroundings—he looked at the thick growth encircling the dark, abysmal hole in the jungle floor to see if there was a rescue in place, to see if there were American troops who were going to come and save them…some glimmer of hope in what now appeared to be a suicide scenario.

Will stopped just a foot away from Vega, who was now between him and Marlowe.

The Mexican official was still holding the small white card in his right hand, over his head.

Abu Adis, with his scraggly beard and wild eyes, stepped away from the other two terrorists and yelled out something Will could not understand—perhaps in his native tongue. Then Adis started to laugh, and was joined by the other two terrorists and by Damon Lynch.

"You go first—I get to take you," Lynch shouted at Will. "I wanted to do it slow, and have some fun—but we're busy guys. I got things to do."

And then he raised his weapon and pointed it at Will's forehead. Lynch's face had a twisted, demonic look—not like pleasure—or even pain—but something beyond that.

The near-gale-force winds were so wild that Will was having a hard time keeping himself standing, as he looked down the barrel of the automatic weapon. *This is holy ground*, he muttered out loud in a frantic prayer.

Then there was a crack. A sound. From somewhere. Lynch, for only a millisecond, gave Will a dazed, blank look. Then he dropped to the ground like a bag of bricks. Blood was surging from the sniper shot to the side of his head.

Adis and the other terrorists whirled instantly, only to be struck by a hail of bullets from the edge of the jungle, which cut them down before they could get off a single shot.

Within seconds, Master Sergeant Rockwell and the members of the BATCOM unit charged onto the site with guns poised at Lynch and the three terrorists, whose bodies were sprawled on the ground.

Then another group came running up behind the BATCOM squad—a small group of Mayan rebels being led by Juan Oxla Tulum, who had aided in the assault.

Caleb Marlowe then turned to Vega and reached his hand out toward him.

"Give me the card, Vega. This is the end of the show," he shouted, steadying himself against the near-hurricane winds.

But Vega only sneered, and with the small card flapping, he stepped backward toward the gaping edge that opened on the black, watery depths below.

His left hand was still raised above his head with the card, his right hand still in the pocket of the raincoat that was whipping in the storm.

As Rockwell and his men checked the bodies of Lynch and the terrorists to make sure they were dead, Juan Oxla Tulum ran, head down against the wind, directly toward Vega, lifted his revolver, and pointed it at the other man's heart.

"Put it away, Juan," Marlowe yelled. "Put it away now. This is not your operation. We're taking this man in. We're doing this our way."

"No—I'm sorry, Colonel Marlowe, but this man belongs to me. He's tortured and killed my people. And now he's going to die."

The American held a hand out to stop the Mayan leader. His voice was barely audible over the roar of the wind.

"This is not the way we're doing this," he pleaded loudly.

"You should talk!" Tulum shouted above the tempest blowing through the jungle. "You—the professional killer backed by the American government—*you* should lecture *me* on killing?"

"I kill only when I must—and only when I can justify it before God."

But in his plea to Tulum, Marlowe had turned away from Vega, and in so doing had opened up an opportunity. Vega squeezed the trigger of the revolver that was hidden in his left pocket—there was a flash of fire out of his coat, and the colonel was thrown to the ground by the impact of the bullet fired at him from a point-blank range.

Tulum's eyes had never deviated from Vega, and he quickly put two rounds into the other man's heart, throwing him backward off the edge and down into the black waters that lay at the bottom of the Sacred Well of Sacrifice. In the raging roar of the hurricane, no one heard the splash as Vega's body hit the depths below.

But the hand holding the card had released it as he fell, and the wild wind had picked it up and slammed it against Will's chest. He grabbed frantically at the small piece of paper, as if he were wrestling some invisible force—falling to the ground as the card began to fly off into the air. He snatched at the card with both hands and then caught it, closing his hands around it.

Rockwell and Staff Sergeant Baker were already huddled over their commander's body, and Rockwell was yelling into his headset, calling for medivac. Marlowe's face was white, his eyes dull.

Chief Petty Officer Dorfman raced up to Will, reached over to unclasp his hands, and retrieved the small card. Will could see a picture of a tomb prominently displayed...perhaps a card from a Mexican cemetery.

"I'll take care of this, sir," Dorfman shouted at the top of his voice, after he had extracted the card from the other man's grip.

"Marlowe—what happened to Marlowe? How is he? Is he badly hurt?" Will was yelling at the top of his voice as the approaching hurricane reached its full cacophony.

"I'm sorry, sir," Dorfman yelled back, shaking his head. "You're going to have to come with me."

He quickly escorted Will to a helicopter waiting in the clearing. Then he yelled into his headset. "We have the code—but the coral snake is dead. And Marlowe's down."

As he climbed in, Will saw two medics racing from their helicopter back toward Marlowe's position, where he lay terribly wounded.

As their aircraft lifted off, it was buffeted violently by the high winds. But soon they were high over the undulating canopy of the jungle, and as they traveled due north, the winds—though still powerful—began subsiding.

Will did not know it then, but he would not see Colonel Caleb Marlowe again before the funeral, which would be held ten days later.

81

THERE WAS MUCH THAT WILL CHAMBERS would never learn. Like the meaning of the small card with the tombstone that Vega had been holding—and that Marlowe and the American operatives wanted so frantically to obtain.

Its deeper meaning was lost on Will. He was just glad he had caught it in the hurricane-force wind. He had been an outfielder in his high-school baseball days, but here he could claim no athletic talent in the save. The catch had been nothing short of divine intervention.

However, by the time Will and Fiona, Tiny Heftland, Professor Redgrove, Jacki Johnson, and the rest of Will's law-office staff would attend Colonel Marlowe's funeral in his small hometown in the panhandle of West Virginia, some facts would have surfaced in a major splash of headlines and television talk shows.

The news would electrify and shock the American public. A plot against the United States Supreme Court had been foiled...

On a day scheduled for Supreme Court oral arguments, a man in a small, dingy apartment in DC rose very early. This man's left leg had been amputated, and taking its place was a prosthesis, which the man strapped on. He had an important day ahead of him.

His plan was to attend the oral arguments. He intended to obtain a visitor's pass using forged Supreme Court bar credentials. He was to seat himself as close as he could manage, to the front row of seats just behind the counsel tables that faced the bench. Then he was to detonate the prosthesis, which contained deadly VX gas. If all went as planned, several of the sitting justices would be exposed, at a minimum—and would die within twenty-four hours.

The man had not known—until the day before Vega's death at Chichén Itzá—what his target would be. Manuel Abdal Vega had communicated it to Abu Adis, who in turn had informed the man which site had been selected for the poison gas attack.

"The tomb" is what the message had said. It had been transmitted by passing on one of the cemetery cards—like the one carried by Vega. That was the cryptic denotation for the white-marble Supreme Court building...

The little card that had been caught by Will had let the FBI know, with certainty, where the attack would take place.

What Will would learn—along with the rest of the world—was that the man with one leg would be captured on the steps of the Court's outer courtyard, before even reaching the front doors. FBI agents would drag him immediately into the back of a sealed decontamination vehicle and lock him in. There he would detonate the device—killing only himself.

That is what Will, Fiona, and the world would discover.

But as the little group of friends gathered at the small country graveside service for Colonel Marlowe, something else occupied their minds. They thought about his bravery...and wished they could have said farewell to his body...but it was a closed casket. They found it disappointing that there was no military honor guard—except the BATCOM unit led by Master Sergeant Rockwell. The sergeant seemed strangely detached.

Fiona had been teary-eyed, but she started to sob gently when Rockwell walked over to Will and placed the folded flag from the coffin in his hands. After receiving that honor, Will put his arm tightly around Fiona, thinking about the battle account he had looked up before the funeral. The book of Joshua recorded the second battle of Ai as a successful ambush against the unsuspecting enemy—who had been drawn out from their ancient fortress and into the open. Only...in that battle, Joshua, the commander, had survived.

≈   ≈   ≈

It would be several months before Will would again consider the fate of his client—and his friend—Colonel Caleb Marlowe. It was on a Saturday.

Will and Fiona had been working around the house. That morning Will had caught the news on the television—including the oil deal struck between Russia and the United States. That did not stop Warren Mullburn from becoming the world's wealthiest man with his Mexico project…though it did take a few billion dollars off his profit margin.

Will greeted the news with a different perspective. The intruder who had threatened Fiona had never been linked to Mullburn. But no one could convince Will that the billionaire had not been the sinister force behind it.

Afternoon came, and he was still thinking about that, and about Fiona's safety, and about the mystery of both forgiveness and punishment for evildoers, when he took the winding walk down the hill that would bring him to their mailbox at the road. It was a bright, beautiful day. The mountaintops, off in the hazy distance, were drenched in sunlight.

At the mailbox, Will reached in and pulled out a few magazines. And bills—always the bills.

Fiona was up on the porch, looking out for her husband. She spotted him and waved and threw him a big, exaggerated kiss that he couldn't miss.

Then Fiona saw Will looking, without moving, at something in the pile of mail. She was too far away to know that Will was looking at a postcard. Or to know why he read it, then reread it, and then read it again. But that was when Will felt a lump in his throat. And he looked up into the sky, and laughed out loud, and wiped his eyes with his knuckle.

The front of the postcard was a simple picture of the American flag. It had been mailed from Istanbul, Turkey, five days after the funeral.

The postcard bore no note—except for a Bible verse. As he had read it, Will had swallowed hard and then smiled as he understood its coded message.

It was Second Corinthians chapter four, verse twelve.

"So death works in us, but life in you."

Will would wonder, long after that postcard, when he would ever hear from Caleb Marlowe again.

THE CHAMBERS OF JUSTICE SERIES
by Craig Parshall

The Resurrection File

When Reverend Angus MacCameron asks attorney Will Chambers to defend him against accusations that could discredit the Gospels, Will's unbelieving heart says "run." But conspiracy and intrigue—and the presence of MacCameron's lovely and successful daughter, Fiona—draw him deep into the case...toward a destination he could never have imagined.

Custody of the State

Attorney Will Chambers reluctantly agrees to defend a young mother from Georgia and her farmer husband, suspected of committing the unthinkable against their own child. Encountering small-town secrets, big-time corruption, and a government system that's destroying the little family, Chambers himself is thrown into the custody of the state.

The Accused

Enjoying a Cancún honeymoon with his wife, Fiona, attorney Will Chambers is ambushed by two unexpected events: a terrorist kidnapping of a U.S. official...and the news that a link has been found to the previously unidentified murderer of Will's first wife. The kidnapping pulls him into the case of Marine colonel Caleb Marlowe. When treachery drags both Will and his client toward vengeance, they must ask—*Is forgiveness real?*

Missing Witness

A relaxing North Carolina vacation for attorney Will Chambers? Not likely. When Will investigates a local inheritance case, the long arm of the law reaches out of the distant past to cast a shadow over his client's life…and the life of his own family. As the attorney's legal battle uncovers corruption, piracy, the deadly grip of greed, and the haunting sins of a man's past, the true question must be faced—*Can a person ever really run away from God?*

The Last Judgment

A mysterious religious cult plans to spark an "Armageddon" in the Middle East. Suddenly, a huge explosion blasts the top of the Jerusalem Temple Mount into rubble, with hundreds of Muslim casualities. And attorney Will Chambers' client, Gilead Amahn, a convert to Christianity from Islam, becomes the prime suspect. In his harrowing pursuit of the truth, Will must face the greatest threat yet to his marriage, his family, and his faith, while cataclysmic events plunge the world closer to the Last Judgment.